faking it

Jenny Crusie is the author of *Tell Me Lies*, *Crazy for You*, *Welcome to Temptation* and *Fast Women*, as well as nine award-winning romances. She teaches writing and literature at Ohio State University.

jenny crusie

faking it

PAN BOOKS

First published 2002 by St. Martin's Press, New York

First published in Great Britain 2002 by Macmillan

First published in paperback 2003 by Pan Books

This edition published 2004 by Pan Books
an imprint of Pan Macmillan Ltd
Pan Macmillan, 20 New Wharf Road, London N1 9RR
Basingstoke and Oxford
Associated companies throughout the world
www.panmacmillan.com

ISBN 0 330 42030 5

1 3 5 7 9 8 6 4 2

A CIP catalogue record for this book is available from
the British Library.

Printed and bound in Great Britain by
Mackays of Chatham plc, Chatham, Kent

For
PAT GAFFNEY

for her magnificent novels,
limitless patience, and
unconditional friendship,
and because she totally gets
the Buffy the Vampire Slayer thing

$\mathcal{M}$Y THANKS TO

CATHERINE AIRD,
who supposedly said the quote I gave to Gwen, but since
I can't find documentation of it, I can't attribute it to her.
And anyway, I like her books.

ANN TWOMEY
for giving me the best book covers in the business.

THE FACULTY OF THE DEPARTMENT OF ART, BGSU, CIRCA 1971,
for trying to teach me to paint. Maybe if it hadn't been the
seventies . . .

DACHSUND RESCUE OF OHIO
for fixing me up with Wolfgang, aka Steve.

DEBORAH LANATA
for explaining police procedure to me over and over again,
for reading this book in manuscript, and for maintaining
my bulletin board on YahooGroups.

THE JENNIFERCRUSIEFANS BULLETIN BOARD
for critiquing my first chapter, giving me movie quotes in my
darkest hour, and putting up with me in general.

JOHN KARLE

for being the best of all possible publicists, who has never once told me to fix my own damn problems even though he must have been sorely tempted.

THE PEOPLE WHO HELPED ME FIGURE OUT THIS BOOK,

including Val Taylor, Teresa Hill, Judy Ivory, Jen Badger, Mollie Smith, and the XromXCraft Link.

JEN ENDERLIN

for once again being an editor whose intuition is superb, whose patience is legendary, and whose taste is exquisite

and

MEG RULEY

for ten thousand things, culminating in just being Meg.

If you can't be a good example,
you'll just have to be a horrible warning.

—Gwen Goodnight

faking iT

CHAPTER · ONE

MATILDA GOODNIGHT STEPPED BACK FROM HER LATEST mural and realized that of all the crimes she'd committed in her thirty-four years, painting the floor-to-ceiling reproduction of van Gogh's sunflowers on Clarissa Donnelly's dining room wall was the one that was going to send her to hell. God might forgive her the Botticelli Venus she'd painted in the bathroom in Iowa, the Uccello battle scene she'd done for the boardroom in New Jersey, even the Bosch orgy she'd painted in the bedroom in Utah, but these giant, glaring sunflowers were going to be His Last Straw. "I gave you a nice talent," He was going to say to her on Judgment Day, "and this is what you did with it."

Tilda felt her lungs tighten and stuck her hand in her pocket to make sure she had her inhaler.

Beside her, Clarissa wrapped her thin little arms around her size two chenille sweater and squinted at the brownish-yellow flowers. "It's just like his, isn't it?"

"Yes," Tilda said with regret and handed her the museum print of the original.

"The flowers look so . . . angry," Clarissa said.

"Well." Tilda closed her paint box. "He was nuts."

Clarissa nodded. "I heard about that. The ear."

"Yeah, that got a lot of press." Tilda shrugged off her paint shirt. "So I'll take my completion check—"

"Did you sign it?" Clarissa said. "You need to sign it. I want everybody to know it's a real Matilda Veronica mural."

"I signed it." Tilda pointed the toe of her paint-stained canvas shoe at the bottom where she'd scrawled "Matilda Veronica." "Right there. Now I have to be going—"

"You didn't sign it 'van Gogh,' did you?" Clarissa bent down. "Wouldn't that be forgery?"

"Not unless he had a Kentucky mural period we don't know about." Tilda tried to take a deep breath. "So I'll take that check—"

"Write your name bigger," Clarissa said, straightening. "I want everybody to know you painted this. I'm going to keep the magazine right here, too. So they know that it's a real Matilda Veronica—"

Clarissa's enthusiasm for her as a brand name had lost its appeal many days before, so Tilda changed the subject. "Well, Spot was certainly a champ about the whole thing." She nodded at Clarissa's elongated little dog on the theory that people were always pleased when you talked about their animals.

"His tail is almost hiding your name," Clarissa said.

Tilda let her glasses slide down her nose a little and looked over the rims at Spot, quivering at her feet.

She'd done some dog face-lifting in the mural since Spot's beady eyes almost met over his long knife-edged nose. She'd softened the gray that streaked his dark, shaggy coat, too, so he didn't look so much like a very small, mutant wolf.

"You have to sign it again," Clarissa said. "Sign it up at the top. Bigger."

"No," Tilda said. "Everyone will see it because they'll be comparing Spot to the painting. People always do that, look at the dog and then look at the painting—"

"No they won't," Clarissa said, triumphant. "He goes back to the pound today."

"You're taking your dog to the pound?" At Tilda's feet, Spot pressed against her, shedding on her jeans.

"He's not my dog," Clarissa said. "You always put dogs in your murals—"

"No I don't," Tilda said.

"—it said so in the magazine, so I had to have one, too, or people wouldn't think it was a real Matilda Veronica, so I went and got the only purebred they had."

"Spot's a purebred?"

"Silver dapple, longhaired dachshund," Clarissa said. "He'll be fine back at the pound. He's used to it. I'm the third person who's adopted him."

Tilda pulled out her inhaler and inhaled.

It made sense when she thought about it. Clarissa was exactly the kind of woman who'd go to Rent-A-Dog and get a designer second for fake warmth in her faux Postimpressionist wall painting. Spot looked up at her now, shaking, almost as pathetic as he was ugly.

I am not going to rescue you, Tilda thought, capping her inhaler. *I can't save everybody, I'm asthmatic, and I don't want a dog, especially not one who acts like he snorts coke and looks like he rolls in it.*

"Sign it again up here," Clarissa said. "I'll get you a Sharpie."

"No," Tilda said. "I signed it. It's done. And I'll take the completion check now, thank you."

"Well, I don't know, that signature—" Clarissa began, and Tilda pushed her glasses up the bridge of her nose and turned steely eyes on her. Clarissa nodded. "I'll go get that check, then."

Left alone with Spot—a hell of a name for a dog that had none—Tilda tried to think of something besides the pound. There was the mural, another success, another chunk of money off the family debt, another two weeks painted from her life by ripping off art history—

Her cell phone rang and cut short her stab at optimism. Tilda flipped open the cover. "Hell-o."

"Tilda," her mother said, "we have a problem."

"Really," Tilda said, staring at the sunflowers. "Who'd have guessed?"

"It's bad," Gwen said, and Tilda stopped, taken aback by the seriousness in her mother's voice. Gwennie did muffins and Double-Crostics, not serious.

"Okay, so whatever it is, we'll fix it." She looked down at the dog again, and he gazed back at her, desperation in his eyes. "What is it?"

"Nadine sold a Scarlet."

Tilda jerked her head up as her stomach cramped. In the background on the phone, she heard her sixteen-year-old niece say, "I still don't get what I did wrong," and she went cold all over.

"There aren't any Scarlets." Tilda tried to draw a deep breath while not throwing up. "Dad sold them all."

"Not the first one," Gwen said. "Remember? He couldn't because it was of our building. Nadine found it in the basement. And the woman who bought it won't give it back. I asked."

Clarissa came back with the check and Tilda took it. "Thank you," she said to Clarissa and then spoke into the phone. "Ask again."

"I tried. She hung up on me and I called again and Mason Phipps answered. She's staying with him." Gwen's voice grew slower. "Mason was an old friend of your father's. He's the one who told her about Scarlet and the gallery. And he invited me to dinner tonight."

"Oh, good. One of us will have a hearty meal."

"So I thought I'd go and distract them and you could sneak in and steal it," Gwen said. "And then we can bury it in the basement again."

Tilda turned away from Clarissa and whispered into the phone. *"You do realize you don't get muffins in prison!"* She tried again for a deep breath, fighting back the nausea. "And when we get it back, we're *burning it*. If I'd known it was down th—"

"Something wrong?" Clarissa said from behind her.

"No," Tilda said to her. "Everything is peachy." She

spoke into the phone. "I'm coming home. I'll be there in four hours. Do not do anything until I get there."

"We never do," Gwen said and hung up.

"I certainly hope everything's okay," Clarissa said, looking avid.

"Everything is always okay," Tilda said bitterly. "That's what I do. I make everything okay." She stuffed the check in her shirt pocket and looked down at Spot, trembling on her foot. "Which is why I'm taking your dog."

"What?" Clarissa said, but Tilda had already scooped Spot up, his long body drooping over her arm while his feet tried for purchase on her hip.

"Just saving you a trip to the pound," Tilda said. "Have a lovely day."

She carted her paint box and the dog out to her beat-up yellow van, simmering with exasperation and another emotion she didn't quite recognize but thought might be fear. It put an acrid taste in her mouth, and she didn't like it. Once on the passenger seat, Spot simmered, too. "Oh, calm down," she said to him, as she put the van in gear. "Anything's better than jail." Spot looked at her strangely. "The pound. I meant the pound." She talked to him all the way home, and by the time she pulled into the fenced lot behind the Goodnight Gallery, Spot was asleep and she was calmer. When she shut off the motor, he jerked awake, his eyes like marbles, and she carried him, now heaving with anxiety, into the shabby gallery office and deposited him on the floor in front of her mother and niece, both of them looking blonde and blue-eyed and cute. *So not like me,* Tilda thought. Behind them, Gwennie's bubbler jukebox played "No, No, Not Again," by the Three Degrees.

"This is Spot," she said to Gwen and Nadine. "I'm finding him a home where people will treat him with dignity and not sell him down the river while his back is turned."

"Well, I'm *sorry,*" Nadine said, her pretty face defiant under her mop of pale curls. She was wearing a black T-shirt that said BITE ME in Gothic letters, but she still looked like Shirley Temple in a snit. "Nobody told me we couldn't sell paintings. We're an art gallery, for cripe's sake." She crouched down on the worn Oriental rug to pet Spot, who backed away, still heaving, his eyes peeled for a getaway. "What is wrong with this dog?"

"So many things," Tilda said. "About the painting?"

"While you were in Iowa," Gwen said to her, "Nadine broke curfew and Andrew sent her down to clean the basement as a punishment."

Tilda took a deep breath and thought of a few choice things to say to her ex-brother-in-law.

"You can stop looking so mad," Nadine said. "Dad didn't let me in the locked part. I still don't know what's in there."

"Storage," Tilda said.

"Right." Nadine rolled her eyes.

"Nadine." Tilda pushed her glasses up the bridge of her nose and looked down at her, and Nadine swallowed and sat up a little straighter. "You are not in a position to push your luck here. The painting."

"Dad made me clean the back storeroom," Nadine said. "It was full of furniture painted with animals. Dad said you did it when you were my age. It was pretty cool, especially the bed when we'd cleaned it off and set it up—"

"We?" Tilda said.

"Ethan and me," Nadine said. "You didn't think I cleaned that whole place out by myself?"

"So Ethan knows." Tilda consigned Andrew to the lowest circle of hell for criminal stupidity, in sending not only his daughter down there but also her non-family best friend.

"Well, he knows there's furniture down there, yeah," Nadine said. "What is it with you and the basement? It's *furniture.*"

"Right." Tilda realized her lungs were closing up again and got her inhaler out. "Are we close to the painting yet?"

"It was in there," Nadine said. "It was wrapped in paper and stuck in a cabinet, the one with the turquoise monkeys on it. Did you really paint all those animals?"

"It's junk. I was going through a phase." Tilda hit the inhaler. "So you pulled the painting out and then what?"

"We thought it was good," Nadine said.

"So you sold it," Tilda said.

"No. We put it back in the cabinet and put dustsheets on everything and went to Cup O' Joe's. And then today, Grandma had to go to the bank, and this Mrs. Lewis came in and asked if we had any paintings by somebody named Scarlet, and I said no, all we had was Dorcas Finsters." Nadine turned to Gwen. "Are we ever going to get rid of those? I know she lives here, but they're really depressing, and I think we could—"

"*Nadine,*" Tilda said.

"*Okay.*" Nadine crossed her arms. "And Mrs. Lewis said no, she wanted paintings that looked like a kid had painted them, and she started talking about checkerboard skies and stars, and Ethan was here and he said, 'That's like the one we found in your basement,' and she would *not* leave until we showed it to her."

"Ethan said that," Tilda said.

"Or maybe me." Nadine squinted at the ceiling. "I'm not sure. Ask Ethan."

"Like Ethan wouldn't lie down on burning coals for you," Tilda said. "So you went and got the painting . . ."

"And she offered me a hundred dollars for it and I said no," Nadine said virtuously.

"And yet, the painting is not here," Tilda said.

"She kept offering and I kept saying no and when she got to a thousand I caved," Nadine said. "Now will somebody tell me why that was bad?"

"No." Gwen sank down on the couch next to her granddaughter, looking much like Nadine was going to look in forty years, pale-eyed, graying, and gamine.

"Where's your mom?" Tilda asked Nadine. She turned to Gwen. "Why wasn't Eve watching the gallery?"

"She had a teacher's meeting," Gwen said. "Summer school. She's aiding again. Look, this Lewis woman is not going to return it. And the more fuss we make, the more suspicious we look."

"Suspicious about *what*?" Nadine said. "Nobody tells me *anything*." She reached down and scooped Spot off the faded rug, and his tremors picked up again. "If you don't tell me stuff, you can't blame me when I screw up."

She stuck her chin out at Tilda, defiant as she patted the dog, and Tilda thought, *She's right*. She pulled out the ancient desk chair so it was facing Nadine and sat down, wincing as it creaked. "Okay, here it is."

"No," Gwen said. "She's sixteen."

"Yeah, and how old was I?" Tilda said. "I can't remember a time I didn't know."

"Hello?" Nadine waved. "I'm right here. Know what?"

"Do you remember how successful the gallery used to be, when Grandpa ran it?" Tilda said.

"No," Nadine said. "I was a kid when he died. I wasn't really into the gallery thing then." She relaxed her hold on Spot, who struggled out of her lap, hit the rug with a splat, and recovered by putting his paws up on Tilda.

"Well, one of the reasons we were successful was that Grandpa sometimes sold fakes," Tilda said flatly.

"Oh," Nadine said.

"That's good," Gwen said, her hands gripped together in her lap. "The more people who know *that* the better."

"I won't tell," Nadine said.

"Some of the paintings that were real were by a man named Homer Hodge," Tilda plowed on, "and Grandpa made a lot of money off him legally. But then he and Homer had a fight, and Homer stopped sending him paintings, so your grandpa got the bright idea of inventing a daughter for Homer named Scarlet, and he sold five paintings by her, making a big deal out of the fact that she was a Hodge."

Gwen slumped back against the couch and stared at the ceiling, shaking her head.

"Invented a daughter?" Nadine said. "Cool."

"No, not cool." Tilda picked up Spot, needing something to hold on to for the next part, and Spot sighed and curled his long, furry body to fit her lap. "The painting you sold was the first Scarlet, a fake painting by a fake artist. And that's fraud and we could go to jail. And people are going to realize it's a fake because Homer was from a farm in southern Ohio, and the painting you sold is of this building."

"I thought it looked familiar," Nadine said.

"So once they figure out that one's a fake, they're going to come back to the gallery and ask questions." Tilda felt her stomach twist again. "They might look at all the paintings Grandpa sold them for thousands of dollars and find out that some of them are fakes, and they're going to want their money back, and we don't have it. And we could go to jail for that, too, and lose the gallery and this whole building which means we'd all be out on the street."

"Wait a minute," Nadine said, perking up, evidently undeterred by the news her grandpa was a crook and she might soon be living in the gutter. "I didn't know it was a fake. The only person who knew it was a fake was Grandpa. So we're off the hook. We can blame him. He's dead!"

"That's been pretty much my plan for the past five years," Gwen said, still staring at the ceiling.

"Nice try, but no," Tilda said, feeling sicker. "The gallery as a business is still liable. And there's one other person who knew and could go to jail. The person who painted them."

"Oh." Nadine grew still. "Who painted them?"

"I did, of course," Tilda said, and got out her inhaler again.

IT HAD TAKEN Davy Dempsey four days to track his ex–financial adviser from Miami, Florida, to Columbus, Ohio, and now he leaned in the doorway of a little diner and watched his prey pick up his water glass, survey the rim, and then wipe it with his napkin. Ronald Abbott, aka Rabbit, was born to be the perfect mark: pale, semichinless, and so smug about his superiority in all things having to do with money, art, and life in general that he was a sure thing to con. Which made it doubly annoying that he had taken all of Davy's money.

Davy crossed the diner and slid into the booth, and Ronald looked up in mid-sip and then inhaled his water in one horrified gasp.

"Hello, Rabbit," Davy said, enjoying the gargle. "Where the hell is my three million dollars?"

Ronald continued to choke, strangling on tap water, guilt, and terror.

"You know, a life of crime is not for everybody," Davy said, taking one of Ronald's French fries. "You have to enjoy the risk. You're not enjoying the risk, are you, Rabbit?"

Ronald swallowed some air. "It's your own fault."

"Because I shouldn't have trusted you?" Davy nodded as he chewed. "Good point. I won't do that again. But I want it back, Rabbit. The whole three million. And change." He took another fry. The diner didn't look like much, but the cook clearly knew his way around a potato.

"It wasn't your money. You stole it." Ronald looked around, apprehensive. "Where's Simon? Is he here?"

"Simon is in Miami. I will be beating you up on my own. And you know it was my money, you saw me make it playing the same stocks you did—"

"The million you started with wasn't yours," Ronald said, and Davy grew still, struck by the three-year-old memory of a beautiful, enraged blonde.

"Clea." Davy shook his head. "Did you have a good time, Rabbit?"

"See, you don't even deny it." Ronald was virtuous in his indignation. "You stole that poor woman's inheritance from her father—"

Davy sighed and reached for the salt. If Rabbit had embezzled in the heat of Clea, it was going to be difficult to cool him down again. "That woman is not poor, she's greedy. She inherited a chunk of change from her first husband and the last I heard she'd married some rich old guy in the Bahamas."

"You stole her money," Ronald said, sticking to the high ground. "She's innocent."

Davy pulled Ronald's plate over to his side of the booth and reached for the ketchup. "Rabbit, I know she's a great lay, but not even you could believe that."

Ronald drew himself up. "You're talking about the woman I love."

"Clea is not the kind of woman you love," Davy said grimly. "She's the kind of woman you think you love, but then it turns out you were just renting her until somebody else came along with an option to buy." He dumped ketchup on Ronald's remaining fries.

"I believe in her," Ronald said.

"You also believed the tech ride was going to last forever," Davy said. "Like my daddy always says, if it seems too good to be true—"

"We're not talking about money," Rabbit said. "She loves me."

"If you're talking about Clea, you're talking about money. It's all she cares about."

"She cares about her art," Ronald said.

"Her art? That's what she calls one cult movie and two porn flicks? Art?"

"No," Ronald said, looking confused. "Her art. That's how I met her, at her family's art museum when I was helping value her late husband's collection."

"*Late* husband?" Davy laughed. "Imagine my surprise. Rabbit, her family doesn't have an art museum, and she turned to you when she found out you had access to my accounts. What'd the last guy die of?" He held up a fry. "No, wait, let me guess. Heart attack."

"It was very sudden," Ronald said.

"Yeah, it always is with Clea's husbands," Davy said. "Word of advice: don't marry her. She looks really good in black."

Ronald stuck out what little chin he had. "She said you'd speak badly of her. She said you'd threatened her, and that you'd spread lies about her past. You lie for a living, Davy, why should I believe—"

Davy shook his head. "I don't have to lie on this one. The truth is grim enough. Look, if you want to commit suicide, dying in Clea's bed is as good a way to go as any, but first I need my money back. I don't like being poor. It limits my scope."

"I don't have it," Ronald said, looking affronted. "I returned it to its rightful owner."

Davy sat back and looked at him with pity laced with exasperation. "You already gave it to her. So when was the last time you saw her?"

Ronald flushed. "Four days ago. She's very busy."

"You gave her the money as soon as you got it, and then she got busy."

"No," Ronald said. "She's collecting, too. It's part of our plan, to build a collection—"

"Clea's collecting *art*?"

"See," Ronald said smugly. "I knew you didn't understand her."

"There's not enough fast money in art." Davy frowned as he pushed away Ronald's empty plate and picked up Ronald's coffee cup. "Plus it's a bigger gamble than tech stocks. Art is not a good way to make money unless you're a dealer without morals which entails working." The coffee was lukewarm and did not go well with the fries. Rabbit had no taste.

"It's not about the money," Ronald was saying. "She fell in love with folk paintings."

"Clea doesn't fall in love," Davy said. "Clea follows money. Somewhere in this there is a guy with money. And a bad heart. How's your heart, Rabbit? You in good health?"

"Excellent," Ronald said acidly.

"Another reason for her to dump you," Davy said. "You lost your fortune in the tech slump and you're not going to be easy to kill. So who's the guy she's spending time with? The guy with a lot of money, a weak heart, and a big art collection?"

Ronald sat very still.

"You know," Davy said. "I'd feel sorry for you if you hadn't ripped me off for three million. Who is it?"

"Mason Phipps," Ronald said. "He was Cyril's financial manager. Clea saw his folk art at a party at his house in Miami."

"And shortly after that she saw the rest of him." Davy sat back in the booth, his low opinion of humanity in general, and Clea in particular, once again confirmed. "What a gal. She's learning about art so she can dazzle him into marriage and an early grave."

"Mason's not that old. He's in his fifties."

"The one I saw her kill was in his forties. I gather Cyril was her latest victim?"

"She did not kill her husband," Ronald said. "Cyril was eighty-nine. He died of natural causes. And she didn't make porn. She made art films. And she loves m—"

"*Coming Clean*," Davy said. "Set in a car wash. She's billed as Candy Suds, but it's Clea. Don't believe me, go rent it yourself."

"I don't—"

"But first you're going to help me get my money back."

Ronald drew himself up again. "I most certainly am not."

Davy looked at him with pity. "Rabbit, you can stop bluffing. I have you. If I tell the Feds what you've done, you're back on the inside. I understand why you fell for Clea, I wasted two years on her myself, but you have to pick yourself up now. I'm going to get my money back, and you're either going to help me or you're going to go away for a very long time. Is she really worth that to you? Considering she hasn't called you since she got the money?"

Ronald sat motionless for the entire speech and for a few moments after, and Davy watched his face, knowing wheels were turning behind that blank façade. Then Ronald spoke.

"*Coming Clean?*"

Davy nodded.

"You and she . . ."

Davy nodded.

"You think she and Mason . . ."

Davy nodded.

"I don't know how to get the money back," Ronald said.

"I do," Davy said. "Tell me about Clea and art."

Ronald began to talk about Mason Phipps and his collection of folk paintings; how Clea had followed Mason to begin her own collection and was staying with him now; how she had promised to call, would call, as soon as she had a chance.

"She's very busy with the collection," Ronald said. "It's taking a lot of her time because Mason has to teach her so much."

How you ever made a living from crime being this gullible is beyond me, Davy thought, but he knew that wasn't fair. Clea was the kind of woman who flattened a man's thought processes. God knew, she'd ironed his out a time or two.

Ronald went on about Clea the Art Collector, and Davy sat back and began to calculate. All he needed to do was con her address and account number out of Ronald, get her laptop, go into her hard drive, find her password—knowing Clea, she used the same password for everything—and transfer the money. It wasn't a con but it was semirisky, and it appealed to him a lot more than it should have. He was not looking forward to breaking the law. He was straight now. He'd matured. Crime no longer excited him.

"What?" Ronald said.

"I didn't say anything."

"You're breathing heavy."

"Asthma," Davy lied. "Give me her address and her account numbers."

Ronald furrowed his brow. "I don't think that would be ethical."

"Rabbit," Davy said, putting steel in his voice. "You have no ethics. That's how you got into this mess. Give me the damn numbers."

Ronald hesitated and then took a pen and notebook from his inside jacket pocket, flipped to a page, and began to copy numbers down.

"Thank you, Rabbit," Davy said, taking the page Ronald tore from the notebook. He stood up and added, "Don't leave town. Don't steal anything else. And do not, for any reason, call Clea."

"I'll do anything I damn well please," Ronald said.

"No," Davy said. "You will not."

Ronald met his eyes and then looked away.

"There you go." Davy patted him on the shoulder. "Stay away from Clea, and you'll be fine. Nothing but good times ahead."

"At least admit you stole her money, you crook," Ronald said.

"Of course I did," Davy said, and went off to rob the most beautiful woman he'd ever slept with. Again.

*

BREAKING INTO Mason Phipps's house had been a bad idea, but Tilda hadn't been able to think of a better one. Now, creeping through Mason's halls in the dark of night, she was reconsidering. She really wasn't cut out for this kind of work. She was a retired art forger, not a thief. Plus, the place was deserted except for a caterer in the kitchen and Gwennie's Dinner Party from Hell in the dining room, and it was spooking her out. "Drama Queen," her dad would have said, but she had reason to be spooked. She'd searched an empty billiard room, an empty library, and an empty conservatory, and now she stood in the barren hall, thinking, *I'm knocking over a Clue game. Miss Scarlet in the hall with an inhaler.* Those were the days, the Golden Age, when men were men and women didn't have to do their own second-story work. What she needed was one of those old-fashioned guys who rescued women and stole things for them.

Oh, pull yourself together, she told herself. She crept upstairs and opened the doors to one empty room after another until she found a bedroom full of silky things tossed everywhere, perfume scenting the air, the kind of room that fit the kind of woman that Tilda would never be. For one thing, she'd never have enough money.

Something glowed on a desk. Tilda squinted at it through her glasses and realized it was the edge of a laptop computer. Clea Lewis had closed her laptop without shutting it down. *Careless,* Tilda thought, looking around at everything the woman had and didn't take care of. Really, she didn't deserve to own a Scarlet.

Downstairs, a phone rang, and Tilda picked up speed, making a circuit of the room in the dim streetlight that filtered through the curtains, checking behind furniture and under the bed, feeling her way when the shadows were too deep to see. The Scarlet wasn't that small, she thought as she turned to the quartet of paneled closet doors along one wall. Where the hell had Clea stashed it?

She opened the first two doors and shoved the clothes apart to search the back of the closet.

A man stood there.

Tilda turned to run, and he slapped his hand over her mouth from behind and yanked her against him. She kicked back and connected with his shin, and he swore and lost his balance and dragged her to the carpet as he fell.

He weighed a ton.

"Okay," he said calmly in her ear, while she struggled under him, trying to pry his hand from her mouth before her lungs collapsed. "Let's not panic."

I can't breathe, Tilda thought and sucked in air through her nose, inhaling a lot of dusty carpet.

"Because I'm really not this kind of guy," he went on. "There's no criminal intent here. Well, not against you."

He had a grip like a vise. Her lungs seized up as his hand pressed against her mouth, her muscles clenched, the world got darker, and the familiar panic overwhelmed her.

"I just need to be sure you're not going to scream," he said, but she was going to suffocate, she'd always known she would someday, her treacherous lungs betraying her like everything else in the Goodnight heritage, but not like this, not in the middle of breaking the law while being mugged by some deadweight lowlife, so as her lungs turned to stone and his voice faded away, she did the only thing she could think of.

She bit him.

CHAPTER · TWO

Downstairs, Gwen smiled over the last of dinner at sweet, chubby Mason Phipps, trying to keep her thoughts on the landscape that Mason was showing her and not on her youngest daughter, roaming somewhere in the house looking for evidence of her misspent youth.

"What do you think?" Mason said, and Gwen yanked her attention back to him. "It's a Corot." He stroked the top of the frame with one finger. "Tony wasn't sure, but I said, 'No, that's a Corot.' And when I had the canvas tested, I was right. It's a Corot."

It's a Goodnight, Gwen thought, but she said, "It's very beautiful."

"Those were the good old days, collecting with Tony," Mason said, and Gwen thought, *Tony sure thought so.* She listened with one ear while Mason waxed on and on about the old days. This dinner was lasting for months. She could have done an entire Double-Crostic by now. A hard one.

"I prefer folk art," the blonde at the other end of the table said, and Gwen turned to look at Clea Lewis, lovely as a spring morning, if spring had been around for forty-odd years but had taken really, really good care of itself.

"Folk art," Gwen said politely. "How interesting."

"Yes, I'm still collecting it," Mason said. "But it's not the same without Tony. He really had the life, buying art, running the gallery, hosting all those openings." The envy in Mason's voice was palpable, and Gwen thought, *Yeah*, Tony *had a good time.*

"And living with you and the girls, of course," Mason added, smiling at her. "Little Eve and Matilda. How are they?"

Eve's been divorced since her husband came out of the closet, and Tilda's given up forgery for burglary. "Fine," Gwen said.

"You were always the best part of his life, Gwennie," Mason said. "You don't mind if I call you Gwennie, do you? It's what Tony always called you. It's the way I always think of you."

"Of course not," Gwen said, thinking, *Yes, I mind, and a fat lot of good it does me.*

"Mason and I first met at a museum opening," Clea said, looking beautifully reminiscent, all dreamy blue eyes and creamy soft skin and silky blonde hair. Gwen thought about throwing a plate at her. "My late husband's grandmother founded the Hortensia Gardner Lewis Museum," Clea went on. "It was Cyril's passion." She smiled at Mason. "I find passionate men irresistible."

"Cyril was a good man," Mason said. "We were more

than business associates, we were great friends. I helped him the way Tony helped me."

Oh, God, I hope not. Gwen picked up her glass of wine. "The Lewis Museum?" She tried to remember if Tony had ever sold them anything. Private museums could be so gullible.

"It's a small museum," Mason said, adding, "Of course it got larger when I gave it my Homer Hodge collection."

Gwen choked on her wine.

"And now I've come home to finish the last of my new collection with a southern Ohio painter, Homer's daughter, Scarlet," he said while Gwen tried to turn the choke into a cough. "Do you remember Scarlet Hodge?"

"Uh," Gwen said, and hit the wine again.

"According to a newspaper interview Tony did back in eighty-seven, she only did six paintings." Mason leaned closer to Gwen. "In fact, as I remember, Tony had exclusive rights to her work."

"Are we having dessert?" Gwen said. "I love dessert."

"You eat dessert?" Clea said, clearly appalled, and Gwen turned to her gratefully.

"Every chance I get," she said. "If possible, I eat it twice."

"Good for you," Mason said. "I was hoping to come by and look at your records. I'd like to contact the others who bought Scarlets."

"The records are confidential," Gwen said. "Couldn't possibly. Unprofessional. So, dessert?"

Clea had been tapping on her water glass, evidently trying to summon the caterer who showed up now, looking like Bertie Wooster in his white jacket and slicked-back dark hair.

"Dessert, Thomas," Clea said.

Thomas exchanged a look with Gwen, not the first of the evening.

"Confidential, of course," Mason was saying. "But perhaps you could contact them for me. Let them know someone is interested in buying. For a commission."

"Really, Mason," Clea said. "The woman came for dinner, not to be harassed."

Mason looked across the table, his face suddenly hard, and Clea shut up. "But what would really help," he went on, turning back to Gwen, "would be to meet Scarlet. I'd like to do an article on her, nothing professional, of course." He laughed self-deprecatingly, and Gwen thought, *Article! Oh, no.* "Do you know where she is?" Mason asked.

Upstairs burgling your mistress. "I think she's dead," Gwen said.

"But she was so young," Mason protested. "In her teens. How did she die?"

Gwen thought about Tilda, throwing the last canvas at Tony and walking out the door seventeen years before. "She was murdered. By an insensitive son of a bitch." She smiled cheerfully at Mason. "And I have no idea what happened after that."

"That's fascinating," Mason said, leaning forward.

"Not if you're Homer or Scarlet," Gwen said, as

Thomas brought in the cheesecake. "Then it just stinks. Oh, good, chocolate. My favorite."

Beside her, Clea contained her scorn, and Gwen cut into her dessert and prayed that she'd heard the last of Homer and Scarlet Hodge.

"So when can I come by the gallery and talk more with you about Scarlet?" Mason said.

"Excellent cheesecake," Gwen said, and kept eating.

DAVY HAD been braced for Clea, so he was pleasantly surprised when he fell on somebody soft and padded. *Definitely not Clea*, he thought as he pinned her to the carpet in the darkness and tried to reason with her, one adult to another. It was a fine manly show of control for the ten seconds before she bit him. Then he jerked his hand away, swallowed his scream, and resisted the urge to deck her. A fistfight was not in his best interest at the moment, especially with somebody who fought dirty.

"Have you had your shots?" he whispered to her as he rubbed his hand.

She stayed under him, braced on one hand, gasping for breath as she fumbled for something in her pocket, the bill of her baseball cap shielding her face in the dark. He heard a *whoosh* and another gasp and leaned over her to see if she was all right, and she whispered savagely, "Touch me and I'll scream."

"No you won't," he whispered. "If you were going to scream, you'd have done it already."

She exhaled hard and pushed herself up from the floor, a blur in the darkness as she knocked him back, and he caught her sleeve as he rolled to his feet.

"*Easy,*" he whispered. "I can't let you go yet. I haven't—"

"I don't *care.*" She was whispering, too, as she tried to tug her sleeve away from him. "Let go, I have to get out of here."

"No." He pulled her arm closer and caught a hint of her scent, something sweet. "The thought of you on the loose discussing this with the cops does not—"

"*Look,* you idiot." Her whisper was savage as she tried to pry his hand from her arm. "I don't know who you are. I don't even know what you look like. How can I possibly tell anybody about you?"

"Good point." Davy dragged her over to the window and pulled back the drape to let the streetlight in, keeping to the shadow so she couldn't see him.

"*Hey.*" She was wearing a sloppy Oriental jacket buttoned to her throat, and she glared up at him, her strange light eyes glowing behind huge hexagonal glasses that made her look like a bug. "Are you *insane?*" she hissed at him. "What if somebody's out there?"

She jerked away from him again, and he let go of her arm before she dislocated it. "What are you dressed for?" he whispered. "Chinese baseball?"

She shoved past him, and he pulled off her baseball cap and held it above her head, feeling disappointed when her hair was too short to come tumbling down. She took another deep breath and turned back to him.

"Has it occurred to you that *this isn't a game*?"

"No." Davy stared at her dark, loopy curls, standing up like little horns. "It's always a game. Why else would you do it?"

"Give me that hat," she whispered, and when he held it higher, she pushed her glasses up the bridge of her nose and glared at him.

"No," he said. "And that was a question. Why are you here?"

She frowned at him, glaring harder.

"What?" he said. "Speak."

She shook her head, clearly frustrated. "Oh, *forget* it. *Keep* it."

She headed for the door and he caught her around the waist and pulled her back against him. "Tell me what you're up to, Mulan," he said in her ear as she tried to squirm away. "I'd like to be a gentleman, but the stakes are high."

She stopped struggling so suddenly that he drew in his breath. *Cinnamon.* Her hair smelled like cinnamon and vanilla, like the rolls his sister used to make on Sunday mornings. Then she turned in the curve of his arm to face him, which was nice all on its own.

"An old-fashioned gentleman," she said, her voice low, and Davy felt a stirring of alarm. "I could use one of those."

"I'm not." Davy loosened his hold and backed away toward the closet. "Twenty-first-century cad, that's me."

She stepped closer, and he tripped over Clea's shoes and stumbled backward.

"I need a favor," she whispered up at him as she backed him through Clea's clothes and up against the wall, and her low, husky voice would have set up a nice hum in his blood if she hadn't been so stiff as she pressed against him.

You want to seduce me, you have to melt a little, he thought, but she smelled like the best mornings of his life, so he didn't push her away.

"I'm not good at this kind of thing," she whispered, putting her palms on his chest, her hands trembling a little.

No kidding, Davy thought. He'd held two-by-fours that were more yielding.

"While you clearly are—" she clutched his shirt "—good at this."

"Okay, you really are no good at this," he told her, keeping his voice low. "So cut to the chase. What do you want?" He heard her sigh in the darkness, and there was a tremor in it, and he realized she was afraid and put his arm around her. "It's okay," he told her, without thinking.

"There's a painting," she said. "Eighteen inches square. A city scene with a checkerboard sky with lots of stars. It's somewhere in this house."

"A painting," Davy said, knowing what was coming next.

"Steal it for me," she whispered, and his hands tightened on her automatically, feeling all that warm softness under her slippery jacket.

Okay, the chances of her delivering what she was

promising were nil, and she was a thief which couldn't be good, and she was asking him to steal which was worse than anything she'd done to him up until then including the bite and the shin kick. A smart man would say no and escape, dragging her with him so she couldn't rat him out.

But life had been so boring lately.

And she was afraid.

"Please?" she said, pressing closer, her lips parted.

"Sure," he said, and kissed her lightly, wanting her to taste like cinnamon, surprised to find her mouth cool like mint, even more surprised a second later to find her kissing him back, rising to meet him, the tip of her tongue touching his, and he tightened his arms around her and kissed her as if he meant it.

"Vilma Kaplan," he said when he broke the kiss, and she jerked back, and then he heard it, too, the step outside the door, and almost knocked her off her feet trying to get the closet door closed before someone came in.

Okay, that's an omen, he thought. *Stay away from this woman and her tongue.* Then a moment later she sighed beside him and he put his arm around her again.

Thank God, she's a brunette, he thought as he listened to Clea rustle out in the bedroom. *It's the blondes that screw up my life.*

FIFTEEN MINUTES earlier, Clea Lewis had been watching Gwen Goodnight slurp cheesecake and thinking of ways to permanently separate her from Mason, with an ax if necessary, when the caterer interrupted her.

"Excuse me, Mrs. Lewis?" he said from the doorway, and Clea turned to look at him, keeping her face pleasant because Mason liked it when people went out of their way to be nice to the help. Also, they might need a caterer again. You never knew.

"There's a telephone call for you," the caterer said.

"Thank you, Thomas." Clea turned back to Mason and the threat from the gallery. "I'm so sorry," she said, radiating graciousness.

"Perfectly all right," Mason said, happy because he was talking about art again. Mason wasn't hugely attractive, but he was hugely rich, so the smile Clea gave him was genuine.

Gwen Goodnight widened her pale blue eyes that couldn't compare to Clea's, which Clea knew because she'd compared them. "No problem," Gwen said to Clea. "Tell whoever it is we said hi."

Clea nodded and slid her chair back, keeping her eye on Gwen. Gwen had crow's-feet and her jawline was going, but she knew art, and more than that, Mason thought she was charming. "Gwen Goodnight," he'd said when he'd taken her phone message. "Charming little woman. I'd almost forgotten her. I invited her to dinner." And now here she was.

Fortunately, Gwen looked her age, which was just careless of her.

"Hello?" Clea said when she'd picked up the phone.

"Clea? Clea, darling?" a man said.

"Who is this?" she said, annoyed. The last thing she needed was Mason hearing some man calling her "darling."

"It's Ronald," the voice said, clearly hurt.

"What do you want?" She stretched to see into the dining room. Mason was still leaning toward Gwen. Honest to God, she'd gotten the man a caterer for the evening—well, she'd hired the man who showed up at the door canvassing for odd jobs after she realized Mason expected her to handle dinner—and now he was using the dinner party she'd arranged to flirt with another woman. Where was loyalty? Where was appreciation?

"I know you said not to call," Ronald was saying, breathless, "but this is important. Davy Dempsey has found us."

"What?" Clea looked around to make sure Davy wasn't standing there, flashing that lousy grin.

"He tracked us down somehow," Ronald said. "He even knew where you were, I don't know how. He threatened me to keep me quiet, Clea, but I had to tell you, I don't care if he beats me up, I had to tell you because I love you."

"How did he follow me here?" Clea said, her voice like a lash. Honest to God, she had a *genius* for picking men who would let her down. Davy, Zane, Cyril . . . "He didn't know where I was. He followed *you.* What did you do, leave a forwarding address?"

"I'm taking a great risk telling you this at all," Ronald said, his voice thick with hurt. "He's *dangerous.* He threatened to *kill me.* If I didn't love you so much—"

"He's a con man, not a hit man." Clea thought about Davy—good-looking, shifty, and implacable—and glanced around the empty hall again, thinking fast. He could be anywhere, the bastard, looking for his money. She had to get rid of him. Ronald should do that. He owed her. It was his fault Davy was here. "If he's so dangerous, why did you send him after me?" Clea let her voice tremble. "Oh, Ronald, I'll never be able to trust you again—"

"*Clea*—" Ronald's voice strangled on his panic.

"—unless you help me." Clea let her voice drop, deepening with promise. "Unless you prove you love me by saving me, Ronald. If you did that, I'd know we—"

"Anything," Ronald said, his breath coming quicker. "*Anything*. We should talk about it. Let me see you. If we could—"

"You have to prove you love me first." Clea craned her neck to make sure Gwen hadn't crawled into Mason's lap. God, you just could not trust men.

"I'll meet you," Ronald said breathlessly. "We'll—"

"I can't possibly meet you while Davy is around."

"Clea, please—"

"Get rid of Davy and then we'll talk," Clea said. "I have to go—"

"Wait, wait, I have a plan for that," Ronald said. "I think I can get him to agree to leave you the million he stole from you and only take the money he made with it. The first million is rightfully your—"

"It's *all* mine," Clea said, outrage making her louder.

Honestly, where was this man's mind? How long did he think a million would last her in this economy? Well, in any economy. She dropped her voice again, this time to the purr that had made stronger men than Ronald twitch. "You *know* that, Ronald darling, you *know* that's true."

"Of course," Ronald said automatically. "But if he'll leave—"

"He won't leave," Clea said. "I know him, he's impossible. Get rid of him, and then you and I can be together forever. I only have a few more paintings to buy, Ronald. Another month at the most and then we'll be together again. With a beautiful art collection."

"A month?" Ronald took a deep breath. "I don't—"

"But only if you get rid of Davy," Clea said. "As long as he's around, we'll *never* be together."

There was a silence on the other end of the line, and Clea stretched to see what was going on in the dining room now. Gwen was laughing at something Mason said. The woman was practically a hyena. And her jawline was definitely going. Clea put her fingers under her chin and pushed. Still firm, but for how long? There was a limit to plastic surgery, after all. Too much and you started to look like—

"What exactly," Ronald said slowly, "do you mean by 'get rid of'?"

In the dining room, Gwen put her hand on Mason's arm, and Clea said, "Get him *out of the picture*."

"You mean, *kill him*?"

Clea stopped glaring at Gwen and Mason to think about it. Death was a little more drastic than she'd intended, but it would get Davy out of the way permanently. Maybe Ronald could pin his murder on Gwen. That would solve all her problems.

On the other hand, it was Davy. He'd been good to her a long time ago.

Oh, hell, let Ronald figure it out. "Ronald, either you love me or you don't."

"He has *family*," Ronald was saying. "Real family, he calls his sister every week. I don't think I can—"

"Then you don't get me," Clea said. "If you won't take care of a little thing like this, I can't trust you to take care of me, which means I can't spend the rest of my life with you. You betrayed me, Ronald, you sent that horrible man here and now you won't save me. I'm so upset, I can't even talk to you anymore."

"Clea—"

"Good-bye forever, Ronald," Clea said and hung up in the middle of his pleading, hearing the crack of desperation that meant she had him.

Now all she had to do was wait for Ronald to push Davy under a bus or deport him or something. Ronald loved her, he'd do it. Not a problem. As long as Davy wasn't already in the house. He couldn't be in the house already, could he? She should have asked Ronald for more details.

Clea took one more look in the dining room and went upstairs to her bedroom to make sure Davy wasn't ripping her off. That's the kind of world it was: a woman had to do damn near everything for herself.

OKAY, OKAY, Tilda thought as she stood as still as she possibly could. *There's a way out of this. I just have to slow down and think.* She drew in a deep breath. Oxygen was important, especially if you were asthmatic. Lack of it made you unconscious and vulnerable. She breathed in again, and the kissing bandit beside her put his arm around her.

That was sweet. He must think she was a complete idiot. Or a complete slut. She'd kissed him. She'd sunk into the dark anonymity of the closet and thought, *Oh, thank God, he's going to help me,* and kissed him back. She was an idiot slut. Of course, he was a thief, so it wasn't as though he was in a position of superiority there. *I have to get out more,* she thought. Six months of celibacy and she was swapping tongues with burglars in the middle of felonies.

Outside, Clea Lewis slammed a drawer shut, and Tilda froze. The bandit pressed her shoulder, and she tried not to feel comforted. He was a crook, for heaven's sake, which strangely enough did not lessen his appeal. *Goodnight blood,* Tilda thought. Like calling to like.

He shoved at her gently and she realized he was trying to get her to move down into the other part of the closet, away from the first set of doors.

Right. She stepped sideways, and he eased down the

wall with her, his hand now warm on her back as the closet door opened.

She heard Clea shove the clothes aside where they'd been standing, and her entire life passed before her eyes: faked paintings and forged murals interspersed with glimpses of family. She moved her head a fraction of an inch toward the man standing between her and ruin, just enough that her forehead touched his shoulder in the dark. She was always the one who rescued, but tonight, he could do it. He was as bad as she was, probably worse, he needed the good karma points, he could get them out.

Clea stopped pawing through her clothes and shut the closet door, and Tilda inhaled in shuddery relief, smelled soap and cotton, and tried not to shake. When she heard the door close outside, he said, "Here," and opened the closet door. *But it's so safe in here,* she thought, and followed him out.

"Well," she whispered when they were out in Clea's bedroom again, "I really apprec—"

"*Fuck,*" he said, and she followed his eyes to the desk. The laptop was gone. "Sorry," he said to her, keeping his voice low this time.

"Are you kidding?" Tilda said. "I've been wanting to scream that for the past eight hours." She drew a deep breath. He was wearing her black baseball cap, the one she'd borrowed from Andrew, the one embroidered with BITCH on the front in white. That was okay, he could have it to remember her by. "Well, it's been great, but—"

"There's a diner three blocks east of here," he said. "I'll meet you there."

"What?" Tilda whispered. "Why? Listen, if this is about the kiss, I apologize, I—"

"The painting," he whispered back, trying to push her toward the door.

"You know," Tilda said, resisting the push, "I was wrong. This is not your problem. I'll—"

He leaned closer, large in the dim light, and she stopped. "Vilma, I don't know what you do for a living, but it's not theft. Go wait in the diner."

"No, really."

"You want to stay and search the place?"

The darkness closed in around her, and she felt her lungs start to tighten. She was such a geek. "No."

"Then go away." He steered her toward the door. "And if you get caught? You never met me."

"I wish," Tilda said, and slipped out the door, feeling like a fool and a failure.

WHEN GWEN got back to the gallery, she went straight to the cabinet above the counter and pulled out the vodka bottle. It was empty.

"Damn," she said and dropped it in the trash, prepared to savage whoever had finished it. It wouldn't be Andrew or Jeff; they kept their booze in their apartment. Eve wouldn't have finished off the bottle. And Nadine knew better.

Must have been me, Gwen thought. *Good, just what*

I always wanted to be, a middle-aged amnesiac drunk.
She looked for something soothing on the jukebox and
settled for "Do You Know the Way to San José?"
Dionne was always good. San José would be good, too.
Anywhere but here.

She sank down on the leather couch and tried not to
think about Tilda trapped in that damn house. She
needed a vacation, although it was going to be a while
before she could leave. A year before Eve finished her
teaching degree. Three years before Nadine went to
college.

Andrew came in holding a glass, Spot on his heels.

Twelve years before the dog died.

"There you are," Andrew said, putting the glass on
the counter.

It had about half an inch of clear liquid in it, and
Gwen said, "Is that vodka?"

Andrew smiled at her and said, "Yep," missing the
hint. He looked like one of those blond movie hunks
from the sixties, although that may have been due to
the eye makeup. "Nadine says Tilda's back and she
brought this." He gestured to Spot who gave a shuddery
little whine and collapsed on the carpet. "Did she leave
again?" He opened up the below-counter refrigerator
and took out a carton of orange-pineapple juice. "Oh,
and the bank called."

Twenty-six years before the mortgages were paid off.
That meant she'd be seventy-nine, probably not in the
mood to leave anymore. It also meant she was going to
need about three hundred Double-Crostic books to pass

the time before death. There probably weren't that many. Well, she was not going to descend to word searches no matter how bad it got. She had standards, damn it.

"Gwennie?" Andrew said, pouring juice into his glass.

"You still have mascara on."

Andrew nodded. "Work was hell. Eve decided to leave the Double Take while she was still Louise, and I had to pry her off a guy on the way out. Louise has *no* taste in men."

"No, she just doesn't have your taste in men," Gwen said.

Andrew sat down beside Gwen on the couch. "God, it's good to be home. Hey, Nadine told me she sold a painting for a thousand dollars. Some kid we raised, huh? She sells about six hundred more, Eve can stop being Louise four nights a week and you'll be safe here forever."

"Eve likes being Louise," Gwen said. "And it was a Scarlet. Tilda's at Mason Phipps's house, stealing it back now."

"Oh, crap, Gwennie." Andrew looked exasperated. "I thought Louise was our major problem."

"Louise is not a problem," Gwen said. "And if you're not going to drink that screwdriver, give it to me. I've had a terrible night and it's getting worse. Tilda's still in that house, and for all I know, they've caught her. And it's going to be hard to explain why she's there without pulling this whole life down around us." She looked around the ancient office. "I'd be okay with that if it didn't mean I'd go to jail."

Andrew handed over the screwdriver.

"You're a good boy, Andrew," Gwen said. "Now go get the bottle."

TILDA SAT in the diner, drumming her fingers on the table next to her coffee cup until the guy in the booth next to her asked her to stop. She turned her head to look at the clock on the back wall. It had been over an hour. Maybe Clea Lewis had caught him. Maybe he was telling her that a woman had tried to steal the painting. Maybe he had given the police her baseball cap. Maybe—

"Hello, Vilma," he said, sliding into the booth across from her. "Miss me?"

TILDA PULLED HER FOOT FROM UNDER THE DUFFEL BAG he dropped under the table. "Do I know you?"

"Yep." He settled into the booth. "You stuck your tongue down my throat about an hour ago. Did I thank you for that?"

She squinted at him through her glasses. At first glance, he was average looking, a mild-mannered, dark-haired, Clark Kent kind of guy with horn-rimmed glasses in a beat-up nothing-colored jacket; the only notable thing about him was Andrew's "Bitch" base-ball cap that he'd swiped from her back at Clea's.

On second glance, the glint in his eye and the set of his jaw made her twitch.

"Did you want this?" he said and she felt something bump her leg under the table.

When she reached down, she felt paper wrapping and under that, the edge of a painting, and the relief that rolled over her was so intense that she closed her eyes. "*Thank you.* I forgive you for everything."

"Everything what?" he said. "Saving your butt?"

"For mugging me in a closet." One corner of the

paper was torn back, and Tilda could see the stars in the checkerboard sky beneath it. Definitely her stars. *Thank you, thank you.*

"You jumped me," he was saying. "I was there first. Technically, it was my closet, Vilma."

"Who's Vilma?" Tilda said, her interest in his glint diminishing.

"Nobody watches the late movies anymore. I blame cable."

Oh, good, he was colorful. Tilda smiled at him brightly. "Well, gee, this has been great. Thanks for all your help." She started to slide out of the booth and he put his foot on the bench, trapping her.

"Hold it," he said. "You owe me. Who are you and why were you hitting Clea's closet?"

"No," Tilda said and pushed at his foot.

"Yes," he said, keeping his foot where it was.

"If I create a scene," she began and then stopped as she saw the problem. She was sitting in a booth with a hot painting. She couldn't afford a scene. Somebody would come up and say, "What is that?" and then she'd have to explain and anything was better than talking about the Scarlets, anything, even this yahoo and his glint.

"There you go," he said. "The good news is, I don't care what you're up to, I just want information. Who are you and—"

The waitress came by with the coffeepot, and he shrank into his jacket a little more. "Hamburger?" he said to her, and she took out her pad without even looking at him. If anybody asked tomorrow, she wouldn't remember a thing about him which was amazing because he really was a piece of work. "Coffee," he said. The waitress nodded, put her pad back in her apron pocket, topped up Tilda's cup and left, still not looking at him.

"Now," he said to Tilda. "Your name."

Tilda sat back and thought fast. "Call me Vilma. The painting is mine. Mrs. Lewis took it and wouldn't give it back, so I had to go in and get it."

"She stole it?" he said. "That doesn't sound like her."

"She bought it," Tilda said, "but she didn't pay for it."

"That sounds like her," he said and Tilda thought, *You know her well.* Her thoughts of Clea, never warm to begin with, grew colder.

"So who are you?" she said. "And what were you doing there?"

"I'm a consultant for an elite law enforcement agency," he said, looking at her over the top of his horn-rims. "Call me Bond. James—"

"Funny," Tilda said.

The waitress brought his coffee, and when she was gone, he said, "So why didn't you call the police?"

"That would be so unpleasant." Tilda lifted her chin. "And she could say she had the painting on approval."

"So you turned to B and E to avoid the unpleasantness." He nodded. "We'll come back to that. Who taped the door for you?"

"What?" Tilda said, widening her eyes the way Gwen and Eve always did when they wanted to look innocent.

He snapped his fingers. "Betty Boop."

"What?" Tilda said again, this time for real.

"That's who you remind me of. Curly hair, bug eyes, Kewpie-doll mouth. My sister dressed up like her for Halloween once."

"Fascinating," Tilda said, her eyebrows snapping together over the "bug eyes" part. "Can I go now?"

"No, Betty, you can't. When I got to Clea's, I tried the doors and they were all locked except one at the side. The latch was taped down so it wouldn't lock. Who did that for you?"

"I have no idea what—"

"Betty, you can stop lying. I just want to know who you know on the inside so I can know him, too."

The waitress brought his hamburger and slapped the check on the table and then wandered off again.

"I don't know anybody inside," Tilda said as he began to work his way through the sandwich at the speed of light. "I went in during the day and taped it."

He looked at her over the top of his glasses and she stopped. "Here's some advice," he said, threat palpable in his tone. "Don't lie to me. It's a waste of your time and my patience."

"Oh, please," Tilda said, unimpressed.

He nodded and bit into the hamburger again. "That tough stuff never works for me," he said when he'd swallowed, his voice light again. "Which is odd because I really can be a bastard."

He smiled at her, and Tilda saw menace in his eyes and felt her throat close up.

"Want to push your luck?" he said.

"No," Tilda said. "Okay, here's the truth. Somebody taped it for me but that person does not work inside. I don't think anybody works there. I think it's just Mason Phipps and Clea Lewis, and I don't think there's any time when the house is empty for sure."

He sat back and regarded her with something that might have passed for approval. "So you set up a dinner party. Not stupid."

"Thank you." Tilda tapped his shoe. "May I go now?"

"No," he said, not moving his foot. "Clea bought the painting from you. Why?"

"No idea," Tilda said. "I guess she liked it."

"Why do you have to have it back?"

"No," Tilda said. "That will not help you."

"And yet I feel sure it would." He pushed his empty plate away, and Tilda blinked her surprise. He must have been starving to inhale a hamburger like that. "Let's take this from the top."

"Let's not." Tilda sat up straighter. "Look, I know you've got me, but I have no connection with Clea Lewis, I've never even met her, and I'm done telling you things." She stuck out her chin. "So if that's not enough, go ahead and turn me in."

He looked at her sadly. "Betty, I am not the kind of guy who turns people in." Then he stopped, as if he'd remembered something. "Well, I'm not the kind of guy who turns people like you in." He picked up his coffee cup and smiled at her.

"Thank you," Tilda said, ignoring the little leap her pulse gave. "You're a real prince. Move your foot."

He sipped his coffee, never taking his eyes off her. "You're not a thief. You'd starve to death trying to steal for a living, and you clearly haven't been starving."

"*Hey,*" Tilda said.

"That wasn't an insult. That was an observation made while bouncing you on the carpet." He moved his foot off the seat and slid out of the booth, taking off Andrew's baseball cap and dropping it crookedly on her head as he went. "Okay, this conversation is not over." He reached under the table for the duffel bag. "Stay here, Betty. When I get back, we're going to start all over again."

Oh, no we're not, Tilda thought and watched him go toward the back, his shoulders hunched, unremarkable. She straightened her cap as he turned into the hall where the restrooms were, gave him an extra minute to be sure, and then slid out of the booth and headed for the door, the painting clutched firmly under her arm.

The waitress caught her on the way out. "Wait a minute. Who's paying for the hamburger?"

"He is," Tilda said.

"He's gone," the waitress said, blocking her way. "Went out the back door."

"The son of a bitch," Tilda said, outraged. "He stuck me with the check?"

"That's a guy for you," the waitress said. "With the coffee that's nine eighty-seven."

"Jerk." Tilda dug in her purse for the money, kicking herself. She'd actually had semiwarm thoughts about the bastard, which just went to show how pathetic she was. Well, the good news was, he was out of her life.

And her Scarlet was back. She felt slightly sick at the thought but it was all good, having it back. It really was.

"Thank you," she told the waitress and headed out the door, grateful for her narrow escape.

ACROSS THE street, Davy lounged against the side of a building, hidden in the shadows. *Sorry about that, Betty,* he thought as he saw the waitress catch her by the door. She looked up and down the street, undoubtedly gunning for him, and he stayed motionless in the shadows, watching her sling her bag over her shoulder and anchor the painting under her arm before starting off, taking long strides and making people turn to watch as she walked by. *Clearly not cut out for crime,* he thought as he began to follow her.

Four blocks later she cut down a side street and he picked up speed to catch her, only to find himself alone in an alley. Kicking himself for not watching her closer, he went back out into the street and looked around.

There was nothing of interest on the street except for a dingy brick storefront that had dim light filtering through its windows. Davy walked over and looked through the glass. The shop was dark, but at the back was a door with a window in it and people moving around inside. And through the shadows in the front of the store he could see two well-executed but depressed-looking seascapes.

Paintings.

That is not a coincidence, he thought, and stepped back to scan the peeling sign over the storefront. It was hard to read because the gold letters had faded, but after a minute he'd spelled it out: THE GOODNIGHT GALLERY.

So Betty the art thief had connections to an art gallery. He caught sight of a smaller sign in the lower corner of the show window and moved closer to read it.

"Furnished Apartment for Rent," it said. *"Inquire within."*

He looked over his shoulder, suddenly cautious, remembering his dad: if things seem too good to be true, get out. Michael Dempsey wasn't much of a father, but as a survivor, he had no peer.

Davy considered the situation. If some human being wasn't setting him up for a fall, fate was. He thought about Betty, her pale blue eyes clueless behind those bug glasses, failing miserably at seducing him at Clea's, stonewalling him with no finesse at all in the diner. The chances that she'd led him here on purpose seemed slim to none.

Fate, on the other hand, could very well be trolling for him. He'd been a pool player long enough to know that if you had to choose between skill and luck, you chose luck; a con man long enough to know that if you had to choose between a great plan and fate on your side, you picked fate. And here he was, up to his ass in skill and plans.

The situation required some thought and he needed some capital, so he went to find a bar with a pool table. Betty could wait.

After all, he knew where to find her.

FIVE MINUTES earlier, Tilda had let herself in the back door of the gallery and then into the office. Gwen was stretched out on the beat-up leather couch, her blonde hair picking up some flame from the bubbler jukebox, which was playing the Cookies's "Don't Say Nothin' Bad About My Baby," but Spot leaped to his feet from the threadbare carpet and launched himself at Tilda. She caught him as Gwen sat up so fast she almost slid off the leather couch.

"Where have you been? My God, I thought you'd—"

"I know." Tilda tried to control Spot's flailing rear end without dropping the painting. "It's solved. Look!" She held up the paper-wrapped square, and Gwen sank back down onto the cushions.

"Thank God." Gwen lifted her eyes to the ceiling.

Tilda dropped the painting on the couch and hauled the frantic dog up to her shoulder to comfort him as he began to hyperventilate again. "I know," she said, patting him like a baby, enjoying his blatant need for her. "I can't believe it's all over."

"It's not," Gwen said.

The office door opened again before Tilda could say

anything, and Andrew came in, Eve padding behind him in purple pajamas and fuzzy slippers. "We heard you come in," he said, pulling Tilda into a bear hug and crushing Spot in the process. "We've *missed* you, delinquent." Tilda leaned against him for a moment, loving his arms around her, and then Spot gave a strangled moan and Andrew let go.

"Now me." Eve shoved aside her ex-husband to hug, too, her curls brushing Tilda's chin. "We missed you *so much*," she said, her voice muffled in Tilda's neck.

"I missed you, too," Tilda said, patting her back. "You have no idea how much I want to talk to you."

Eve pulled away. "What's wrong? If it's money, we're okay. Nadine sold an old painting for a thousand dollars!"

"Yeah," Tilda said. "Not good. It was a Scarlet."

"So?" Eve's eyes went to the painting on the couch, the paper torn even more now so that most of the sky was visible. "Is that it? Why is it back?"

"Because it's a fake," Tilda said flatly.

"Why?" Eve picked up the painting and began to pick at the tape that bound it. "Because you signed it 'Scarlet'? So?" She shrugged. "It's a stage name. Like my 'Louise.' Writers do it, don't they?" She looked at Tilda. "Write under fake names for their privacy? You were just painting in private."

"We told people Scarlet was Homer's daughter. They bought her paintings because of Homer."

"I think her paintings were wonderful." Eve tugged

at the tape. "I think that's why they bought them, not because of that old poop Homer."

"Oh, Homer wasn't that bad," Gwen said.

Tilda lifted her chin. "It doesn't matter now. We're safe."

"No we aren't," Gwen said.

Eve gave up on the tape and began to tear the paper off.

"Mason is looking for the rest of the Scarlets," Gwen said, and Tilda held the dog tighter as her stomach went south again. "He wants to write about Scarlet. All he can find about her is that one interview your father did, so he wants me to tell him all about her. He wants to *talk* to her."

"You don't remember *anything*," Tilda said, as Spot squirmed in her arms. "We've got the painting back, so—"

"I don't think so," Eve said, looking at the canvas as she dropped the paper on the floor.

"What?" Tilda said, and Eve turned it around so they could see.

"The one Nadine told me about had our building in it." She pointed to the fat little cows that dotted the landscape. "She didn't mention cows."

Tilda looked at the painting and felt her lungs go.

Cows.

Gwen looked at Tilda. "That's not the painting Nadine sold Clea Lewis. You stole the wrong painting."

"I *knew* that guy was trouble," Tilda said, still

staring at the cows as she put Spot on the floor. They weren't even her cows; they'd been her father's idea.

"Guy?" Andrew said. "What guy?"

Her father had said, "Scarlet is a country girl. She doesn't live in our building, for God's sake, are you *trying* to blow this whole deal? She paints, I don't know, cows. Go paint cows." And Tilda had, fat little cows with gold filigree wings that flitted all over the landscape that Eve was holding up.

The landscape that somebody had bought.

Legally.

She felt for her inhaler in her pocket again. She was using it too much. Her asthma was out of control.

Cows.

"*What guy?*" Andrew said.

"This yahoo I met in Clea's closet." Tilda took the painting from Eve and propped it up against the wall on her father's old mahogany desk. "He stole it for me."

"Somebody *else* knows about this?" Gwen said. "Somebody *else* stole this?"

"He was already burglarizing the place." Tilda touched the painting, remembering the fun she'd had painting the fat blocky cows and their impossibly fine wings, the thin strokes of gold paint looking like lace on the checkerboard sky. They'd been difficult, but they'd been such joy.

"Where is he now?" Gwen said. "Is he going to talk?"

"No." Tilda turned away from the cows. "He's history. Focus on the real problem."

"He stole the wrong painting," Andrew said. "That

can't be good. That's a felony or something. I'll ask Jeff."

"No you won't," Tilda said, back in charge again. "This is one of the many things Jeff will not want to know about. Not until I get arrested and I need him to defend me, then we tell him." She looked at the cows, winging their way home, and resisted them. "This one's a Scarlet, too."

Gwen sat back. "I thought so. It's Mason's. He said he was collecting them."

"Then he's going to be really mad when he finds this one gone," Andrew said.

"It's okay, Andrew," Tilda said. "You got a Get Out of Jail Free card with the divorce. You don't have to play with the rest of us."

Eve said, "Andrew?" and he went over and sat down beside her.

"I'm here, honey," he said, putting his arm around her. "Always will be. Tilda knows that, she's just being cranky."

Yeah, Tilda thought. *That's probably why nobody puts an arm around me.*

Andrew frowned a little. "I can't speak for Jeff, though. You know lawyers."

"Jeff will stick," Gwen told him. "He loves you. You don't leave the people you love." She made it sound like a life sentence.

"Don't worry," Tilda said. "I'll figure something out. I will fix this." She picked up the painting.

"Maybe you can get that guy in the closet to steal again," Eve said.

Right, that guy who'd called her Vilma. She turned to her mother. "Gwennie, have you ever heard of Vilma Kaplan? Somebody from the late movie?"

"Sure," Gwen said. "Vilma Kaplan, Bundle of Lust. It's from an old Mel Brooks movie."

Tilda closed her eyes. Oh, good. Along with everything else that she'd screwed up, she'd necked with a comedian. "I am never going to see that guy again," she said to Eve, and went downstairs to bury the cows with the rest of her past.

LEANING AGAINST the wall in one of the Brewery District's up-scale pubs, Davy punched numbers into his cell phone while the mark he'd been playing pool with gloated over the twenty bucks he'd just won. "I may need help," he said when his best friend answered.

"Beating up Rabbit?" Simon said, his faint British accent slurring over the line.

"No. Rabbit is no longer the problem."

"He's not dead, is he?" Simon said, not sounding as though he cared.

"No, just terminally stupid. He gave all my money to a woman."

"Fair enough. Didn't you take it from a woman in the first place?"

"That's the woman he gave it to."

"Which explains why he robbed you and not me," Simon said. "He thought he was righting a wrong. Good old Rabbit. The blockhead. What is it you need? I'm in the middle of something here."

"Anyone I know?"

"Rebecca."

"Brunettes," Davy said. "You need a twelve-step program."

"Whereas your fetish for blondes is—"

"Just good taste. I convinced Rabbit to give me Clea's account numbers. Now I need her password which I can get from her laptop."

"I know nothing about computers."

"But you know everything about theft," Davy said.

There was a long silence, and then Simon said, with barely suppressed envy, "You're going to steal her computer?"

"No," Davy said. "I just want some time alone with it. Clea's staying with her next husband, so I went into his place and looked—"

"What do you mean, you went in?" Simon asked, his accent flattening as his voice went tense. "You went in when there were people there?"

"That's why I got in," Davy said patiently. "If there hadn't been people there, the place would have been locked."

"This is why amateurs should never turn to crime," Simon said. "You just confessed to aggravated burglary. Are you on a land line or your cell phone?"

"Cell," Davy said. "And I didn't steal anything." Much.

"You were a burglar the moment you entered -

uninvited. And the presence of people there made it aggravated. Normally that would put you in real trouble, but since you didn't attack anyone, a good lawyer could probably get you off with only a couple of years."

Davy thought about bouncing Betty on the carpet and decided not to share.

"The problem is," Simon was saying, "you'd have to spend those years in *prison*, you fool. Tell me you wore gloves."

"It was a spur-of-the-moment deal."

"AFIS has your prints. Imagine how thrilled the Bureau will be to know their freelance fraud consultant has turned to second-story work. Tell me where you are and I'll come consult in person."

"*No.* You're on the wagon. What I need to know—"

"I'm not leaving the wagon," Simon said. "But I'd rather give advice in person than over a bloody cell phone. Besides, I want to meet Clea. If she managed to seduce both you and Rabbit, she has a wide range. Exactly how good is she?"

"In bed?" Davy conjured up the memory again. "Phenomenal. But then you die."

"You lived. Where are you staying?"

Davy thought about the APARTMENT FOR RENT sign. Maybe it was time to trust in fate. "Right now, nowhere. Tomorrow, over an art gallery, a couple blocks from Clea. German Village."

"Why there?"

"Strangely enough, there's a brunette I need to know better. Looks like Betty Boop."

"Really." Simon sounded amused. "Perhaps I can help with that, too."

"No. You're bored out of your mind and burglary is the only high that does it for you."

"Whereas you followed Rabbit to Ohio because you have no interest in crime."

"I came to get my money back," Davy said virtuously.

"If you wanted your money, you'd have called the Bureau. You're there because you want the rush. Completely understandable. I'll be there tomorrow."

"No you will not," Davy said. "Stay there and tell me how to get into this damn house."

"Does it have an alarm?"

"I don't think so. No stickers."

"Break a basement window at the back of the house," Simon said. "They'll find it eventually but by then the crime scene will be so old, it'll be useless. Wear gloves. And make sure the apartment you rent has two bedrooms."

"No," Davy said, but Simon had already hung up.

Davy jammed his phone in his jacket pocket.

"You gonna play this second game or not, son?" his mark called to him from the pool table.

"Oh, yeah, I'm coming," Davy said, feigning reluctance. "But I gotta win my money back here. How about upping the stakes?"

"You bet," the guy said, happily clueless, and Davy tried to ignore the surge in his blood. Hustling pool was not illegal. He was still on the straight and narrow. There was no reason for excitement.

"Your break," the mark said, and Davy felt his pulse leap and picked up his cue.

DEEP IN the cool basement of the Goodnight Gallery, Tilda stopped at the locked door to her father's old studio, Spot snuffling anxiously at her feet. She looked at her cows again and heard her father say, "Well, it's not real painting, but the idiots who liked Homer's work will buy it."

Somehow the thought of locking her cows in there seemed wrong. Her father had been right, it hadn't been real painting, but still . . .

She crossed the hall, Spot close behind, and opened the door to the storeroom that filled the other half of the spotlessly white basement. When she flipped on the light, there were dustsheets everywhere but no dust; Nadine had been thorough and the air cleaner was doing the rest. She pulled on the nearest sheet and uncovered a wing chair painted with undulating snakes that made funky green and purple and blue stripes across the frame and upholstery. Their hot little eyes winked at her and their tongues curled around their little snakey cheeks, and Tilda grinned back, charmed in spite of herself. She went from dustcover to dustcover, peeking under them to find all of her pre-Scarlet work: a table painted with red dogs with floppy ears, a chest of drawers scrolled with chartreuse snails, several

mismatched chairs painted with conga lines of yellow
and orange butterflies that flirted at her with pale blue
eyes. Spot followed her patiently while she looked
under the rest of the covers, finding a different animal
batting its eyes at her, daring her to laugh, and she told
herself it was just a kid's junk while she smiled.

Then she remembered her father, finding the pieces
in the storeroom when she was sixteen. "I spend ten
years teaching you to paint," he'd said. "And *this* is
what you do?"

"Junk," she said now and covered it up again.

In the back, she found the last piece she'd done, the
one Andrew had called the Temptation Bed, its leaf-
covered frame now all set up thanks to Nadine and
Ethan, with the mattress on it and the quilt Gwen had
made to go with it folded at the head. Spot jumped up on
the bed and sat down at the foot, shivering a little in the
air-conditioning, and Tilda petted him while she
considered the work she'd done before she'd become
Scarlet Hodge and Matilda Veronica. The headboard
was covered with the leafy spreading arms of the Tree of
Knowledge of Good and Evil, and beneath its branches a
naked blond Adam grinned at a naked dark Eve, her
short curls growing like little question marks around
her head. Behind them in the painted bushes, animals
prowled, the purple snakes and blue monkeys and
orange flamingos from the other pieces of furniture, all
winking and grinning at the first human figures Tilda
had ever painted that weren't copied from the Old

Masters. Everything was free and wild and wrong, not real painting at all.

I couldn't paint like this now, she thought. *I know too much.* It was like making love: once you learned how much you had to lose, you could never be completely free doing it again.

She sighed and propped the cows up against the headboard under the tree, and thought about the other five Scarlets, out roaming wild with Mason stalking them, and faced what she'd known since Gwennie had dropped her bomb: she wasn't going to be safe until she had them all back.

"Oh, hell," she said, and Spot put his nose under her hand and flipped it up, breaking her concentration. "I'll find a home for you tomorrow," she told him, patting him, and then she jumped when Eve said from behind her, "We're not keeping him?"

"You scared the hell out of me," Tilda said, clutching Spot.

"Sorry." Eve threaded her way through the dust-covers to sit down at the foot of the bed, her purple pajamas clashing nicely with the leafy green footboard. She was holding a large Hershey's Almond Bar, Tilda noticed with interest. "Nadine's really set on keeping him." She broke the end of the bar off, tearing the paper, and tossed the rest of it to Tilda. "She named him Steve."

Tilda put the dog down on the bed and picked up the bar. "Steve?" She looked down at the beady-eyed, needle-nosed little dog staring avidly at the chocolate in her hands.

"He's not hungry," Eve said. "Nadine got him designer dog food and four kinds of biscuits."

"Yes, but *Steve*?"

"Nadine and Ethan and Burton were watching *Fargo* again, and she decided he looks like Steve Buscemi."

Tilda broke a chunk off the bar and squinted at the dog. "Not much." She bit into the chocolate, felt the waxy sweetness rush her mouth, and twenty years fell away, and she and Eve were back in bed, whispering over torn brown wrappers with silver letters. The bars had definitely been bigger. And she definitely felt better. "Who the hell is Burton?"

"Nadine's latest. Very pretty. No sense of humor. Has a band. She's singing."

"He won't last if he doesn't laugh." Tilda sat down at the head of the bed, and the dog moved up beside her.

"I hope he doesn't. He's a pill." Eve made kissing noises at the dog. "C'mere, Steve." The dog crawled slowly across the bed to her, and she stretched out and propped her head up on one hand, scratching the dog behind the ears with the other.

"So," Eve said, looking innocent. "Tell me everything, Bundle of Lust."

CHAPTER · FOUR

TILDA CHOKED ON HER CHOCOLATE. "NOTHING TO tell," she said when she'd gotten her breath back. "What's up with you and Andrew?" She picked up the quilt and shook it out until it settled over Eve and the dog, its pattern of appliquéd leaves looking like a forest floor across the bed.

Eve looked up at her and smiled. "Come on, Vilma . . .".

Tilda broke off another piece of chocolate. "Really, what's Andrew upset about?"

"Louise," Eve said. "There was this guy at the bar and he looked like fun and I was done for the night so I had a drink. Well, Louise had a drink. I don't think I'd be his type. I never am." She shrugged that off. "Andrew's just overprotective."

"He's overpossessive," Tilda said. "He wants you home being safe little Eve."

"Then he shouldn't be paying me to be dangerous Louise," Eve said, rolling onto her back. "I hate it when he makes me feel guilty. He was never jealous of you and Scott."

"He's never jealous of me at all," Tilda said, wiggling her fingers at the dog.

"He knew Scott was all wrong for you. He knew it wouldn't last." Eve held out her hand. "Give me the chocolate."

Tilda tossed the bar down to her. "Scott was perfect." She patted the quilt. "Come here, Steve."

The dog romped down the length of the bed to her, landing in her lap with a clumsy splat, and she laughed because he liked her so much.

"See, his name *is* Steve," Eve said. "And I don't think you want a perfect guy. I think you've got some Louise in you. I think you want a burglar in the night."

Tilda petted the dog. "I am so not Louise."

"Like Barbara Stanwyck in *The Lady Eve*," Eve went on as if she hadn't spoken. "She says she wants a guy to take her by surprise like a burglar." Eve rolled up on her elbow, chocolate on her mouth, her blue eyes wide and innocent. "So tell me about your burglar. Was he hot?"

"So Andrew's mad at you," Tilda said, gathering the dog up in her arms.

"That good, huh?" Eve broke off another piece of chocolate. "Was he perfect?"

"No." Tilda thought about his kiss in the closet and shivered. "Not even close."

"Oooh," Eve said, grinning at her. "Perfect."

"See, this is why I should never talk to you about boys," Tilda said. "You encourage me to be bad, and I get into trouble."

"You bet," Eve said.

"Give me the damn chocolate," Tilda said, letting Steve settle back onto the bed, and Eve tossed it to her.

"So why did he steal the painting for you?"

"I think he felt sorry for me." Tilda broke off another piece.

"And the Bundle of Lust part?" Eve said. "Come on. Give it up."

"There's nothing," Tilda said primly, but she started to grin in spite of herself.

"*Til*-da's got a *se*-cret," Eve sang, her perfect voice making even that sound good, and Steve pricked up his ears.

"And you're how old?" Tilda said, trying to sound mature.

"Thirty-five, but I'm not meeting burglars and doing God knows what."

"Kissing," Tilda said and then laughed when Eve shrieked in delight and Steve jerked back.

"More," Eve said.

"There's not much to tell," Tilda said, trying to sound offhand. "I opened a closet door, and he jumped me and gave me an asthma attack, so I bit him. Then he criticized my clothes and told me he was no gentleman and kissed me."

"Ooh, ooh," Eve said. "How was it?"

"Pretty damn hot," Tilda said, feeling safe enough in the basement with Eve to tell the truth. "I frenched him."

"*Yes*," Eve said, and Tilda laughed again.

"It wasn't my fault," Tilda said, breaking off another

piece of chocolate. "I was scared and he was standing between me and disaster."

"For which you say, 'thank you very much,' not 'let me lick your tonsils.' "

"It was the adrenaline. It had to go somewhere and it ended up in my mouth. Plus I knew I was never going to see him again, and we were in a dark closet so it was like it wasn't me." Tilda felt cheered by how reasonable it all sounded.

"That was the last you saw of him?" Eve said, disappointed.

Tilda nodded. "Except for about twenty minutes in the diner when he threatened me, told me I have bug eyes, and stuck me with the check."

"Edgy," Eve said. "Iconoclastic. Not your mother's Oldsmobile."

"Right," Tilda said, deciding they'd talked enough about her sins. "So does Gwennie seem a little odd to you lately?"

"Gwennie always seems odd to me," Eve said, sitting up, "which is one of the many reasons I love her. Did I tell you she went to the Eddie Bauer outlet and came back with five sweaters, one for you, one for her, one for Nadine, one for me, and one for Louise? I said, 'Gwennie, that's two for me,' and she said, 'Don't be ridiculous, dear, you'd never wear black.' "

"Which is true," Tilda said. "Although I never thought of Louise as an Eddie Bauer girl."

"Which is why you need this guy and not Scott," Eve said. "You need a burglar in the night, not a lawyer in the day. The Louise in you needs him like the Louise in me needs a black sweater."

"There is no Louise in me." Tilda felt a little depressed about that. She stood up, handed Eve the last piece of chocolate, and put Steve on the floor.

"There's a little Louise in every woman." Eve leaned down the bed and straightened the painting where it rested against the headboard. "Just because yours is nicknamed Vilma doesn't mean it isn't really Louise."

"And I do not need a burglar in the night." Tilda thought back to her disgraceful behavior, asking him to rescue her. "That guy brings out the worst in me."

"That's your inner Louise," Eve said, approval in her voice. "Set her free. Really, I don't know what I'd do without Louise. Just about the time I think I'm going to start screaming, it's Wednesday night and there she is, blowing off all my steam."

"Right," Tilda said. "I don't teach elementary school, I paint murals. It's very peaceful. I have no steam to blow."

"Just remember the three rules," Eve said as if Tilda hadn't spoken. "She only comes out four nights a week, she never has sex at home, and she never tells anybody she's you."

"It's not too late to get therapy," Tilda said. "I'm sure your school insurance covers it."

"Why?" Eve stood up and straightened her pajamas. "I'm happy. And I got two sweaters."

"Good for you," Tilda said. "Look, the guy in the closet was not that hot, I was exaggerating."

"You know," Eve said. "You keep talking yourself out of all the good stuff, you're never going to get any."

"I got some," Tilda said, annoyed. "Scott and I had great sex. I came *every time*." Steve put his paws on her leg and she picked him up. "They should put that man's name in lights."

"He was too calm," Eve said. "Did you ever feel ravished? Did you ever feel as though if you didn't have him, you'd die?"

"For the last time, I have no inner Louise." Tilda looked back at the bed. "I don't even have an inner Scarlet anymore." She handed the dog to Eve and flipped the dustcover back over the bed, hiding the headboard, the quilt, and the painting. "I have responsibilities. I have to be smart. I have to steal a painting." She felt a little sick at the thought, but that might have been the chocolate.

"Which is another reason why you shouldn't have let the burglar go," Eve said.

"I didn't let him go. He let go of me." She forced a smile. "And thank God for that."

"Yeah," Eve said. "Because all that good kissing would have gotten old eventually. I think there's more chocolate upstairs, Vilma."

Tilda sighed. "Lead me to it, Louise."

AT NINE the next morning, Gwen poured herself a cup of coffee, punched up a nice Bacharach medley on the jukebox, pulled a pineapple-orange muffin from the bakery bag Andrew had dropped off on his way to jog, and then went out into the gallery to the marble counter and her latest Double-Crostic. To her right, the sun streamed through the cracked glass pane above the display window, and a loose metal ceiling tile bounced silently in the breeze from the central air. Behind her, Jackie DeShannon sang "Come and Get Me," and Gwen thought, *Fat chance. I'm stuck here forever.*

The clue for *G* was "once a popular make of automobile;" that was always "Nash." Why they never varied that clue was beyond Gwen. It wasn't as if there weren't other formerly popular automobiles. That gave her two of four letters for the word in the quote—*R*, blank, *N*, blank—which could be "rang," or "rank," or "rant," or "rend," or "ring," or "rung," or "runs" . . . *Kill me now,* Gwen thought.

Okay, *H.* "Nineteen fifty-four Ray Milland movie." Fourteen spaces. "Damn."

"Language, Grandma," Nadine said from behind her, and Gwen turned. Nadine was sporting a black leather jacket, spiky black hair, mime-white makeup with raccoon eyes, Steve in her arms, and her boyfriend du jour, Burton, looking his usual, sullen Goth self, at her side.

"It's June," Gwen said to Nadine, deciding to ignore Burton since her day was already irritating. "Maybe not the leather jacket."

Burton made one of those all-purpose cut-me-a-break sounds, and Gwen ignored him some more. He'd have been such a good-looking boy if it hadn't been for the sneer.

Ethan came out of the office, eating a muffin, not looking pretty. "I snagged one, Mrs. Goodnight," he said, his bony face cheerful under his bright red hair. "What do I owe you?"

Gwen's mood improved slightly. "I'll spot you the muffin if you can tell me a 1954 Ray Milland movie, fourteen spaces."

"*The Lost Weekend*," Ethan bit into the muffin.

"You're a good boy, Ethan," Gwen said and filled in the space.

"That's what the 'damn' was for?" Nadine put the dog down and took a corner from Ethan's muffin as the gallery door opened. "A 1954 movie? You know you'd have gotten that eventually."

"Ray Milland makes it harder." Gwen turned to face whoever was lost enough to come into the gallery and thought, *Uh-oh.* Six feet, dark hair, horn-rimmed glasses, dusty jacket, and dustier duffel bag, and even with all of that, you paid attention. "Loser," Burton said under his breath, and Gwen looked into the newcomer's sharp, dark eyes and thought, *No, but trouble just the same.*

"Ray Milland, 1954?" he said.

"Yes," Gwen said, as Steve barked once, a low tremulo that slid up the scale at the end.

"Steve," Nadine said, delighted. "You're musical!"

"*Dial M for Murder.*" The newcomer stuck out his hand. "Hi. I'm Davy Dempsey."

Gwen frowned at him and shook his hand and thought, *He's charming. That can't be good.* She squinted at her book. *Dial M for Murder* made the word in the fourth line "never" instead of "nevew." "That's a help."

"Sorry," Ethan said. "Should I give the muffin back?"

"No," Gwen said. "You're sixteen and you came up with a Ray Milland movie. You get muffins for life."

"So, you want to buy a painting?" Nadine said to Davy, openly appraising him.

He studied the closest Finster, a pale oil of three depressed and evil fishermen closing in on a dyspeptic tuna. " 'A foul and depraved-looking lot, Bailiff.' "

" 'Those are just the spectators, Your Honor,' " Ethan said, and the two of them grinned at each other.

"What?" Gwen said, not reassured. That smile, that confidence, that glint in his eye. *Who does this guy remind me of?*

"Movie quotes," Nadine said, affection in her voice. "Ethan just found another film geek to play with."

"Losers," Burton said under his breath.

"So what are you here for?" Nadine said to the stranger, focused as always.

"You have a room to rent?" He nodded toward the sign in the window as Steve crept closer and sniffed his shoes. "I'll take anything, even the attic."

"Aunt Tilda has the attic," Nadine said. "She's not good with the sharing."

"Efficiency apartment," Gwen said. "Furnished, clean, neat, eight hundred dollars, two months' rent in advance. Don't worry about the dog. He doesn't bite." *We hope.*

"You going to stay for two months?" Nadine said, eyeing his duffel with suspicion.

"Probably not," Davy said, grinning at her. "Basically, I'm on my way to Australia."

"*Support Your Local Sheriff,*" Ethan said.

"I don't know that one," Nadine said, shoving her hand at Davy. "I'm Nadine and this is my grandmother, Gwennie." She nodded over her shoulder. "That's Burton and that's Ethan, and that's Steve, sniffing your foot."

"Hey," Ethan said, waving his muffin. Burton glowered. Steve sat down and scratched behind his ear.

"Can we *go* now?" Burton said.

"No," Nadine said, and Burton shut up.

"Can you give me references?" Gwen said to Davy.

"Not from here," Davy said. "I can give you several in Florida. Miami."

Florida, Gwen thought. Sparkling blue water. Cool white beaches. Alcoholic drinks with little umbrellas. She'd kill to be in Florida even if it was June.

"We gotta go *now,*" Burton said, slinging his arm around Nadine's shoulders. Nadine looked annoyed while Ethan munched his muffin, ignoring Burton completely.

"The jacket," Gwen said to Nadine. "It's Louise's. If you sweat in it, there'll be hell to pay."

"You're right." Nadine shrugged off the jacket and Burton's arm at the same time. "Take the hair, too," she said, and pulled off the black wig, freeing the damp blonde curls matted around her face. "June is not a Goth month."

Burton was disgusted, but then he always was, Gwen thought. Clearly Nadine had inherited the Goodnight women's legendary taste for impossible men. She looked back at Davy again. Perhaps Louise should not meet this one.

"See you later, Australia," Nadine said, and went out the door, Burton's arm around her once again. Ethan ambled behind them both, finishing off his muffin.

Davy leaned on the counter and watched them go. "She does know she's with the wrong guy?"

"I don't know," Gwen said. "Nadine is a very deep child."

Back in the office, the jukebox started to play "Wishin' and Hopin'."

"Dusty," Davy said, lifting his chin to listen. "Good omen. Am I renting?"

Sixteen hundred dollars. "Yes," Gwen said.

He nodded. "Now, there's just one problem."

I knew it.

"I got my pocket picked in a bar last night," he was saying. "Dumb of me. I've got money coming in later, but I had to cancel all my credit cards, so for right now all I have is a hundred bucks."

He smiled at her again and her lips quirked automatically. A hundred bucks was a start, and it wasn't as if there was anything in the apartment worth stealing.

She let her eyes slide sideways to Dorcas's beautifully painted but depraved fishermen.

Or in the gallery.

"But I can have a friend wire me the rest by tomorrow. Is that all right with you?"

"Yes," Gwen said, giving up.

He said, "You are a good person," and handed her five twenties.

Gwen took them. "The room's on the fourth floor. I'll get the key and take you up."

She backed into the office and fished in the desk for the key to 4B, across the hall from Dorcas in 4A. She could have put him in 2B, but that would have put him across from her apartment. Dorcas was always expecting the worst anyway. If he turned out to be an ax murderer, he could reinforce her theory of life. She took the keys out to him.

"Thank you," he said, taking the key ring. "You won't regret this." Then he must have seen something in her eyes because he stopped and added, "Really. It's okay," and for a moment she felt that it was, that whatever he was, it would be fine.

Then she realized who he reminded her of. Tony. Right down to the "You won't regret this," when he'd proposed and she'd accepted, not knowing much about him except he appeared to be crazy about her and she was starting to appear to be pregnant with Eve.

"Hello?" he said, and she realized she'd been staring at him.

"Right this way," she said, and steered him out of the gallery before he turned into Tony and sold her a Finster.

*

DAVY WASN'T sure what he'd said to make Gwen Goodnight stare at him as if he were the Angel of Death, but she seemed to be dealing with it as she led him up the three flights of stairs to the apartment. The hall could have used some paint but it was clean and well lit which was more than Davy could have said for a lot of the places he'd lived in. His landlady didn't have much money, he deduced, but she was hardworking. Or at least somebody was hardworking. Probably not Nadine.

He grinned a little to himself, thinking of Nadine's curly hair and pale blue eyes; clearly she was somebody who swam in Betty's gene pool. And Gwen, too. If you lined them up, all three of them with those weird eyes, they'd look like an outtake from *Children of the Damned*.

"So I've met your granddaughter," Davy said to Gwen, as they reached the top of the second set of stairs. "When can I meet your daughter?"

"When you've had time to rest," Gwen said without looking back. "My daughters can wear on a person."

More than one, Davy thought, and almost ran into Gwen who'd stopped on the stairs above him.

"How'd you know I have daughters?" she asked him.

"Well, Nadine had to come from somewhere."

"Maybe I had a son."

"Lucky guess," Davy said.

Gwen did not look appeased, but she went up the next flight of stairs and gestured to the door on her left. "Four B."

Davy put the key in the lock and turned it, but before he could go in, the door to 4A opened and a ghost stood in the doorway, arms akimbo.

"Dorcas," Gwen said, smiling brightly. "This is Davy Dempsey, your new neighbor. Davy, this is Dorcas Finster."

Dorcas was tall, thin, patrician-looking, and smelled of turpentine and linseed oil, but mostly she was white: short white hair, dead-white skin, huge white artist's smock. An equally white cat twined around her ankles and then sat down on the landing.

"And Ariadne," Gwen said, nodding to the cat.

"Nice to meet you, Dorcas," Davy said, not sure it was.

Dorcas looked him up and down. She did not have pale blue eyes, Davy noticed, which was some relief. She shook her head. "Watch out for Louise," she said, and shut her door. Ariadne sat on the landing, unperturbed about being stranded.

"Louise?" Davy said to Gwen. "Who's Louise?"

"Dorcas likes to be colorful," Gwen said, and Davy looked at her in disbelief. "So there's your room."

The apartment held a shabby blue couch, a table painted in blue stripes, two blue chairs, and through an archway, a bed covered in a blue and purple crazy quilt with a framed sampler over it. When he opened the door next to the bed, he found a small bathroom with a shower. The place was small, shabby, clean, close to Clea, and even closer to Betty. "Perfect," Davy told Gwen, who looked around at the room to see what she'd missed.

"You're easy to please," Gwen said, heading for the door. "Let me know if you need anything."

"I certainly will," Davy said, as she shut the door, thinking, *Send up your daughters, I think I met one of them last night.* He dropped his bag on the floor and sat on the bed, expecting the rattle of ancient bed springs as he bounced on it and hitting a solid mattress instead. *Bless you, Gwennie,* he thought and then wondered again what he'd said to her to put her off. The bed quilt distracted him, and he tried to make sense of the pattern, a crazy quilt with lots of yellow lopsided diamonds lined with sharp white triangles that looked like teeth. Which meant that either he was deeply disturbed or the quilt maker was.

He got up to unpack his bag and glanced at the sampler. It was worked in blues and greens, neat rows of alphabets and numbers and a scene of a house flanked by two trees. Davy looked closer at the lettering:

"Gwen Goodnight. Her Work. 1979."

He looked at the blues and the purples in the quilt and then back to the blues and greens in the sampler. There was something around the base of the trees in the sampler, and he leaned in again to see it.

Wolves. Little purple wolves with tiny, sharp white triangle teeth.

Gwen was definitely Betty's mother.

He unpacked his duffel and went out to reconnoiter Clea's basement windows, eat lunch, and call Simon, who was suspiciously absent. By the time Davy got back to the gallery, it was afternoon, and he stretched out on the bed to consider his situation and fell asleep. He woke up when someone knocked on the door.

When he opened it, Betty stood there, holding out a stack of towels. "Gwennie thought you—" she said, and then her eyes widened, and he yanked her into the room.

She tripped and lurched into him, and he stumbled backward and caught her as she lost her balance. She said, *"Ouch!"* and he slapped his hand over her mouth and pulled her with him onto the bed.

"Okay, we've been here before," he said to her, keeping his hand over her mouth as he pinned her to the quilt. "Unless you want everybody in this place to know you're a burglar, keep your voice down." She glared at him over his hand, and he said in a more conversational tone, "No kicking. No biting. And don't have an asthma attack."

She brought her knee up and he rolled to avoid her and caught sight of Dorcas through the open door, watching them, as unperturbed as Ariadne. Tilda shoved him away and herself off the bed with one motion, and stood out of arm's reach, looking frantic. "How did you get here? How did you find me? What are you *doing here*?"

"Renting a room?" Davy said.

"No you're not," she said and shot out the door. He went after her, but she was fast on her feet, and Ariadne got in his way, so he didn't catch her until they were on the ground floor.

"*This,*" Betty said, as she fell through a door with him right behind her, "is the guy from last night."

Three people stared at him: Gwen, a pretty little blonde who looked a lot like Nadine, and a tall blond man who had clearly decided to dislike him on sight. Behind them, Steve the dog eyed him warily in front of a huge pink and orange bubbler jukebox playing some woman singing "I'm into Something Good."

"Hi," Davy said, not sure what to do next.

"You rented the room to a *thief,*" Betty said to Gwen.

"Actually, I'm not a thief," Davy said.

"Oh." Gwen nodded. "I knew there was something wrong with you."

"You're the burglar in the closet." The little blonde dimpled at him.

"The guy who stole the wrong painting?" the tall guy said, hostile as hell.

"The burglar thing was a one-time deal," Davy told the little blonde.

"Evict him," Betty said to Gwen. "Refund his rent."

"We could use him," the blonde said, and Davy thought, *Whatever you want, honey.*

Then the other shoe dropped. "Wrong painting?" Davy said.

The little blonde held out her hand. "I'm Eve."

I'm Adam. "I'm Davy." He took her hand. "*Very* pleased to meet you."

"I'm Nadine's mama," she went on, more wholesome than he'd thought possible in a woman over twenty. "And Vilma's sister."

"And this is Andrew, Nadine's father," Gwen said pointedly.

Damn, Davy thought and let go of Eve's hand. He nodded to Andrew who did not nod back, which made sense since he'd been ogling Andrew's wife.

"And you know Tilda," Gwen said.

"Tilda?" Davy said, turning back to Betty, starting to grin. "As in Matilda?"

"Yes," she said, her voice like ice.

Davy shook his head. "And you got mad when I called you Betty."

"I didn't get mad," she began. "I—"

"How important is it that we get the painting back?" Andrew said to Tilda, and Tilda abandoned Davy in a nanosecond to focus on him.

"Very important," Tilda said. "But I can do it."

Andrew shook his head at her. "No. You stay out of there. Let this guy do it."

"Gee, thanks," Davy said. "But no."

"No?" Eve looked crushed. "Can't you wait to go to Australia?"

"What?" Davy said.

"Nadine said you were on your way—"

"Oh." Davy shook his head. "No, it's not Australia."

It would have been fun to comfort Eve, but Andrew already didn't like him. "I stole you a painting already, remember?" Davy said to Tilda. "Everything you asked for, square board, night sky, stars . . ."

"It wasn't your fault," Gwen said, her voice fair. "They do look—"

"I said a *city scene*," Tilda said. "The one you stole had cows in it." Her tone was not warm.

"Be nice, Tilda," Eve said. "Describe the one you want him to steal and send him after it and all our problems will be over."

"Honey," Davy said to Eve, "if I could steal another painting, I would, just for you, but I can't get back in there."

"Why not?" Tilda said, and he transferred his attention back to her.

"Because there may be people in the house," he said. "And I have recently learned that's a very bad idea."

"So if there weren't any people in the house, you could do it?" Gwen sounded as if she were heading for something, and Davy focused on her.

"Yes," Davy said.

Behind them, the jukebox changed records and someone who was not Linda Ronstadt began to sing, "You're No Good."

"Because I might be able to get them out of that house," Gwen said. "Mason wants to look at the files. If we take out all the Hodge files first, I could invite him over, and Clea would follow him to keep an eye on him, and he could shuffle through the records as much as he wanted. And his house would be empty."

Tilda rounded on Davy, switching tactics so fast he was surprised she didn't leave skid marks. "You didn't get what you wanted, either. You could go in and get the painting and whatever—"

"No." Davy stared her down. How Eve's pale blue

eyes could be so sweet, and Tilda's same blue eyes so icy was beyond him.

"Why not?" Tilda said.

"Because I'm not letting four complete strangers send me off to commit a crime for them," Davy said. "That would leave me pretty exposed, don't you think?"

"You can trust us," Eve said earnestly.

"You, maybe," Davy told her. "But your sister has conflicted feelings for me. She's tried to maim me several times now, so ratting me out to the cops wouldn't bother her at all. She goes with me."

"It's okay," Tilda said to Gwen. "I looked in most of the rooms already, it'll only take a few minutes. I checked every place but Clea's closet and the third floor."

"You didn't check the closet?" Davy said.

"I was attacked when I tried," Tilda said.

"Because I didn't look there, either," he said. "I found the cows on the next floor up. Big room, full of wrapped and packed paintings. I took the first one I saw that was the right size and shape and had stars."

"I would have done the same thing," Eve said, nodding at him, and Davy thought, *What a sweetheart.*

"So it's probably in her closet." Tilda took à deep breath. "Let's do it."

"I'll call Mason," Gwen said and headed for the gallery.

Davy smiled at Eve, and Andrew took her arm.

"We have things to do," Andrew said, keeping an eye on Davy as he dragged Eve from the room.

Davy turned to look at Tilda, now standing all alone in front of the jukebox, eyeing him as though he were something hissing the dog had dragged in.

"So, Betty," he said cheerfully. "Let's get to know each other."

"Oh, hell," Tilda said, and collapsed onto the couch.

CHAPTER · FIVE

THE LAST OF "YOU'RE NO GOOD" TAILED OFF, AND Davy looked around to see what he'd gotten himself into. It was a medium-sized room filled to capacity by a huge old leather sofa and an equally huge old walnut desk that looked as though it might have once been valuable. They flanked the jukebox and a large round oak table with beat-up, mismatched chairs that didn't look valuable at all, everything including Steve the dog sitting on a very beautiful and very worn Oriental rug.

"Cash flow problem?" Davy said to Tilda.

"It's not that I don't appreciate what you've done for me," Tilda said. "It's that I think it's *creepy* that you know where I live." She frowned at him, her blue eyes cold behind her bug glasses, her Kewpie-doll mouth flattened to a tense line.

"I followed you home last night," Davy said, and went over to a row of photos on the wall.

"I'm supposed to be reassured by that?" Tilda said as he looked at the array of school portraits and holiday snapshots. "You *stalked* me."

"That'll teach you to neck in closets," he said.

"Aren't you supposed to be doing something with files?"

She was quiet behind him for a minute and he tensed, but then he heard a chair scrape as if somebody had yanked it across the floor and then a file drawer open, and he went back to the pictures, fairly sure she wasn't going to attack him.

The pictures must have been up in no particular order since there was one of an angelic-looking blonde baby next to one of three teenage girls in fifties bubble hair and big skirts, leaning together with their chins out, over a pen scrawl that said "The Rayons." One looked like Eve, but that couldn't be, she was much too young to have been a teen in the fifties, and on the other side—

"My God, you're wearing a poodle skirt and big hair in this picture," he said, turning to look at Tilda. "How old are you?"

"None of your business," Tilda said, bent over a card catalog. Steve glared at Davy from her lap. "Get away from my family."

"There's no reason to be bitchy," Davy said. "If you'd told me your name when I asked nicely, I wouldn't have had to stalk you."

"It was a high school talent show." Tilda slammed the drawer and opened the next one. "Nineteen eighty-five. Retro kitsch."

"And your talent was . . ."

"Singing. And no, I'm not very good at it."

"The Rayons?"

She took a deep breath. "Gwennie raised us on girl group music like the Chiffons. You know, this is *really creepy*, having you here."

"Vilma, you frenched me in the dark, and now you're upset I followed you home?"

"You didn't follow me home for that," Tilda said, looking at him over her glasses. "You're up to something."

"You know me well." Davy went back to the pictures. "Who's the third girl? Louise?"

The silence behind him was deafening.

"Louise?" she said.

"Yeah," Davy said. "Dorcas warned me about Louise. Who is she?"

"My . . . cousin," Tilda said. "She works with Andrew at the Double Take. She's not here very often. She doesn't live here." She was close to babbling, which meant she was lying. Again.

"What's the Double Take?"

"Andrew's club," Tilda said. "The floor show is impersonators, all kinds, and people come dressed up like other people, and there's a Karaoke Night on Tuesdays that really . . ." Her voice trailed off as if she'd realized she was talking too much. "You should go there sometime," she finished. "Nobody there is what they seem to be, either."

He turned back to the Rayons photo. "Louise doesn't look much like you and Eve."

"That's not her," Tilda said. "That's Andrew."

"No, the girl in the middle." Davy looked closer. It

was Andrew. A teenage Andrew in big hair and a puffy skirt, but still Andrew, looking prettier than either Eve or Tilda. "Oh. He makes a really good-looking girl."

"He makes a really good-looking guy," Tilda said.

"So does your sister know you have a thing for her husband?" Davy asked.

"Had," Tilda said.

"No, it's still there." Davy moved down to look at a more recent picture of Andrew, this time dressed as Marilyn Monroe.

"She *had* a husband," Tilda was saying. "They're divorced. And I *had* a thing, but it's over."

"I don't think so," Davy said, moving on to one of Nadine's grade-school pictures. Very cute. "Why'd they get divorced?" He went down the line of photographs until he found their wedding picture. "Did you get grabby?"

Tilda opened the last file drawer. "Andrew fell in love with somebody else."

"Andrew has no brains," Davy said, looking at Eve, smiling like a dewy angel, her face fresh and clean under her blonde curls.

"Andrew is gay," Tilda said, "and Jeff is a great guy."

"Andrew didn't know this before he married Eve?"

"He says not. He says it was God's way of making sure there was a Nadine." She took a card out of the last drawer and tipped Steve gently to the floor as she stood up. "That's it for here. I have to go downstairs. You are not invited, and you can't stay here."

"Tell me about this painting." Davy swung around to confront her. "Why are we stealing it?"

"You do not need to know that," Tilda said, starting past him.

"Oh, yes," Davy said, catching her arm. "If I'm stealing it, I need some information. Who painted it?"

Tilda took a deep breath and then turned those eyes on him, glaring with intent.

"What?" he said.

"You know," she said coldly, "there are people who are afraid to cross me."

"And what a shame none of them are here," Davy said. "Who painted it?"

She sighed. "Scarlet Hodge."

Davy looked at her, dumbfounded. "Somebody named a helpless baby Scarlet Hodge?"

Tilda pulled her arm out of his grasp.

"Of course, Gwennie named you Matilda," he said, reflecting.

"My father named me Matilda," Tilda said. "After my great-grandmother, so show some respect."

"Uh-huh. And your middle name?"

"Veronica." When the silence stretched out, Tilda added, "After Ronnie Spector. 'Be My Baby.' "

"You have my sympathies," Davy said.

"It was almost Artemesia Dionne," Tilda said. "You may keep your sympathies."

"Okay," Davy said. "So Scarlet painted them and Clea bought one. Where'd the other one come from?"

Tilda shrugged. "Mason Phipps, I guess."

"So we take that one back." He watched her stiffen. "Betty, you're keeping things that don't belong to you," he said sternly. "That's bad."

Tilda stared back at him, unblinking, as Gwen came in radiating tension and said, "It's set. They'll be here at eight. Mason is *thrilled*." She sounded not thrilled. "Did you get the files?"

"Going down after them now," Tilda said, equally tense. They both looked miserable.

"Not used to crime, huh, girls?" Davy said.

"Good heavens, no," Gwen said and went back out into the gallery.

"You may go now," Tilda said to him, and he thought, *I could be chasing divorced Eve right now.* Then the light caught Tilda's crazy blue eyes again, and she looked stubborn and difficult and exasperating and infinitely more interesting than Eve, if he could keep her from maiming him. And he already knew she could kiss.

"So," he said, sliding down the door to sit on the floor. "Talk to me, Matilda Veronica. Tell me all about it."

ACROSS TOWN, Clea sat at her bedroom vanity and fumed, mostly so she wouldn't panic. Mason was besotted with that horrendous Goodnight woman.

If Gwen had been twenty, it would have made sense. Clea looked in the vanity mirror. Forty-five years of taking exquisite care of herself couldn't make her twenty. The way she'd squandered her youth appalled her. Rich men had wanted her, but she'd wanted to be an actress. She'd wanted to show everybody she was somebody.

The problem was, you needed money to be somebody.

You don't have much time, she told her reflection savagely. *You made stupid choices and now the clock is ticking. This one has to be the one. Do something, you dumb bitch.*

The contempt she felt for herself was making her frown. That added a good ten years right there. She smoothed out her forehead, shoving away her anger, and with the anger gone, all that was left was panic.

No. Clea straightened on the vanity bench and smiled at herself. Her competition was not a twenty-year-old, it was Gwen. Gwen was *old*. So maybe it wasn't the woman, maybe it was the gallery. In which case, why didn't he buy a damn art gallery? Honestly, *men*.

The phone rang and she picked it up, ready to mutilate whoever it was on general principles.

"Clea!" Ronald said. "Darling!"

Darling, my ass. "Tell me Davy Dempsey is on his way to Tibet," she said through clenched teeth.

"Why would he go to Tibet?" Ronald said.

"You were supposed to get rid of him, Ronald," Clea said. *"You're failing me, Ronald."*

"I don't know where he *is*," Ronald said, panic making his voice rise. "But it's okay. I talked to somebody—"

"I don't want you to talk to somebody, I want you to *get rid of him*," Clea said. "Do not call me again until he is *out of the way*."

"But I did—"

Clea hung up on him, taking savage satisfaction in smacking the receiver down hard. Those phones where you pushed the button to hang up were never going to last. People need cradles to smash receivers into to let fools know they were pushing their luck. Fools like Ronald. Her eyes narrowed. And Gwen Goodnight.

She needed a contingency plan. She tapped her foot for a moment and then picked up the phone and hit star 69. "Ronald?" she said a moment later, her voice much softer. "I'm sorry. I'm just so worried about Davy." On the other end of the phone, Ronald made soothing noises. *Yeah, yeah, yeah*, Clea thought. "There is one way you could help. You know so many things, so many people. Could you be my darling and find out everything you can about Gwen Goodnight and the Goodnight Gallery? *Especially* Gwen Goodnight." Ronald babbled all over himself. "You could? Oh, thank you, darling. I'll be thinking about you."

She hung up and thought, *He'll get something*. That was one good thing about Ronald. He was efficient. She caught sight of herself in the mirror. Frown lines again. She looked *forty*. Her face blanked out in panic—she was not aging, not yet, she didn't have any money, she wasn't going to be *alone and poor*—and then she took a deep breath and looked again, smiling.

An angel smiled back from the mirror.

"Don't do that again," Clea said to the mirror, and went to her closet to find something to wear that would make Mason forget all about galleries and Gwen Goodnight.

TILDA FROWNED at Davy, sitting calmly against the door to her escape, looking pretty damn good for a stalker-thief. "I don't want to talk to you. Move."

Davy smiled up at her. "So tell me, Matilda, was Dad slightly crooked?"

"*Hey!*" Tilda straightened, flustered with what she hoped looked like indignation. "Listen, you, my father had an *impeccable* reputation, my whole *family* does, for *generations*. We're *Goodnights*."

"Good for you." For the first time, Davy looked a little taken aback. Steve walked over and sniffed him, and Davy scooped him into his lap and held him there like a shield.

"He used to *warn* people about some of the paintings," Tilda said, on a roll. "He'd tell them to wait, to get more documentation—" She broke off as Davy perked up.

"Documentation. That's how he knew if a painting was real?"

"He traced its provenance," Tilda said, her voice full of forged virtue. "He found out where it originated, who sold it first, got letters from people who had owned it. He—"

"He was trusting a lot of people, then," Davy said,

patting Steve. "All he'd need is one crook in the bunch and only the artist would know for sure."

Tilda snorted. "You can't even trust the artist. They used to take paintings to Picasso for verification, and if he'd painted them and he didn't like them, he'd deny them. But if somebody else had painted them and he liked them—"

"He'd claim them," Davy said. "That makes sense."

"Only if you're dishonest," Tilda said virtuously.

"But there are other ways of telling? Science. Chemical analysis."

"For some things," Tilda said, growing more cautious. "Good forgers scrape down old canvases and grind and mix their own paints. You can still get them on trace elements so if people take their time and get the results back before they buy, they can walk away. But if they've already bought it, even if the evidence comes back—"

"They don't want to hear it," Davy said.

"Right." Tilda frowned at him. "You know about this?"

"People don't like to be made fools of," Davy said. "So they'd rather keep believing the con than go after the guy who swindled them."

Tilda shrugged. "I can't feel sorry for them. If they really fell in love with the painting, what difference does it make if it's real or a fake or a forgery? And if they didn't like it, they shouldn't have bought it."

"So they deserve to be swindled," Davy said. "I've heard this before."

"No." Tilda jerked her head up. "*Nobody* deserves to be swindled."

"You said a fake or a forgery," Davy said. "I thought they were the same thing."

Tilda looked at him, trying to think how she could get rid of him. "A forgery is corrupt from the beginning," she told him. "A fake is something that began honest and then somebody corrupted it to make it look like something else. And now, I really have to go."

"You know a lot about this." Davy's smile was open and honest. Clearly a forgery.

"Family business. Nobody knows how the crooks work better than the legit people in the same business. Look, I have work to do."

"So what's the best art con?" Davy said, keeping his seat against the door. "What's the surefire fake?"

Tilda frowned at him. "You planning on going into art fraud?"

"The fake that can't be caught," Davy said. "Tell me and I'll let you out."

"It's not a fake," Tilda said. "It's a forgery. A contemporary forgery." When Davy shook his head, she added, "A forgery painted at the same time the real painter was painting."

"What if you didn't have an ancestor who forged and left you his work? What's the next best thing?"

Tilda sighed. "There was one guy, Brigido Lara. He forged an entire civilization."

Davy grinned. "My kind of guy."

"Yes," Tilda said. "He was exactly like you. He had no morals and no fear."

"What'd he do?"

Tilda hesitated, and he folded his arms.

She sighed again, trying to shame him into letting her go. "Okay, when pre-Columbian pottery got hot in the eighties, he made beautiful ceramics and then spread the word that they were from a newly discovered tribe, and he was the greatest living expert."

"I'm impressed," Davy said. "How'd they ever catch him?"

"They didn't," Tilda said. "He finally came clean."

"And even then, a lot of people didn't believe him," Davy said.

"It was really beautiful pottery," Tilda said. "Lara became an expert on pre-Columbian fakes, if you can believe it. The old 'set a thief to catch a thief' bit."

"Hard to believe," Davy said, not meeting her eyes.

"My dad had a Lara piece for a while until somebody talked him into selling it."

"But he told them it was a forgery," Davy said.

"Of course," Tilda said, tensing again.

"So Matilda," Davy said, watching her closely. "Are we stealing back a fake or a forgery?" Tilda froze, and Davy shook his head. "Look, babe, it has to be one or the other. There's no other reason for you to be so desperate to get it back."

"The Scarlets are real," Tilda said. "What are you stealing?"

"We're not talking about me," Davy said.

"We are now," Tilda said. "Unless you'd like to agree that neither one of us really needs to know what the other one is up to."

"Maybe we'll talk later." He leaned forward to get up as Steve scrambled out of his lap to follow Tilda.

"Maybe we won't," Tilda said. "For us there is no later. You're out of here once we get back. Have a nice time in Australia."

Then she opened the door, hitting him in the back with no guilt whatsoever.

DAVY WATCHED Tilda unlock the basement door, Steve on her heels, and then pull it shut behind them, neatly cutting him off from following her. A locked basement. Clearly the Goodnights had secrets. He tried to think if there was any way that could help him and decided that whatever was down there was Tilda's problem, not his, and that was the way it should stay. A better plan was to go eat. The way his luck was going he'd be in jail by midnight, so he might as well take advantage of German Village's good restaurants.

At seven-thirty, he went back to the apartment, keeping the door ajar so he could hear Tilda when she came to get him. He turned on his cell phone and called Simon again, but there was still no answer, so Davy left a message that he needed fifteen hundred dollars FedExed to Gwen, sparing a moment to wonder where Simon was. Somewhere brunette, undoubtedly. Then since it was Friday, he dutifully punched in his sister's number, and his niece answered on the second ring. "Hey, Dill, it's me," Davy said.

"Excellent," Dillie said. "I need some advice from a guy."

"Right," Davy said. "I reserve the right to bail from this conversation at any time."

"Don't be wimpy," Dillie said. "Jamie Barclay quit the softball team. She says boys don't like girls who compete with them. Mom says that's garbage. But she would say that. I mean, you know Mom. But Jamie's mom says it's true. And she's been married to a lot of guys. So I need to know. Is it true? And don't give me any of that after-school-special stuff."

"Well, yes and no," Davy said, following with some difficulty. "Some guys don't. That's not the point. You like softball, right?"

"Yes," Dillie said. "*But—*"

"Well, what kind of loser guy would make you give up something you liked so he could feel better?"

"Yeah, I know," Dillie said. "That *sounds* good, but—"

"Got your eye on a seventh-grader, too?"

"No," Dillie said. "He's in my grade. His name's Jordan."

"And he doesn't want you to play?"

"I didn't ask. He doesn't know I like him. He doesn't know I *exist*."

"Okay, I've got it." Davy thought for a moment. "I think you have to look at the big picture here, Dill. This guy, whoever he is, is a practice swing."

"Huh?"

"Very few people mate for life with the people they fall for at twelve. Doesn't mean it isn't real, doesn't mean it doesn't hurt, doesn't mean it doesn't matter, but basically, we're talking a practice swing in the big game of love."

Dillie groaned.

"So he's temporary. But softball is permanent. You can play softball forever if you want to. Softball is not a practice swing. The things you love are never practice swings."

"Okay, yeah, that's good," Dillie said, sounding overly patient, "but I *like* Jordan. You know?"

"Right." Davy looked at the ceiling and sighed. "I'm going to explain something to you, so listen carefully. And don't ever tell your mom I told you. Or God knows, your dad. They'd never let me near you again."

"Okay," Dillie said. "Cool."

"You can get anything you want from people if you approach them the right way. But you have to think it through and watch the other person very carefully. You have to think more about the other person than you think about yourself. You have to *know* the other person."

"Is this some kind of Golden Rule thing?" Dillie asked, her voice skeptical.

"No," Davy said. "Not even close. This is the basic, uh, sales pitch that every Dempsey knows in kindergarten. Five steps. Memorize them. Don't write them down, *memorize* them."

"Okay," Dill said. "Shoot."

"One, make the mark smile. In your case, Jordan is your mark."

"Got it. Make him smile. How?"

"Smile at him. People usually smile back. And once they smile, they relax."

"Okay. One. Smile."

"Two, get him to say yes. To anything. Ask him if he watches the WWF or if he has a game after school. Anything, but get him to *say* it."

"Okay," Dillie said. "But I don't get—"

"If you can get somebody to say yes to something, he's likely to keep on saying it. You're setting up a pattern so that he associates talking with you with saying yes. Then, three, make him feel superior to you. It increases his confidence and he'll get careless."

"So I do what?"

"Ask him a question he can answer. He'll feel smarter than you."

"Okay," Dillie said. "That's sort of girlie, isn't it?"

"No," Davy said. "This is not a girls-are-dumb, boys-are-smart thing. This is lulling him into a false sense of security. This is you running a . . . sales pitch on the poor schmuck. Which is really unfair because you're holding all the cards because you're the girl, but you're also a Dempsey, so it's his tough luck."

"Okay," Dillie said. "One, smile, two, yes, three, superior."

"Now he's feeling pretty good around you," Davy said. "So you want to reinforce that. So on four, you give him something. Like a compliment. Or half of the candy bar from your lunch. Something that makes him think he's the one who's ahead in the conversation."

"Okay," Dillie said, sounding confused.

"Then you move in for the kill," Davy said. "On five, ask for what you want but do it so that he thinks you're doing him a favor by taking it."

"I want to know if he likes me."

"Translate that into something concrete. Do you want him to take you to the movies? Walk you home? Give you his ball cap? What?"

"I want him to like me," Dillie said.

"He probably does, you're a likable kid. That's too fuzzy a goal. Figure out specifically what you want. And in the meantime, practice it on people until it works. Just not on any people named Dempsey."

"Jamie Barclay," Dillie said.

"Good," Davy said. "But don't ever push it. If it's not working, drop it and find another way in on another day. And do *not* tell Jamie Barclay. This is for Dempseys only."

"Right," Dillie said. "I love you, Davy."

"I love you, too, Dill," Davy said. "If the practice swing turns out to be a loser, I'll come beat him up for you. Now let me talk to your mom."

"She's not here," Dillie said. "She's at a meeting."

"Okay, tell her I said hi. Tell her I'm all right and I'll call next week."

"She'll be mad she wasn't here," Dillie said. "You better give me your number. And not your cell phone.

You always turn it off and that makes her mad. What's the number where you're staying?"

"I don't think so," Davy said, imagining Sophie talking to Tilda. "Tell her I wouldn't give it to you."

Dillie was quiet for a minute, and then she said, "Yeah, *that'll* get me off the hook. I can see Mom saying, 'No problem, I'll just *trust* him because he's never lied to me.' "

Davy grinned into the phone. "Very funny. Tell her I'll be down to visit soon."

"You're coming to visit?"

"Yep," Davy said.

"Good," Dillie said. "Then you can teach me more of this neat stuff. I never learn stuff like this in school."

"I can well believe it."

"It's too bad I can't tell anybody, but I won't because I know you're right. You're always right."

Davy looked at the phone and laughed.

"What?" Dillie said innocently.

"I told you, never push it," Davy said. "But that wasn't bad. You hit four before I caught on."

"It was easy," Dillie said smugly. "I almost had your phone number."

"Not even close, Dill. It's not horseshoes. If you don't get all five, you get nothing. You pushed it too hard and you didn't think about your mark. I'm always right? Come on."

"Oh," Dillie said. "I should have stuck with how cool you are."

"Ouch," Davy said.

"This really is neat," Dillie said. "But I think I'm going to make mistakes. I mean, I'll know *if* I screwed up, but I'll need you to tell me what I did wrong like you did just now."

"Dill?"

"Yes, Uncle Davy."

"I told you, stop trying when the mark gets suspicious. I'm not giving you my phone number so you can call me for advice. And I changed my mind. Do *not* tell your mother I called. We did not talk. Wipe this from your mind."

"Wipe what?" Dillie said and hung up.

"Well, that was illuminating," Tilda said, and Davy clutched the phone and turned to see her lounging in his doorway. "Who were you talking to?"

"My niece," Davy said, turning off the phone. "It's rude to eavesdrop."

"How old is this kid?" Tilda said.

"Twelve," Davy said.

"And what exactly is it you do for a living?"

"Sales," Davy said. "So how was the basement?"

Her smile vanished and she straightened, tense again. "Mason and Clea just pulled up. Could you get a move on?" She looked impatiently down the stairs. "I want to get this over with. And you out of here."

He put his phone in his jacket pocket and folded his arms, watching her. She still looked like a bug. He had an old-fashioned urge to rip her glasses off and say, "Why, Miss Goodnight, you're lovely," but she'd probably dislocate something of his and take the glasses back before he could finish the sentence.

"*Now* what are you doing?" she said.

Also, she wouldn't be lovely. That was sister Eve. This one was . . . He tilted his head at her, trying to think of the right word.

"*Could you please—*"

"Betty," he said, cutting her off. "I have stolen one painting for you and I am about to help you steal another, even though I don't need to, even though I have fish of my own to fry. So I'm waiting for you to ease back on the hostility. It's annoying and, frankly, boring." He watched her take a deep breath, the furrow in her forehead disappearing. He still couldn't think of a word to describe her, but she was definitely fun to watch.

She nodded. "You're right." She came in to sit on the bed beside him, making him bounce a little as the mattress sank down. "This is making me crazy. I hate relying on other people to save me, I hate being clingy, I *hate it*, and every time you show up, I lean on you."

" 'Clingy' is not the first word that comes to mind when I think of you," Davy said.

"So I'm taking it out on you. You don't deserve that. I apologize." She looked at him. "Really. I'm sorry."

Davy nodded, taken aback by her honesty, not to mention her proximity. "Accepted."

"And I hate stealing stuff," she said miserably.

"Well," Davy said. " 'I've always believed that if done properly, armed robbery doesn't have to be an unpleasant experience.' " She looked at him as if he were insane, and he added, "It's a movie quote. *Thelma and Louise.*"

"A movie quote."

"It's a family hobby."

She looked almost sweet sitting there beside him, her eyes wide behind her bug glasses, her dark curls all tumbled and soft, and then she said, "It's so odd to think of you having family."

"What did you think?" Davy said, annoyed. "That I was raised in a petri dish?"

"No, no, I didn't mean that," Tilda said hastily. "I meant that you seem like such a loner. Kind of a Liberty Valance thing."

"Thank you," Davy said. "I've always wanted to be a vicious killer."

Tilda looked genuinely puzzled. "What vicious killer?"

"Liberty Valance. Lee Marvin."

"No, I meant Gene Pitney."

Davy frowned at her. "Who's Gene Pitney?"

"The guy who sings 'The Man Who Shot Liberty Valance.' " They stared at each other in incomprehension until she said, "Never mind, I take it all back. Can we go?"

"So you're thinking of me more as John Wayne than Lee Marvin." Davy shrugged. "Okay." He stood up and gestured to the door. "Want to go steal stuff, Thelma? Or would you rather be Louise?"

She looked up, startled. "I don't know who I want to be," she said, and went past him out the door.

"That makes two of us," he said, catching the faint scent of cinnamon as she passed. "I don't know who I want you to be, either."

Chapter · Six

"I can't believe we broke a window," Tilda said
half an hour later, trying not to panic as Davy closed
Clea's bedroom door behind them. "Even if it was a
basement window. That's vandalism."

"I broke the window," Davy said. "I climbed inside.
I let you in. And yet, so far, no thank you."

"Thank you," Tilda said. "Oh, God."

"You're not good at this, Betty," Davy said. "Go look
in the closet. If the painting's not there, you'll have to
go upstairs."

He went to Clea's bureau and began to go through her
drawers, and Tilda opened the closet doors again.
"Bleah, this perfume."

"Obsession," Davy said, opening the next drawer.

"You can tell from over there?"

"No, that's what she wears." Davy lifted up a pile of
something silky and expensive.

"Known her long?" Tilda said, feeling annoyed.

"Yep. Find a painting yet?"

Tilda took a deep breath and pressed into the closet.
The damn thing was huge, and she moved to the back,

trying to avoid Clea's shoes, feeling around for an eighteen-inch-square piece of evidence she'd been a forger. She heard Davy push the clothes back, and she said, "I need a light," just as he closed the doors.

"Hey," she said, turning and he put his hand over her mouth.

"Shut up, Betty," he whispered in her ear. "There's somebody in the hall."

Tilda froze as she heard Clea's bedroom door open. *Great,* she thought. They'd asked Gwennie to do one little thing, and—

Davy took his hand off her mouth, and she sucked in air, staving off panic, which would lead to asthma. He moved his hand to the small of her back and patted her there, the way she patted Steve to calm him down, and Tilda pressed closer to him, trying not to wheeze, her heart pounding.

Outside a drawer slammed shut with a bang, and Tilda jerked and clutched Davy's shirt. He patted a little faster, and she thought, *As long as I'm in here, I'm safe, nobody knows I'm here, nobody but him,* and she put her arms around him, grateful he was there. He stopped patting, and they stood like that for eons while Tilda grew warmer and whoever was outside rustled and shuffled. She felt Davy's fingers slide against the small of her back, felt his palm go flat there, not pressing, just flat and hot there, and something kicked up low in her solar plexus and spread, waiting for him to pull her close. When he didn't, she lifted her face through the darkness, and when he bent closer, her breathing went ragged, and when his mouth brushed hers, her body stuttered and when she closed that last inch between them, his arms tightened around her, and she kissed him in a closet again.

He was a damn good kisser, and Tilda felt breathless as she leaned into him, good breathless as she pressed him against the back wall of the closet and sank into all that good heat. *I don't do this enough,* she thought as she came up for air, and then she went back for more, unleashing her inner Louise, or at least her inner Vilma.

Then the closet door opened and somebody pawed through Clea's shoes and grabbed her ankle, and she kicked back hard on panicked reflex, and connected with something hollow and something heavy hit the floor.

"Oh, great." Davy let go of her and shoved the clothes apart, kneeling to see whoever was on the floor. "Damn it." He stepped over the body and dragged it out of the closet by its shoulders.

Tilda followed him out, trying not to panic. "Is he dead?"

"No," Davy said, "but he's unconscious. You have a kick like a mule, Matilda."

"I was tense. He grabbed my ankle."

"Something I must remember not to do. Christ, you really nailed him." Davy stood up and frowned. "Do you know who he is?"

Tilda bent cautiously to look at the guy. He was a weedy thirty-something with dark hair and a bleeding lump forming on his temple. "No. I never saw him before."

"Okay." Davy took her arm and moved her toward the door. "Out."

"What?" Tilda tripped as she tried to see back over Davy's shoulder. "We can't just leave him—"

"You can." Davy kept her moving into the hall and down the stairs, his hand on her arm like a vise. "This just changed from a small heist to a major crime. Get out of here, walk straight home and do not talk to anybody."

"What about you?" Tilda said, trying to keep her feet on the stairs as Davy picked up speed. "I'm not leaving you—"

"That's very sweet." Davy steered her down the hall and into the kitchen and opened the back door. "Goodbye."

He shoved her out the door and slammed it behind her, and she was left on the back steps, shivering in the warm June night, with nothing left to do but go home.

MEANWHILE, GWEN was thinking envious thoughts about Tilda, who was only breaking and entering, much preferable to being stuck with Mason and Clea.

"Man, the times we had here," Mason said, looking around the gallery. "I can almost hear that big booming laugh of Tony's. What a guy."

What a guy, Gwen thought, and put the files for 1988 on the table in front of him. Across the table, Clea watched her like a hawk, for what, Gwen had no idea.

"Remember that opening for the New Impressionists he did? Nineteen eighty-two." Mason smiled at Gwen. "Tony wore a blue brocade vest, and you had on a black halter dress and gold hoop earrings the size of dinner plates. I'll never forget it."

Gwen straightened a little, startled by the memory.

"You were amazing, Gwennie," Mason said, his face softening as Clea's hardened. "You moved through the crowd, and people smiled looking at you, and Tony and I stood at the back of the gallery, right by the door over there—" he nodded at the office door "—and we watched you. You know what he said?"

"No," Gwen said, trying to hold on to her memory of Tony-as-son-of-a-bitch.

"He said, 'I'm the luckiest son of a bitch in the world,'" Mason said. "And I said, 'You sure as hell are.'"

The early Tony came back to her, laughing down at her, wrapping her in love and excitement, and she tried to push him away, to get back to the later Tony, desperate because the gallery wasn't doing well, growing grimmer, laughing less, making Tilda paint the Scarlets.

"He was a great guy," Mason said. "And he built a great gallery."

"Yeah," Gwen said. "So the records for eighty-eight are right here. That's when we sold the Scarlets."

"Wonderful." Mason pulled them over in front of him. "I've always wanted to know how the gallery worked, how Tony did it. The building's an asset, too, isn't it? Real estate is always a smart move."

Maybe we should let the creditors have it, Gwen thought. *Maybe we should burn it down, set everybody free.*

"So what other assets does the gallery have?" Mason said, picking up a new folder.

"What?" Gwen said.

"Assets," Mason said. "Besides the building and the inventory. How does a gallery work? What other assets are there?"

"Uh, none," Gwen said, confused. "The paintings are on consignment."

"Well, the good name, of course," Mason said.

"Oh, yeah," Gwen said. The good name of the Goodnights.

"God, I envied him," Mason said. "His gallery, his parties, his charm." He smiled at Gwen. "His wife."

Clea stirred.

Gwen smiled back stiffly and thought of Tony, introducing her: "This is my wife, Gwennie." One night she'd said to him, "Just once, can't you introduce me as Gwen, your wife?" and he'd stared at her, not comprehending.

"I couldn't believe it when I heard he'd died," Mason was saying. "It didn't seem possible. I wrote, but there wasn't really anything I could say."

"Your letter was lovely," Gwen said, not remembering it. There'd been so many.

"You'll probably never get over him," Clea said sadly, and they both turned to look at her, surprised. "Real love is like that." She put her hand on Mason's sleeve and smiled at him dreamily, and Mason looked at her, incredulous.

I hope she's good in bed, Gwen thought.

"It must be hard running the place on your own," Mason said to Gwen, picking up the first file.

"I have family," Gwen said, trying to sound brave. "So the records . . ."

An hour later Mason said, "These are all the records for 1988? Are you sure?"

"Pretty sure," Gwen said and then realized if he was done, he'd go home. "But you know, Tony was a pretty sloppy recordkeeper. Better check eighty-seven and eighty-nine, too. I'll get them."

Mason nodded happily, Clea sighed, and Gwen headed for the office. *Hurry up, Tilda,* she thought. *I can't keep them here forever. It's too damn painful.*

WHEN TILDA got back to the office, she saw Gwen out in the gallery with Mason and Clea. She sat down on the edge of the couch, still shaking, and Gwen came in with a backward glance at Mason, followed by Steve who spotted Tilda and lunged for her in ecstasy.

"I don't know what's wrong with that man," Gwen said, as Tilda scooped up the little dog. "He's looking at every old file in the place and he's *enjoying* it. He's like a kid. It's like his whole life, he's always wanted to look at gallery files." She stopped when she got a good look at Tilda. "What's wrong?"

"Everything." Tilda sank down on the couch, holding on to Steve's long wriggling body for comfort. "There was a man there. I never saw him before, I knocked him out by accident. Davy's still there, fixing it, and he's going to get *caught*."

"Okay," Gwen said, looking rattled. "Be calm. Because you're never like this and you're scaring me."

She went to the cupboard and got out the vodka and poured a healthy shot into a glass.

"Oh, God, yes, thanks." Tilda let go of Steve and held out her hand in time to see Gwen knock back the glass.

"You want one, too?" Gwen said.

"Yes," Tilda said. "Listen, I can't do that again, go into somebody's house and steal. I am not designed for that. I'll fix this some other way."

"Okay." Gwen handed over the glass and the bottle. "Okay. We'll think of something else. Where's Davy?"

"I told you, he's still there." Tilda heard her voice crack from guilt. "He told me to go. Oh, Gwennie, he's a mess, but I don't want him in jail because of me." She poured the vodka with a shaking hand.

"He's not a mess," Gwen said. "Do you think he—"

"Gwennie!" Mason called from the gallery. "Did you know Tony sold to the Lewis Museum?"

"Really?" Gwen called back. "Imagine." She turned back to Tilda. "He's driving me crazy. He thinks this dump is Disneyland. Do I still have to keep him here?"

"*Yes,*" Tilda said. "Until Davy gets back safe. It's the

least we can do for him since he's out there . . ." She knocked back her own shot and felt the alcohol seep into her veins, calming her a little. "You want another one?"

"No." Gwen looked through the glass door at Mason. "I have to go pretend nothing's wrong. I have to go pretend I like it here. I have to go pretend that I don't want to throw up when he talks about the good old days."

"Gwennie?" Tilda said, taken aback by the anger in her voice.

Gwen shook her head. "I'm having a bad night."

"Me, too," Tilda said as Steve crawled back in her lap. "I am *not* cut out for a life of crime."

"You always were more my daughter than your father's," Gwen said, and went back to the gallery.

"No I wasn't," Tilda said miserably, but Gwen was already gone.

Davy came into the office and kicked the door shut behind him, looking frazzled and carrying a brown-paper-wrapped eighteen-inch-square package, and Tilda forgot everything else and let Steve slide onto the couch as she sprang up to meet him.

"Are you okay?" she said, pressing the glass and bottle into his chest.

"Yes." He held up the painting so she could see the torn corner with the sky and the edge of a brick building, and then he put it on the table and took the vodka.

"I can't believe you stayed," Tilda said. "I can't believe—"

Davy drank a belt straight from the bottle, and she offered him the glass as an afterthought.

"What happened?" she said. "Did he come to? Did you get caught? Are you okay?"

"Shut up, Betty." He slopped some vodka into the glass and handed it to her. "I dragged him into an empty room, found your painting, and left. I am not cut out to be a thief. Let's not do that again."

"Oh, God, no, let's not," Tilda said. "And you got the painting. You're a good, good man."

"I looked before I took," Davy said. "Stars and houses."

Tilda clutched her vodka, her eyes closed in gratitude. She didn't even want to see the painting, she never wanted to see any of them again, she just wanted her old, boring, mural-painting life back. "Thank you, God."

"Hey!" Davy said and pointed to himself.

Tilda opened her eyes to look at him. "Thank you, too. I'm sorry I was so bitchy, I'm sorry for every lousy thing I ever said to you, I'm sorry—"

"I got it," Davy said. "You're sorry." His voice was calm now, and he had a rueful half-smile on his face. "You're an interesting woman, Matilda Veronica."

"No, Matilda Veronica is a bitchy control freak." Tilda turned away from him to look into the gallery.

"That, too," Davy said. "Where's Gwennie?"

"Out front," Tilda began, and then she stopped.

Clea Lewis was looking through the window in the door, her face slack-jawed in surprise.

"Where?" Davy said and then followed Tilda's eyes. "Hell." He lifted the bottle in a toast to the door. "Hey, babe," he said, and Clea's eyes narrowed and she jerked her head toward the street door to the gallery. "Oh, yeah, I want to talk to you," he said, but he put the bottle down on the table. "I'll be right back," he said to Tilda and went out the side door.

Tilda sat back on the couch and caught Steve as he scrambled up beside her and licked her on the chin. There was something to be said for a male who loved you desperately, was always glad to see you, and never made you mad. "I'm glad we're keeping you, Steve," she told him as she cuddled him close. "You're the only good man I know."

CLEA STOOD out on the sidewalk, tapping her foot with impatience. "What are you *doing* here?" she snapped as Davy came out the side door. "Are you trying to ruin my life?"

"I have no interest in your life," Davy said. "I want my money back." He looked her up and down slowly, and Clea braced herself for the insult. "You're looking really good, Clea."

"Thank you," Clea said, slightly mollified. He looked really good, too, for a treacherous son of a bitch. Hot memories came back and she stifled them. "Look, it's my money," she told him. "You stole it from me three years ago, you know you did. It's mine."

"Not all of it." Davy folded his arms and leaned

against the storefront. "And you owed me. You dumped me, I took your money, that made us even until—"

"I left you years ago. *Get over it.* Move on."

"You betrayed me," Davy said, his voice tensing.

"Oh, I did not," Clea said, exasperated. "Look, I'm beautiful, I'm charming, I'm expensive, and I give the best head in America."

"True," Davy said, looking taken aback. "But—"

"But I'm not faithful," Clea said. "I never was. There's no point in it. If somebody who can take better care of me comes along, I'm going with him. That's just sensible."

"It may be sensible," Davy snapped, "but it's pretty damn hard on the other guy in the relationship."

"What relationship?" Clea said, mystified. "What made you think we had a relationship?"

"We were living together," Davy said. "I thought—"

"No you didn't." Clea folded her arms. This was why men were a pain in the ass. They only thought of themselves. "You didn't think at all. You looked at me and saw what you wanted to see, a faithful hottie of a girlfriend. You didn't want to know me, you just wanted to *have* me. Well, you had me. It's over." He was looking at her as if she were speaking Chinese, so she spelled it out for him. "I'm not responsible for you not knowing me, Davy. It's not my fault you never looked—"

"Oh, come on," Davy said. "We were *living together.*"

Clea shrugged. "I saved a lot on rent. I don't see what that has to do with this. I mean, did I ever say, 'Davy, you're the only one'?"

"No," Davy said.

"Did I ever say, 'I'll never leave you, this is forever, you're the love of my life'?"

"This is really depressing," Davy said, leaning against the storefront again.

"So you're mad at me for not being what you wanted me to be," Clea said. "Well, I'm mad at you, too. I wanted you to be rich, and you weren't, and I ended up with that bastard Zane."

"If you'd been faithful to me, you wouldn't have," Davy pointed out.

"If you'd had money, I wouldn't have," Clea said. "It's your fault. But am I still blaming you? No. I've moved on. You should, too."

"I'd love to," Davy said. "Give me my fucking money back."

"It's *mine*," Clea said, amazed that he couldn't see the justice of it all. "You *stole it* from me. You took *my family home* from me."

"Oh, please," Davy said. "You'd have burned the family home to the ground if you could, you hated that place."

"It was worth *money*," Clea snapped.

Davy went on, ignoring her the way he always had. "And I stole a third of what you took. Keep the original stake, but I want the rest of it back. Hell, Clea, you were married to two rich guys, you don't need it."

"You don't know what I need." Clea stepped back. She hadn't been married to two rich guys, she'd been married to two *poor* guys, at least they'd been poor when they died, and she didn't need that thrown in her face, thank you very much. "It's my money, and I need it." She looked through the gallery window and saw Mason take Gwen's hand. "I want to get *married*," she said savagely, "and rich men do not marry poor women."

Davy followed her eyes. "You think you're going to marry this guy? No. Guys like him marry Jackies, not Marilyns. He's stringing you."

"Very funny," Clea said. "No, he's going to marry me. He brought me home to Ohio with him."

"Which does not make him the first man to transport you across a state line for immoral purposes," Davy said. "I've done it myself."

"But you never will again," Clea said. "Now go away."

"You *really* think I'm going to?" Davy said.

"You don't have any choice." Clea stuck her chin out. "There's nothing you can do."

He smiled at her and she felt a chill. Davy had been good at a lot of things, she remembered, many of them illegal. "Don't spend my money," he told her. "I'm coming for it." Then he went back inside.

"Oh, well, that's just fine," she said to the empty street. It wasn't enough that she was broke and aging and being ignored for a woman ten years older than she was, now she had Davy Dempsey on her ass. Well, she'd just have to be nicer to Ronald so he'd keep an eye on Davy, except that this was Ronald's fault for telling Davy where she was. It was Davy's fault for not taking care of her in the first place. It was Mason's fault for not taking care of her now, she should have been *married* to him by now. She looked through the gallery window to see him talking seriously to Gwen, leaning close.

"*Men*," she said and went back inside to retrieve her future.

WHEN DAVY came back into the office, Tilda was on the couch with Steve and her third shot of vodka, this one cut with orange juice for flavor. "You know, you never did tell me what you were looking for in her room," she said, trying not to sound cranky.

"Money." Davy picked up the vodka bottle. "My money. Clea seduced my financial manager into embezzling my entire net worth."

"You had enough money to have a financial manager?" Tilda said, impressed.

"He was a colleague," Davy said, looking for a glass.

Tilda got up and got him one from the cupboard while Steve fibrillated with separation anxiety on the couch. "So what is it that you do? With this colleague?"

"Consult." He took the glass. "He told me he could show me how to double my money and instead he tripled it," Davy went on as he poured. "His name is Ronald Abbott. Unaffectionately known as Rabbit for his ability to burrow into other people's accounts. I was grateful and I got careless."

It still didn't sound right to Tilda. "How could he get into your accounts?"

"Rabbit is a genius with money," Davy said. "Bank accounts are like toy boxes to him. He likes to open them and play with their insides. I cannot pretend to know the things he knows, I can only tell you that I made money in the market when I did what he told me to."

"I can see where that would lead you to trust him," Tilda said, sitting down again so Steve would calm down. "I guess. I mean, most financial managers aren't crooks, right?"

"Actually, Rabbit has a record," Davy said. "Guys who make a lot of money usually cut corners someplace."

"He had a record," Tilda said, incredulous. "You trusted somebody you knew was crooked?"

"Everybody's crooked," Davy said. "The trick is to find out how they're bent. Then you make sure the consequences are so great they stay straight anyway."

"Oh," Tilda said, trying to look unbent. "Which clearly didn't work with Rabbit."

"Oh, it worked," Davy said. "Until somebody came along with a bigger carrot than my stick."

"That big," Tilda said. "Imagine. Do I know this person? Can I get to know him?"

"Clea," Davy said, nodding toward the gallery where Clea was smiling at Mason.

"Oh," Tilda said, following his eyes. "Well. Yes. She does have a big carrot."

Davy frowned. "You know, the visuals I'm getting on this are—"

"So why not call the police?" Tilda said.

"Good idea," Davy said. "You call them about the Scarlet first."

Tilda wanted to say, *So there is something crooked here*, but that would mean admitting that the Scarlets were bent, so she dropped that one. "Or have Rabbit steal it back. He took it—"

"Yeah," Davy said. "That's what I want, to get trapped in a conspiracy charge with Rabbit. Because he's got so much backbone, he'd never rat me out. No."

"You have a problem," Tilda said.

"I have many. But I'm working on the money first."

Tilda nodded and took another drink. "Good choice. The money will probably solve all the other problems. It sure as hell would solve all of mine."

"No it wouldn't," Davy said.

Tilda looked through the door to the gallery again, to where Clea was now dragging an unhappy Mason to the door. "Why you?"

"What?" Davy said, putting the bottle back in the cabinet.

"Why did Clea send him after you?"

"I had money."

"Lots of people have money," she said, the skepticism heavy in her voice.

"And some history with Clea," Davy said, watching the minidrama through the door. "And some history with Rabbit."

"You slept with Rabbit, too?" Tilda said, feeling bitchy.

"No, I disagreed with Rabbit once," Davy said. "We'd made another killing in tech stocks, and I watched the numbers and said, 'This is too good to be true.' And that made me think of my dad."

"Your dad," Tilda said. "The one in sales."

"Michael Dempsey," Davy said, turning back to her. He saluted the air with his glass. "God bless him wherever he is now, as long as he's not with me." He considered that. "Or my sisters. He has many faults, but stupidity is not one of them. He always says, 'If it looks too good to be true, get out.' "

"Your dad sounds a lot like you."

"No," Davy said flatly. "He is nothing like me. And I am nothing like him."

"Oh-kay," Tilda said, and took another drink.

Davy nodded. "So I said, 'Rabbit, get me out of there.' And he argued, but in the end he put me in blue chips and bonds. And then he sneered at me for six months while the market boomed and he made millions."

"Wow," Tilda said.

"Yeah, and then the tech market crashed and he lost everything and I still pretty much had it all." Davy sighed. "He never really forgave me for that."

"So he embezzled it."

"And gave it to Clea, which is why I turned to theft for the one and only time in my otherwise blameless life," Davy said.

So he really wasn't a crook. Tilda found that

depressing. "Did you get your money back tonight?"

"No. I found your painting and ran."

"And now she's seen you. She knows you're here after the money."

"Yes."

Tilda leaned back, suddenly exhausted. "So we've completely screwed up your life."

He looked down at her, and he didn't look upset. "No, I'd pretty much done that before I met you, Vilma."

Some of the warmth she'd felt for him in the closet began to ease back, or maybe it was vodka and relief. Whatever it was, it was a huge improvement over panic and guilt, and she drank some more to celebrate.

"I thought they'd never leave," Gwen said, coming in from the gallery. "If Clea hadn't thrown a fit, they wouldn't have. That man was fascinated with—" She saw Davy and stopped. "Oh, good, you're back. Tilda was so worried."

"Were you?" Davy said, looking down at Tilda.

"Not at all." Tilda toasted him with her glass and a weak smile. "I'd have felt no guilt at all if you'd been sent up the river for saving my butt. Again." She sighed. "Oh, God, never again."

"Did you get—" Gwen began, and Tilda gestured to the paper-wrapped square on the table.

"He got what we needed," she said. "He didn't get what he needed."

"The night's young yet," Davy said, his eyes still on her.

"You're not going back there," Gwen told him. "We'll help you get whatever it is you need, but you are not going back there tonight. They'll be home any minute."

Davy patted her shoulder. "Relax. I'm fine."

"Oh, well, *good for you*." Gwen picked up her puzzle book. "I've had a terrible evening. That man was absolutely rabid about this damn place and he wants to come back. I don't think I can stand that again. I'm going to bed with a Double-Crostic and forget any of this happened."

"Good plan," Tilda said, keeping a wary eye on Davy, who was pretty chipper for somebody who was still broke. A little vodka and he was back to his old self. That couldn't be good.

When the door had closed behind Gwen, Davy sat down on the couch beside Tilda and took her glass. "How much of this have you had?"

"I don't remember," Tilda said. "I think two. Why?"

"Are you drunk?"

"No," Tilda said. "I know how—"

"Good." Davy put the glass on the table.

"—to drink—"

"Bully for you." Davy slid his arm around her.

"—and . . ." Tilda's voice trailed off as he leaned closer. "Okay, if this is about the closet—"

And then he kissed her.

CHAPTER · SEVEN

DAVY'S KISS TASTED LIKE VODKA AND DISASTER, AND even while she kissed him back, Tilda thought, *I'm never going into a closet with this man again*. He slipped his hand under her T-shirt, and she said, "You know," as his hand slid up to her breast, but the only thing left to say was, I'm not that kind of girl, and of course she was.

She felt his thumb slide under her bra and thought, *Louise would love this guy*, and it occurred to her that maybe if she faked being Louise, she'd finally have the wild, screaming, carnal, criminal sex that Louise always had. *Call me Scarlet*.

He dropped his head, his mouth hot on her neck.

No, that wasn't right. *Call me Louise*.

His hands slid around to her back and pulled her closer as he eased her T-shirt up and she nestled into his arms, feeling warm because somebody was holding her close.

And if she was pretending to be Louise, maybe she wouldn't lose her mind and scream out, "I painted the Scarlets," when she came.

He bit her neck gently, and she drew in a short, shuddery breath.

Because if she said anything, Davy was the kind of guy who'd notice. And remember.

He began to press her back against the arm of the couch.

Louise never screamed out, "I'm Eve." It could work.

Steve jumped off the couch onto the rug and looked at them with what might have been contempt.

Yeah, I'm appalled, too, Tilda thought, and then Davy kissed her again, another deep, warm kiss, and she cuddled closer, but the wildness wasn't there, she missed the closet, if they'd only done it in the closet . . .

He pressed her back against the arm of the couch and she shifted a little as he kissed her stomach, trying to fit her butt into the space between the cushions as she drifted back from the warmth, thinking, *This isn't going to work.*

Not unless he wanted to neck all night. Maybe he—

His hand slid between her thighs, and she thought, *Nope, doesn't want to neck.*

At least he hadn't made it inside her bra yet. Maybe she could say yes just to keep him holding her but convince him to do it fully clothed—

He unsnapped her bra—one-handed, too, she gave him points for dexterity—and began to lick his way up her rib cage, clearly headed north to her breasts.

No, she thought, *this isn't working,* and pulled her T-shirt down, connecting her fist smartly with the top of his head.

"Ouch!" he said.

"I was thinking," she began.

"Well, stop," he said and kissed her again, and she remembered how she'd ended up on the couch in the first place. The man had an excellent mouth.

Oh, just do it, Louise, she told herself. *You could use this.*

He moved his hand under her bra, and she considered a moan, which was better than heavy breathing because if she breathed too heavy, she'd end up in an asthma attack, and that would be the end: topless geekdom. She pushed her glasses back up the bridge of her nose. Definitely moaning.

Then his mouth moved to her breast, gentle and hot, and she clutched at him and said, *"Oh!"* for real, a lot louder than she'd meant to.

He lifted his head and met her eyes. "Sorry," she said, and felt a blush start.

Davy smiled at her, the smile of a man about to have sex. "Not a problem." He stretched over her head and pounded at random on the buttons on the jukebox. The music started as he slid back down to her. "What is this, anyway?"

"What?" Tilda said, panicking that he'd realized something was wrong with her.

"This song," he said, as the surf rolled on the jukebox.

Tilda listened. " 'Wonderful Summer,' " she said as Robin Ward started to sing. "It's one of my favorites."

"Never heard of it," Davy said, and Tilda felt

annoyed. Then his mouth was on hers again, and she wrapped her arms around his neck and tried to coax herself back into all that heat she'd felt in the closet. But no matter how she tried as the minutes passed, she couldn't get beyond conflicted warmth. Then Davy's hand was on her zipper, and that was dangerous. She had too much to lose to let somebody like Davy Dempsey in.

Robin belted out the last line about the most *wonderful summer* of her *life*, and the surf rolled, and the room was silent again, and the sound of her zipper reverberated everywhere.

"Hold that thought," Davy said, as he moved back up to the jukebox, and Tilda thought, *You don't want me to hold my thought. You want me to hold the one you're having.*

He reached over her head and smacked half a dozen buttons at random. The Essexes kicked in the opening bars of "Easier Said Than Done," and Tilda said, "You know—"

"Later," Davy said and slid his fingers into her jeans.

"Oh. Hey." Tilda closed her eyes and decided to push him away in a couple of minutes. Or maybe not at all. If he kept doing that for about half an hour, she'd even take off some clothes.

Davy pushed up her T-shirt, narrowly missing her chin, and she yanked it back down again as he pulled her hips down to his. The pressure there was nice as long as she kept her eyes closed and thought, *LouiseLouiseLouise.* Then he stopped kissing her long enough to strip off her jeans and slide between her legs. *Maybe not*, she thought, as he shoved off his jeans. *Birth control, we didn't—*

"Wait," she said, opening her eyes, careful not to look down. "I don't have—"

He held up a condom and went for her mouth again, and she thought, *If I say no, he'll stop, and then we'll have to* talk *about it, and that'll be terrible*, and he did feel good, if she could just get her head straight—

Come on, she told herself, and tried to work herself into the mood, concentrating on how solid his arms were around her, how wonderful it was to be held, how good his mouth felt, finally generating enough heat that when he pulled her hips to his and she felt him hard against her and then hard inside her, it didn't hurt—*there's a recommendation for you*, she thought: *it didn't hurt.*

She moaned for effect, more surprised he was inside her than shocked—this is what happened when you didn't pay attention, they got ahead of you, and there you were—and it wasn't that she wasn't ready, exactly, it was more that Louise would have felt more. There would have been gasping with Louise, she was sure of it.

Of course, Louise wasn't asthmatic.

She began to move with him, trying to pick up his rhythm, which was hard because she kept slipping down the couch. *Oh, hell*, she thought, and moved her hand to brace herself on the back of the couch and caught him across the nose.

Don't have a nosebleed, she thought, *please don't have a nosebleed*, but he just said, "Ouch," and kept going.

Single-minded, she thought. *Okay, there is no Louise, Louise is like the Easter Bunny, so just breathe heavy and get this over with and never go near this man again.*

She took deep breaths, not even trying to match his because they were never going to be in sync, and once she stopped trying and started breathing, things got better. He picked up speed, and Tilda tried to imagine the tightening of her muscles and did a damn good job with those moans as the minutes passed and her pulse picked up. Then he shifted against her and hit something good, and she sucked in her breath and thought, *Wait a minute, this could*—but even as she had the thought, he shuddered in her arms and that was it. *Just hell*, she thought, and finished off with an oh-my-god-that-was-good moan-sigh combo.

So much for channeling her inner Louise. He was semimindless on top of her now, so she held him, patting him on the back while he caught his breath and Pippy Shannon sang "I Pretend" on the jukebox. *Our song*, Tilda thought.

Steve dozed on the rug beside the couch, oblivious to both of them. He had the right idea. She should have taken a nap instead.

Then Davy pushed himself up on one arm and looked in her eyes, nose to nose. "So what was that?" he said, still breathing hard, looking mad. "A fake or a forgery?"

"Hey." She tried to sit up, and he shook his head.

"You're a terrible actress," he said, and collapsed on top of her again.

"Your foreplay was okay," she said crushingly to the top of his head. "Your afterplay sucks."

"Sorry," he said, clearly not, and eased away from her, and she looked at the ceiling as she pulled up her jeans, and he got rid of the condom and got dressed.

"Well, gee, I can't thank you enough," she said when they were both clothed again. She made her eyes wide. "What a good time."

He shook his head and turned away from her. "Good night, Tilda. I'll see you in the morning."

Ouch, she thought, and then he turned back and said, "Look, don't fake. It's lousy for everybody."

"Gee, *you* sounded like you were having a pretty good time," Tilda said, stung.

He started to say something and then shook his head again and headed for the door.

When he was gone, Steve jumped up on the couch again and Tilda patted him and tried to blame everything on Davy, but fairness got in the way. Okay, so it hadn't been good. That was her fault. She wanted to be Louise and she wasn't. She was a fake, she just wasn't a hot fake.

Although she was sure as hell a *tense* fake, damn it.

And if he were any kind of a lover, he would have known something was wrong.

She punched buttons on the jukebox and decided to forget about Davy and concentrate on the comfort of music. She lay down on the couch and Steve climbed on top of her stomach and stretched out, his nose underneath her chin. "Lotta guys doing that tonight," she told him and when he looked at her adoringly, she relented and patted him. "You're a good man, Steve. Needy, but good."

That was one thing Davy wasn't. She had to give him that. Completely self-sufficient, didn't need her for anything. Davy would never tell her she had to choose between him and her family. Of course, Davy would never propose, either. That was the problem with independence. It so rarely went well with commitment. Which she didn't want anyway because she had enough people to take care of.

Maybe that's why I don't miss Scott, she thought and then shoved Scott and Davy and uncompleted sex—not that that was bothering her—out of her mind and let the music fill the void until she heard Andrew and Louise come in the back door and hit the stairs. If they were home, it was past midnight.

She got up as the jukebox began to play "The Kind of Boy You Can't Forget," and picked up the painting from the table. "Well, let's look at you," she said. "You're the one that started this mess." She tore the paper off and then stopped, staring at the cupped yellow flowers that rioted under the checkerboard sky while the Raindrops burbled, "I ain't got over it yet."

Flowers. Not houses, *flowers.* He'd stolen the wrong damn painting *again.* Her already tense system split down the seams, and she headed for the stairs.

She stomped on every tread as if it were Davy's head as she climbed the three stories to his door, Steve trailing dutifully behind her. *"Open up!"* she said, pounding on it, not caring who heard.

After a minute he opened the door, wearing nothing but black boxers, looking sleepy and annoyed. "Look, if this is about the couch, I don't want to hear—"

She shoved the canvas at him. "I said *a city*!" Snapping at him felt wonderful, really, she just wanted to rip him apart. "These are *flowers*."

He took it and shoved it back at her, pointing at the houses in the distance. "Those are *houses*. See? Those little red things? *That's a city*."

"Yes, *little*," Tilda spit back. "In the background. Everybody knows if you say *city*, it means a big city, it means what the picture is *about*."

"That's true," Dorcas said from the doorway behind them as she peered at the painting from her doorway. "That's a painting of flowers."

"Thank you, Dorcas," Tilda said. *"Go away."*

"This is so like you," Davy said, ignoring Dorcas. "It's all about what you know and I don't. I don't know who Gene Pitney is, so it's my fault."

" 'Town Without Pity,' " Gwen said from below on the stairs. "What's going on?"

Davy jerked his head back from Tilda. "Why are you here?" he asked, looking down the stairwell at Gwen.

"I live here," Gwen said. "Why are you shouting about Gene Pitney?"

" 'True Love Never Runs Smooth,' " Louise said

from behind her, her black china-doll wig swinging away from her stage makeup as she stretched to see the painting.

" 'Only Love Can Break a Heart,' " Andrew said, from behind Louise.

" 'One Fine Day,' " Dorcas said, from behind Tilda.

"That's the *Chiffons*," Tilda said to Dorcas, fed up with everybody. "Will you people please go back to bed?"

"I wasn't the one screaming in the hall," Dorcas said and shut her door.

"She has a point," Gwen said. "What's going on?"

"Did Davy say something bad about Gene Pitney?" Nadine said, from farthest down the stairs. "Because I think *he* has a point."

"It's not about Gene Pitney," Davy said, fixing Tilda with cold eyes. "It's about people who do not give other people the information they need to get the job done."

"What job?" Louise said, her eyes dark behind black contacts. "Is that the painting?" Tilda turned it so she could see it. "Oh. No. It isn't."

"You got the wrong one *again*?" Gwen said.

"Hello," Davy said, squinting at Louise in the dim hall with interest. Suddenly he wasn't nearly as sleepy or annoyed, and Tilda wanted to kick him.

"Hello." Louise handed the painting back to Gwen, looked him up and down and smiled, and then faded down the dark stairs in her four-inch heels, probably trying to get away before he noticed she was Eve.

Davy stretched his neck to watch her go as Tilda took

the painting back from Gwen. "If you're all finished yelling at me," he said, when Louise was history, "I'd like to go to bed. *Alone.*"

"*Not a problem,*" Tilda said, and he slammed the door in her face.

"So, the evening went well, did it?" Gwen said.

"No," Tilda said. "The evening sucked. But don't worry, I will figure out a way to get the right painting back." She went down the stairs, Steve on her heels once more, slammed the office door behind them, threw the painting back on the table, and plopped herself down on the couch, determined not to cry. It had been a horrible, horrible night. She felt her face crumple. It had been—

Louise came in, leggy in her heels. "You okay?"

"No," Tilda said, ready to burst into tears.

"Jeez." Louise sat down beside her and put her arm around her, her long red nails looking like petals on Tilda's T-shirt. "That bad. What did he do?"

"It's not him, it's me." Tilda tried to smooth out her face and crumpled it more in the process. "God, I'm hopeless."

"Better not be," Louise said. "You're holding the rest of us together. What happened?"

Tilda drew a deep shuddering breath. "Lousy sex."

"*Really.*" Louise looked thoughtful as she sat back. "I thought he'd be hot. He's got that look going on in his eyes. And a *very* nice body."

"He probably would have been great with you," Tilda said, defeated. "I just wasn't in the mood."

"Well, why didn't you say no?"

"Because I was in the mood when we started," Tilda said. "I really was. Except that it's Davy, and he sees everything so you can't let your guard down, plus, the embarrassment factor. I mean, I hardly know him." She turned to look at Louise. "That sounds stupid, doesn't it?"

"No," Louise said. "It's the reason Eve never has sex. She keeps thinking she doesn't really know this guy, and then there's Nadine, what will she think, and of course Andrew will hate him, and it just doesn't seem worth it to her."

"Eve has sex," Tilda said flatly. "She just has it when she's you."

"I have sex whenever I want," Louise corrected her. "Eve never does. I don't think she'd even know what to do, it's been so long." She cocked her head at Tilda. "You know, you should really think about getting a Louise."

"I *tried*," Tilda said, annoyed. "That's how I got into this mess. But I couldn't make it work. I kept thinking, *What if I come and scream out 'I'm an art forger'?* We'd all be dead."

"Stop thinking." Louise stretched out on the couch, put her sequined high-heeled feet in Tilda's lap, and surveyed her red ankle straps with pleasure. "So it was hot at first, huh? Where did he screw up?"

"Well, there was the lag time," Tilda said bitterly. "I kissed him in a closet, and he said wait a minute and sent me home and stole a painting and then came back here and had a drink and talked to Clea Lewis and—"

"The guy's a moron," Louise said. "Why didn't he jump you in the closet while you were hot?"

"Because we would have ended up in prison," Tilda said, guiltily remembering the guy she'd knocked unconscious. "I actually do get that part."

"Okay, so you cooled off, and he came home. Why didn't you say, 'Not tonight, Dempsey?' "

"Because it felt so good to be held," Tilda said, feeling pathetic even as she said it. "And because I wanted to be Louise. He was out there flirting with Clea Lewis instead of me, and then he came in and he looks *really* good, you know—"

"I *know*," Louise said with enthusiasm.

"And he kissed me and I thought, *Oh, what the hell,* and then it turned out to be hell." She wiggled her toes. "And now I'm *mad.*"

Louise shrugged. "Take care of it and get back to business. Where's your vibrator?"

"That's not it," Tilda said. "I'm mad at him for the painting, not for not coming."

"I don't think so. You'll feel much better if you finish yourself up. Or go bang on Davy's door and make him finish what he started."

"He did," Tilda said. "We are completely finished. You can have him." She clenched her jaw. "He's all yours."

"Not a chance." Louise swung her feet off Tilda and pushed herself up from the couch. "He's yours. I do not poach."

Someone hammered on the street door and they both

turned to look through the window in the office door. "Don't answer it," Tilda said, "it's late," but Louise was already on her way, so Tilda followed.

"Hel-*lo*," Louise said when she opened the door, and Tilda peered past her and thought, *She has a point*.

He was dark and tall, he had one of those classically beautiful faces with cheekbones, and his clothes were impeccable. Tilda had a brief moment when she thought that getting mugged by this guy would be a step up from sex with Davy.

"Would you like to buy a nice seascape?" Louise said, channeling Mae West as she stood back to let him in.

He looked at the nearest Finster as Steve sniffed his shoes. "No, thank you."

"Wise move," Tilda said.

He smiled at her, a lovely matinee-idol smile, and said, "I'm really here to bail out my friend Davy Dempsey. He is staying here, right?"

"You're Davy's friend," Tilda said.

"And he owes you this," the lovely man said and handed her an envelope.

When she opened it, there were fifteen crisp hundred-dollar bills in it. "Oh. Yes, he does," she said, thinking, *I had to sleep with the wrong guy, I couldn't wait until the right one showed up.*

"Is he here?" Davy's friend said. "The name's Simon, by the way."

"Davy didn't mention you." Louise moved closer.

"He never does, love," Simon said, looking deeply into her eyes and smiling. "He never does."

Tilda sighed, and Simon transferred his smile to her.

"Two brunettes. Which one of you did Davy meet first?"

"Tilda." Louise linked her arm through his. "I'm Louise. I'll take you up to his room."

"Thoughtful of you," he said, smiling down at her with intent.

Tilda thought about intervening, and then decided there was no point. She was here and Davy was up in his room, so unless Louise raped him on the staircase, Simon was safe. And they had fifteen hundred dollars. She put it in the cash box in the office after Louise had started up the stairs with Simon, and then she caught sight of the flower painting again.

Just hell.

Sooner or later, Mason was going to notice he was leaking paintings, and he probably wasn't going to buy the explanation that Davy was dumb as a rock. The thought of Davy made her clench her jaw, which was ridiculous. It wasn't his fault.

It was just that at the end, there'd been that possibility. The thought alone was making her warm all over again. She tapped her feet on the floor faster.

Really, just *hell*.

She took the flower painting down into the basement and stuck it under the quilt with the cows, and then she went up the stairs with Steve on her heels one more time and paused at Davy's door. Maybe Louise was right, maybe if she said, "You know, I was close," he'd be interested in giving it another shot. Maybe—

Inside, Louise giggled, and Tilda froze. When Louise giggled like that—

Davy must have gone out. Not even Louise would do a three-way. Probably. Oh, hell. Tilda went upstairs and opened her dresser drawer and found Eve's Christmas present from ten years before. *Thank God Louise picked it out*, she thought as she plugged it in. *At least somebody around here knows what she's doing.*

BEATING ANOTHER sucker at pool had partially restored Davy's good humor, so when he went into his apartment and saw Louise and Simon in bed, all he said was, "Of course, that's perfect," before he went back out and stood, bedless, in the hall. Somebody was going to pay for his lousy night. After a moment's reflection, he climbed the stairs to Tilda's attic, knocked on the door, and went in.

"Jesus," he said when he'd stopped inside the door.

The room ran the length of the building and the whole place was white—ceiling, walls, floor, the heavy old four-poster bed in the center of the space—and Tilda sat in the middle of it all, looking tired but relaxed in the soft glow from the skylights, wearing what looked like a white T-shirt, her hair the only dark thing in the place. It was the coldest room he'd ever seen. Which figured.

"It looks like a meat locker in here," he told her.

"Come in," Tilda said, frowning at him. "Don't

bother to knock. It's only my room." Steve poked his head out from under the white quilt as she spoke and looked at him with deep suspicion.

Davy shook his head at Tilda. "A white T-shirt. You are what you sleep in." He closed the door behind him and looked at Steve again. "And what you sleep with."

"Thank you," Tilda said. "I feel Steve is a big step up from the last guy I slept with. Why are you here?"

"Because Louise is showing Simon more than my room," he said. "I thought about sleeping in the hall, but she's loud. Which made me think of you."

"I know." Tilda sighed. "I should have stayed with them, but I didn't think she'd jump a complete stranger."

"What makes you think she's the one who jumped?" Davy moved to the side of the bed, unzipped his jeans and shoved them off. "Simon has moves. Which side of the bed do you want?"

"We'll take the left," Tilda said, sliding over and taking Steve with her. "And Louise has moves, too."

Davy crawled in beside her. The sheets were warm where she'd been. Or where Steve had been, it was hard to tell. "If Louise has moves, why didn't she move on me?"

"You slept with me," Tilda said. "She also has loyalties."

"How does she know we had sex?"

"I told her."

"Thoughtful of you."

"We're close." Tilda lay back and stared at the skylight. "I should have shown Simon that room. He's much more my type."

"It wouldn't have done you any good." Davy put his arms behind his head. "Simon has loyalties, too."

Tilda turned to look at him. "How could he know I slept with you? He just got here."

"He may have picked up an intention."

"An intention." She went back to looking at the ceiling. "*Very* nice."

Davy started to grin in spite of himself. "Fixed each other good, didn't we?"

"It wouldn't have made any difference," Tilda said, sliding back under the covers. "You and I are doomed to be the best friends."

"Huh?"

"It's always been that way. Louise is Meg Ryan and I'm Carrie Fisher. She's Melanie Griffith and I'm Joan Cusack. She's the beautiful heroine who gets the beautiful guy, and I'm the wisecracking friend who gives the good advice."

"Ruth Hussey in *The Philadelphia Story*." Davy turned his head to look at her. Her hair lay in little question-mark curls on her pillow and the quilt settled roundly over her, and he was finding it difficult to stay mad at her. Also, he was pretty sure she was naked under that T-shirt. "The best friends are always more fun. I could never see what Cary saw in Katherine Hepburn when Ruth was standing there wisecracking with that camera. Much more grit."

Tilda frowned. "I thought that was Celeste Holm?"

"Wrong version," Davy said. "Celeste was in *High Society*. But also gritty."

"I don't think Cary was looking for grit," Tilda said. "I think he was probably going for beauty and sex appeal."

"Ruth and Celeste were sexy," Davy said. "Celeste was the kind of woman you could count on. Celeste would hit somebody with that camera for you."

"Okay, fine," Tilda said. "And you are Ralph Bellamy in *His Girl Friday*, a good, dependable man." Her tone said, *See how you like that.*

"I am *not* Ralph Bellamy," Davy said. "I'm Cary Grant. Pay attention, woman."

"If you're Cary Grant, what are you doing in bed with Celeste Holm?"

"Wising up," Davy said. "Katherine Hepburn probably turned out to be a pain in the ass."

"But the sex was great," Tilda said. "Which is more than you can say for us."

"I had a fairly good time," Davy said mildly. "And now that I'm here, I'm willing to try again. How about you?"

"Right," Tilda said. "As we speak, I'm feeling an overwhelming urge to scream, 'Ravish me, Ralph.'"

"Merely an offer," Davy said.

"Thank you, no," Tilda said. "It would upset Steve. Good night, Ralph."

"Good night, Celeste. Your loss."

Tilda rolled away from him, leaving Steve nestled

between them. They lay there in the soft glow from the skylight for a while, until Davy heard her sigh.

"Look, if you can't sleep with me here, I can go back downstairs," he said, feeling guilty. "They can't take much longer."

"You don't know Louise," Tilda said, keeping her back to him. "It's okay. You can stay."

Davy stared up at the skylights, thinking about strangling Simon, and then Tilda rolled over, her face as pale as ever in the moonlight, her crazy eyes reflecting soft light.

"It was my fault," she said.

"What? Simon? You couldn't know he has no morals."

"No. The lousy sex." She propped herself up on one elbow to look into his eyes. Everything shifted under her T-shirt, and suddenly he wasn't mad at all anymore. "I know it seems like I'm in control," she said to him, her voice earnest, "but it's a fake. I'm a big fake at everything. I was born to fake."

"Matilda," Davy said, "you weren't born to do anything. You do what you do when you do it because that's where you are at the time. When you're ready to have great sex, give me a call. Until then, lie back down and stop moving around under that shirt."

"Sorry," Tilda said and slid back down under the quilt, disturbing Steve.

Yeah, she disturbs me, too, Steve, Davy thought. *I'm never going to get to sleep now.* Maybe he could count sheep. Or paintings, there seemed to be a hell of a lot of those around. "Tilda?"

She rolled back over.

"These Scarlet Hodge paintings. How many are there?"

She hesitated. "Six."

"So I could conceivably screw this up three more times before I got the right one."

Tilda sat up. "You're going to try again?"

He looked at her T-shirt, round in the moonlight. "Oh, yeah."

"Because I have the records for them all," Tilda said, her voice eager. "We can figure out where the rest of them are."

Davy stopped staring at her T-shirt. "You want them all."

"Yes," Tilda said, her voice intense. "I didn't before, but I realized tonight that I need them all." Her voice trailed off and Davy thought, *Here comes a lie.* "They're defective," she said. "I know it's too much to ask but—"

She bent closer as she talked, and he caught the faint scent of cinnamon and vanilla and heat, and he missed part of what she said.

"—sorry I was so awful," Tilda finished. "I mean it, I've been horrible to you."

It took everything he had not to reach for her. "You can make it up to me later," he said and rolled over, and felt her slide back down under the covers next to him. *Sweet Jesus,* he thought. *I have to get out of here.*

"I mean it," she said, over his shoulder. "I'll help you get your money back. I swear."

"Good," he said. "Why do you smell like dessert?"

"What? Oh. My soap. It's called Cinnamon Buns."

"Good choice," he said. "Go to sleep."

"Thank you," she said. "I'm really grateful."

How grateful are you? he thought and then tried to remember her drawbacks: she was prone to biting and kicking, she was bad in bed, she was brunette—

"I'm *really* grateful," Tilda said, her voice very small.

He was definitely going to try again.

WHEN TILDA woke up the next morning, she was sandwiched in between Steve, whose back was to her stomach, and Davy, whose back was to her back. *Forty-eight hours ago, I didn't know either one of these guys,* she thought, and tried to decide if the current situation was an improvement or not.

She propped herself up on her elbows. Steve was lying with his head back, breathing through his nose, his tiny little Chiclet teeth protruding over his lower lip. *Overbite,* Tilda thought. *Too much inbreeding.* She looked over at Davy. He had a five o'clock shadow and he was breathing with his mouth open, but everything else looked good. No inbreeding. In fact, there was nothing wrong with him at all. Except for the arrogance and the lousy sex and the tendency to turn to theft to solve his problems.

Of course, those were also her faults. And thanks to the asthma, she probably snored, so he was actually ahead on points. She shook her head and crawled over

Steve to get to the bathroom. When she came out after her shower, Davy was still out cold, but Steve hung his head over the edge of the bed, looking at her with mournfully beady eyes. "Come on," she whispered, buttoning her paint shirt. "I'll take you outside."

Ten minutes later, she went into the office for orange juice and found Nadine in her cow pajamas investigating the milk carton.

"Hey," Tilda said, getting the juice out of the fridge as Steve rediscovered his food and water bowls. "How's the new boyfriend?"

"Burton." Nadine sniffed the milk carton and made a face. "He has a very good band, and he doesn't freak at the stuff I wear, so I'm thinking he's a keeper."

Tilda put two pieces of toast in the toaster. "Your mom says he has no sense of humor."

"He has one." Nadine shoved the milk carton at Tilda. "It's just not hers. Sniff this."

Tilda sniffed the carton. "Dump it. Is his sense of humor yours?"

"Not really." Nadine poured the milk down the sink and rinsed out the carton. "But I'm keeping him anyway so don't preach. When did you know you wanted to be a painter?"

"I didn't." Tilda reached over her head to get the peanut butter down. "I was told I was going to be one. Don't change the subject. If you're not laughing with him—"

"But you're really good at it," Nadine said.

"Yeah." Tilda shoved the silverware around in the

drawer but could only find a butter knife. She held it up. It looked like a palette knife. Bleah. What the hell, it would spread peanut butter. "That was just a lucky break," she said, slamming the drawer shut.

"But you like it," Nadine prompted.

Tilda picked up the peanut butter and began to unscrew the lid. She was starving. A little lousy sex the night before could really lower a woman's blood sugar.

"You do like it, right?" Nadine said.

"I used to," Tilda said. "Yeah, I like it."

"You used to." Nadine leaned against the cabinet. "But not anymore."

Tilda shrugged. "It used to be fun. Learning to paint. And then painting the furniture." *And the Scarlets.* She unscrewed the jar lid the rest of the way, slowly. "I think the murals are getting to me. Like the one in Kentucky?" She shook her head. "Have you any idea how awful van Gogh's sunflowers look blown up ten times their real size behind a reproduction Louis Quinze dining room table? It was a crime against art."

"So are you going to quit?"

"No." Tilda's toast popped, and she picked it out with the tips of her fingers, trying not to get singed. "We have a mortgage to pay off and the murals are doing it."

"But you don't like it," Nadine said. "So how long before you can quit and be happy?"

"If I keep doing one every two weeks?" Tilda stabbed her knife into the peanut butter. "Oh, fifteen years or so. When your mom gets her teaching certificate next year, that'll speed things up. And the Double Take's doing better."

"Fifteen years. You'll be forty-nine," Nadine said.

Tilda frowned at her. "How did we end up on murals instead of Burton?"

"I have to choose the right career," Nadine said. "I don't want to get stuck doing something I don't want to because the family has to eat." She looked at the peanut butter jar. "I don't mind supporting them, but it has to be something I like."

"You don't have to support them." Tilda handed her the first piece of peanut butter toast. "I've got it covered."

"Well, you can't do it forever," Nadine said. "Let's face it, I'm up next."

"No." Tilda stopped in the middle of spreading the second piece of toast. "No you are not. You do not have to—"

"Keep Mom and Dad and Grandma from the poor-house?" Nadine said. "If not me, who? The Double Take barely pays for itself. Teachers don't make that much. Grandma hasn't done anything but Double-Crostics since Grandpa died, and the Finsters aren't selling. You're going to be nuts from doing murals by the time I'm out of high school. It's me."

"I'll take care of it," Tilda said seriously. "Nadine, really. You are not going to—"

"It's okay," Nadine said. "I want to. But it has to be something I like. I don't want . . ."

"What?" Tilda said, knowing she wasn't going to like what was coming next.

"I don't want to be as unhappy as you are," Nadine said. "I want to still be laughing when I'm thirty-four."

"I laugh," Tilda said.

"When?" Nadine said.

Tilda turned back to her toast. "I laughed at *Buffy the Vampire Slayer* last Tuesday. I distinctly remember chortling."

"I like singing," Nadine said. "And Burton's band is good, even Dad thinks so and he doesn't like Burton. And Burton's good to me. So I'm thinking that might be the way I can support us."

"You picked Burton because you want to make money as a singer?" Tilda shook her head and picked up her juice glass and toast plate. "I'd think about that some more. Listen, I have to go downstairs and get ready for next week's mural. Can you take Steve?"

"Sure," Nadine said, looking down at Steve's furry little head. "He can watch me get dressed."

"Close your eyes, Steve," Tilda said. "Oh, and if you see Davy, will you tell him that the notes about the rest of the paintings are in the top desk drawer there?"

"Sure," Nadine said. "Rest of the paintings?"

"You don't want to know," Tilda said and headed for the basement, balancing her glass on her plate. She stopped in the doorway. "Nadine, I'm not unhappy."

"Yeah," Nadine said, clearly humoring her.

"Right," Tilda said and went to work.

CHAPTER · EIGHT

DOWN IN THE BASEMENT, TILDA FLIPPED ON THE LIGHT in her father's studio and noticed for the first time how the white walls and cabinets gleamed back at her, glossy and sterile. "This place looks like a meat locker," Davy had said when he'd walked into her white bedroom, and now, looking around the spotless studio, she could see his point. Monochromatic white was a great look for a studio full of paintings, not so good for empty rooms. Maybe she'd take a week off and paint a jungle in the attic, thick green leaves that covered her walls and headboard, only this time, no Adam and Eve, they were too hokey, she'd paint a jungle for Steve to hide in.

Then she shook herself out of it. She wasn't going to have a week off for years, and when she did, she wasn't going to paint a jungle, that was for kids, Nadine would paint a jungle. No, she'd paint the walls a nice light blue, maybe some stars on the ceiling, maybe some clouds on the walls, too, so she could sleep in the sky . . .

That was ridiculous, too. Time to get practical. She

put her breakfast on the drawing table, went to the drawers along the side of the room, and pulled open the one marked "19th Century." Flipping through the prints stacked there, she found one of Monet's water lilies, coming soon to a bathroom wall in New Albany. At least the Impressionists didn't take nearly as long to forge as the Renaissance painters, so maybe she would have time to paint her room week after next. Maybe yellow. With her kind of sunflowers lining the walls, only with real suns for heads . . .

"Oh, for heaven's sake," she said out loud. She was not going to paint sunflowers in her room. She laid the print on the table, put Melissa Etheridge on the stereo, and turned on the lamp clamped to the edge. It cast a clean white light, nothing to taint the colors in the print, and Tilda began to eat with one hand and make color notations with the other, concentrating on the job at hand, the one that made the money, while Melissa sang "I'm the Only One." It was a good job. She was her own boss, and she got to paint, she liked to paint, she'd spent fifteen years building a rep as a great painter. Of mural-sized forgeries.

Life could be a lot worse. She could be dependent on somebody else, she could be answerable to a boss, she could have to pretend she liked somebody in order to eat, that would be hell. She was lucky.

She looked at the print in front of her and thought, *I hate Monet*. And then she went back to work.

THREE BLOCKS away, Clea sat at the breakfast table, tapping her fingernail against her coffee cup. It was the closest she could come to throwing the damn thing at Mason and still project loving warmth, the kind of woman he'd want to face over the breakfast table for the rest of his life.

"Could you stop doing that?" Mason said over his paper.

"Oh, I'm sorry," Clea said, pulling her fingers back. "I was thinking."

"Don't," Mason said and went back to his paper.

Not good. Not good at all. First she'd had to spend the entire evening sitting in that ratty little art gallery watching Mason get all excited about old papers with Gwen Goodnight. Then Davy Dempsey had shown up, and worst of all, when they got home, Mason had said he was too tired for sex. Something had to be done.

"You're tapping again," Mason said, closing his paper.

"I'm sorry." Clea pushed the cup away and smiled brightly. "So what are we going to do today?"

"Well, I'm going to work on my Scarlet Hodge research," Mason said. "I don't know what you're going to do."

"Oh." Clea tried to sound bright and independent. "I think I'll go to the museum and look at their primitives. I want to see how they compare to Cyril's collection."

"Very well," Mason said dryly. "Cyril's collection wasn't exactly museum quality."

"He thought it was," Clea said, maintaining her smile at great cost. At least, Ronald had told Cyril it was before his death. Ronald had probably gotten that wrong, too, not that they'd ever know with the insurance company dragging its feet.

"Yes, and after he died, nobody else thought much of what was left, did they?" Mason pushed back his chair and stood up. "I'm sorry, Clea, I don't mean to be disrespectful of your late husband, but he really wasn't a good collector."

"He was a good man," Clea said, surprising herself and Mason at the same time.

"Yes, he was," Mason said, smiling at her for the first time that morning.

"Let me know if I can help you." Clea leaned forward a little, projecting wifeliness and giving Mason a nice view down the front of her blouse.

"You know what would be a help?" Mason said.

Clea leaned forward a little more.

"If you could make breakfast," Mason said. "We've been making do with toast and coffee for a week now. Can you make omelets?"

Clea felt her smile freeze on her face. "Omelets?"

"Never mind." Mason turned away. "Maybe we should get that caterer in full time. What was his name?"

"Thomas," Clea said, her smile still locked in place.

"Maybe *Thomas* does breakfasts," Mason said and went upstairs.

Clea sat back in her chair. Breakfast. He wanted her

to cook. She had flawless skin, she wore a size four, she knew every sexual position that a man over fifty could want, she was unfailingly cheerful, supportive, complimentary, and passionate on demand, and now he wanted *breakfast*?

Honest to God, if she had enough money, she'd give up men forever.

The doorbell rang, and Clea got up to answer it. Maybe it was Thomas, looking for work again. If they kept him full time, he could answer the door, too.

She opened the heavy oak door and blinked at the man on the step. Tall, weather-beaten, black hair graying at the temples, wintry gray eyes, angular jaw, shoulders a woman could lean on . . . not Thomas. *It would be so nice if you had money*, Clea thought, and then took the rest of her inventory: beat-up tweed jacket, worn jeans, boots that had seen better days . . . not rich. She let her eyes go back to his face. "We're not buying anything."

She started to close the door, but he put his foot in the way. "Clea Lewis?"

"Yes," Clea said, feeling a chill. She was positive she hadn't seen this man before, but—

"Ronald Abbott sent me," he said. "About your problem."

"Problem?"

"It would be better if I came in," the man said slowly. "The longer your neighbors watch me on your porch, the better witnesses they'll make."

"Witnesses?" Clea said faintly. *Oh, God, I told Ronald to get rid of Davy.*

The man smiled at her. It wasn't pleasant. "If anything goes wrong," he said.

I do not deserve this, Clea thought. *This is not the way my life is supposed to be.*

"Mrs. Lewis?" the man said.

Clea opened the door.

DAVY WOKE up feeling cheerful. It was a feeling he hadn't had in months, and it persisted even when he rolled over and remembered where he was: broke and alone and about to go looking for four paintings he didn't care about. He found Tilda's bathroom, showered, shaved, and dressed at full speed, stopping only once, on his way out the door, when he caught sight of a sampler hung over Tilda's white desk. He looked closer and saw a naked Adam and a naked Eve standing under a spreading cross stitch tree surrounded by tiny animals with tiny teeth, and under them a verse:

> When Eve ate the apple
> Her knowledge increased
> But God liked dumb women
> So Paradise ceased.
> Gwen Goodnight. Her Work.

Remember to be nice to Gwennie, he thought, and then he took the stairs two at a time to find Tilda and breakfast, not necessarily in that order.

Instead he found Nadine drinking juice in the office, dressed in a vintage housedress printed with little red teapots. She had a red ribbon threaded through her blond curls and red lipstick on her Kewpie-doll mouth, and she was wearing bobby socks with red heels. Steve sat at her feet, fascinated by the bows on her shoes, nudging them with his nose, clearly thinking about chomping one.

"You're looking very Donna Reed today," he said. "Where's your aunt Tilda?"

"Working in the basement," Nadine said. "Steve, stop it. She said the notes you wanted about some paintings are in the top desk drawer. And I was going for Lucy Ricardo. Donna wasn't much for prints. Want some juice? It's orange-pineapple. Grandma's very big on Vitamin C."

"Wise woman," Davy said. "Pour, please." Nadine got a glass out of the cupboard, and Davy had to grin, she looked so fifties housewife. "So you're dressed for . . . ?"

"The dentist," Nadine said, pouring. "Dr. Mark likes all things retro. He has the coolest neon and all these old dental ads. Lucy is for him."

"A retro dentist." Davy detoured around the table to get to the desk drawer. "Of course."

"He's also a painless dentist," Nadine said. "First things first. Goodnights are very practical."

Davy looked around at the stills from the Rayons and the Double Take. "Yeah, I can see that." He pulled open the desk drawer and found six cards, banded together, the top one headed "Scarlet Hodge."

Nadine slid his juice to him across the table. "As Grandma says, don't confuse flair with impracticality." She looked at him severely over the juice glass. "Very different things."

Davy picked up the cards and shut the desk drawer. "So basically, you're a forty-year-old masquerading as a sixteen-year-old."

Nadine shook her head. "I am a free spirit. Don't judge me by conventional standards."

"That would be a mistake." He stuck the cards in his shirt pocket and tasted his juice. It was sweet but with a kick. Sort of like Tilda.

Andrew came in and nodded at Davy, clearly not happy to see him. He dropped a bakery bag in front of Nadine. "When's your appointment?"

"Half an hour," Nadine said. "I'm walking. Fresh air. Very healthy."

Andrew nodded and gestured toward her dress. "Nice Lucy."

"Thank you," Nadine said, beaming at him.

Good dad, Davy thought.

"Want to rehearse that Peggy Lee medley with me tonight?" Andrew went on.

"No," Nadine said, developing a sudden interest in the ceiling.

"Date with the doughnut, huh?" Andrew shook his head at Davy. "Wait until you have a daughter and she starts bringing home boys. All you can think of is 'Where did I go wrong?'"

Maybe when you dressed up like Marilyn, Davy

thought and then felt ashamed even as Andrew threw him a patient look.

"You didn't go wrong at all," Davy said to make up for it. "She's a great kid."

"Wait'll you meet the doughnut," Andrew said.

"This is Burton?" Davy said and Andrew nodded. "Met him. You have my sympathies."

"Make yourself some whole wheat toast," Andrew said to Nadine as he headed out the door again. "You need fiber."

"I had a piece with Aunt Tilda. And *he's not a dough-nut*," Nadine said to her father's back, sounding like a teenager for the first time since Davy had met her.

"Doughnut?" Davy said.

Nadine sighed and opened a cupboard, taking down a loaf of whole wheat. "According to Grandma, there are two kinds of men in the world, doughnuts and muffins."

"Is there anybody in your family who's sane?"

"Define 'sane'." Nadine dropped two pieces of bread in Gwen's yellow Fiesta toaster.

"Never mind," Davy said. "Doughnuts and muffins."

"Doughnuts are the guys that make you drool," Nadine said, taking a jar of peanut butter from the cupboard. "They're gorgeous and crispy and covered with chocolate icing and you see one and you have to have it, and if you don't get it, you think about it all day and then you go back for it anyway because it's a doughnut."

"Put some toast in for me when yours is done," Davy said, suddenly ravenous.

Nadine pushed the bakery bag toward him. "There are pineapple-orange muffins in there."

Davy fished one out. "You have a thing for pineapple-orange?"

"We have a thing for tangy," Nadine said. "We like the twist."

"I picked that up," Davy said. "So doughnuts make you drool."

"Right. Whereas muffins just sort of sit there all lumpy, looking alike, no chocolate icing at all."

Davy looked at his muffin. It had a high golden crown, not lumpy at all. He shrugged and peeled the top off and took a bite. Tangy.

"And while muffins may be excellent," Nadine went on, "especially the pineapple-orange ones, they're no doughnuts."

"So doughnuts are good," Davy said, trying to keep up his end of the conversation.

"Well, yeah, for one night," Nadine said, as her toast popped. She dropped in two more pieces for Davy and then dug into the peanut butter, slathering it on her bread like spackle. "But then the next morning, they're not crisp anymore, and the icing is all stuck to the bag, and they have watery stuff all over them, and they're icky and awful. You can't keep a doughnut overnight."

"Ah," Davy said. "But a muffin—"

"Is actually better the next day," Nadine finished. "Muffins are for the long haul and they always taste good. They don't have that oh-my-God-I-have-to-have-that thing that the doughnuts have going for them, but you still want them the next morning." She bit into her toast with strong white teeth that were a testament to Dr. Mark.

"And Burton is a doughnut," Davy said.

"The jury is still out," Nadine said through her peanut butter. "I find him quite muffiny, but I may be kidding myself."

"You're kidding yourself."

"Maybe not," Nadine said as Davy's toast popped. "I think he gets me."

"In that case, hold on to him." Davy leaned across the table and took his toast. "He's one in a million."

"That's my plan." Nadine put her glass in the sink. "I have to go brush my teeth. It was lovely talking to you. Oh, and I met your friend Simon on the stairs this morning. He's lovely, too."

"Thanks, I'll tell him," Davy said. Then, unable to resist the impulse, he said, "So what am I? Doughnut or muffin?"

"Jury's still out on you, too," Nadine said as she came around the table. "Grandma thinks you're a muffin pretending to be a doughnut. Dad thinks you're a doughnut pretending to be a muffin."

"And your aunt Tilda?"

"Aunt Tilda says you're a doughnut and she's on a diet. But she lies about the diet part." Nadine eyed him carefully. "So if you're a doughnut, you should probably leave although we might miss you."

"You might?" Davy said, surprised.

"Yes," Nadine said. "You may blend nicely. It's too

soon to tell. So be a muffin." She patted him on the shoulder and headed for the door.

"I'll try," Davy said, slightly confused. "Hey, Nadine."

Nadine stuck her head back through the door.

"What's Simon?"

"Doughnut," Nadine said. "With sprinkles."

"You're too young to know about sprinkles," Davy said severely.

Nadine rolled her eyes. "You have no idea what I'm too young for, Grandpa," she said and turned, only to run into Simon.

"Hello, Nadine," Simon said, faintly British and perfectly groomed.

Nadine blushed and nodded and then ran up the stairs, coming back again to say, "Davy, can you watch Steve while I'm at the dentist?"

Davy looked down at Steve who looked back at him with patent distrust. "Sure. We shared a bed last night. We're buddies."

Steve drew in air through his nose and honked.

When Nadine was gone, Simon said, "Did I say something rude to make her blush?"

"No." Davy handed him the bakery bag. "Have a muffin."

"It's too early for sweets," Simon said. "Is there a decent restaurant nearby that serves breakfast?"

"I keep forgetting what a pain in the ass you are," Davy said. "You've lived in America for twenty years. Eat badly, damn it."

"Bad night?" Simon said, pushing the bag away.

"It would have been better if you hadn't co-opted my bed," Davy lied.

"Louise," Simon said, his voice heavy with respect. "I love American women."

"Louise may not be representative," Davy said.

"Louise may be anything she wants," Simon said. "Extraordinarily gifted."

"Oh, good for you." Davy finished off his juice and went around the table to put his glass in the sink.

"What are you so grumpy about? Didn't you spend the night with your Betty Boop?"

"Tilda," Davy said. "And yes, I did."

"Oh," Simon said. "I gather my sympathies are in order."

"I'm working on it," Davy said. "Why are you here?"

"I got a phone call from Rabbit." Simon settled in at the table. "He seemed a trifle upset."

"I never touched him." Davy put the juice away.

"He seems to think someone has put out a contract on you, old boy."

Davy closed the refrigerator door and considered it. "A hit? On me? Nah."

"He implied it was an angry woman which made it more plausible. He also seemed especially concerned that we knew that he had nothing to do with it."

"That's Rabbit for you," Davy said. "He hears about it and wants his ass covered. But I'm not buying it. Tilda isn't that mad." Then he remembered the night before. "Oh. Clea."

"Exactly."

Davy leaned against the table. "Well, she does like men doing things for her. But I don't think so. It's not her MO."

"He seemed fairly serious, so I flew up," Simon said virtuously.

"You were bored so you flew up," Davy said. "And what are you planning on doing, now that you're here? Because I don't have time to entertain you, even if you did pay my rent."

"I thought I'd visit some old haunts—"

"Like the jail?"

"—and then see if you needed any help later with—"

"No," Davy said.

"Solely in an advisory capacity," Simon said.

"You get caught again, they'll throw away the key. And as much as you annoy me, having this conversation on a phone looking at you in an orange jumpsuit would be worse."

"Are you going to break in again?" Simon said, his voice serious.

"Yes," Davy said. "I don't want to, but there are still things in there I need. But not right away. I shot off my mouth to Clea and got her all worked up. I'm going to have to wait a couple of days until she's distracted with something else."

"You're going to need me," Simon said.

"Maybe for the burglary," Davy said. "But not on site. You can advise from Miami."

"And leave Louise?" Simon said.

Davy heard a sound from the doorway and turned to
see Eve, blonde, blue-eyed, and fresh-scrubbed in a pink
T-shirt that made her look younger than her daughter.
"Morning, Eve," he said, smiling at her. "This is my
friend Simon."

"Oh." Eve looked up at Simon and blushed and
turned away. "Welcome to Columbus."

"Thank you." Simon smiled at her back, avuncular.
"It's a beautiful city."

"German Village is nice," Eve said, a little inanely.
She took a muffin from the bag and retreated to the
door. "Have a nice stay," she said over her shoulder.

"And who was that?" Simon said.

"Eve," Davy said, watching her go. "Nadine's mama.
And quite the cupcake."

"Don't go there, my boy," Simon said. "Never sleep
with a mother. It can only lead to grief and guilt."

"Odd rule," Davy said. "Mine's simpler: Never sleep
with sisters." He shook his head. "But you have to
admit, Eve is beautiful."

"Very," Simon said. "But she's no Louise."

WHEN CLEA had seated Ronald's hit man in the living
room, she cleared her throat and said, "I'm not sure
what Ronald told you, Mr. . . ."

"Brown. Ford Brown. He said you had a problem that
needed taken care of." He leaned back in the Chippen-
dale chair. It creaked.

"Well, there is this man," Clea said, lacing her

fingers together in her lap to keep them from shaking. "From my past. But I was hoping that *Ronald* would take care of him."

"He did," Ford Brown said. "He sent me." He stretched out his legs and folded his arms across his chest. "What do you want me to do?"

Well, there it was. All she had to do was say, "Kill Davy Dempsey," and her problems would be over. This man could do it, she had no doubt. He'd probably killed dozens of people. And now here he was, Ronald's present to her. She was going to have to have a long talk with Ronald.

"Mrs. Lewis?"

"Can you keep him away from me?" she said. "This man. Can you stop him from coming near me?"

"Permanently?"

Clea shifted in her chair. "Well, I don't want to see him again. Ever."

The man shook his head at her. "You have to tell me what you want."

"I want you to stop him from coming after me," Clea said, trying to sound like a poor, threatened woman. "I don't know what that would cost—"

"Mr. Abbott already paid my retainer," the man said. "The final bill pretty much depends on what you need."

Clea thought about it. What she needed was Gwen Goodnight pushed off a bridge and Davy Dempsey shoved under a bus and here was the guy who could do both. She bit her lip and looked at him again. He looked very efficient. She'd finally met a man she could count on, and he was a killer. One damn thing after another.

"Mrs. Lewis—"

"I'm *thinking*," Clea said. Okay, maybe they could take this one step at a time. "I need you to watch him for me. His name is Davy Dempsey. If he tries to come after me, if he tries to come into this house, I need you to stop him. To protect me. He's associating with this woman, Gwen Goodnight. I think they're trying to swindle my fiancé, so I need you to watch her, too."

"A woman?"

"I said *watch*," Clea said. "Just *watch* her. If she gets close to Mason, if he goes to see her, I need to know so I can protect him."

"Uh-huh," the guy said. "You want me to watch."

"Both of them," Clea said. "Let me know if they do anything that looks suspicious. And keep them away from me and Mason." She sat back. That sounded good. Nobody dying, and her alone with Mason. "That's it. Oh, unless you can find out anything illegal or immoral about Gwen Goodnight. That would be good. Anything you can get on Gwen." He didn't look impressed so she added, "So I can protect Mason from her. And from Davy. It's part of your job."

"Where are they?"

"She runs the Goodnight Gallery," Clea said and gave him directions. "That's the last place I saw Davy, too."

"And if I have expenses?" Brown said.

"Ronald will take care of it," Clea said, standing. "Do you have a number where I can reach you?"

"I'll call you with one when I find a place to stay," he said. "First I'll need descriptions of these people."

Clea sat down again, not sure of how to get rid of him.

"Well, Davy is about six feet, dark eyes, dark hair, good build"—she faltered there a little, remembering—"cocky as all hell, thinks he's God. Gwen is about five four, blonde hair going gray, watery blue eyes, not much body, not much of anything, really. She runs the gallery." She smiled at him, trying to look innocent. "I don't know what Davy's doing in town besides stalking me."

"Okay." He hadn't taken any notes, which was probably good. No evidence. Then he stood up to go which was even better.

"So you'll call me if anything happens," Clea said, following him to the door.

"No," he said. "If anything happens, I'll stop it."

"Right," Clea said. "Good man. Best of luck."

She closed the door behind him and breathed a sigh of relief, both that he was gone and that he was going after Davy. God knew where Ronald had found him—Ronald must have depths she wasn't aware of—but now that he had, her troubles were over.

She did spare a thought for what he meant by "I'll stop it," but then she decided that since she hadn't told him she wanted Davy dead in a ditch, it wouldn't be her responsibility if he ended up there.

All in all, a good morning. She started up the stairs to dress for the art museum and then slowed down. Breakfast. She had Thomas's number someplace. All you had to do to make life run smoothly was hire the right people, she decided.

Really, it was so simple.

SINCE IT was Saturday, Gwen slept late, but at noon she opened the gallery, poured herself a cup of coffee, punched up an eighties medley on the jukebox, got the last pineapple-orange muffin from the bakery bag, and took everything out into the gallery to the marble counter and her latest Double-Crostic. To her right, the sun streamed through the cracked glass pane above the display window, and the loose metal ceiling tile bounced silently in the breeze from the central air. She thought, *I have been doing this for too many years*, but there wasn't much push to the observation since she was undoubtedly going to be doing it for too many more. She looked at the Finster-laden gallery and shook her head and then bent over her puzzle.

The clue for *J* was "liable or prone to sin." What the hell was that? Eight letters, possibly starting with a *P*, definitely ending in an *E*. Nothing. She had nothing. Maybe Davy would know; he'd gotten the Milland movie. And she'd bet he had more than a passing knowledge of sin, too.

Thunder boomed on the jukebox for the Weathergirls's intro, the bell rang, and she looked up. The man coming in the door was taller and broader than Davy, his dark hair grizzled around his temples, his face seamed by hard living. "You have a room for rent?" he said, and his voice wasn't as harsh as she'd expected, but it wasn't gentle, either.

"Uh, yes," she said, trying not to step back. It wasn't that he looked threatening as much as it was that he was so much *there*, blocking all the light from the street. "I'll need references—"

"Clea Lewis recommended you," he said. "My name's Ford Brown. You can call her."

"Oh." Gwen let her eyes slide toward the phone. "Uh—"

Then he took out his wallet and opened it and Gwen saw money. Lots of it.

"Eight hundred a month," she said. "Two months' rent up front."

He counted out the bills, several of them hundreds, while she watched. *Ben Franklin*, she thought. *Just lovely*. Where the hell had Clea met this guy?

"Are you from around here, Mr. . . ."

"Brown," he said again. "No."

Gwen smiled at him, waiting.

"I'm from Miami," he said, handing her the bills.

"That must be where you met Clea," she said brightly.

He waited patiently, not smiling, and she thought, *Well, at least he's not charming*. Not like Davy. Who was also from Miami.

"Do you know Davy Dempsey?" she asked.

"No," he said, still patient.

"Because he's from Miami, too," Gwen said, feeling like an idiot. "Like you. And Clea."

"You winter in Florida, we summer in Ohio," he said, completely deadpan.

"Oh." That had to be a joke. Didn't it? "Why would you summer in Ohio?" she said, waiting for him to say, "It was a joke."

"It's cooler here," he said.

She waited for him to say more but he just stood there, huge and patient. It was perverse and Gwen had had enough perverse for one lifetime. She leaned on the counter. "So it's not cool where you live?"

"It's not bad."

"Air-conditioning?" Gwen said.

"No." She waited and the silence stretched out until he said, "I live on the water."

Of course, you do, Gwen thought. *That's why you came to Ohio to stay in a dark little overpriced apartment.* "Ocean-front condo?"

"My boat."

"Your boat." White sands, blue water, alcoholic drinks with little umbrellas. *I want a boat*, Gwen thought and then kicked herself. Where would she put it? The Olentangy?

"Is there something wrong?"

"No," Gwen said. "I was thinking about your boat. I bet the water's blue and the sand is white and all the drinks have little umbrellas."

"Not my drinks."

"Well, no, of course not." Gwen looked at him, exasperated. "This boat has a bed and a kitchen and everything?"

"Yes," he said.

"And you left it to come to Ohio because . . ."

"I have work here. I won't be staying long."

"Oh," Gwen said. "Then why . . ."

"Because renting from you is cheaper than staying in a hotel," he said. "Although not faster."

"I'll get the keys," she said, but it wasn't until she was in the office, rummaging in the desk drawer, that she realized where he was going to be staying.

Two B. Right across from her.

She picked up the phone, finding the paper with Mason's number that she'd pinned to the bulletin board. She dialed and listened to the Weathergirls sing "I feel stormy weather moving in" while she watched Mr. Brown through the glass door to the gallery. He was looking at Dorcas's seascapes. They would help him not miss his boat. Finsters could put anybody off the water for good.

"Hello?" Clea said.

"Clea?" Gwen said. "This is Gwen Goodnight. There's a man here named Ford Brown who wants to rent an apartment from me. He gave you as a ref—"

"I know him," Clea said. "It's okay."

"Oh." Gwen peered through the glass again. He hadn't gotten any less disquieting. "Okay. Thanks."

So Clea vouched for him and he had sixteen hundred in cash. *Well, if he kills me, it'll be what I deserve for selling out,* she thought, and then she went out front, feeling that at least she'd done better than she had with Davy, although Davy had known the Milland movie.

"The outside door is to the left," she said, handing him the keys. "I'll take you up."

He nodded. "Thanks."

He made her uneasy behind her on the way up the stairs, and she thought, *If there was only a sign, something that would tell me this is all right,* and then on an impulse, she turned back to him, her eyes level with his because he was two steps below her. "You don't happen to know an eight-letter word that means 'capable of sin,' do you?"

He looked at her with no expression on his face at all, and then his lips twitched. "No, ma'am."

"Oh." Gwen shrugged, feeling like an idiot. When even the scary guys laughed at her, she had lost it. "Just a thought. I work Double-Crostics and that one's stumping me."

He nodded.

She sighed and went the rest of the way up the stairs, and he followed her to the room, looked around without comment, thanked her for her help, and shut the door, leaving her in the hall, a little rattled by the whole thing.

I rented a room to an ax murderer, she thought. *Who owns a boat.* She turned to see Tilda on the stairs below her.

"Who *was* that?" Tilda said.

"Mr. Brown," Gwen said, coming down the stairs. "He just rented Two B."

"Merciful heavens." Tilda followed her into the office. "Right across from you. Gwennie, your luck has finally turned."

"He's a *tenant*," Gwen said.

"No imagination. I vote you go for it."

"Like you did?" Gwen said, and Tilda shut up.

The gallery door opened, and Nadine came in from the street, running her tongue across her teeth as they went out to meet her. "It always feels weird," she said. "Dr. Mark says hi. Everyone there was thrilled I'd been flossing." She looked at them. "What's up now?"

"Gwennie just rented the last apartment," Tilda said. "To a very hot guy."

"Simon?" Nadine said.

"Who's Simon?" Gwen asked.

"No, a different hot guy," Tilda said, frowning. "Although now that you mention it, it is raining men here."

"Simon?" Gwen said.

"Davy's friend," Nadine said. "He's staying in Davy's room. He paid the rent."

"So where's Davy staying?" Gwen said.

"So about *Mr. Brown*," Tilda said.

"I think he moved in with Aunt Tilda," Nadine said.

Gwen looked at Tilda who looked at the ceiling.

"Right," Gwen said. "Mr. Brown. I'm sure he's a very nice man. He's got that cowboy thing going. His first name is Ford. Maybe his mama was channeling John Ford when she named him."

"Ford Brown?" Tilda said, her eyes back from the ceiling. "Did you get his middle name?"

"No," Gwen said, going back to her stool behind the counter. "But I got his sixteen hundred dollars."

"Because if it's Madox, we've got ourselves a tenant with a fake identity," Tilda said. "Or the descendent of a famous painter, but what are the chances of that?"

Nadine said, "Famous painter?"

Gwen shook her head. "Or his mama loved her Thunderbird. Let's not get too paranoid here." She picked up her Double-Crostic book.

"I have a rehearsal," Nadine said. "Keep me informed on the cowboy painter."

"You'll be the first to know." Gwen turned to her puzzle.

"Davy and I are going to go get a painting." Tilda kissed her cheek. "I'll call if we need bail."

"Oh, good." Gwen ran her eyes down the list of clues as Tilda went out through the office. Thank God for Double-Crostics. There was never anything upsetting there.

J. Prone to sin. Eight letters.

Ford Brown, she thought.

No that was nine letters.

Doughnut.

She moved on to *K.*

CHAPTER · Nine

*U*PSTAIRS, DAVY HAD GONE THROUGH THE SCARLET notes and was now contemplating his future. "I'm starting to like this room, Steve," he said to the dog as they stretched out on the white quilt. "Like its owner, it has infinite possibilities." Steve sighed and put his head between his paws and Davy scratched his ears. "You've really got a thing for her, don't you? Good thinking on your part. She'll never let you down. Dog biscuits and sleeping on the bed for life." Steve rolled his head to one side a little to listen, and Davy thought about Tilda, taking care of everybody, desperate to get those paintings back so people wouldn't find out her father sold forgeries.

That had to be it. There had to be something wrong with those paintings, something dangerous enough to make Tilda turn to crime. Because she wasn't a natural at it, that was for sure. He spared a moment to wonder what Tilda would have been like if his dad had raised her instead of hers. Not much difference, he decided. Some people were straight clean through. They never got that insane buzz that sliding into forbidden territory set up in the blood, when every nerve ending sharpened and hummed, and every sound and scent was magnified. *God, I miss it,* he thought. *Thanks for raising me to be an adrenaline junkie, Pop.* At least he hadn't turned out like his dad. There would be a horror story for you.

There had to be another way to get that buzz. Some way that was legal. *Bungee jumping.* No, that was stupid. *Drugs.* No, that was illegal. *Sex.* That was Tilda. Okay, she wasn't thrilled about the idea, but he could get a second shot and make sure she paid attention this time. She could even bite if she wanted to since, given Gwennie's needlework, it appeared to be a genetic predisposition. He began to think about her instead of crime, and he was feeling fairly cheerful by the time he and Steve heard her step on the stairs.

"We were wondering where you were," Davy said as she came through the door and Steve sat up and wagged his tail.

"Working," Tilda said. "Remember me, Matilda Veronica, Mural Painter? That's what pays the bills here, boy." She made kissing noises at Steve. "Hi, puppy."

"That would be Veronica the control-freak bitch you mentioned last night?" Davy said, trying to imagine her making kissing noises in leather. It was surprisingly easy. He patted the bed beside him. "Come and talk to me about these paintings."

"It's all in the notes." She sat down beside him and Steve climbed into her lap and sighed with happiness.

"The first one was the city scene," she said, scratching the dog behind the ears. "That's the one Nadine sold to Clea."

"The one I keep missing," Davy said, watching Steve stretch his head to meet her fingers.

"The second one was the cows and the third one was the flowers," Tilda said. "You got those." She pushed her glasses back up the bridge of her nose and smiled at him crookedly, her Kewpie-doll mouth askew, the first real smile she'd ever given him, and he leaned toward her a little because she looked so warm.

"Then there were butterflies," she said. "Somebody named Susan Frost bought that. She's in Gahanna."

"Butterflies," he said, and wondered what she'd do if he went for that warm place under the curve of her jaw.

"Then mermaids," she said. "A guy named Robert Olafson got that one. He lives in Westerville."

Maybe he wouldn't wait until he had all the paintings. Maybe—

"And the last one, which I can't *believe* he sold, is dancers," Tilda said. "That one went to Mr. and Mrs. John Brenner."

"Why can't you believe he sold it?" Davy said, enjoying the energy in her voice. "This is your dad we're talking about, right?"

"Because it was smeared," Tilda said. "It was damaged. But my dad sold it anyway."

She looked unhappy, so Davy changed the subject. "Okay, today we get the butterflies."

"Can't we do them all today?" Tilda said. "Can't we just go buy them back?"

"Sure," Davy said. "Unless they don't want to sell. Or they want more than we have to spend. Let's take our time and do it right."

"Oh." Tilda swallowed. "I thought . . . well, that you could do anything."

" 'You rush a miracle man,' " Davy said, " 'you get rotten miracles.' "

She pushed her glasses back up again. "So what do we do if they don't want to sell?"

"We convince them," Davy said cheerfully.

Tilda's face changed.

"What?" Davy said.

"You sound like . . . somebody I used to know," Tilda said.

"Your dad," Davy said.

"No," Tilda said, but she was lying. She really was a terrible liar.

"Who forged the Scarlets, Tilda?"

"The Scarlets aren't forgeries," Tilda said, rising. "But we need to get them back anyway."

"Okay," Davy said, rolling off the bed. "Try not to kick anybody this time."

"Oh, God, I'm trying to forget that," Tilda said, wincing. "That guy's probably okay, right?"

"I didn't see anything in the paper," Davy said. "And he's not exactly in a position to whine. He was breaking in, too. He probably came to and got out of there."

"Right." Tilda opened the bedroom door, leaving

Steve disconsolate on the bed. "You sure you know how to do this?"

"Oh, yeah," Davy said. "I know exactly how to do this."

DOWNSTAIRS IN the gallery, Pippy Shannon sang "He Is," the phone rang, and Gwen discovered to her disgust that the answer to *M*, "sweetheart," was "tootsy wootsy." "Goodnight Gallery," she said, still frowning at the puzzle book.

"Gwen? This is Mason Phipps."

"Oh." Gwen shut the puzzle book and tried to sound bright and innocent. "Hello."

"I wanted to thank you for last night."

"Oh, my pleasure," Gwen lied. "Really. Like old times."

"I'd like to show my gratitude by taking you to a late lunch tomorrow," Mason said. "You can get away from the gallery on Sunday, can't you?"

I'll never get away from the gallery. "I don't know—"

"I would truly appreciate it if you'd join me, say about two?"

Gwen thought she heard some vulnerability in his voice. The poor man was living with Clea. That could leave anybody flayed and bleeding.

But he'd want to talk about Tony.

On the other hand, if she didn't eat lunch with him, she'd be eating it with a Double-Crostic. "Tell me an eight-letter word for 'capable of sin' and I'll go."

"All right," Mason said, sounding taken aback. "Any other clues?"

"Begins with *P*, ends in *E*."

"Give me a minute," he said, and there was a smile in his voice, and she thought, *This is a nice guy. I should go to lunch.*

"It couldn't possibly be 'peccable,' could it?" he said finally.

"Peccable?"

"You know, as in 'impeccable,' only the opposite?"

Gwen opened the crostic book. "Hang on." She filled in the letters and then transferred them to the quote squares. "I'll be damned."

"That's it?" Mason said.

"I'll also be having lunch with you," Gwen said, laughing at the absurdity of it all. "I can't believe you got that. Because I was *never* going to."

"I was motivated," Mason said, the smile in his voice growing bigger.

"You are my hero," she said.

They talked about Double-Crostics for a while, and he thanked her again for the night before, and when she finally hung up the phone, she was looking forward to seeing him again. *I wonder if that's a date,* she thought. *It's just lunch. But Clea isn't coming along. I wonder . . .*

The door opened as Pippy did her big finish, and Gwen saw Ford Brown, now forever a cowboy in her mind with the soundtrack to match: *Do not forsake me, oh, my darling.* "Oh," she said to him, trying to ignore the music in her head. "Is everything all right upstairs?"

"It's fine." He looked around the gallery. "Nice place."

Gwen looked around at the dingy walls and cracked window and dull wood floors. "Uh-huh."

His lips twitched in that not-grin again. "I was being polite."

"That only works when there's some possibility it might be true," Gwen said, wondering what he was up to. She hadn't known him long, but she knew he was being abnormally chatty.

"So why isn't it?" He wandered past the Finsters, his hands in his pockets.

"What? Nice?" Gwen shrugged. "No money."

Ford stopped at the cracked window. "Wouldn't take that much."

"Are you a contractor?" Gwen said.

"You could say that." Ford turned back to her. "I was heading for lunch. What's your favorite restaurant?"

"Lunch," Gwen said.

Ford nodded patiently. "You tell me where the best place to eat is, I'll pay you back by bringing you lunch."

"Do I look hungry or something?" Gwen said. "Because you're the second guy who's offered to feed me in fifteen minutes."

"People eat," Ford said. "Usually about this time. Even in Florida."

"Imagine that. I figured you all lived on the fruit in the drinks with the little umbrellas."

"What is it with you and the umbrellas?" Ford said.

"Just looking for a way out of the rain." Gwen went back to her Double-Crostic. "Try the Fire House. Great seafood. You'll feel right at home."

An hour later he brought her back a piña colada with an umbrella in it. "Extra fruit," he said when he put it on the counter. Then he went upstairs.

"Damn," Gwen said, surprised, and tasted it.

It was delicious.

WHEN DAVY and Tilda got into Jeff's car that afternoon, Davy said, "Here's the way this goes. When we get there, I go to the door. You watch me. You will stay in the car, unless I do one of three things, then you come up with me."

"Three things," Tilda said.

"If I motion you up and call you Betty," Davy said, "be a ditz. I'm the one in charge, I'll patronize you a little bit while you search through your purse."

"Big purse," Tilda said, holding it up. "Is Betty a ditz because I was such a mess in the closet?"

"You were not a mess in the closet," Davy said. "You were Vilma in the closet. If I need somebody to jump my bones, I'll call you Vilma. Unfortunately, I don't think that's going to come up this afternoon. If I call you Betty and say we've been together a year, you put a hundred-dollar bill in the mark's hand and then you look for a second hundred."

"The mark?"

"Pay attention," Davy said sternly. "If I say we've been together one year . . ."

"I put a hundred in the mark's hand and then start digging for a second hundred," Tilda said.

"Right, if I say we've been together for two years . . ."

"I give her two hundred," Tilda said.

"Good girl."

"Why?"

"Because once she has the money in her hand, it's going to be really hard to give it back. If you hand it over while you're looking for the second bill, she'll take it automatically and we'll have her."

"We can't just offer her the money?"

"Yes," Davy said. "We can. That's what I will do. If that doesn't work, you come up."

"Okay." Tilda looked a little uneasy. "One. Betty. Ditz. Money."

"Two is I look at my watch. You come up and tell me we're running late and we have to go."

Tilda nodded. "Am I nice?"

"Take your cue from me. If I call you Veronica and act like I'm afraid of you, be a bitch." Tilda sighed. "If I call you Betty and snarl, you grovel. We're putting a time lock on the deal, and if the mark doesn't hurry up, he'll lose it."

"Time lock. Okay. What's three?"

"I put my hands behind my back, and you come up and be the enemy."

"The enemy," Tilda said.

"If I can't get the mark on my own, I'm going to have

to give him a reason to bond with me," Davy said. "The fastest way to do that is for the mark and me to confront an enemy together. That's you."

"Okay," Tilda said. "What do I do?"

"Take your cue from me again. If I call you Veronica and cringe, say I couldn't get the painting, whatever, bitch me out. Say you knew I couldn't do it. Bully me."

"And that works how?" Tilda said, frowning at him.

"If the person at the door lives with a bully, he'll side with me. Now if the person at the door *is* the bully, I'll call you Betty and you come up whining."

"I didn't whine in the closet."

"No, you didn't. Be as annoying as you can be without challenging me. Put me in a position where the guy at the door thinks I should be bullying you. Whine that we don't need the dumb painting, that we should be spending that money on you."

"Okay, I think I've got it." Tilda sat frowning for a minute and then nodded. "So Betty's a ditz, and Veronica's a bitch, and Vilma's a slut. I had no idea you thought so much of me."

"You're not concentrating, Matilda," Davy said. "I'm going to try to work it so that you don't have to come up at all. It's better if we can just buy the damn things. And no matter how we do it, the fewer recognizable faces associated with this mess the better." He looked into her pale blue eyes and lost his train of thought for a minute. "You are memorable, Celeste."

"Oh," Tilda said. "I can fix that, Ralph. Wait a minute."

She got out of the car, and Davy slid down in his seat and thought, *Now what?* When she still wasn't back fifteen minutes later, he opened the door to go find her and there she was.

She'd slicked her curls down into a smooth bob and taken off her glasses. She was wearing a pink sweater that fit very well and a green dotted scarf around her neck and she looked neat and respectable and sort of Yuppie and completely unlike herself.

"I'm impressed," Davy said. "What did you do?"

Tilda slid back into the front seat. "Mousse, eye makeup, dark contacts, Eve's sweater, scarf, and skirt. Now can I go up to the door with you?"

"No," Davy said. "You still stay in the car. But I am really impressed." *And turned on. Hello, Vilma.*

"Easy," Tilda said, and picked up her bag and pulled out the first card. "Let's go see Mrs. Susan Frost. She has a lovely Scarlet of butterflies for which she paid five hundred dollars. She's in Gahanna. Take 670 east."

TWENTY MINUTES later, Davy pulled up in front of a tidy little ranch house in Gahanna. "Okay. Got the money?"

Tilda opened her billfold and picked out ten very crisp hundred-dollar bills. "Simon isn't a counterfeiter, is he?"

"No," Davy said. "He doesn't have that much concentration. Why?"

"Because these are his," Tilda said. "From your rent."

"His rent," Davy said. "I haven't seen that room

since he got here. Give me five of them in case I can do this without you."

"It's a painting of butterflies," Tilda said, handing over the bills. "You sure you don't want me to come up with you?"

"Nope." Davy opened the door. "Stay in the car and watch me. If you come up, I'm your husband Steve."

"Okay," Tilda said, clearly humoring him.

A tight-lipped woman about Gwennie's age answered the door, and Davy smiled at her and discarded the idea of asking for donations of paintings. This one would want money and she'd gouge them for all she could get. "Mrs. Frost?"

"Yes," she said suspiciously.

"Hi," he said. "I'm Steve Foster. You don't know me but my wife's aunt used to visit you here with a friend." He shook his head. "I can't remember the friend's name."

"So?" Mrs. Frost said.

"I'm sorry, I'm telling this so badly." Davy stuck his hands in his pockets and smiled at her, his best I'm-an-idiot smile. "I guess I'm nervous."

"What is it you want?" she said, but her mouth relaxed a little.

"My wife's aunt's coming into town today," Davy said, going earnest on her. "It's her sixtieth birthday and she's been really good to Betty, and, when she was here years ago, she saw this butterfly painting, and she told Betty all about it, a big checkerboard sky and lots of beautiful butterflies. She said she looked at it the whole visit and she used to dream about it at night. She really loved it."

"I think I remember her," Mrs. Frost said, the suspicion easing from her face a little. "Was her friend Bernadette Lowell?"

"Maybe," Davy said, watching her face, smiling. "That sounds about right. Betty would really like to buy that painting for her aunt, but she's really shy, that's Betty down in the car . . ." He turned and waved at Tilda. "It would make her so happy, and it'd make me so happy to make her so happy—"

"I don't even know what happened to that painting," Mrs. Frost said, distracted, looking behind him.

"Hi," Tilda said, coming to stand beside him, smiling and confident, and he put his arm around her.

"Don't be shy, Betty," he said, and Tilda hunched her shoulders under his arm. "Mrs. Frost isn't even sure she has the painting. She hasn't seen it in a year—"

"Oh, but we'll pay for it," Tilda said, looking slightly goony as she dug in her bag. "I know we're interrupting you—" She came up with a hundred-dollar bill and Mrs. Frost's eyes swiveled right to it. "That's not enough." She jabbed it at Mrs. Frost who took it, and then went back to her bag. "I'm so sorry, I know I have the other one in here . . ."

"Hey." Davy squeezed her shoulder a little. "She's not even sure she has it. Maybe—"

The vague look on Mrs. Frost's face had sheared off into avarice as she looked at the hundred in her hand.

"Let me look upstairs in the attic," she said and was gone, taking the money with her.

"I know it's here somewhere," Tilda said, her head practically in her bag.

"It's okay, honey." Davy patted her shoulder and wondered how she knew to stay in character when he hadn't told her to. Maybe he'd been wrong about Tilda. Maybe Michael Dempsey could have turned her into a crook. Damn good thing she hadn't been born a Dempsey. "Don't worry, she's looking for it," he said and Tilda turned her face to his and smiled, as open as the sun, and he tightened his arm around her and was even more grateful that she hadn't been born a Dempsey.

"Oh, I hope she finds it." Tilda dug in her bag again. "Wait, here it is." She held up another hundred.

"That's good," Davy said. "You hold on to it and try to calm down."

They sat down on the top step and Tilda talked about her aunt and how happy she'd be to see the painting, and Davy left his arm around her and let the sun seep into his bones and thought, *Damn, I'm happy.*

"This it?" Mrs. Frost said from behind them about fifteen minutes later, and Davy looked up to see a dusty eighteen-inch painting, full of the wickedest-looking butterflies he'd ever seen.

"That's it!" Tilda sprang up. "Oh, that's exactly the way Aunt Gwen described it. Oh, this is so wonderful. And look . . ." She held the second hundred out. "I found the other hundred." She pressed it into Mrs. Frost's hand.

"You know, we paid over a thousand dollars for this painting," Mrs. Frost lied through her teeth.

"Oh." Tilda looked devastated as she turned to face him. "Steve, we can't . . ."

"Well, now, wait a minute, honey," Davy said, and got out his wallet. He counted out a twenty, a ten, and four ones. "We can go up to two thirty-four," he said, offering Mrs. Frost the bills. He looked apologetically at Tilda. "We can just eat at home instead of taking Aunt Gwen out to Bob Evans. Your cooking's better than eating out anyway."

"Oh, Steve," Tilda said, putting her head down. Davy could have sworn she blushed.

"Okay," Mrs. Frost said, taking the bills out of his hand, probably to get the two of them off her front porch before they got any ickier. "Here you go."

"Oh, *thank you*!" Tilda said, grabbing the painting. "Oh, my aunt is going to be—"

Mrs. Frost shut the door in her face.

"—so happy," Tilda finished, still sweetness and light.

"Come on, honey," Davy said, taking her arm. "Let's go get Aunt Gwen."

When they were in the car, Tilda said, "She did not pay a thousand dollars for this."

"That's okay. Neither did you." Davy handed the five hundreds she'd given him back to her and started the engine. "About those butterflies."

"Boy." Tilda angled the painting to catch some of the sunlight from the window. "I haven't seen this for fifteen years."

"Scarlet must have been a little annoyed when she painted them," Davy said, pulling out into the street. "They look like they could strip a cow faster than piranha."

"Oh." Tilda looked at them closer. "They are sort of edgy, aren't they? Well, Scarlet had issues."

"You still want to try the next one right away?" Davy said.

"No," Tilda said. "My heart should be out of my throat by tomorrow. That is possibly the scariest thing I've ever done."

Davy looked over at her, surprised. "I couldn't tell. You were really good."

"Really?" Tilda said.

"Quite an actress."

"That's Gwennie," Tilda said, looking back at the butterflies. "Eve and I could both do Lady Macbeth in kindergarten. Nadine could do it even earlier. You should hear 'All the perfumes of Arabia' with a lisp. She was so cute."

"Yeah." Davy stole a glance at her profile as she studied the painting. "Runs in the family."

She turned to him. "You were damn good yourself. Gwennie couldn't do a character better. You were amazing."

You haven't seen anything yet, Vilma, Davy thought.

"I really am grateful," she told him.

"My pleasure," he said and kept his eyes on the road.

*

• 193 •

TILDA HAD braced herself for another pass that night, but Davy left with Simon to do God knew what and she felt oddly bereft. They should have celebrated or something. Nadine showed up shortly after they were gone, on her way to sing with Burton's band, and handed over Steve, who had a bleeding gash across his nose.

"What happened?" Tilda said, appalled.

"He met Ariadne on the way up the stairs," Nadine said, shaking her head at him.

"And she attacked you, poor baby?" Tilda cuddled Steve's little furry body.

"No," Nadine said. "He jumped her and tried to, uh, well, hump her."

Tilda stopped cuddling to look into his beady, clueless eyes. "Steve, she's a cat."

"And he's a guy," Nadine said. "Which reminds me, I'm late to meet Burton. Where's Davy?"

"He and Simon went out," Tilda said, still not sure what to do about Steve. "They'll be back soon."

When Louise got home at midnight, Steve's nose was better, and Simon and Davy were still gone, but five minutes later, they turned up, as if on cue. "That was lucky," Tilda said as Simon and Louise faded upstairs.

"Lucky, my ass," Davy said. "He had one eye on the clock all night. She must have told him when she was getting off work." He went upstairs then, and when she followed an hour later with Steve, he was fast asleep, looking like a fallen angel in her bed.

Right, Tilda thought. *Lucifer, right here in my*

sheets. He did not learn to scam people in heaven. But the next morning, after she'd taken Steve out for his morning Dumpster encounter, she found out Davy might be on the side of the angels after all.

"Good morning," she said to Gwen and Eve when she got to the office. "What's new?" She poured a glass of pineapple-orange juice as Steve attacked his food bowl, and then she turned to find them watching her. "What?"

"Louise had a talk with Simon last night," Gwen said.

"You talked?" Tilda said, raising her eyebrows at Eve.

"He's with the FBI," Eve said, and Tilda sat down hard in the desk chair, gripping her juice glass like death.

"What's he here for?" she said.

"He's here because he's working with Davy," Eve said.

Tilda swallowed. "*Davy's* FBI?"

Eve nodded. "Louise found that exciting. Then I woke up this morning and realized what it meant."

"Tell me you're being nice to Davy," Gwen said to Tilda. "Don't make him mad."

"I'm not making him mad." Tilda bit her lip. "Well, I haven't made him mad lately. You know, that would explain why he was so good at scamming that painting. If he's FBI, he probably knows all there is to know about crime."

"How is he on art fraud?" Gwen said grimly.

"He was asking a lot of questions about it," Tilda said. "But I think it was general information. I don't think he's here for . . . me." She swallowed. "I mean, we met burgling Clea's closet, he couldn't have planned that."

"So what was he doing in Clea's closet?" Eve said. "The FBI is investigating Clea?"

"I don't think so," Tilda said. "He told me she'd made his financial manager embezzle all his money and he's here to get it back. It sounded personal, not professional."

"If he's FBI, why doesn't he have her arrested?" Eve said.

"I don't *know*, Eve," Tilda said, still trying to wrap her mind around the new information. "Maybe it's part of a plan. He's a devious son of a bitch."

"Don't get angry with him," Gwen said. "We need him to like us."

"Well, hell, I *slept* with him," Tilda said. "You'd think someplace in there he'd have mentioned something like the FB-fucking-I. Are we sure Simon wasn't just trying to impress Louise into bed?"

"Louise was in bed," Eve said, looking at the ceiling. "There were handcuffs. Nice ones. Louise asked him where he'd gotten them."

"Great," Tilda said. "Tonight have Louise ask him what he's here for."

"She can't," Eve said. "It's Sunday. She doesn't exist again until Wednesday."

"She's not supposed to exist *here* at all," Tilda said. "Are you going to tell him who you are?"

"No. It turns out he has a thing about sleeping with women who are mothers. If I tell him, he'll be furious." She sighed. "I'm thinking maybe Louise won't be back on Wednesday. I'll leave her at the Double Take."

"Well, figure out where the hell she is tonight because Simon's going to want to know." Tilda put her juice glass down, not thirsty anymore. "Men tend to miss women who get to the handcuff stage by the second night."

"I'm going to miss him, too," Eve said miserably, and Tilda thought, *You're going to? Not Louise?*

"Miss who?" Nadine said, coming in from the hall. "Steve, baby, poochie, how's the nose?"

Steve lifted his head from his food bowl, barked once, and went back to eating.

"Doesn't he have a beautiful voice?" Nadine picked up the orange juice carton. "So who's leaving?"

"Nobody's leaving, baby," Eve said, leaning over to kiss her cheek. "How was singing with Burton last night?"

"The singing part was good," Nadine said, pouring her juice. "The Burton part, not so. He wants to see me today, though, so maybe he's sorry."

"What did he do?" Eve said, moving into dangerous mother mode.

"Well," Nadine said, sitting down at the table. "He *acts* like he's this big rebel, walks on the wild side, but it turns out he's pretty conservative after all. He didn't like the Lucy dress at all."

"What a fool," Eve said. "You look great in the Lucy dress."

"I know." Nadine sounded perplexed. "I think I may have misjudged him. Men are so seldom what they seem to be."

"Tell me about it," Tilda said, thinking of Davy upstairs, asleep in the security of federal employment. She picked up her orange juice glass. "I have to go work. I start that Monet in New Albany tomorrow."

She went down to the basement, Steve with her in case Ariadne decided to come down to the gallery. She really didn't think Davy was going to arrest her, she wasn't even sure he was really FBI, but he was still a danger. She locked herself in her dad's studio, cut a piece of foam core board to dimensions in ratio with the wall in New Albany, and began to lay in the colors for the bathroom lilies while she obsessed on the question. "You'd think he would have told me," she said to Steve, who lay with his chin on his paws, gazing patiently up at her. "I told him I painted murals. But is he honest with me? No, he says he's in *sales*. He *consults*. What the hell is that, *consults*?" She was still obsessing when somebody knocked on the door two hours later.

"What?" she said when she opened the door, and was only marginally relieved to see it was Andrew. "Oh. Hi."

"Can I talk to you?" he said, coming in and pulling the door shut behind him.

"Sure." Tilda went back to the drawing board.

"It's about Simon. And Louise."

"Get a life, Andrew."

"I can't really blame him." Andrew pulled up a stool and sat down beside Tilda. "He seems like a nice guy and Louise probably made the first move."

"She jumped him at the door." Tilda picked up her brush. "Real bundle of lust, our Louise."

"But she's sleeping with him *here*," Andrew said. "Suppose Nadine finds out?"

"Finds out what? Nadine knows about Louise."

"She doesn't know Louise is a . . ."

"Yes, Andrew?" Tilda said, laying in another ultramarine wash.

"She thinks Louise just sings," Andrew finished.

"Andrew, you're a good man, but you're an idiot. Nadine knows exactly what Louise is. Nadine is smarter than the rest of us put together."

"Well, she shouldn't be *seeing* it." Andrew shifted on the stool. "I wish Eve would give up Louise."

Tilda sighed. "Right. Then who headlines the Double Take?"

Andrew blinked at her. "Well, she'd be Louise *there*. Just on stage."

"You know," Tilda put down her brush. "There are times when you talk like a straight guy."

"What?" Andrew said, appalled. "What did I say?"

"You only want Eve to be sexual in service to you," Tilda said. "That sucks, Andrew. You dealt her a lousy hand, and now you want her to play by your rules."

"That's not fair. I didn't know I was gay. I meant it when I said I loved her. I do love her."

"Yeah," Tilda said. "Well, if you love her, respect her for what she is."

"I would," Andrew said, frowning, "if I knew what that was. I don't think she does."

"Well, she's the one who gets to figure that out, not you." Tilda picked up her brush again.

"So it didn't go well with Davy, I hear," Andrew said.

Tilda set her jaw. "I have no idea what you're talking about."

"Eve said you had lousy sex on the couch."

Tilda looked at the ceiling. "Are there families that don't discuss each other's sex lives? Because if there are, I'm going to go live with them."

"Why didn't you marry Scott?" Andrew shook his head. "The sex was good. He was perfect for you."

"And yet, he left me," Tilda said. "Anything else depressing you want to talk about?"

"No." Andrew stood up. "Talk to Eve, will you?"

"I don't need to," Tilda said, keeping her back to him. "She's already decided to keep Louise at the Double Take. All your wishes are granted."

"Well, that's good," Andrew said and went upstairs, much relieved, leaving Tilda below, much annoyed.

At least her next mural was Monet, easy to copy. Even Monet had forged the water lilies, turning them out like a factory. She didn't feel nearly as guilty painting one on a wall. Monet would have done the same if somebody had paid him enough.

Why didn't you marry Scott?

Tilda sat back from the drawing table and looked at

the bank of white cabinets, full of family secrets. "You've mortgaged your life to them," Scott had said, but he didn't get it, and that's why she couldn't marry him. She'd already betrayed enough family by going straight. The least she could do was make sure everybody survived, that everything her father had worked for wasn't lost. It wasn't going to take that much longer. Maybe fifteen years. She could do it. Scott didn't understand.

Of course, that was because Scott didn't know there were three hundred years of bad Goodnight forgeries in her basement.

There was no way she could have told him about the buried gallery of Durers and Bouchers and Corots and God-knew-who-elses, all painted by Goodnights, most of them before they changed the family name from Giordano, and every one a little too wrong to safely sell. She couldn't tell him about those, she couldn't tell anybody, and it was probably a bad idea to marry a guy you couldn't tell everything to.

She stood up and began to clean her brushes for the next day. She had a painting to retrieve that afternoon, and the guy who was helping her get it back might be working for the FBI.

"As God is my witness, Steve," she said to the dog. "Once I get these paintings back, I will never go wrong again." He looked skeptical, so she sighed and went upstairs to get ready to scam with a possible Fed.

CHAPTER · TEN

THREE BLOCKS AWAY, CLEA WENT INTO HER BEDROOM to get her purse for an early brunch with Mason and saw Ronald standing over the unconscious body of Thomas the Caterer.

"What are you doing here?" she said to him, closing the door behind her. "And what did you do to Thomas?"

"He was in your closet," Ronald said virtuously. "I caught him stealing."

Clea forced herself not to frown. Then she forced herself not to beat Ronald senseless with her Gucci bag. "Ronald, you caught him cleaning. He's the new hired help."

"Oh." Ronald looked down at him. "Well, I just tapped him a little."

"With what? A tire iron?" Clea tilted her head to look at Thomas. He was breathing okay and he didn't look unnaturally white or red even though he had a red mark and a bad bruise on his forehead. "Why'd you hit him twice?"

"I didn't," Ronald said. "The first bruise was already there."

Clea straightened. "Well, now what are you going to do with him?"

"I'll get rid of him," Ronald said. "You don't have to worry about a thing."

"You will not get rid of him, I need him to make dinner tonight." Clea shook her head at his general callousness and stepped over Thomas to get to her dressing table. "What are you doing here, anyway?" she said, as she sat down to check her face.

"I had to see you." He beamed at her as he sat beside her on the vanity bench. "Darling, you look beautiful."

"Thank you," she said automatically. "How did you get in?"

"The back door was unlocked." Ronald put his arm around her. "I had to see you. I had to make sure you were all right. I'm taking care of you."

"Yeah," Clea said, disentangling herself from him. "You knocked out my help before he could do my laundry, and you sent me a hired killer. Thanks a bunch."

Ronald looked wounded. "I thought you wanted a hired . . ." He made vague motions with his hand.

"No," Clea said patiently. "I wanted you to send one to *Davy*. Direct trip."

"I wanted you to know I'd come through for you," Ronald protested. "I paid him, you know. All you had to do was tell him what to do."

"That's true," Clea said, "that was nice of you to pay him. Thank you, Ronald."

Ronald relaxed.

"But next time just do it," Clea said. "He was a very scary man, Ronald."

"I wouldn't know," Ronald said. "I talked to him on the phone and wired him the money."

Clea looked at him, exasperated. "So for all you knew, you were sending me some crazed serial killer."

Ronald blinked back at her. "I thought that was what you wanted."

Where do I find these guys? Clea thought. *Do I have some kind of homing device that draws them to me?*

"I thought we could go out and celebrate," Ronald said, moving closer. "Or stay in."

Clea shifted away. "Not a good time, Ronald. Maybe next week." She stood up. "Now really, you have to get out of here." She looked back at the body on the floor. "And do something about Thomas before—"

"Is that one of the paintings you bought?" Ronald said.

She turned and saw the Scarlet Hodge leaning against the wall, back from being framed. "Yes. That's part of the collection."

"I like it," Ronald said. "You have very good taste."

Clea looked at it doubtfully. It looked sort of amateurish to her, and it had a lot of colors. And she already knew how bad Ronald was at valuing art, the dummy.

"The artist has a very distinct style," Ronald went on. "What did you pay for it?"

"A thousand," Clea said, still bitter about that even though she hadn't actually written the Goodnights a check yet. "And she can't have been very good. She only painted six of them before she died."

"She's dead?" Ronald whistled. "That really increases the value. You'll probably make a nice profit on it. We should take it down to Miami where there's real money." He stood up and put his arm around Clea's shoulders. "You really have an eye, honey. Too bad you couldn't get all six."

Clea looked up to tell him not to call her honey, and he kissed her. It was an okay kiss, better than some, worse than others, but his timing was terrible. Still, she let him finish. After all, he was paying Ford. And he'd promised to check up on Gwen.

"So," she said when he was done. "Did you find out anything about Gwen Goodnight?"

Ronald blinked, looking a little taken aback, and then he said, "Well, she's broke. The place is mortgaged to the hilt."

"How is that going to help me?" Clea moved away from his arms.

"Help you what?" Ronald said.

"Get me something better," Clea said. "Find out that she was a hooker or killed her husband or something. Get me something that will bring her down and that gallery with her."

"I don't think she's that kind of woman," Ronald said doubtfully.

Clea stepped close again and looked up at him, and he swallowed.

"Every woman has secrets, Ronald," she said softly.

"Find out Gwen Goodnight's and I'll show you some of mine."

"Okay," Ronald said faintly.

Mason knocked on the door and said, "Clea?" and Clea thought, *Honestly*, and shoved Ronald toward the closet.

"Get in there," she said. "To the back. And to the right, the *far* right, in case he opens the door. And do *not* make a sound."

"But—" Ronald began and then saw her face. He nodded and backed into the closet, and Clea closed the door on him. She remembered the painting and opened the door again to shove it in after him. It was supposed to be a surprise, given to Mason on his birthday with cake and wine and sex in return for a nice ten-carat engagement ring. It was too soon to let him see it. Rushing a man was always a mistake.

Then she turned and almost fell over Thomas.

Honest to God. Well, Mason just couldn't come in her bedroom. She grabbed her jacket, stepped over Thomas, and eased herself through the door so Mason couldn't see inside.

"You ready to go?" he said.

"Absolutely," Clea said, cheerful and supportive.

She looked at Mason from the corner of her eye as they went down the stairs. She could tell him Gwen Goodnight was broke and the gallery was in hock, but would that put him off Gwen or make him decide to rescue her?

"You look lovely," Mason said, smiling at her.

He'd rescue her. Ronald was going to have to dig deeper.

"Thank you," Clea said and kissed him on the cheek.

And she was going to have to try harder. "Too bad you didn't get all six," Ronald had said. That meant Mason would like all six. It would be a fabulous birthday gift. Well, how hard could that be? She could put an ad in the paper, see if anybody had one of the dumb things in an attic.

"I have an appointment after brunch," Mason said as he opened the door to his Mercedes for her. "But this evening, the museum is having an opening. I thought we'd go."

"I love it there," Clea said, and thought, *Oh, hell, more paintings.* When Mason died, her next husband was going to be in something bearable, like fashion. She saw herself in the front row at all the runway shows and smiled.

"You really do, don't you?" Mason patted her hand. "I had no idea."

"Oh, there's a lot about me you don't know," Clea said, and sat back in his Mercedes to plan.

TILDA SEEMED more cautious than usual with Davy when she came downstairs after lunch, and he thought it might have been the hair and the clothes: she was a redhead with dark eyes wearing a blue jacket that looked very businesslike and remote. To cheer her up, he found Shelby Lynne on the radio.

"Terrible jacket," he told her when she was in the car.

"Gwennie's," she told him, keeping her eyes on the radio. "She interviewed for a job once."

"Once?" Davy said.

"Not her thing," Tilda said. "Any instructions?"

"Same as yesterday," Davy said, trying not to stare at her eyes. Funny what a difference dark contacts could make. "I miss your eyes," he said, and she looked over at him, startled, and then she smiled, that great crooked Kewpie-doll smile, and he thought, *Good, I got her back.*

"You can see them again when we get the mermaids," she said, relaxing a little into the car seat.

"Mermaids," Davy said and put the car in gear. "Can't wait."

The Olafsons lived in a neat little foursquare, surrounded by a neat patch of lawn that was rimmed with even neater strips of concrete. A single row of petunias edged the walk, each spaced precisely six inches apart. The only thing that jarred, aside from the whole anal-retentive landscape, was a tire leaning up against the trim white garage.

"Somebody who lives here likes order," Davy said. "And somebody else does not."

"Okay," Tilda said.

"Pray I get the one who doesn't," Davy said, putting on his horn-rims, "and that the one who does is out."

"Praying." Tilda nodded. "I'm on it. I was wondering what happened to those glasses."

"This time I'm Steve Olson," Davy told her. "You're definitely my wife. With any luck, I can do this without you, but if not . . ."

"I'll come up and weed the petunias," Tilda said.

"Do you remember—"

"Betty's the ditz, Veronica's the bitch, and Vilma's the slut."

"Actually, I'm quite fond of all of you," Davy said, and patted her knee.

When Mrs. Olafson opened the door, she was five feet nine and heavy, frowning at him, and Davy thought, *Too much to hope for that I wouldn't get the bully*, and smiled at her. "Hi," he said. "I'm . . ."

"Are you here for the tire?" Mrs. Olafson said, her voice a little weak. "Because I *really* need to have that moved before my husband gets home."

"Oh," Davy said, kicking himself for jumping to a stupid conclusion. "No, I'm not, but if you'd like, I can take it away with me. I've got room in my trunk."

"Oh, that would be wonderful," Mrs. Olafson said, her frown clearing. "He was upset about that. He likes things neat."

"Oh," Davy said. "I know how that is. My wife . . ." He shook his head. "Some days I want to track mud across the linoleum for the sheer heck of it."

Mrs. Olafson drew in her breath and then smiled, and Davy thought, *Bingo*.

"I don't want to keep you," he said. "My wife's aunt is coming into town for her sixtieth birthday, and my wife wants to buy her a painting that she saw here once."

"Here?" Mrs. Olafson lost what little smile she had. "I don't—"

"She came with a friend several years ago," Davy said. "She saw a painting of mermaids—"

"Oh," Mrs. Olafson said, and pressed her lips together. "That's my husband's painting."

Fuck, Davy thought. "My wife really wants that painting, Mrs. Olafson. Do you think your husband would sell it for two hundred dollars?"

"I don't think so," Mrs. Olafson said, resentment clear in her voice. "He seems to like it."

Davy put his hands behind his back. "Oh, boy. I'm going to catch heck for this one."

Behind him, Tilda closed the car door and came up the steps, and Mrs. Olafson frowned again.

"Now, Veronica." Davy turned to Tilda and watched her face contort with rage.

"What *the hell* is taking so long?" Tilda said, slapping her bag against his arm. "Aunt Gwen is going be at the airport *waiting for us*, and you know how I *hate to be late*."

Davy rubbed his arm. "Yes, I know but—"

"I should have known better than to send *you* up here," Tilda fumed. She turned to Mrs. Olafson. "Look, I'm sorry about this, my husband never does anything right. We'll pay you a hundred dollars for the painting. Cash." She smiled, looking very self-satisfied, and Mrs. Olafson shifted closer to Davy.

That's my girl, Davy thought, but he said, "Well, actually, honey," and moved closer to Mrs. Olafson as he ducked his head away from Tilda.

"You offered her more," Tilda said, exasperation oozing from every pore. "Honestly, Steve—"

"I know, Veronica," Davy said. "I know you're upset, and rightly so . . ." He held up his hands. "But Mrs. Olafson says her husband really likes that painting."

"Well, *so does my aunt*," Tilda snarled.

Davy exchanged a helpless look with Mrs. Olafson. "Honey, if you'll give me a chance."

"I'll give you five minutes," Tilda snapped. "Then I'm leaving for the airport without you." She stomped down the steps like a woman possessed, and Davy watched her go, thinking, *There's a woman who's worth her weight in rubies. Real ones.*

He turned back to Mrs. Olafson. "She's really very nice, she's just upset. About the painting."

Mrs. Olafson shook her head in sympathy. "She shouldn't treat you like that."

Davy shrugged. "Well, what are you going to do?"

Mrs. Olafson nodded.

"Listen," Davy said, letting a little desperation creep into his voice. "You think your husband might sell the painting for two fifty? I can tell Veronica I got it for a hundred after all. She wouldn't need to know."

Mrs. Olafson looked torn. "He really likes it." Her face changed. "And it's *disgusting. Naked mermaids*."

"Oh," Davy said, feeling a little more sympathetic

toward Mr. Olafson. "That must be awful for you. To have to look at that every day."

"It is." Mrs. Olafson shook her head. "It's *vile.*"

"Boy, if you could sell it to me, you'd never have to look at it again, and I wouldn't have to . . ." Davy looked back at the car, and Tilda reached over and hit the horn. *I love you, Veronica,* Davy thought. "And he'd have the money, too. That'd be good, right?"

"Yes," Mrs. Olafson said thoughtfully. "He's been wanting to get the driveway cleaned."

Davy looked over at the spotless cement. Mr. Olafson's obsession with cleanliness, control, and disgusting mermaids was not making him someone Davy wanted to meet. "You wouldn't get in trouble, would you?" he said, suddenly feeling guilty about Mrs. Olafson.

"Certainly not," Mrs. Olafson said.

Davy got out his wallet and began to count through the bills. "I have an extra ten here and a five and two ones. That would make it two sixty-seven. Do you think—"

Down in the street, Tilda slammed the car door as she got out and walked around to the driver's side.

"Just a minute, honey," Davy called, panic in his voice.

"I'll get it," Mrs. Olafson said and went inside.

"Really, just another minute," Davy said, going to the edge of the porch to look beseechingly at Tilda.

Tilda started the car and gunned the motor, and Davy began to picture her in leather again.

Mrs. Olafson came back to the door and handed Davy the painting, and he handed over the bills.

"You can count it," he said, glancing back over his shoulder at Tilda.

"I trust you," Mrs. Olafson said. *"Go."*

"Thank you," Davy said and ran down the steps to give Tilda the painting. "Here you go, honey," he said, loud enough to carry back to Mrs. Olafson. "Just one more thing."

Tilda opened the door and took the painting, and Davy started back up the drive. "Where the hell are you going?" she said, her voice like a knife.

"Just a minute, sweetie." Davy picked up the tire and waved to Mrs. Olafson who beamed at him in return. Then he headed back to his shrew of a wife, who popped the trunk open for the tire.

Damn, I married well, he thought and got in the car.

WHEN THEY were almost to the highway, Davy said, "Pull over up here," and Tilda obliged. *An obedient woman,* he thought. *God, she's hot.*

"Okay, what—" she said, and he leaned over and kissed her hard, and she clutched at him and kissed him back, and for a minute, Davy forgot his own name. "Oh," she said, coming up for air. "You're really good at that. What was it for?"

"You are magnificent," he said, trying to get his breath back.

"I am?" She hit him with that crooked grin again.

"You do a beautiful bitch," Davy said. "You got any chains in the attic?"

"You're disgusting," Tilda said cheerfully.

"That reminds me." Davy dragged the painting out of the back seat. It was full of round-bodied, sloe-eyed, rosy-breasted mermaids who swam in a checkered sea, looking inviting and edgy but not unwholesome.

"What?" Tilda said, looking at the painting.

"Mrs. Olafson thought this painting was disgusting," Davy said, imagining the mermaids bobbing in the sea. "I'm not seeing it."

"Bare breasts. And they're not ashamed."

"My kind of women. They do look a little . . ." Davy searched for the word. "Aggressive. But in a good way."

"Poor Mr. Olafson," Tilda said. "He lost his mermaids for a lousy two-fifty."

"I went to two sixty-seven," Davy said, now imagining Tilda bouncing in the sea. "You know, these mermaids kind of look like you."

Tilda took the painting from him. "You're projecting, Dempsey. Keep your mind on the job." She traced one of the foamy waves with her fingertip, looking a little sad.

"You okay?" he said.

"I am magnificent," she said and put the painting in the back seat again.

When they got back to the gallery, they heard voices in the office. Davy followed Tilda in and saw Eve and Gwen and a rotund younger guy he'd never seen before gathered around a tearful Nadine.

"Oh, no," Tilda said, and went straight to her niece.

"What happened?" Davy said, looking for blood or broken bones.

"It's a Poor Baby," Tilda said, not turning around.

"That miserable little tick Burton dumped her," Eve said, standing militant in front of her daughter. "I think he should be castrated."

"Later for that," the new guy said, his arm around Nadine. "Poor Baby first, revenge later."

That's got to be Jeff, Davy thought.

"He was just wrong for you, Poor Baby," Gwen said from Nadine's other side. "He had no soul."

"He was a vampire. Pasty little bastard," Jeff said. "Poor Baby."

"But he was so cute," Nadine wailed.

"This is true," Tilda said.

Gwen glared at Tilda. "You're not helping."

"Poor Baby," Tilda said obediently. "The thing is, Dine, the good-looking ones are always doughnuts. They're so pretty they don't have to develop fiber. Look at Davy. Perfect example."

"Hey," Davy said, faking outrage. "I'm full of fiber."

Nadine sniffed but she stopped dripping tears to look at him.

"I," he went on, "am clearly a muffin."

"As in 'stud'?" Tilda said. "No."

"Hopeless doughnut," Gwen said, and Nadine gave Davy a watery smile.

"Muffin," Davy said, "and to prove it, I'm willing to go find Burton and beat the crap out of him."

"Absolute doughnut," Tilda said, turning her back on him. "So what did this Davy-in-training give as his miserable excuse? Poor Baby."

"Who cares?" Jeff said. "He's scum. You deserve better. Poor Baby."

"He said I was too weird," Nadine said, wincing, and Davy felt like beating up the kid for real.

"Okay," Tilda said to Davy. "Go get him."

"No," Nadine said, sniffing, "I mean, really, that was it for me. I wore the Lucy dress to his gig, and he told me today that I had to stop wearing such weird stuff or it was all over."

"And you said it was all over?" Tilda said.

Nadine nodded, and Eve said, "Oh, that's my girl," while Jeff pounded her on the back and said, "Way to go, kid."

"Clearly not the kind of guy who deserves a Goodnight," Davy said.

"He was only a speed bump," Tilda agreed, "on the great highway of love."

"I know," Nadine said, sniffing again. "I'm not really crying for him. I just needed to get it out, you know?"

"Of course," Gwen said, "you should always get it out," and Davy wondered if there had ever been any emotion that any Goodnight had ever left unexpressed.

Except for Tilda. He watched her comfort Nadine and wondered what she'd been like when she'd been part of the Rayons, when she'd been singing and laughing with Eve and Andrew. If she'd ever smiled all the time like she'd smiled at him today.

"Are you sure you're okay?" Gwen was saying to Nadine. "I can stay."

"Where are you going?" Tilda said.

"She's having a late lunch with Mason Phipps," Eve said, raising her eyebrows to her hairline. "It's a day-yate."

Uh-oh, Davy thought. Clea was not going to be happy about that.

"No it is not," Gwen said. "He wants to talk about the gallery. And I get free food." She turned back to Nadine. "Unless you want me to stay."

Nadine sniffed. "Bring me your dessert if you don't eat all of it."

"Good enough," Gwen said and went out into the gallery.

"Ice cream," Eve said to Nadine. "I'm thinking Jeff drives and we all go to Grater's."

"That would be good," Nadine said, and sniffed again, but Davy got the distinct impression that she was now enjoying herself. Well, good for her.

Jeff stopped by Davy on his way out the door. "Welcome to the family," he said, offering Davy his hand. "Andrew says you're helping Tilda with a problem."

"Family?" Davy said as he shook Jeff's hand.

"Anybody the Goodnights rope into problem solving is family," Jeff said. "Not that I want to know what the problem is until you need bail."

"Jeff's a lawyer," Tilda said.

"Handy guy to have around," Davy said.

"Hey," Jeff said. "Tonight we play poker. It's our

standard Sunday-night family bonding. Do you gamble?"

"Why am I sure he gambles?" Tilda said to the ceiling.

Davy looked down into her weird light eyes, and said, "Yes."

"I play rough," she warned. "Don't bet anything you're not ready to lose."

"Not a problem," he said. "I don't *have* anything to lose."

She grinned that crooked grin at him again, her eyes connecting with his, and he felt dizzy for a moment. There was a possibility that he could lose his shirt to this woman. With a great deal of enthusiasm.

But later that night, sitting around a poker table with Tilda, Eve, Gwen, Jeff, Andrew, and Mason, who had somehow escaped from Clea for an hour, Davy felt back in control. Poker was second only to pool in Michael Dempsey's list of skills his children should have. It clearly hadn't been on Tony Goodnight's or Father Phipps's list at all. The first deal said it all. They picked up cards and sorted them, and every one of them had faces like billboards: Gwen's face fell when she looked at her hand, Eve smiled and then frowned to hide it, Jeff sighed and shook his head and pulled his money in a little, Andrew tried to keep a stone face but was clearly delighted, Mason leaned back and folded his arms because he thought he had something, and Tilda—

Tilda was looking right at him.

She shook her head and picked up her cards, the only other person at the table smart enough to know that poker was about the people you were playing with, not about the cards you were dealt. *That's my girl*, he thought, and watched her play, bluffing nervelessly, losing and winning without batting an eye, and always, always watching the others.

Nadine joined them later and played almost as well as Tilda, but she also had an unfortunate tendency to buy into bluffs. After Davy had taken her for the third time, he said, "Dine, if it seems too good to be true, get out."

"I'm optimistic," she said, her chin in the air.

"Smart is better," Davy said.

The last hand ended when everyone but Eve and Davy were out, even Mason, whose ironclad optimism had been nothing short of astonishing as he lost hand after hand, making a nice match for Gwen who didn't even try to hide her reactions to her cards. Eve tried to bluff Davy out of a pot with nothing, which he knew because when Eve had nothing, she tapped her worst card three times and sighed. It was one of the most blatant tells he'd ever seen, and when she did it this time, he saw Tilda close her eyes in sympathy, and he wondered what it must have been like being the sharp one in the family, the one who watched everybody else and played the smart game while the rest went on their feckless way, having fun.

Maybe it was time she had fun, he thought as he

raked in the last pot. In fact, maybe it was his duty as a guest to make sure she had fun.

It was only the polite thing to do.

"so you're a cardsharp," Tilda said to Davy after he'd turned all his winnings over to Gwen "for the muffins and orange juice I've been bumming off you." Mason had gone home to Clea, and the rest of the family had drifted off to bed. "A real Cool Hand Luke."

"Cool Hand Luke was a convict," Davy said, opening the refrigerator. "Get your allusions right."

"Okay, you're whoever was a really sharp poker player." Tilda tried to think of one. "Maverick."

"Very good," Davy said. "When Gwennie was teaching you to stay in character in kindergarten, my daddy, like Maverick's, was teaching me not to draw to an inside straight." He held out the orange juice carton. "Drink?"

"Yes," Tilda said. "Your daddy sounds like an interesting person."

"With vodka or without?"

"With, please." She went over to the couch and stretched her legs out in front of her. She had four of her paintings back, thanks to Davy. It was almost a miracle, and when she had all six, she'd build a bonfire and wipe out her past entirely. Onward into the future. No more mistakes.

As long as Davy didn't arrest her.

He sat down beside her. "Your drink, Celeste."

She took the glass and sipped. "Very good, Ralph." She smiled at him, grateful for the paintings and the drink and that he was there in general. *He really is a nice guy,* she thought. *Even if it turns out he is the FBI.* "So your dad, what is it he does?"

"He annoys people." Davy relaxed into the leather next to her. "Speaking of parents, what is it with Gwennie and the teeth?"

"Huh?" she said, not expecting that one.

"The quilt in my room had teeth on it," he said, "and so did the sampler. What is that?"

"Oh," Tilda said, regrouping. "Well, I think she had a lot of repressed anger when my dad was alive." She frowned at him. "That's a weird thing to ask."

"They're weird to look at," Davy said. "Repressed anger. This is not something you suffer from, Veronica."

"I'm not living with my dad," Tilda said. "He was sort of domineering. She loved him, but she didn't speak up much. And the older we got, the more he tried to control us and the madder she got, so she took up cross-stitch to relax. She did a couple of samplers the way the graphs showed and then she started changing things, and pretty soon there were all these little animals with teeth in them. Which I thought were neat."

"And the quilts?"

"Toward the end the samplers weren't helping her relax, so she switched to quilting. And for a while she did these beautiful nine-patch quilts, but then she started skewing the nine-patches and they turned into these crooked crazy quilts and then the teeth started showing up again, so she had to quit those, too."

"And that's when she started the Double-Crostics," Davy said.

"No," Tilda said, "that's when she started the paint-by-numbers."

Davy choked on his drink. "What?"

"Paint-by-number paintings," Tilda said, grinning as she thought about it. "The kits. She'd paint them and hang them up in the office and he'd take them down. They drove him *crazy*. But then she started messing with those, too, and eventually—"

"Let me guess," Davy said. "Teeth."

"Yep." Tilda took another drink and watched him. "We must have boxes of those things in the basement. Then she went to crossword puzzles, and when those got too easy, she moved on to Double-Crostics."

"Any teeth yet?"

"Not so far," Tilda said. "Actually, she stopped with the teeth right about the time I moved out, and that was seventeen years ago. And now my dad's dead, so she's not so mad anymore."

"Right," Davy said, smiling at the photos on the opposite wall. He had a great profile, straight nose, strong chin. "You have an interesting family, Matilda."

He had a great smile, too. In fact, when you came right down to it, he had a great everything. And he'd been wonderful all day, working his butt off to get her painting back, offering to beat up Burton, giving Gwennie the muffin money. And all she'd done for him was screw up his chance to get his money back and fake an orgasm with him on the couch and get testy because he might be the law. She should be *grateful* that he was the law. Assuming he didn't send her up the river. "I'm really sorry," she said.

"About what?" Davy said, looking confused. "Your family? I like them."

"About your money. And about Friday. You know." She patted the couch. "Here." She took another drink.

"Get over it, Matilda," Davy said.

"That was an apology." Tilda got up and poured more vodka into her glass, making the orange juice fade. "A sincere, heartfelt apology."

"Have you always had this drinking problem?" Davy said.

"No." Tilda took the bottle back to the couch, drank more of her vodka and orange juice, and then closed her eyes as the alcohol seeped into her bones. "You are great at that. Getting people to give you things."

"Thank you." Davy took the bottle from her.

"It's because you're in sales, right?" Tilda hit the vodka again. *Come on, tell me the truth.*

"Sales?"

"You said you were in sales."

"I said my father was in sales."

"So what are you in?"

Davy looked at her for a moment. "Sales," he said, and topped up her drink.

Tilda sighed. "Like father, like son."

"Not even close."

She sipped again and waited. Okay, he wasn't going to tell her about the FBI. She clearly did not have Louise's skills. At least she was pretty sure she didn't. "So here's a question."

Davy waited, and she smiled at him again, feeling fairly loose in general.

"Question," he prompted.

"Right." She took another drink and steeled her nerve. "How bad was I?"

"You were great." He stretched to put the bottle on the table. Lovely arms, she thought. Lovely lines to his body. That was probably why the FBI hired him. "You have a real flair for reading people," he said as he leaned back. "I think Mrs. Olafson—"

"No," Tilda said. "On this couch the other night. How bad was I?"

"You were fine," Davy said, suddenly cautious.

"Hey," Tilda said. "I deserve the truth. We're partners now. Steve and Veronica. Ralph and Celeste. Whoever that was in the closet and Vilma. Tell me the truth."

Davy sighed. "Okay. You were terrible."

"Ow." Tilda slugged back the rest of her glass. "I was hoping for mediocre. You know. Not so good."

Davy offered her the bottle.

"Thank you." Tilda held out her glass.

"It was my fault, too." Davy poured a quarter inch of vodka in her glass. "I was still on a rush from burgling Clea, and I didn't—"

"It's me," Tilda said.

Davy shrugged. "Well, you know, sex isn't for every-body. Maybe—"

"I want it," Tilda said. "I just don't want it when there are guys in the room."

Davy lifted an eyebrow at her. "Louise looks like she might swing both ways."

"I don't want women, either."

Davy nodded and took a drink. "Do you have it narrowed down to a species?"

"When I'm alone," Tilda said, "I'm very interested in men. *Very* interested." She thought about Davy in the closet and thought, *And sometimes, even with them right there.* "I mean, sometimes I have thoughts that are really, well, wrong."

"These are the thoughts you should share with me," Davy said, over his vodka.

Like sometimes I have this incredible urge to walk up to you and say, "Fuck me," just to get it out of my system. Except that would be wrong, not to mention difficult to explain, like the rest of her secrets. Besides, saying "Fuck me" to the FBI? That couldn't be good.

"No, really, you can tell me," Davy said. "I'm *very* open-minded."

"No," Tilda said. "There are some secrets you can never tell." She sighed. "There are things I'm tempted to do, but when there's another person in the room, there are so many other things to consider."

Davy shook his head. "Short of 'Don't forget the condom' and 'Try not to choke on your spit,' I can't think—"

"Like how well do you really know this person?" Tilda said, giving him another opening. "Because I think you should know him pretty well before you let him inside you."

"I'm the one going in," Davy said, relaxing back into the couch, "so I'm good with strangers."

"Right," Tilda said. "It's my space being invaded."

"You want a guy who won't invade your space?"

"Not in theory. In theory, I want a guy who's all over my space. It's just—"

"In practice."

"In the real world," Tilda agreed. "Space Invaders, not my game."

"Problem is," Davy said, "Space Invaders is pretty much the name of the game. Everything else is just a variation on the theme."

"Maybe I'll never have sex again," Tilda said. "I'm trying to decide if that's a bad thing."

"Tell you what." Davy picked up the bottle again. "Small bet."

"Bet?" Tilda watched as he slopped more vodka in her glass. The pineapple-orange juice was only a pale memory now. "Like poker?"

"I bet you," he said, handing it to her, "that I can make you come, right here on this couch. No Space Invaders."

"Uh-huh," Tilda said dubiously over the rim of her glass. The coming part sounded good, but it was Davy. There was bound to be a catch. On the other hand, it was Davy. And she did want him. Even the FBI thing was a turn-on. Maybe she had some Louise in her after all.

"If you win," he was saying, "I help you get the rest of the paintings. If I win, we play Space Invaders." He thought about it. "Which means that you win either way. This is a great deal for you, Vilma."

"Spare me," Tilda said, willing to be seduced but not scammed.

Davy shook his head sadly. "I've never met a woman who was more afraid of orgasm."

"I'm not afraid of orgasm," Tilda said, indignant. "I've had *plenty* of orgasms. I just—"

"*When Harry Met Sally*," Davy said. "First diner scene."

"That was not a movie quote," Tilda said. "Is everything a game to you?"

"Pretty much." Davy met her eyes and smiled at her, and Tilda thought, *Oh, Lord.* "So, do you want to play or can we go to bed now?"

"There are two more paintings left," Tilda said, her heart picking up speed.

"Fifteen minutes," Davy said. "Time me."

She drank the rest of her vodka and orange vapor, regarding him over the edge of the glass. He was so much fun to look at. And as long as she kept her mouth shut, what did she have to lose besides her dignity? Which, let's face it, had gone with the wind the last time they'd hit the couch. That had to be the all-time low. And if it wasn't Space Invaders, if she wasn't letting him inside, maybe she wouldn't say anything—

"Matilda," Davy said. "I'm growing old here."

Her heart began to pound and she swallowed again. "Fifteen minutes?"

"Yep."

So even if it was bad again, it was only fifteen minutes. And if it was good, it might be Louise. She took a deep breath—there was never enough oxygen around when she started contemplating having sex with Davy—and she nodded. "You're on."

CHAPTER · ELEVEN

HE GOT UP AND LOCKED THE DOORS TO THE GALLERY
and the hallway, and she said, "That was thoughtful,"
as he took her glass away from her.

"You're drunk," he said.

Tilda looked at him with contempt. "Well, duh.
Would I be doing this if I wasn't?"

"Good point." He went over to the jukebox and
started punching numbers at random.

"What are you doing?" She squinted at him through
her glasses as the Exciters started to sing, "Yeah, yeah,
yeah."

"Cover," he said, over the music. "In case you turn
out to be a moaner for real."

"Somehow I thought it'd be more romantic," she said.
"You know. Since we sort of know each other this time."

He came over to her and took her glasses.

"Hey."

"Reality is not a turn-on for you," he said. "Stick
with soft-focus."

"Well, that's a good point," she said, and didn't say
anything at all when he turned the lights off so there

was only the glow of the jukebox behind them. Then he came over, picked up her knees, and swiveled her around so her back was to the arm of the couch.

"Okay, I'm pretty sure you're supposed to be more romantic than this," Tilda said, as he pulled her hips down the leather seat. She managed not to roll off, but he stuck his hand out to catch her, just in case. A real gentleman.

"Here's the deal," Davy said, leaning over her. "You shut up. Both your mouth and your brain. You've probably talked yourself out of coming more times than you've come."

"*Hey*," Tilda said, annoyed, and he kissed her, that mouth on hers, hot and insistent, all that heat going straight into her brain and shorting out whatever it was she'd been going to say. "You do that *really* well," she said, when he moved to her neck.

"I know," he said into her shoulder. "Be quiet."

He began to slide her T-shirt up, and she held onto it and tried to remember if she was wearing a good bra or not, definitely not one with safety pins but hopefully not a boring white one—

"Matilda," Davy said.

"Hmmm?"

"You're thinking."

"Am not."

"You had that look on your face, the one you get when you're counting something."

Tilda shrugged herself down on the couch a little more which brought her into contact with him. Somehow, in all of the sliding around, he'd put himself between her legs. "How did you get there?"

"Practice," he said. "Stop thinking."

"It was sexual. I was wondering if my bra was good."

He stripped her T-shirt over her head before she could stop him, catching it on her ear. She untangled it and looked down. White lace.

"It's good," he said. "Now make your mind a blank. Try not to pass out."

"How long have we been doing this?" Tilda said. "Is my fifteen minutes up?"

He bent and licked her stomach, and she shut up, and then he moved down, flicking her belly button with his tongue as he slid her zipper down, and Tilda felt the heat spread low which was surprising because there he was, right there in the room, dangerous as all hell.

She looked at the ceiling and thought, *This could be good*. As long as she kept her mouth shut. *Positive thoughts*. "I'm positive," she said, surprising herself when it was out loud. "I'm positive I want the most incredible orgasm I've ever had in my life."

"Okay." He eased her jeans down, and she lifted her hips to help him because given the amount of hip he had to negotiate, that was only fair. "What's my standard of reference?"

"Pretty damn good," she said. "Scott knew what he was doing."

"Scott?" Davy looked up at her. "Who's Scott?"

"My former fiancé."

"And you wait until now to mention him?"

"He's former," Tilda said. "Am I making snarky noises about Clea? No."

Davy shook his head. "Okay, if it's only pretty good, you've got it," he said and bent down to her again.

"Talk's cheap," she said, but his hand slid between her legs as his cheek brushed her stomach, and his mouth was hot on her skin, and Tilda felt herself flush with something that wasn't embarrassment. If she thought about it, she'd have to stop, but the deal was she wouldn't think, and when he pushed her knee up, her hips rose to meet his hand and then his mouth. She gasped once as he licked inside her, and she grabbed the arm of the couch over her head to keep from sliding off, and then he licked again and got serious and she gave herself up to the pressure he built slowly in her, thinking, *This boy has a great mouth. Don't think about where it is.*

Behind her, Betty Everett sang, "It's in his kiss," and Tilda relaxed into the familiar lyric and Davy's unfamiliar mouth, thinking, *I'll never hear this song again without remembering how this felt,* easing into heat, breathing in pleasure. When she was breathing pleasure so hard they could have heard her in the hall, Davy pulled back.

"Nice try," she said, as Betty trailed off behind her.

"Quitter." Davy bit her inner thigh.

She pushed herself up on her elbows. "The deal was—"

Davy pointed his finger at her. "Fifteen minutes. And you'd be quiet."

The thought of where that finger had been made her blush. Not to mention where his head was now. "Well, what—" she began, trying to brazen it out, but then the jukebox started the Sisters, and by the time they'd finished the first line of "All Grown Up," Davy's head was back down, and he began to slowly lick all that heat back into her. She shivered and felt the tension start in her again, as tight as it had been before, and she slid back down the couch, closer to him, she hadn't lost anything, and this time the heat rose much faster so that when the Ladybugs finished "Sooner or Later," and Davy pulled away again, she smacked his shoulder and said, "Don't *stop*."

He shook his head. "I should have gagged you," he said, and kissed her stomach, and she shivered under him. He slid down again, and then stopped as the Shirelles began to sing "Will You Love Me Tomorrow?" "This music," he said, sounding exasperated, and then he bent back to her and started the heat all over, kicking it up higher, each time he stopped it went higher, only this time he kept going, this time his hands were rough on her hips, this time she felt the heat come welling up, and she squirmed and clenched and gasped and thought, *Don't say anything*, until finally she broke, her body arching under his mouth as she bit her lip, and the aftershocks made her jerk even after he slid up to kiss her neck. When she'd stopped, still clinging to him, he said in her ear, "And a minute to spare. I win."

"Uh," she said, realizing vaguely that the Shirelles were gone and Damita Jo was singing "I'll Save the Last

Dance for You," and Davy was hard against her, and then he pushed her knee up again and slid inside her— *Space Invaded*, she thought—and he felt good as she relaxed into afterglow, holding him absentmindedly while he moved and shuddered and came, and she felt warm but not really involved in what he was doing.

When he pulled away from her, she wasn't sure what to say, so she tried, "Thank you," and tugged her jeans back on and looked for her T-shirt.

"You know, you have a really short attention span," he said, as he got rid of the condom. "You come once and you're gone."

"I faked it," Tilda said, pulling her shirt over her head, and when he laughed, she gave up. "Okay, you won." She closed her eyes and tried to hold onto the leftover warmth. "Thank you."

"I'm feeling fairly grateful myself," he said, his voice as calm as ever.

I didn't even make a dent in his concentration, she thought. It had felt good, okay great, but not great enough to get rid of this damn weird feeling that always hit her afterward. *You don't know me. You think you've had me, but you don't know me.*

Of course, it was a damn good thing he didn't know her. She was going to have to stop saying yes, or he'd get to know her. Maybe she needed therapy. Maybe she and Gwennie and Louise could go, and they could get a family deal.

"You're thinking again," Davy said as he pulled his pants back on.

Tilda opened her eyes and forced a smile. "Just that you're off the hook for the rest of the paintings now."

"Oh, we'll get the rest of the paintings." Davy stood up, dressed again. "But it'll have to be quick. I'm on my way to Australia."

"Right," Tilda said, not surprised that the other paintings were still a sure thing. Davy kept all his promises and got everything he went after. Which was why from now on, she had to be something he wasn't going after. He was just too damn dangerous.

Behind her, the Paris Sisters sang "I Love How You Love Me," evidently not the kind of women who ever had weird thoughts after sex, and Tilda felt depressed and wondered why. Maybe it was just exhaustion. Long day. Strong orgasm.

"You've got that look again," Davy said.

"Really tired." Tilda stood up and zipped her jeans. "Well, good night."

"Celeste, we're sharing the same bed," Davy said as she unlocked the door.

"Right," she said. "See you there, Ralph." Then she took the steps two at a time while he stood at the bottom, shaking his head.

TILDA GOT up the next morning careful not to wake Davy. She couldn't find Nadine, so she turned Steve over to Gwen for baby-sitting while she went to work. Gwen didn't seem to mind. "Variety," she said, looking down at the little dog. "I live for it."

"Are you okay?" Tilda said, taken aback.

"Fine," Gwen said.

"Mason was sweet last night at poker," Tilda said, prodding a little. "How was lunch?"

"Nice," Gwen said.

"Gwennie?"

"We talked about the gallery. He appears to yearn for it." She flipped open her Double-Crostic book.

"Maybe *we* should talk about the gallery." Tilda picked up a little yellow paper umbrella Gwen had stuck in her pencil holder. "Drinking on the job?"

"Don't you have to paint today?"

"Just the base coat," Tilda said, looking at the crostic book. Gwen had been doodling little umbrellas in the book margins. "And then Davy and I are going after a painting. What is it with you and umbrellas?"

"So how is Davy?" Gwen said. *"Happy?"*

"Asleep." Tilda put the umbrella back and escaped out through the office.

But when she opened the door to the van, Nadine was sitting in the passenger seat.

"Hello?" Tilda said.

"I want to come along," Nadine said, and she still looked a little rocky from the Poor Baby, so Tilda said, "Sure," and climbed in.

"Here's the thing," Nadine said when they were heading north. "With Burton gone, so is the singing gig."

"There are probably other bands," Tilda said. "You have a great voice, Dine."

"I didn't like singing with the band," Nadine said. "I know that's where the money probably is, but it was noisy and a lot of the songs were stupid and nobody really listened anyway. It wasn't really music."

"Okay," Tilda said. "Do you want me to talk to your dad about the Double Take?"

"It wouldn't do any good," Nadine said. "I'm underage. I can't sing there for another two years even if he wanted to let me which he doesn't. But that's okay. I'm thinking I might want to be a painter."

"Oh," Tilda said, light dawning. "Well, today is not going to be very interesting. I'm painting the base coat and looking at color samples under the light there. Tomorrow I'm doing the underpainting. You can help with that if you want."

"That'd be good," Nadine said. "Because you make pretty good money doing this, right? I mean, you were in that home magazine and everything."

"That helped," Tilda said, thinking of Clarissa Donnelly and her sunflowers, the magazine left strategically nearby. "But it's not exciting work, Dine. It's a lot like you and the band. It's painting, but it's not art. I'm copying other people's art to make wallpaper."

"But it makes money," Nadine said.

"You do not have to support this family," Tilda said.

"Right," Nadine said. "You think I could learn to do this?"

"I think you can do anything," Tilda said.

"Cool," Nadine said, and sighed. "So what's this about Mr. Brown?"

"What?" Tilda said.

"Mr. Brown. When he moved in, you told Grandma you thought his name was fake. Should we worry?"

"No," Tilda said. "If that becomes a problem, I can take care of that, too."

"You know, I can help," Nadine said, sounding exasperated.

"Why don't you be a kid instead?" Tilda said. "Enjoy it while you've got it."

"You obviously don't remember what being a kid is like," Nadine said and slumped down in her seat.

Being an adult has its drawbacks, too, Tilda thought, and took the exit for her next mural.

BACK IN Tilda's bedroom, Davy woke up feeling less than triumphant, especially when he rolled over and she was gone. He squinted at the clock. It was after ten, she'd had to start a mural today, it didn't mean anything that she wasn't there, but still . . .

Yeah, like you've ever wanted to wake up with a woman you've slept with, he told himself. Especially one who seemed less than pleased with the night before, which was really confusing because she'd definitely made it that time. Complicated woman, Celeste.

Maybe getting the fifth painting that afternoon would work the kinks out of her. That was the problem with women, they were high maintenance, needed attention all the time, flowers, phone calls—

"Oh, hell," he said, remembering his sister Sophie.

She'd probably tried to call him. He crawled out of bed and found his cell phone in his jacket pocket and clicked it on to check his messages. It rang almost immediately and he looked at the number. Nobody he knew. "Hello?" he said.

"I've been calling you for days," Ronald said. "You should leave that cell phone on."

"So I can talk to you?" Davy said, sitting back down on the bed. "No."

"I'm trying to help you," Ronald said. "I wanted you to know that Clea knows you're in town."

"Yeah, I know," Davy said.

"Well, *I* didn't tell her," Ronald said.

"Blow me, Rabbit."

Ronald exhaled loudly into the phone, apparently in disgust. "I'm trying to *help* you. She's really angry. You're in danger."

"Am I?" Davy said.

"She's hired a hit man, Davy," Ronald said.

"Good to know," Davy said, checking his watch.

"I didn't tell you this before," Ronald went on, "but one of the reasons she had to have your money is that her husband didn't leave her anything. She needs that money, Davy. You should get out of town."

"She's lying to you, Rabbit," Davy said tiredly.

"No," Ronald said. "It's true. He had a great art collection and the warehouse it was in burned down, and the insurance company is refusing to pay. He was wiped out. She really needs your money. Let her have it and go."

"A torched warehouse? Christ, that's the oldest fraud in the book. I can't believe she—" Davy said, and then stopped. "Wait a minute. How do you know he had a great collection?"

"I told you, I helped Clea value it after he died. That's how we met. She turned to me in her grief and—"

"The warehouse burned before he died, Rabbit. You just said so."

"Oh," Ronald said. "Well, yes, I helped value it before he died. But nothing happened between us until—"

"My ass," Davy said. "You helped Clea burn an empty warehouse to collect the insurance. Where are the paintings now?"

"I have no idea what you're talking about," Ronald said. "I'm trying to save your life. I'm not kidding."

"I know," Davy said. "You have no sense of humor. Tell Clea I said hi and not to burn any more storage facilities. Does she still do that thing with the feather and the ice cube?"

"What?"

"Oh, Rabbit, don't tell me you gave her three million dollars and she never pulled out the feather and the ice cube."

"I don't know why I called you," Ronald said. "You don't deserve to be saved."

"You called me because if somebody tries to kill me, you want to be sure you don't go down for it," Davy said. "You're covering your ass, as usual. And I don't deserve most of the stuff that happens to me, including having all my money stolen by a Judas of a friend."

"It wasn't your money," Ronald said automatically.

"Good-bye, Rabbit," Davy said. "Call me if Clea hires anybody else. I live for these updates."

"She hired some help around the house," Ronald said, trying to be snotty. "I'll call you if she gets a dog."

"Around the house," Davy said, straightening. "Does this help live in?"

"I think so," Ronald said. "Why?"

Oh, fuck, Davy thought. They should have gone after the last painting sooner. Now he had a third person to get out of the house, and it wasn't likely Mason and Clea were going to let Gwen invite the kitchen help to the gallery for the night.

"Davy?"

"What does the help look like?" Davy said.

"Thin. Dark hair. Rather foolish looking. Not anybody Clea would sleep with," Ronald said, sticking to the essentials and ignoring the fact that if he'd said "blond" instead of "dark hair," he'd have been describing himself.

"I think I know him," Davy said. *I think I dragged him into an empty room after Tilda kicked his head in.*

"He didn't look very competent," Ronald said. "But then it's hard to get good help."

"Yeah, I know," Davy said. "They embezzle from you." He hung up and tried to work out a plan to get the help out of the house. Maybe he could find out the guy's night off. There was always a way. Life could be a lot worse. He could be Rabbit.

"No, I couldn't," he said and went to shower.

★

DAVY WAS waiting when Tilda came back for lunch, and they took off for Clintonville and the fifth painting with Tilda as a redhead again. The Brenner house was a four-square, maintained but not rehabbed, with a front porch crowded with pots of greenery that Davy recognized under the generic heading of "grandmother's houseplants." The woman who opened the door would have fallen under the heading of "nice old lady" had Davy been a nice young man. Instead, he looked at her and thought, *Mark*.

"Hi," he said, smiling his best nice-young-man smile, and sure enough, Mrs. Brenner smiled back. *Such a nice young man.* "My name is Steve Brewster, and I'm collecting for Art for Masses. We ask for donations of old paintings and framed artwork which we sell to benefit the homeless." She nodded, smiling back at him. "There was an article in the *Dispatch* not too long ago," Davy lied. "Maybe you saw it?"

"Why, yes," the woman said, adjusting her glasses.

God protect this woman, Davy thought, but he said, "We were wondering if you might have an old painting or two hanging around." He grinned. "So to speak."

"Oh, dear," she said. "I did have an attic full of them, but my husband's nephew Colby cleaned it out for me. I think he hauled all of them to the dump."

Hell. "That was thoughtful of him," Davy said.

"Not really," the woman said, losing her smile. "He charged me quite a bit for it. And then there was the fee at the dump. After all that, I almost wished I'd left them up there."

Fee at the dump, Davy thought, and immediately downgraded the nephew from good human being to classic cheating mark, the guy who deserved to go down. "I don't suppose he told you which dump?" Davy said. "We do a lot of salvage."

"No," the woman said, shaking her head, "but it was an expensive one."

"Could I have your nephew's phone number?" Davy said, trying to keep his voice from growing grim. "That dump sounds like a good place for us. For charity."

"Of course," the woman said and disappeared back into the house, leaving her door open.

Oh, honey, Davy thought. *Get a Doberman.*

"Here it is," she said, coming back to the door with a slip of paper and a five-dollar bill in her hand. "He's up in Dublin."

The creep lived in upper-crust Dublin but he was still ripping off his aunt? *Take this guy for everything he's got,* Davy's lesser self whispered.

"I'll give him a call," Davy said, turning his inner con man back to the job at hand. "And I'll make sure to send you a receipt so you can claim the donation on your income tax." He tried to take the paper without the bill, but she shoved both at him.

"Oh, no, I'm just sorry I couldn't help more," the woman said. "Please take this, too. I'm sorry it can't be more—"

Jesus, Davy thought. "Absolutely not," he said,

sliding the slip of paper out from under the bill in her hand. "Our charter only allows us to accept artwork. You're much too generous."

"Well, I still have my home," she said. "And they don't, poor things. Are you sure you won't take this? Why don't you use it for your lunch? You should be rewarded, too."

Davy gazed at her sadly. The urge to say, "Look, never give to anybody door to door, never leave your door unlocked especially when there's a strange guy asking for money on your porch, and never, ever, *ever* let your nephew in the house again," was overwhelming. "I really can't," he said. "But the gesture is appreciated. You have a really nice day."

"Thank you," she said, holding the five to her chest with a gesture that told Davy all he needed to know about how much she would have missed it. "You have a good day, too."

The screen door banged closed behind him as he went down the cracked concrete steps, and he gave serious thought to calling Colby in Dublin and offering to sell him some nice land in Florida. Instead he got back in the car and called the number on his cell phone.

"What are you doing?" Tilda said. "I don't get to play on this one?"

Davy waved her off as a bored-sounding woman answered the phone. "He's not here," she said when Davy asked. "He won't be back until late."

"I'll call back later," Davy said. "I'm interested in some paintings he took to a dump. You don't happen to know which dump, do you?"

"He didn't take any paintings to a dump," the woman said, sounding outraged at the thought. "He sells stuff like that at the flea market on South High."

"Is that where he is now?" Davy said, keeping the grimness from his voice.

"He's at work," the woman said. "The flea market opens Thursdays."

"Right," Davy said, but she'd already hung up.

"What's wrong with you?" Tilda said.

"These guys are *scum*," he said. "The guys who rip off people who can't afford it. The bullies and the grifters and the snakes. I *hate* them."

When she didn't say anything he looked over at her. She looked pale, her eyes huge behind her glasses.

"Hey," he said. "It's okay. I'll take care of him. But we are not giving him money."

"Okay," she said faintly.

"Take it easy, Betty," he said, patting her knee. "You just aren't cut out for crime."

"Oh, no," Tilda said. "I'm really, really not."

What a shame, he thought, and put the car in gear.

TILDA WENT upstairs to bed that night at eleven, with both Steve and Davy behind her, determined to say no if Davy made his move. And he was going to, he had that cheerful look in his eye. Steve was looking fairly cheerful, too, for a change, but on the third-floor landing, as they passed Dorcas's room, the door opened, and Dorcas peered out.

"Could you guys keep it down a little?" she said.

"What?" Tilda said, startled. "We didn't say anything."

"Not now," Dorcas said. "Friday and Saturday night." She shook her head at them. "All that moaning and screaming. I couldn't paint."

"That wasn't us," Davy said regretfully. "That was Simon and Louise."

"Simon?" Dorcas said, as Ariadne walked out on the landing.

"A friend of Davy's," Tilda said. "And it was only the weekend. Louise isn't—"

Ariadne swatted Steve, claws bared, three times fast.

Tilda scooped up the startled dog and held him out of harm's way as Dorcas said, "Ariadne!"

"What the hell was that for?" Davy said.

"Past crimes." Tilda propped Steve on her shoulder and he looked down at Ariadne, eyes wide. "It's okay, Steve. She'll get over it. I'll tell Louise, Dorcas." She started up the stairs again, and Davy followed her.

"What did he do to Ariadne?"

"He made a pass," Tilda said, trying to keep the discussion PG.

"Oh." Davy looked back down at Ariadne on the landing. "Doesn't he get points for being open-minded?"

Tilda gave up on the PG. "He tried to hump her."

"Steve, you dummy," Davy said. "You gotta buy her a couple of drinks first, get her liquored up."

Tilda had a momentary vision of Steve leaning up against the landing wall, asking Ariadne if she came there often, and laughed.

"Then when you've got her laughing," Davy said to Steve, "make your move."

"I too have claws," Tilda said.

"And teeth. But I am not afraid."

"You and Steve have a lot in common." Tilda handed the dog to him.

"Speaking of dangerous females," Davy said, slinging the dog under his arm, "where has Louise been? Simon's starting to think she's a figment of his imagination."

"She'll be back at the Double Take Wednesday night. She has Sunday, Monday, and Tuesday off." She opened the bedroom door and saw her bed, looking vast and white in the moonlight.

"She takes three nights off from sex?"

"From the Double Take," Tilda said. "Tell Simon to be patient." *Really patient, she's not coming back here.*

"That's two days from now." Davy put Steve on the floor. "I don't know if he has that much patience. I don't even think I do."

"Develop some," Tilda said.

"So that's a no," Davy said.

"If the question is what I think it is," Tilda said "then, yes, that's a no."

"You know, Vilma, playing hard to get can backfire."

"I'm not playing," Tilda said and locked herself in the bathroom to change into her pajamas. She liked sleeping in T-shirts better, but they had an adverse effect on Davy.

When she came out, he was already in bed, looking annoyed. She crawled in beside him, perversely glad he was there, and held up the quilt for Steve to tunnel under. *Cozy*, she thought as she felt the dog snuggled up to her through the sheet. She glanced over at Davy who was fighting with his pillow and looking not cozy.

"So tell me, Vilma," he said, punching the pillow again. "If you're not playing, why do you let me back in your bed?"

"In my bed," Tilda pointed out. "Not in me. There are limits here."

"In your dreams." Davy shoved his pillow behind him. "If I wanted to be in you, I'd be in you. You have lousy pillows. Why is that? Is Gwennie antipillow?"

"*How* would you be in me?" Tilda looked at him with contempt. "You would not be in me."

"I have charm." Davy shoved the pillow again. "Tomorrow I'm getting you better pillows."

"You do not have charm," Tilda said and then honesty made her add, "well, you don't have that much charm."

"I have charm you haven't experienced yet," Davy said. "Unplumbed depths of charm not yet unleashed on you." He punched the pillow again.

"Well, let me know if you plan to unleash it," Tilda said, snuggling down against her own pillow. "I want to brace myself."

"Won't do you any good," Davy said. "I'll get you anyway. How do you do that?"

"What?"

"Sink down into that pillow." He frowned at her. "You gave me the lousy pillow."

"I didn't give you anything. You took it."

"Let me see." Davy jerked her pillow out from behind her and Tilda's head bounced on the bed. He punched it a couple of times and shook his head. "No, this one's lousy, too." He dropped it on her face, and as she pulled it off she heard him say, "Tomorrow we get new pillows."

"I like *this* pillow."

"You think you like that pillow," Davy said, trying to get comfortable again. "Once you try the new pillows, you'll spit on that pillow."

"I will still like this pillow."

Davy leaned over her and Tilda blinked at how suddenly close he was. "Work with me here," he said. "This is vitally important."

"Pillows are vitally important," Tilda said.

"Yes," Davy said, so seriously she had to smile.

"Can you admit," he said, "that there is a slim possibility that there might, just might, be a better pillow than the one under your head right now?"

"Well—"

He leaned closer. "*Possibly*, maybe, might be, yes?"

"Yes," Tilda said.

"Then tomorrow I am getting you new pillows."

"I like these pillows."

"Did you know that after a year, half the weight of a pillow is dust mites?"

Tilda sat up, almost bumping into him. "What?"

"I swear to God it's true," Davy said, leaning back. "How old are these pillows?"

"They were here when I moved back home five years ago," Tilda said, looking at her pillow in horror.

"We get new pillows," Davy said, and tossed his on the floor.

"Oh, gross," Tilda said and shoved hers after his.

"Of course, now we have nothing to sleep on," Davy said. "Want to have sex?"

Tilda grinned at him. "*That's* your boundless charm?"

"No, I spent all my charm talking you out of the pillows." Davy got out of bed, picked up his shirt from the chair, and wadded it into a ball as he came back to her. "I thought I might get you on the momentum."

"You're pathetic," Tilda said.

"So that's still a no."

"Yes," Tilda said. "That's still a no."

"Confusing." Davy stuffed his shirt under his head and rolled away from her.

Tilda looked at the lovely strong line of his shoulders in the moonlight. "I know," she said and rolled away from him.

GWEN OPENED the gallery on Wednesday morning, poured herself a cup of coffee, punched up a Shirelles medley on the jukebox, got a pineapple-orange muffin from the bakery bag, took everything out into the gallery to the marble counter and her latest Double-

Crostic, and thought, *Someday I'm going to die, and my body will still do this. And nobody will notice.*

To her right, the sun streamed through the cracked glass pane above the display window, and the loose metal ceiling tile bounced silently in the breeze from the central air, while the Shirelles sang "I Met Him on a Sunday." She should mention the cracked window to Simon who'd evidently exhausted the entertainment possibilities of Columbus without Louise, and was now poking around the building, making notes to update the security. "This place is a burglar's dream," he'd told her. She'd gestured to the Finsters. "And he'd steal what?"

Davy had been grumpy for the past two days, too, which had to be either his money or Tilda, Gwen wasn't sure which but she was sure it wasn't good. "He's FBI," Gwen told Tilda. "Make him happy. Whatever it takes." "Mother of the Year, you're not," Tilda said. He was also spending a lot of time playing pool somewhere with people who had deep pockets. "You could earn a living doing that," Gwen told him when he came in one night and gave her more muffin money. "And then it wouldn't be fun anymore," he said, and went upstairs to Tilda's room.

And then there was Ford, who had brought her piña coladas every day without once breaking into an expression, although he did stay to talk about the gallery. It was flattering how much he wanted to know about her and sad how little there was to tell. The piña coladas helped ease the shame considerably. She had four umbrellas now, pink, blue, green, and yellow, and she kept them in her pencil holder where she could see them because she figured they were as close as she was ever going to get to blue water and white sand.

That's pathetic, she thought, which made her think of Mason, who'd called both Monday and Tuesday to thank her for going to lunch and then talked about the gallery wistfully. He was working up to asking her something, and she was pretty sure she knew what it was: he wanted to buy the gallery. *Heaven,* she thought, except that she couldn't, so no point in thinking about it. But at least her life was expanding. Now instead of looking forward to a Double-Crostic every day, she could look forward to a Double-Crostic, a phone call from Mason, and a paper umbrella from Ford. "Whoa, Nellie," she said, "now I'm really getting somewhere," and slapped open her Double-Crostic book.

By noon, having written in "ophidian" for "snake-like," "nimiety" for "redundancy," and "enswathe" for "wrap as a bandage," she was feeling much better. Of course anybody who would use "dofunny" as an answer for "gadget" was clearly insane, but that was puzzle-makers for you. She was still annoyed with this yahoo for spelling "toffee" with a *y.* And that "heavily built birds" clue that turned out to be "rough-legged hawks" was just—

"Grandma?"

Gwen looked up from her book. Nadine stood there, looking solemn with Ethan behind her.

"I thought you went to paint the mural with Tilda," Gwen said.

"I did," Nadine said. "Yesterday. We painted the underpainting. It was boring so I'm not going to be a muralist."

"Probably a good idea," Gwen said. "So now what?"

Nadine looked at Ethan. "Well, Ethan and I were concerned about Mr. Brown."

"Why?" Gwen said.

"Because Aunt Tilda said he had a fake name," Nadine said.

"She was kidding," Gwen said, going back to her Double-Crostic.

"I don't think so," Nadine said. "Ethan and I bugged his phone."

Gwen jerked her head up. *"Nadine."*

"It's okay, Mrs. Goodnight," Ethan said. "We didn't hurt the phone."

"It was really easy," Nadine said. "I'm thinking maybe I'll be a detective."

"I'm thinking you'll go to jail," Gwen said. "That's illegal. You stop it right now."

"We're not the ones going to jail," Nadine said, and Ethan nodded. "Not after what we heard."

"What?" Gwen said, not really wanting to know. She liked those little umbrellas. And the piña coladas were good, too.

"Mr. Brown is a hit man."

"Oh, hell," Gwen said, and closed her Double-Crostic.

Chapter · Twelve

"Okay, explain this to me again," Tilda said later that afternoon when she got home after underpainting too damn many water lilies. "Ford Brown is a contract killer?"

"Nadine bugged the phone in his apartment but didn't put a tape recorder on it," Gwen said, holding an ice pack to her forehead with her right hand and a drink with a purple umbrella in it in her left. "She swears she heard him talking to Clea Lewis about Davy and that it sounded like they were talking about killing him."

Tilda sat down next to her on the couch. "Well, I suppose it's possible. She took his money and she knows he's coming back for it. And I think it's a lot of money. But isn't there some horrible penalty for killing an FBI agent?"

"Oh, God," Gwen said. "And I rented a room to him." She looked at the drink, sighed, and drank a slug of it. "Hard to believe that a week ago, I thought any change would be good."

"You know, it just doesn't seem *probable*," Tilda

said. "Of course, neither does the FBI thing. What did Davy say?"

"He's been gone all day," Gwen said. "I don't know where . . ." She straightened. "You don't suppose he's already—"

"No," Tilda said. "I don't think he's that easy to kill. I'll talk to him when he comes in."

Gwen put the compress down. "Exactly what is going on with the two of you?"

"Exactly nothing," Tilda said. "We're helping each other recover lost property. Then he leaves for Australia and I go to Cleveland to paint a *Starry Night* in a bedroom."

"I'm sorry," Gwen said and offered her the compress, but not the drink.

"Don't be," Tilda said. "This is exactly the way I want it. Men screw everything up."

"Yeah," Gwen said, looking at the umbrella in her drink. "I know that. I just wasn't expecting a killer doughnut."

"Well," Tilda said. "There's always Mason. I know he's with Clea, but that's not going to work out, he's too sweet."

"Mason wants the gallery, not me," Gwen said. "I'll stick with Double-Crostics. They're annoying, but they don't court you for real estate or try to kill your tenants."

"Good point," Tilda said and watched her mother drift back out to the gallery.

*

BY TEN that night, even Tilda had begun to fret, so she was relieved when Davy came in the bedroom door, carrying two big plastic bags.

"Pillows," he said, emptying the bags on the bed. "Four of the best that money can buy."

"Thank you," she said. "That was thoughtful. Is it possible that somebody might have hired someone to kill you?"

"That's the rumor." Davy stripped off his shirt. "Hell of a day."

"Nadine already talked to you?"

"Nadine?"

"Nadine tapped Ford Brown's phone and now she thinks Clea Lewis hired him to kill you."

"The cowboy?" Davy said. "Huh. Could be."

He went into the bathroom and turned on the shower, and Tilda thought about throwing something at him. She picked up a pillow and then decided it was too good to waste on him and went downstairs to find pillowcases instead. By the time she came back, he was in bed and Steve was under the covers again.

"Come here, Vilma," he said, patting the sheets.

"I have a headache," Tilda said. She tossed him two pillowcases and began to cover the two that were left.

"You know, I've never heard a woman actually say that until now," Davy said, picking up a pillow.

"New experiences are good," Tilda said, and covered the second pillow. Then she slid into bed and sank back. "Oh, these are *really* good."

"So am I," Davy said. "You want to tell me what's

wrong here? Because I could have sworn you made it Sunday night." He flipped one covered pillow behind him and started on the next one.

"I did." Tilda slipped a little farther under the covers. "Thank you. Good night."

"Matilda," Davy said. "Talk."

Tilda frowned at him. "Me, talk? I tell you a guy two floors down is going to kill you and you don't bat an eye. What is it again that you do for a living?"

" 'I killed the president of Paraguay with a fork,' " Davy said.

"*Grosse Pointe Blank,*" Tilda said. "This is not a movie."

"I find it hard to believe that Ford Brown is trying to kill me."

"And that's because . . . ?"

Davy shrugged. "What's he waiting for?"

Tilda thought about it. "Instructions?"

"That must be it," Davy said. "Since this may be my last night on earth, how about—"

"No," Tilda said.

"You want to explain this to me?"

She tried to frown at him but the sheet was in the way. "Hey, I can not want to."

"Yes, you can," Davy said. "I just want to know why. Come on." He smiled at her. "Talk to me."

Tilda shook her head, her mouth under the covers. "I'm much too worried about Ford gunning you down. If I was under you, he'd get me, too."

"He's too efficient for that." Davy leaned closer, his

smile still in place. "Tell you what. *Ten* minutes. I'll beat my own best time."

"Really not in the mood."

"Five minutes."

"*Davy.*"

He sighed and pushed himself up in the bed until he was leaning against the wall, the new pillows bunched behind him, and he looked damn good shirtless in the moonlight. "Okay, then tell me why, so I don't make whatever terrible mistake I made again."

"You know you didn't make a mistake." Tilda slid deeper into the bed, and Davy pulled the sheet down so her face was uncovered.

"It's hard to hear you under there. Come on up and talk."

Tilda closed her eyes. "I have to paint tomorrow, and I need my sleep."

"So tell me and get it over with. Where'd I screw up?"

Tilda thought, *Tell him something so he'll shut up,* and shoved the covers down. "Okay, if I tell you, you have to promise not to get insulted or wounded or mad."

"Oh, this is going to be good," Davy said, sounding unconcerned.

"Listen, there's a reason people lie to each other," Tilda said, feeling waspish. "It keeps them from *killing* each other."

Davy pulled her pillows out from under her head.

"Hey!"

Then he piled up her pillows against the headboard

and patted them. "Come on. My ego can take damn near anything."

"Well, that's true." Tilda sat up and scooted back against the pillows. "Okay, but you asked for it. I tried to be polite. It's embarrassing."

"Well, spit it out and get it over with."

"No, that's it. That's what's wrong. You. Sex. The whole thing. It's embarrassing. And dangerous." She turned to find Davy looking at her with his "you're insane" look. "I don't know you very well, okay? I met you five days ago. I don't know anything about you and all of a sudden there you are."

"There I am," Davy said, sounding mystified.

"You know." Tilda pointed to the south. "There."

"That's where the good stuff is. You're overthinking this."

Tilda looked straight ahead. "I know what I feel."

"Because," Davy went on as if she hadn't spoken, "if you think about it too much, you'll never do it."

"Not true," Tilda said, exasperated.

"I mean, when you think about what you're actually doing—"

"Which I don't want to."

"—let alone what you sound like—"

Tilda winced. "I hadn't thought about that."

"—it makes you wonder how anybody can videotape themselves—"

"Oh, *God*." Tilda sank down into the bed, trying not to imagine a videotape of the couch.

"—although I'm up for that if you are."

Tilda sat up. "*Are you nuts?*"

"Why?" Davy said, startled.

"Do you pay any attention to me at all?"

"Well, I'd like to," Davy said. "But you have a headache."

"Not that kind of attention," Tilda said, warming to her subject, "although I could point out that you don't pay a lot of attention there, either."

"*Hey*," Davy said. "I paid attention."

"Yes, to what you were doing," Tilda said. "Not to me."

"You *were* what I was doing."

"It's not like you talked to me. It's not like you made eye contact."

"My mouth was full," Davy said, sounding annoyed. "And my head was between your thighs. You want eye contact, you're gonna have to lean down."

"I told you that you wouldn't like it," Tilda muttered, settling back against the pillows.

"Okay, let's cut to the chase," Davy said. "You came, right? No faking."

"Yes." Tilda stared at the skylights.

"And it was good, right? No small stuff. The real thing."

"Yes."

"Well, I guarantee I'll get you there again," Davy said, exasperated.

"I don't want you to," Tilda said. "That's my point."

"You don't want to come."

"I don't want to come with you," Tilda said. "I don't

know you, and you're a stranger, and you're dangerous and you're . . . down there . . . and I'm moaning and acting like an idiot and saying God knows what and then you're inside me and the next day I can't even look at you."

"Okay, so we won't talk during the day," Davy said, the voice of reason.

Tilda glared at him. "Is that supposed to be funny?"

"No," Davy said, mystified. "I'm trying to be accommodating. It's not like you're seeing anybody else who's doing this for you."

Tilda turned back to the skylight. "I can do it for myself."

"Not like I can do it for you," Davy said, and she turned to him, amazed by his arrogance.

"Hey, I can give myself orgasms that blow me out of bed, thank you. My vibrator's *electric*. It *plugs in*, Sparky. Now can I get some sleep?" She stopped when she realized she'd finally made him speechless. "Look, don't take it personally—"

"You'd rather have a vibrator than me," Davy said.

"It's a good one," she said, trying to soften the blow. "It's not battery-operated. It plugs in." When he didn't say anything, she added, "Eve gave it to me for Christmas ten years ago, so I've had it a while and . . ." She trailed off as she watched his face.

"You're in a long-term relationship with an appliance," Davy said.

"Hey." Tilda straightened. "I never have to talk to it,

it never makes me feel embarrassed, and it never lets me down."

"You know, you could say the same thing about me if you weren't so uptight," Davy said. *"Jesus."*

"I am not uptight," Tilda said.

"Louise is not uptight," Davy said. "You are winched to the eyebrows." He shook his head. "Eve gave you the vibrator. What did Louise give you? A sailor?"

"They went in on it together," Tilda said icily. "So now you have your answer. Satisfied?"

"Oddly enough, *no.*" He took a deep breath. "Look, this is not a problem. I'm an open-minded man. How about a threesome?"

"What?" Tilda said, outraged.

"You, me, and the machine," Davy said.

"No," Tilda said, heroically refraining from throwing something at him. "I do not want a threesome. Now, may I please go to sleep?"

"Honey, I don't think you ever wake up." Davy got out of bed.

"Oh, right, because I don't want you, I must be half-dead." Tilda slid down in bed. "Your ego astounds me."

Davy stopped at the end of the bed. "When was the last time you had sex?"

"Sunday," Tilda said savagely, under the covers.

"With somebody besides me," Davy said with exaggerated patience.

"That is none of your business," Tilda said.

"You can't even remember." Davy picked his jeans up off the floor. "You're so damn busy running around being good, you can't even remember the last time you were bad."

"I remember the last time *you* were bad," Tilda muttered into the blankets.

"Okay, *fine.*" Davy zipped up his pants and grabbed his shirt. "Where's your purse?"

"What?" Tilda sat up as he shrugged on the shirt and found her purse on the dresser. "What are you *doing*?"

"Taking twenty bucks," Davy snapped. "You'll have it back by morning."

"That's my money!" Tilda said, trying not to notice how good he looked with his shirt open.

"You're going to sleep," Davy said. "You're not going to need it tonight. Not unless you tip the vibrator."

"I knew you couldn't take that," Tilda said. "I knew you'd be this way." When he opened the door without answering her, she said, "*Wait a minute*, where are you going?"

"To play pool," Davy said. "I'm going to sink *something* in a pocket tonight." Then he slammed the door, taking her twenty with him.

"Men are so *sensitive*," she yelled at the door, trying not to think about how good he'd looked, enraged in the moonlight. She punched the pillow he'd given her. She was really tired of his nothing-bothers-me routine, and he was way too dangerous to bed, but . . .

He was damn fun to look at when he was mad. She could tell he was mad even before he started yelling, just watching the muscles in his arms. And he did have skills.

Oh, hell, she thought. If he'd stuck around for another couple of minutes, he could have talked her into the threesome. Which was why he was so dangerous; he could talk her into anything. The more she thought about him, the madder she got, and the madder she got, the more she tapped her toes on the foot of the bed, until she finally gave up and pulled out her dresser drawer and plugged in her longest-running relationship.

Say what you would about General Electric, it got you where you needed to go without taking your money and slamming the door.

DAVY QUIT when he was a hundred ahead, mostly because he was so mad, he was playing stupid. "That's what happens when you let women in your head," he muttered to himself, and his mark said, "Ain't that the truth."

The walk back to the gallery didn't help, and when he was standing in the downstairs hall, going up to Tilda didn't appeal, either. What the hell was her problem, anyway?

He looked at the basement door. There was something down there that she kept locked up. Well, that was Matilda for you, nobody got in below. "Except me," Davy said and went upstairs to bang on the door of the room he'd rented.

"What?" Simon said when he finally answered, looking sleepy.

"Take a break," Davy said. "I need you to open a lock. Louise can spare you for five minutes."

"Louise isn't here," Simon said. "I have high hopes for tomorrow, however. What do you want unlocked?"

"Basement door."

"Not a problem," Simon said and went back inside the room.

When he came back with his tools, it took him longer to walk down the two flights to the ground floor than it did to open the basement door.

"It really is a shame you're retired," Davy said. "You're an artist."

"I know," Simon said. "But I really dislike prison. So you're expecting to find something interesting down there?"

"I have no idea," Davy said. "Let's go."

He flipped on the light at the head of the stairs, prepared to encounter one of those pit-of-hell basements that are usually under very old buildings, and saw white cement steps leading down to an immaculate hallway, so brightly lit the place glowed.

"There is definitely something interesting down there," Simon said.

Davy frowned. "Already you know?"

"Somebody spent money," Simon said. "Not on this lock, but . . ." He pushed past Davy and went down the steps and Davy followed him. The stairs ended in a short hall painted as white as Tilda's bedroom, and Simon stopped to listen. "Air cleaner."

"It's cool." Davy looked around. There were two

doors facing each other across the hall and a row of empty bookcases at the end but otherwise the place was empty.

"Temperature controlled," Simon said. "They're storing something valuable down here."

"Paintings?"

"That's the obvious guess," Simon said, looking at the door on the left. "Hello."

"Hello what?" Davy said. "This was supposed to be my good time."

"This lock they spent money on," Simon said, bending down.

"Can you get in?"

"Given enough time and enough motive, yes," Simon said. "I don't have either. It'd be a bugger. Go seduce the combination out of Tilda. It'll be a lot faster."

"You don't know Tilda." Davy turned to the other door. "How about this one? Can you pick it?"

Simon reached over and turned the doorknob, and it opened. "The first rule of B and E. See if it's unlocked."

"Is there a *reason* everybody's busting my chops tonight?" Davy said, and shoved the door the rest of the way open. He flipped on the light and the big room glared back at him, stretching half the length of the building, full of white sheets draped over God knows what, the walls, floor, and ceiling all the same flat white. "This family's aversion to color is downright scary."

Simon nodded. "Louise wears red. I think. It's hard to see color in the dark."

Davy raised his eyebrows. "Louise doesn't like the lights on?"

"It's the only thing she doesn't like," Simon said. "Considering everything else she's said yes to, it's not much to ask."

"You're an accommodating man." Davy pulled on the first dustcover. "Jesus."

Snake eyes stared back at him from a blue and green wing chair. What he first took for stripes were snake bodies, undulating over the wings and down the seat, each body striped again in more colors, purple and silver, their little snaky heads turned toward him, grinning at him dark-eyed with evil intent.

"Reminds me of Louise," Simon said.

Davy pulled the next sheet off and found a chest of drawers painted pink with blue-eyed daisies lined up innocently across the drawers, their curly yellow petals making them look like happy little suns.

"Reminds me of Eve," Davy said.

He lifted the next sheet and found a table painted with sly-looking blue flamingos while Simon uncovered several chairs from different dining sets covered in campy yellow and orange butterflies. They moved through the room, finding a table painted with red spotted beagles, a chest of drawers slathered with lime-green snails, at least a dozen footstools painted with frogs and fish and mice, one perversely decorated piece of furniture after another until they reached the back wall and flipped back the last and largest dustcover and found a bed with a tree painted on the headboard, its spreading branches framing two human figures, one blond, one brunette.

Davy started to laugh. "Okay, I'm getting this bed for my sister."

"Why?" Simon said.

"Because that's her and the stuffed shirt she married," he said. "She'll love it and he'll hate it. It's perfect."

"I don't think that's Sophie," Simon said. "I think that's Tilda. And Andrew."

Davy stopped laughing. "Oh." Then he shook his head. "I don't think it's anybody, but it's going to be Sophie and Phin."

"Handpainted bed," Simon said. "That's about a thousand bucks you don't have."

"What?" Davy said, suddenly alert.

"Handpainted furniture," Simon said. "It's expensive."

"How expensive?" Davy said.

Simon shrugged. "It's labor intensive. I'm sure they'll give you a break on the price . . . What?"

Davy scanned the room, trying to count while his thoughts climbed all over each other to reach the same conclusion. "How many pieces of furniture are down here?"

Simon shrugged. "Forty. Fifty. Why?"

"I think the Finster Era is over," Davy said and headed for the door.

★

TILDA WAS deep asleep when Davy turned on the light and said, "Rise and shine, Snow White, we need to talk."

"No," she said, half-asleep, putting her pillow over her head to shut out the light. "No, I don't want to have sex, no."

"Surprisingly, neither do I." He sat on the bed and pulled the pillow away. "Wake up, Judy, we're gonna put on a show in the barn."

CHAPTER · THIRTEEN

"DAVY, I HAVE TO WORK TOMORROW." TILDA SQUINTED
at the clock. "Oh, hell. I have to work today. It's past
midnight."

"The furniture in the basement," Davy said and she
sat up, awake and breathless.

"What were you doing in the basement?"

"We're going to sell the furniture down there," Davy
said, as Steve poked his nose out from under the quilt
to see what was going on.

Tilda tried to take a deep breath. "How did you *get in*
the basement?"

"Door was unlocked. Pay attention. You have a lot of
furniture down there."

"It was not unlocked," Tilda said, wheezing a little
on "was," and he bent over her and covered her mouth
with his hand.

"Listen to me very carefully," he said. "We are going
to have a show of that furniture very soon. And we are
going to invite Mason to host it. And Clea will come
with him. And . . ."

Tilda pushed his hand away. "And we can go steal

our stuff back. Why can't we just invite them to dinner?"

"Because they now have staff," Davy said. "In fact, you've met the staff. You kicked its head in."

"Oh." Tilda sat up a little more, making Steve shift over, trying for deeper breaths. "But what—"

"You're going to need a caterer for the opening. You'll hire him."

Tilda shook her head. "There's got to be an easier way—"

The wheeze was more pronounced on "easier," and Davy opened her bedside table drawer and got out her inhaler. "Not one that will also make you money," he said, handing it to her. "You've got a small fortune down there."

She hit the inhaler and frowned at him. He looked sincere, but then he always did, even when he was lying through his teeth. "Davy, nobody's going to want to buy that furniture. I painted that when I was a kid."

"You painted it?"

"Yes," Tilda said, not in a mood to be sneered at. "Why?"

"It's really good."

"And that's a surprise?"

"I thought you only did the murals," he said, backing off a little. "And I've never seen one of them. I had no idea how good you were. Oh, and I'm buying the bed."

"Why?" Tilda said, now really wary as she put the inhaler back in the drawer.

"My sister's anniversary," Davy said. "I'll pay you after I get my money back."

Tilda waved her hand. "Take it. You've more than earned it this week. But about this show—"

"You need the money, we need the diversion, and all it's going to cost us is some paint and advertising," Davy said, stripping off his shirt. "It's a no-brainer."

"Paint for *what*?"

"The gallery." He shoved off his jeans and crawled into bed beside her, making Steve shift again. "You'll never con people into paying a hundred bucks for a footstool with the place looking the way it does now. Perception is reality, babe. We have to bring this place back from the dead." He settled into his new pillows, looking very pleased with himself.

"No." Tilda's breath went at the thought.

"Yes," Davy said. "I don't know why you want the gallery to fail, but you've got to get over it. We need a successful opening to keep Mason busy, and you need the money."

"I don't want the gallery to fail." Tilda felt the familiar scraping wheeze begin in her lungs.

"Right," Davy said. "You're the only one with the brains and the push to make this place work, and you spend all your time on the road, leaving Gwennie to sell Finsters. You've done everything but put a stake through its heart."

"I have not—" She tried to take a deep breath.

"Which I wouldn't care about but it's a pretty sweet setup, Tilda. It's a crime to let it go to waste."

Tilda heard "crime" and reached for her inhaler again. "I'm not much of a salesman. Woman. Person."

"I am," Davy said. "We're selling the furniture in the basement."

"Is that why you want to do this," Tilda said. "Because it's a sweet setup and you're a salesman?"

"No," he said, looking unsure for the first time since he'd ruined her sleep. "Matilda, I want to sell that furniture. You're not doing anything with it. How long has it been down there?"

"Seventeen years," Tilda said.

"Give me one good reason why we shouldn't do this."

Because anybody with any kind of an eye at all could tell that furniture was painted by the same person who painted the Scarlets. Tilda's stomach heaved at the thought.

"I'm waiting," Davy said.

On the other hand, there were damn few people who had seen the Scarlets. Davy had, and he hadn't figured it out. Clea had, but she didn't appear to have much of an eye. Mason had, but he was so caught up in the fine-art thing, he wouldn't want to believe Scarlet had painted them.

"Okay," Tilda said. "Okay. But you're going to be the one who tells Gwennie." She fell back against the pillows. "I'm sure this is a mistake."

"You have no faith." He leaned over and picked up his jeans from the floor and pulled something from the pocket, and then he slid his hand under her chin, warm on her skin, and before she could say, "Hey," he'd stuck something papery down the neck of her T-shirt.

"Off." She batted his hand away and pulled the neck of her T-shirt open to see two twenties and a ten on her chest. "I don't take cash."

"That's your cut from the twenty I borrowed," Davy said. "Half my winnings."

"Maybe I should just send you out to play pool," Tilda said, fishing the bills out of her T-shirt.

"We'll use that as a backup," Davy said. "First, we're going to sell furniture."

WHEN TILDA woke up the next morning, Davy was gone, but he'd left a note that said, "Don't forget to tell Gwennie." *Great,* she thought, and went downstairs with Steve to get orange juice and ruin Gwennie's day.

"Hi," Gwen said when Tilda came into the office. "Davy still alive?"

"Yes," Tilda said. "And that's not funny."

Eve waved at her from the table, her mouth full of muffin. "How's Monet?" she said when she'd swallowed.

"Boring as ever," Tilda said, as Steve went to sit at Eve's feet in hopes of muffin. "He deserves to be on a bathroom wall. Oh, and speaking of Davy, he wants to do a gallery show of my old furniture and I said yes. Well, gotta go to work." She headed for the door.

"*Hold it,*" Gwen said, sounding panicked, and Tilda sighed and turned back to get orange juice and fill them in on the night before.

"He's convinced this is the way to get everything back," Tilda said as she finished. "I argued, but—"

"Don't argue." Eve hauled Steve onto her lap to pet him better. "They're FBI. Which I actually find sexy."

"That's Louise," Tilda said. "Pull yourself together. Or in your case, separate yourself better."

"I'm against this," Gwen said gloomily.

"I know," Tilda said.

"Mason's going to be thrilled," Gwen said, even gloomier. "He'll be all over the place. There'll be dozens of people all over the place. I'll never finish another Double-Crostic again."

"I know," Tilda said.

"At least Mason isn't a hit man," Gwen said.

"Plus there's all those free lunches he shells out for," Eve said helpfully. "A man who pays for food is good."

Gwen frowned at Tilda. "Is there any chance that the four of them are toying with us? Like this is a plot they're doing together?"

Tilda looked at her over her glasses. "Any chance that Davy, Simon, Ford, and Mason decided to drive us crazy at random? Sure, why not. I have to go. Give Steve to Nadine for the day, be nice to Davy when he comes back, and don't let Ford kill him. The last thing we need here is a murder investigation."

"I won't be here," Gwen said. "I'm having lunch with Mason. Someone else will have to draw the chalk outline." She got up. "This is going to be a disaster."

She went out to the gallery, and Tilda frowned after her. "We should do something about her."

"Like what?" Eve said, still cuddling Steve. "The only thing that would make her happy is a nice trip somewhere on a boat—"

"A boat?" Tilda said.

"—and you know she wouldn't go. She won't leave us."

"Why a boat?"

Eve shrugged. "I don't know. She's doodling boats on everything now. And her pencil cup has five little paper umbrellas in it. She says she's saving them for a rainy day."

"Boats and umbrellas." Tilda sighed. "Well, at least it isn't teeth. I have to go to work. Davy has plans for after lunch."

"Naked plans?" Eve said.

"No," Tilda said. "We're not doing that anymore."

"Me, neither," Eve said, and didn't sound happy about it.

"Simon misses you," Tilda said helpfully.

"Simon misses Louise." Eve put Steve on the floor. "He doesn't know me."

"His loss," Tilda said.

"I don't know." Eve pushed her orange juice glass away and sat back. "I'm not that interesting. Not like Louise."

"Eve, you *are* Louise," Tilda said. "You know, maybe you should pull yourself together after all. Tell Simon the truth."

Eve closed her eyes. "There's a part of me that wants to. I think, 'He's great in bed and he likes Nadine and he'd be the perfect lover and husband and father to my kid,' I mean, he's the guy who really could pull me together."

"So tell him."

Eve tilted her head back so she could meet Tilda's eyes. "Are you going to tell Davy you're Scarlet?"

"Never," Tilda said.

"Yeah, that's what the other part of me says." Eve stood up. "Especially with Simon's damn mother rule. Maybe I should do what you do, bury Louise in the basement and never let her see the light of day."

"Hey," Tilda said. "There's only one me. Nobody's buried in the basement."

"Tell that to Scarlet," Eve said.

AT NOON Clea met Ronald for lunch. "This better be good, Ronald," she said as she sat down at the patio table, already annoyed because Mason had left for another business meeting without telling her where he was going. He'd been having a whole hell of a lot of business meetings, and she was pretty sure he was having them with Gwen Goodnight. And now Ronald was taking her to lunch in the sun, but her picture hat kept most of it from her face, and she looked wonderful in picture hats, so that was better. She relaxed into her chair and looked around at the other women, chatting away while the rays destroyed their skin. What were they thinking?

"It'll be good," Ronald said. "It's the best restaurant in German Village. Well, one of the best. It—"

"Not the food," Clea said. "What have you got on Gwen Goodnight?"

"Oh." Ronald sat back. "So that's why you wanted to meet."

"Ronald," Clea said, "I'm having a very, very bad week. Tell me Gwen Goodnight had a sex change and is really a retired shoe salesman from Des Moines."

"No, she's Gwen Goodnight," Ronald said, looking puzzled. "Her maiden name was Frasier. She was an actress and a dancer."

"Good," Clea said, feeling cheered. "There must be something shady in her past, then."

"Not really," Ronald said. "Her first daughter was born six months after she was married, but that's not really scandalous anymore."

Clea stared at him coldly. "Ronald. You're not helping me."

"There was a lot on the Goodnights," Ronald offered. "They changed the family name in 1948 from Giordano. They moved here in the sixties."

"I need dirt, Ronald," Clea said.

"One of them went to prison for art forgery," Ronald said helpfully. "That's when they changed their name."

"In 1948," Clea said. "Do you have anything from this century?"

"Not really," Ronald said. "They haven't done any-thing since Gwen's husband Anthony died. I told you, the gallery's on its last legs. There's nothing there."

Clea resisted the urge to slap him. It wasn't his fault there was nothing there. Also, she was beginning to suspect that Ronald liked being abused. "Well, thank you for trying, Ronald."

Ronald leaned forward. "I'll do anything for you, Clea, but really, can't we forget this whole thing, go back to Miami—"

"No," Clea said. "My art collection is here, Ronald." *My future husband and his money are here, Ronald.*

"Did you find the rest of the Scarlet Hodge paintings?"

"No," Clea said, feeling bitter just thinking about it. "But I found two people who had sold them. Somebody else is collecting them."

"Why?" Ronald said.

Clea blinked at him. It was a damn good question. The only person who wanted them was Mason, but he didn't fit the descriptions of the buyers, tall men with dark hair and very different wives . . . Clea sat up slowly. "Davy Dempsey."

"Why would he want paintings?" Ronald said. "He has no interest in art."

"He's living at that gallery," Clea said. "You said Gwen Goodnight had been an actress, right? It was the two of them. He's running some con at that gallery."

"He's gone straight," Ronald said.

"Oh, sure, like you did." Clea bit her lip, and Ronald breathed faster. "No. He's up to something with Gwen Goodnight. I bet they're scamming Mason. They're going to use those paintings to get him to propose to her. Then Gwen will pay off Davy."

"That's not Davy's kind of con," Ronald said.

"Davy is capable of anything," Clea said.

"No," Ronald said, and Clea looked at him, surprised. "I'm sorry, but that's not his con."

"Well then, why does he want the paintings?" Clea said.

"I don't know," Ronald said.

"Find out," Clea said and picked up her menu, feeling much better now that they were making progress.

"No," Ronald said.

Clea frowned. "It was interesting the first time you said it, Ronald. Now it's just annoying."

"I'm not hired help, Clea," Ronald said. "I'm your lover. I deserve some respect."

Clea thought about it. On the one hand, life would be simpler if she let him storm off into the sunset. On the other, he was useful. And he was going to pay for lunch.

"You're right, Ronald," she said, smiling at him ruefully. "You're absolutely right." She leaned toward him, bathing him in her smile and her cleavage. "But you will find out what Davy's up to, won't you? For me?" She breathed in deeply.

Ronald breathed deeply, too. "Of course."

"Oh, good," Clea said and went back to the menu.

THAT AFTERNOON, Davy borrowed one of Simon's shirts for the flea market, trying to look prosperous but not rich, somebody Colby would buy as honest.

"It has to be *my* shirt?" Simon said.

"Tilda doesn't have anything that fits me," Davy said.

"Boy, one night without Louise, and you're a mess."

"Four nights," Simon said. "Does that strike you as odd?"

"That a woman would avoid you for four nights? No."

"I checked her out through the bureau," Simon said.

"You *what*?"

"I was curious. I did it informally."

"Oh, good," Davy said. "You know damn well Tilda's up to something, and you alert the FBI."

"They were already alerted," Simon said. "Someone's up here looking into them."

"Fuck," Davy said.

"It's part of something larger," Simon said. "Some rich old man who died after a warehouse burned down. His grandson is insisting it's arson. But the Goodnights are definitely on the list."

"Keep an eye on that list," Davy said. "If they start to look like they're going for anybody here, let me know."

"Certainly," Simon said. "I don't have anything *else* to do."

Downstairs in the gallery, Tilda was also annoyed.

"I don't get to come?" she said when Davy got the car keys from Jeff. "I leave work early and you're doing this without Betty and Veronica?" She stopped. "Oh, good, I sound like an Archie comic."

"Stay close to the phone," Davy said. "If I need you, I'll call. Oh, and you," he said to Nadine, who was trying to get a sock away from Steve. "You stay here, too. We may need you."

"For what?" Nadine said, looking up. "I get to play?"

"This is not play, my child," Davy said. "This is art."

"Uh-huh," Nadine said and went back to retrieving her sock.

Colby was on the edge of the market when Davy finally found him, directed there by an exasperated woman in a pink My Little Pony T-shirt who was trying to sell "real old handmade reproductions" of advertising signs. He looked like he was trying not to fit in, his polo shirt neatly pressed and tucked into Dockers that failed to disguise his paunch. He was at the age when his hairline was gathering strength to recede, and he smirked under its creeping edges, smug in the knowledge that he was better than everybody else there.

Take him for everything he's got, Davy's inner con whispered.

Davy strolled over and began to leaf through the prints that Colby had displayed in a V-shaped easel.

"Those are all original artwork," Colby said, which was such a blatant lie that even Davy was taken aback.

"I'm really more interested in paintings," Davy said.

"Got those, too," Colby said, sweeping his hand behind him to show a selection of framed artwork, very few of which were actual paintings.

"Something colorful," Davy said, and Colby offered him a still life of throbbing purple grapes and a portrait of a clown that looked as though it had been painted in orange Kool-Aid.

"You know what my wife likes?" Davy said. "Dancers. And wouldn't you know it, I can't ever find a dancer painting."

"Don't have one," Colby said with real regret.

Oh, hell. "Got anything close? People dancing in the air. Flying?"

"Got just the thing," Colby said. "It's got no frame, though." He began to dig under the table, and Davy thought, *There is no chance that this—*

And then Colby was holding up the Scarlet, this one a checkerboard sky with two people with smeared heads who were sure as hell not dancing, not with that body language. Scarlet got more interesting with every painting.

"It's a little weird," Colby said. "But it's colorful."

"It's smudged," Davy said. "Their heads are all messed up. I don't know. How much do you want for it?"

"Well, this is an original artwork," Colby said. "So it's five hundred dollars."

Davy shook his head. "It's messed up."

"It's original," Colby said.

"Let me think about it," Davy said and walked away before Colby could come down on the price. He crossed over to the next lane where he could see Colby between the booths while he punched in Tilda's number on his cell phone. Colby was not a happy art dealer.

"It's me," he said when Tilda answered. "He's got it. Get Nadine and get ready."

"Okay," Tilda said. "Andrew said he'd watch the gallery. Anything we should know?"

"Colby's an idiot," Davy said. "Let him look down your blouse and you've got him. He's also big on frames. Listen, when I pick you up, I don't want to recognize either one of you."

"Okay," Tilda said, a little more slowly. "Any special requests? Fishnet stockings? Funny hats?"

"Nadine should look like a normal teenager," Davy said, trying not to think of Tilda in fishnets. "I know that's a stretch but she should be completely unmemorable."

"Okay," Tilda said.

"And you should look like an art dealer. Look professional and successful and bored. Be Veronica with money."

"Story of my life," Tilda said. "Except for the money. Come and get me."

"That's my plan," Davy said.

NADINE HAD outdone herself in jeans, a Britney Spears T-shirt, and a honey-brown wig with a ponytail. She'd done a clumsy enough job on her makeup that she looked completely authentic, a perfect replica of a teenager.

"She looks normal," Davy said to Tilda when they were back at the flea market and he'd given Nadine her instructions and sent her off to Colby.

"I know," Tilda said. "We were all so proud when we saw her. It's a triumph of illusion."

"You did pretty good yourself." Davy surveyed

Tilda's red silk separates and razor-cut wig. "I hadn't thought of you as a blonde. You look like Gwennie. With a lot more edge."

"Blondes are hot," Tilda said, watching as Nadine approached Colby. "I am cool. All she has to do is leave the print there?"

"Yep," Davy said. "Hot, huh? I don't suppose you'd consider wearing that wig—"

"In bed with you? No." Tilda squinted across the market. "She's there."

Davy turned back and saw Nadine slow in front of Colby's booth. He sprang to life, smiling at her until she began to talk, gesturing to the painting. Then Nadine held up her print to show him, and his smile disappeared as he shook his head.

"What is that print?" Davy asked Tilda.

"It's a Finster," Tilda said. "One of her damaged proofs."

"You're going to convince Colby a Finster is valuable?" Davy snorted. "Good luck. We're doomed."

"No," Tilda said. "Dorcas is really good. She's just depressing."

Nadine talked on, and Davy imagined her with her eyes widened and her voice lightened, channeling Marcia Brady. "I hope she doesn't overplay it."

"Oh, relax," Tilda said. "None of us overacts. We could underplay in the cradle."

Across the way, Nadine held up her finger in the universal "Wait a minute" sign. She dropped the print on

Colby's table and started off down the fairway while he gestured to her to take it.

"Give him a couple of minutes," Davy said. "Then go over there and discover the print. It's worth a lot of money, but you're cagey about it."

"But Colby catches on," Tilda said.

"Then you confess that it's worth thousands."

"Thousands," Tilda said doubtfully.

"Well, a lot of hundreds then," Davy said. "You're the art expert here. You'll give him a lot of money for it."

"What if he sells it?"

"He won't," Davy said. "Nadine's coming back and he knows it. He'll tell you it's on hold or something and ask you to come back."

"I don't see how we're getting the Scarlet," Tilda said.

"You don't need to," Davy said. "Go over there and convince him that you'll pay a lot of money for that thing."

"Right," Tilda said, and he watched her thread her way through the crowd to Colby.

Colby definitely perked up when she arrived, and it wasn't just because she looked like money. *You're married, you jerk,* Davy thought as Colby leaned closer to Tilda. Tilda laughed up at him, compounding the problem. What the hell was she doing? She was supposed to be a cool art dealer, not a fairway floozy. She looked over the paintings Colby showed her, clearly as uninterested in them as she was fascinated by him, and he expanded under her come-on. *Come on*, Davy thought. *Enough of this already.* Then Tilda stopped, her body language changing from pliant to alert. She picked up Nadine's print, and Davy watched Colby's face shift from lust to greed. It was like watching a silent movie: Tilda pulling back as Colby questioned her, her shoulders slumping as he got her to admit the print was valuable, his shoulders hunching as Tilda looked up and down the fairway for the phantom owner of the print.

"She's good, isn't she?" Nadine said, making Davy jump.

"Yeah," he said. "So are you."

"Thank you," Nadine said. "So now what?"

"You wait until she leaves," Davy said. "And then you go pick up your print. He'll offer you some ridiculously small amount of money for it. You say no, it's worth more than that, your grandma told you it was worth a lot, although maybe if he has something to trade, does he have anything that would be nice and bright for your room because that's what you're here for. You let him talk you into trading it for the Scarlet, and then you meet us back at the car and we're out of here."

"Excellent," Nadine said. "Now?"

Davy looked back at the booth. Tilda was gone.

"Give him a minute," he said. "Let somebody else talk to him. Then go."

Two browsers later, Nadine took off for the booth, and Tilda came back, eating a hot dog. "How's it going?" she said, handing him one, too.

"Thanks. It's going the way it always does." Davy unwrapped the hot dog and bit into it. "Just the way I planned it."

"It's so odd seeing these paintings again," Tilda said.

"You and Scarlet close, were you?" Davy said, not really caring. Across the way, Nadine came back for her print.

"Don't know her at all," Tilda said, following his eyes to Nadine. "Is this it?"

"Umhm," Davy said, his mouth full.

They finished eating while Nadine toyed with Colby. She smiled and he leaned forward. She dug her toe in the dirt, he reasoned with her. She shrugged and he tried harder. Finally, Nadine lifted her shoulders and pointed to a blue bowl.

"What?" Davy said, feeling his heart clutch. "Not the bowl, you dummy."

Colby evidently felt the same way because he shook his head. Nadine shifted her hip, clearly agitated, and pointed to the Scarlet. Colby leaned in and they began to negotiate.

"You give a woman a simple instruction," Davy began.

"Oh, for heaven's sake," Tilda said. "She knows what she's doing. Give her some space."

Colby was shaking his head, but he was also handing Nadine the blue bowl.

"Oh, that's great," Davy said. "Now we have a bowl and no—"

Then Nadine handed him the print, and he passed over the Scarlet.

"See?" Tilda said again. "I told you so."

Nadine bounced happily down the fairway, and Colby looked with satisfaction at his ticket to riches.

"Now what?" Tilda said.

"Now we meet Nadine at the car and go home," Davy said. "Although I would really like to do something else to Colby."

"I'm sure you'll think of something," Tilda said.

He looked at her to see if she was laughing at him, but she gazed back at him, completely serious. "You think?"

"I think Colby's dead meat," Tilda said. "And I think I don't ever want you coming after me."

"Wouldn't that depend on what I was after?" Davy said, grinning at her.

"You're hopeless," Tilda said and headed for the car.

"Got it," Nadine said, when she climbed into the back seat a minute later. "And look at this cool bowl."

"The next time I send you out to get something," Davy said sternly, as he pulled out of the parking lot, "do not improvise."

"Let me see," Tilda said, reaching over the seat to hand Nadine her hot dog. Nadine traded her for the bowl.

"I think it's pretty," Nadine said, unwrapping lunch. "It sat there in the middle of all that junk and glowed at me."

"You have to keep focused," Davy said. "Not that we're going to do this again, but—"

Tilda turned it over and looked at the bottom. "It's Rookwood. Way to go, Nadine."

"Oooh," Nadine said around her sandwich. "What's Rookwood?"

"Something good, I gather," Davy said, still disgruntled.

"Cincinnati art pottery," Tilda said, handing it back across the seat to Nadine. "Very collectable. The dumbass never even looked at the bottom to see the potter's mark. He knows zip about art."

"That I could have told you," Davy said. "He put a lot of emphasis on frames."

"Some frames can be worth a lot of money," Tilda said. "Especially if it's the original frame to a good piece of art."

"Which he doesn't have," Davy said.

"So how much is this Rookwood worth?" Nadine said, sticking to basics.

"It depends on the piece and the age," Tilda said. "There's a code on the bottom that tells what year it was made. The size and the shape affect value, too. And condition, but that one looks good."

"The older it is, the better?" Nadine said, squinting at the bottom.

"First condition," Tilda said. "Then age. Then the rest. When you're collecting something, condition is everything. It's like location in real estate."

"So how much?" Nadine said.

Tilda shrugged. "The mark's from 1914. Probably somewhere between five hundred and a couple thousand."

Davy almost drove off the road. "For a *bowl*?"

"Cool," Nadine said.

"For art," Tilda said. "For a thing of beauty that is a joy forever."

"The possibilities for graft in this business must be huge," Davy said, trying not to think about it. It was like discovering a great new sport and not being able to play. When he realized Tilda hadn't said anything, he added, "Because that would be terrible."

"I wouldn't know," Tilda said, turning to look out the window.

"That was a very good plan, Davy," Nadine said, clutching her bowl to the Britney on her T-shirt. "How did you know how to do that?"

"Good question," Tilda said, turning to squint at Davy through her glasses. "How *did* you know how to do that?"

"Read about it in a book," Davy said. "So now we have five, right? One to go?"

"Clea's." Tilda stripped off her wig and rubbed her forehead. "The final frontier."

"A week from tonight then," Davy said.

"We could do it earlier if we could get rid of the help," Tilda said. "Mason really wants to get into Gwennie's files."

"That's not all Mason wants to get into," Davy said.

"Let's hope Gwennie moves fast and Clea hasn't noticed."

"Mason wants Grandma?" Nadine said from the backseat.

"Grandma is hot, kid," Davy said. "Which is good news for you because it means you will be, too, when you hit fifty plus."

"That's eons from now," Nadine said, going back to her bowl.

"It comes faster than you think," Tilda said.

"It's good news for you, too, Celeste," Davy said.

"Not me," Tilda said. "I'm my dad's daughter. The Goodnight women are fierce but troll-like."

"Nope," Davy said, looking at her loopy curls and icy eyes. "You're Gwennie all over again."

"No I'm not," Tilda said, making it sound final.

"Right," Davy said. "So about next week. We go in and get your painting and my money, and then we go home and celebrate by making a killing at the preview. That's going to be pretty much a perfect day." He patted her knee. "I'm going to hate to leave."

"What preview?" Nadine said.

"Leave?" Tilda said, the lilt going out of her voice.

"I have to go to see my sister next weekend," Davy said, talking faster to get past the "and I'm not coming back" part. "She's mad as hell at me already, I can't put her off anymore."

"Right," Tilda said, nodding a little too fast.

"What preview?" Nadine said.

"We're going to sell the furniture in the basement," Tilda said to her.

"Cool," Nadine said. "Can I help?"

"Yes," Davy said. "I see you as essential."

"That's the way I've always seen me, too," Nadine said.

"So," Tilda said to Davy, "any instructions for next Thursday? Want me to be anybody in particular?"

"Yeah," Davy said. "Be Vilma and wear that slippery Chinese thing again. I have good memories of that."

"And they're going to stay memories," Tilda said, looking out the window.

"Slippery Chinese thing?" Nadine said.

"Your aunt is a woman of many faces," Davy said, watching Tilda out of the corner of his eye.

"So you're leaving after that?" Nadine said. "Australia, I suppose."

"Yep," Davy said, looking away from Tilda. "Australia."

TILDA PUT the painting down in the basement and didn't say anything else about the con, so Davy began to plan the show, enlisting everyone to scrape paint and wash windows, even Simon who had plenty of energy to work off since Louise hadn't shown up again. "Did you hear anything else about the Bureau looking around up here?" Davy asked him on Friday.

Simon shook his head. "But they definitely have somebody here."

This family needs a keeper, Davy thought and went

upstairs to shower. He came out of the bathroom, having washed off a lot of paint chips, and met Tilda.

"We're watching *The Lady Eye* tonight for the hundredth time," she said as she walked past him to the bathroom. "It's Louise's favorite movie. If you want to watch, too, you'd better call your sister now."

"Right." Davy watched the bathroom door close behind her, the FBI receding from his mind. A minute later the shower came on, and Davy thought about joining her. Then he thought about how much pain she could inflict on him and picked up the phone instead.

"Hey," he said when Sophie answered. "What's ne—"

"Where *are* you?" she exploded. "I can't believe you talked to Dillie and didn't—"

"Columbus," Davy said, moving the phone a little farther from his ear.

"—leave your num—*Columbus?* That's *two hours* from here."

"I know," Davy said. "Stop shrieking at me, woman. What's wrong with you?"

"I'm having the week from hell," Sophie snapped, "and the one person whom I would actually *welcome* seeing is two hours away and hasn't even bothered to stop by. How long have you been there?"

"About a week," Davy said, shaving some time off.

"*A week?*"

"Okay, you stop yelling now, or I'm hanging up. How's life?"

Sophie groaned. "Don't ask."

"Okay, how's Dempsey?"

"He's teething," Sophie said. "What are you doing in Columbus?"

"Nothing you want to know about. So what's new with you?"

"I thought you were going straight," Sophie said, caution making her voice soft again.

"I am," Davy said. "For me, I'm practically a Boy Scout. So what's making you nuts? Tell me everything."

"Well," Sophie said, mercifully distracted by her own problems. She talked on and Davy listened to the water running and thought about how round Tilda was, and how much fun she'd be covered in soap. Uncovered in soap.

"Are you listening?" Sophie said.

"Yes," Davy lied.

Sophie went on and Davy went back to listening to Tilda and the water. *Someday I'm going to be in there with her*, he thought, and then realized he wasn't. By the time someday got there, he'd be gone.

"Wait a minute," Sophie said, and the water stopped, so Davy brought his mind back to the conversation. "Dillie says hi and she loves you." Sophie dropped her voice. "She brought home this boy after school last week so he could help her with her softball swing—"

"Really," Davy said, trying to sound innocent.

"—and the kid has been over here every night after school, so—"

Sophie talked on as Tilda came out of the bathroom, swathed in a bulky white robe, and pulled the towel from her hair, and Davy watched the little ringlets spring up around her face, shining damply in the lamplight.

"—and I can't remember if Amy and I started doing boy-girl things at twelve. Did we?"

"I don't think that matters," Davy said. "The question is, do they do that now? Hold on a second." He covered the receiver. "When did Nadine start bringing home boys?"

"Birth." Tilda crawled up beside him on the bed. "She's Gwennie's granddaughter."

"Right. You're no help at all." He uncovered the receiver. "Look, they're playing softball. Let them alone."

"Who's there with you?" Sophie said. "Is it a woman? It's a woman, isn't it?"

"Is that your sister?" Tilda said.

"There's a woman there," Sophie said. "I can hear her."

"My landlady." Davy looked down the front of Tilda's robe. "She's asking for my rent. I have to go give it to her."

"You wish," Tilda said.

"*Wait*, don't hang up, when are you coming down here?" Sophie said.

"Next Sunday," Davy said, watching the curve of Tilda's terry-cloth-covered rear as she rolled off the bed away from him. "I have some things to finish here first. But I will be there next Sunday. I swear. I have a present for you."

"Forget the present, bring your landlady," Sophie said.

"I don't think so," Davy said, as Tilda disappeared into the bathroom again. "She's not a biddable female."

"I like that in a woman," Sophie said.

"So do I," Davy said. "So do I."

Chapter · Fourteen

*T*ILDA WENT DOWNSTAIRS THE NEXT MORNING TO FIND Davy standing across the street from the gallery. He looked wonderful in the sunlight, big and dependable and . . . leaving. Why should I care? Tilda thought, and cared.

"Now what?" she said when he motioned her across the street.

"Gwennie's been a little frosty to me lately," he said. "What's up with that?"

"She doesn't want to attach in case Ford kills you," Tilda said. "What are you doing out here?"

"She doesn't want this show, does she?" Davy said.

Tilda sighed. "Not particularly."

"Why? She hates the place, you'd think she'd be happy about—"

"She doesn't hate the place," Tilda said, surprised.

"—anything that would get her closer to freedom."

"Hey, this is her *home*," Tilda said.

"I think she wants to leave the nest," Davy said.

"Is this the boat thing?"

"Boat thing?"

"Never mind. Gwennie will get over it. What are you doing out here?"

Davy squinted at the storefront. "Do you remember what colors the gallery used to be? The kids did a good job of scraping, but they didn't uncover much original paint."

"Blue," Tilda said, squinting at the gallery front, too. "Sort of a midnight-blue trimmed with a red oxide. And the letters were gold, I think they were actually fake gold leaf."

"Sounds expensive," Davy said.

"It is," Tilda said. "Although not like real gold leaf. It's hard to put on, too."

"Too bad," Davy said. "Because we're going to have to do it."

"Can't we do something new?" Tilda said. "I thought maybe black and white—"

"No," Davy said. "Your dad had a reputation in this town and we're building on it. We're restoring, babe. Not to mention there's already enough white in your life."

"Funny," Tilda said. "Listen, I really—" but he'd already started across the street.

He dragged her to a paint store and they bought gallons, a soft white for the interior—"It's a gallery, Davy, it's supposed to be white"—and a light blue and green Tilda talked him into—"We're not selling what Dad would have so we should be us"—and gold leaf for the letters, along with brushes and scrapers and another ladder. "Who's paying for this?" Tilda said, and Davy said, "Simon, on loan. You can pay him back out of the till on opening night. Or you could have Louise stop by. That would cheer him up enormously." When they got back to the gallery, Nadine was inside with Gwen, Ethan, and a new boy, this one dressed in a button-down shirt and immaculate khakis.

"This is Kyle," Nadine said. "We met him working at his father's furniture store in Easton."

"Nice to meet you, Kyle," Tilda said, a little taken aback when he shook her hand. Behind him, Gwen rolled her eyes and went back to her Double-Crostic.

"My pleasure," Kyle said, every inch the gentleman. He turned back to Nadine. "I have to go to work, but I'll call you later." He kissed her on the cheek and nodded politely to Tilda and Davy. Ethan, he ignored.

"That kid is up to no good," Davy said when he was gone.

"Oh, *please*," Nadine said. "He was a perfect gentleman."

"What were you doing in a furniture store?" Tilda said.

"Davy sent us out to look at prices on handpainted stuff. And Kyle's father's store was the biggest." Nadine smiled at the memory.

"He's Eddie Haskell," Davy said. "Carry Mace."

Ethan nodded. "Don't get me wrong when I tell you that Kyle, while being a very nice guy, is the devil."

"What?" Tilda said.

"*Broadcast News*," Davy said. "Try to keep up."

"Cut me a break." Nadine picked up a scraper. "You

guys are worse than my dad." She went out the door and sat down in front of the gallery to finish scraping the front, the top of her curly blonde head just visible through the gallery window.

"And yet, we're right," Ethan said, picking up a scraper, too.

"Do the two of you have any particular knowledge of this kid you want to share?" Tilda said, as exasperated as Nadine. "Because he looked pretty boring to me."

"It's a façade," Davy said.

"He's evil," Ethan said.

"And the two of you are insane," Tilda said and went out front to help Nadine.

"Do you believe them?" Nadine said when Tilda was scraping beside her.

"I know," Tilda said. "The thing is, they're usually right."

"I know," Nadine said. "But his dad runs this huge furniture store, and Kyle really knows what he's doing. He's not fooling around."

"You're dating him for his furniture store?" Tilda said.

"He could teach me a lot," Nadine said. "I'm thinking about retail as a career."

"Nadine, it's not a good idea to date as a career move."

Nadine raised her eyebrows. "And you're not dating Davy to get your paintings back?"

"I'm not dating Davy at all."

"You're just sleeping with him."

"Only in the literal sense," Tilda said. "We're not lovers."

Nadine looked through the window at Davy. "Why not?"

Tilda followed her eyes to where Davy was looking at something in a newspaper Ethan was showing him. He looked sure and strong and hot.

And very Federal.

"I have my reasons," Tilda said.

Davy shook his head at Ethan, and they came out to the street to hand her a sheet of newspaper.

"I was spreading them out so we could paint inside," Ethan said to Tilda. "And that name jumped out."

He pointed to a want ad that said "Scarlet Hodge" in inch-high letters, and Tilda clutched it to look closer. "Wanted: any paintings by Scarlet Hodge," the copy underneath read and gave a phone number. Tilda looked up at Davy. "Mason?" The word came out on a wheeze.

"Or Clea." Davy pulled the top of the paper up so he could read the date. "It's Wednesday's paper. Thank God Colby doesn't read the want ads."

"I hope none of them do," Tilda said. "Or they're going to be really mad." She tried to pull air into her lungs but they were too tight, and when she felt in her pocket for her inhaler, it wasn't there. She drew in another shallow breath.

Davy took the paper from her, folded it up, and handed it back to Ethan. "That's all right. Somebody's always mad at me." He hauled her to her feet and turned her toward the door. "Go get your inhaler before you pass out. We're going to be fine."

"But—" Tilda began and then stopped. He'd said "we're." *We're* going to be fine.

"Miracle man," Davy said, pointing to himself. "Go breathe. We have work to do."

"Right," Tilda said and went to get her inhaler, feeling comforted.

BY THE next day, the outside of the gallery was scraped and ready to paint, the inside had a first coat on and no longer looked like a flophouse, and Davy was feeling not only a sense of accomplishment, but real anticipation. The place would be a gold mine for a gifted grifter; the possibilities were endless. And from what Gwen had told him about the art field, the possibilities weren't even illegal. It wasn't even a game of chance. It was like playing poker with the Goodnights.

"So there's a poker game tonight," Simon said, coming into the gallery and interrupting his thoughts.

"Yes," Davy said. "Every Sunday. And except for Tilda, they're all terrible players. Try not to take their money."

"Why, so you can?" Simon said. "Doesn't matter. I'm just in it for Louise."

"It's Sunday night," Davy said. "Louise is gone on Sundays."

"No, she's staying over," Simon said, smiling.

"She showed up last night, huh?" Davy said.

"Congratulations. I've never seen you wait around for a woman before. This must be the one."

"Not even close," Simon said. "She's skilled, but—"

"Not somebody you'd want to marry?" Davy said. "Imagine my surprise."

"I'm never getting married," Simon said. "I'm a cad, remember?"

"As are we all," Davy said, watching the gallery door open.

It was Kyle, looking very natty in a shirt and jacket, come to pick up Nadine.

"Kyle," Davy said genially, thinking, *This kid is definitely up to no good.* "Date tonight?"

Kyle nodded. "Nadine wants to see the store after business hours," he said, smiling a little. "She wants to see everything."

"She's very career oriented," Davy said, disliking Kyle even more. He'd seen that smile before. In his mirror.

A few moments later, Andrew and Jeff came in from the street, carrying grocery bags.

"Sunday-night-poker food," Jeff said cheerfully. "It's the only reason I play the game."

Andrew slowed as he saw Kyle. "You're here to pick up Nadine?"

"Yes, sir." Kyle stuck out his hand like a gentleman. "I'm Kyle Winstock. Of Winstock Furniture."

Andrew shook it, looking deeply suspicious. "I'll tell Nadine you're here."

"Thank you, sir," Kyle said, his smile fading. He

looked around at the four of them and added, "I'll wait outside."

When he was gone, the four men looked at each other.

"Doughnut," Davy said.

"Absolute doughnut," Jeff said.

"My daughter has an affinity for doughnuts," Andrew said.

"What?" Simon said.

"Two kinds of men in the world," Davy told him. "Good guys and the guys who are only after one thing. Good guys are muffins and—"

"He's a doughnut," Simon said.

"Is Mace illegal?" Andrew said. "I know Gwennie keeps some behind the counter."

"Why don't we just talk to Nadine?" Jeff said, once again the voice of reason.

"You go," Davy said. "We'll wait here."

When they were gone, Simon said, "Nadine is not the person I'd converse with on this."

"Shall we?" Davy gestured to the street where Kyle waited.

"After you," Simon said and followed him out.

"Kyle, old boy," Simon said when they were outside, and Kyle turned around, his face a polite mask. "A word with you."

"Yes, sir?" Kyle smiled at them, citizen of the year.

"About Nadine," Davy said. "Make a move and we'll break all your fingers."

Kyle's smile froze in place.

"You see, Kyle," Simon said, still affable, "we know you."

"Hell, Kyle," Davy said, "we *are* you."

"And we care deeply for Nadine's health and happiness," Simon went on. "We are, if you will, honorary uncles."

"With police records," Davy added helpfully.

"Uh," Kyle said.

"So we wanted your assurances," Simon said, "that Nadine will have a pleasant evening."

"That won't involve her Macing you," Davy said.

"Because we would take it amiss." Simon smiled at him.

"Which is where the broken fingers would come in." Davy smiled, too.

"Uh," Kyle said again, and Nadine came out of the gallery.

"I'm ready," she said brightly, looking like a present waiting to be unwrapped.

"Touch her and die," Davy said to Kyle softly.

"Great," Kyle said, looking from Davy to Simon and back.

Nadine looked at them, too, suspicion dawning in her eyes. She took Kyle's arm and said, "I forgot to tell you, do not talk to these guys."

"Uh-huh," Kyle said and let her steer him toward his car, casting one wary look back over his shoulder as they went.

"I feel fairly good about that," Simon said.

"Me, too," Davy said. "We've got an hour before poker. How about a drink?"

"After you, old boy," Simon said, opening the door. "Are you really going to break his fingers?"

"Nah, I'll let Nadine do it," Davy said, seeing Tilda through the office door. "These Goodnight women are nobody to mess with."

THAT NIGHT the poker game got two new players: Louise and Ford. Ford was exactly the poker player that Davy had figured him for—alert, smart, and ruthless—but he sat down at the table with a handicap: Gwennie. His concentration was fine until she'd move or speak and then, for a moment, he'd be gone. Davy was torn between interest in the situation in general and concern for Gwen in particular. He didn't know who Ford was, but he was certain he wasn't a fuzzy bunny.

Of course, neither was Gwennie, all appearances to the contrary. There were those teeth, for example.

Louise provided the other wrinkle. She distracted Simon so Davy had no competition there—Simon would have gratefully turned over his entire wallet if he could have gotten her upstairs immediately—but something about her was bothering everybody else, too, except for Jeff. Davy was developing a fine appreciation for Jeff; he was like the control in an experimental group of reality-challenged divas. Louise was also distracted, much more interested in Simon than she was in her cards, and the result was that after four hands, Davy was annoyed. He didn't mind winning if there was some skill involved, but with all the tension at the table, he could have just reached over and taken their money and they wouldn't have noticed. Even Tilda, he noted with disgust. They were starting their fifth hand, and he was about ready to quit and go play pool when Nadine came in, her face stormy. Davy tried to look innocent, but Nadine honed in on him with eyes like blue-white lasers. It was like having Tilda mad at him. He felt right at home.

"You're back early," Andrew said as he dealt the cards.

Gwennie reached up and patted Nadine as she came to stand beside her. "Didn't it go well, honey?"

"It would have gone better," Nadine said, staring at Davy, "if somebody hadn't threatened my date."

Gwen looked at Ford, who looked back at her, calm as ever, while Davy ignored Nadine to pick up his cards. A queen, a nine, a six with a four and a deuce showing. Garbage.

"Davy?" Tilda said from beside him.

"Not my bet," Davy said. "Gwennie's up."

"*About the date*," Louise said, turning to look at Simon. "Which one of you—"

"They both did," Nadine said, transferring her scowl from Davy to Simon and back to Davy. "They said they'd beat him up."

"*Davy*," Tilda said.

Davy put his cards down. "We did not say we'd beat

him up. Exactly. And it was necessary. That kid was up to no good."

"No doubt about it," Simon said.

"Bring home a good one," Davy said to Nadine, "and we won't interfere."

"I get to decide who the good ones are," Nadine said.

"I don't think so," Davy said. "You picked out Burton and Kyle."

"Daddy," Nadine said. "Talk to them."

Andrew lifted his chin. "Nadine is allowed to date whomever she wants as long as he's not over eighteen and doesn't have a police record."

Ouch, Davy thought, watching Simon try not to flinch. Ford remained impassive.

"And we never interfere in her life because we trust her and admire her," Andrew said.

Nadine nodded.

"Except for this time because that kid really was up to no good." Andrew stuck his thumb up. "Way to go, guys."

"Thank you," Davy said. "We're playing poker, Nadine. It's a game of chance, much like the way you date. Go get your piggy bank."

"Wait a minute," Louise said, sounding fiercely maternal, "is this a Poor Baby?" and Nadine shook her head.

"They're right," she said, pulling over a chair. "He was awful about music. He'd never heard of Dusty Springfield, if you can believe it."

"Told you," Davy said to Tilda.

"*Could we play poker?*" Simon said, and the rest of the table turned to look at him.

"In a hurry, old boy?" Davy said. "Just shove your money across the table to me. That's where it's going anyway."

"First, you promise never to do that again," Nadine said to him. "To my dates, I mean."

"What good would promising do?" Davy said. "I lie. You in this game or not?"

"I'm in," Nadine said.

Davy threw his cards in the middle. "Redeal, Andrew. Your daughter wants in so she can give me her allowance."

Andrew gathered up the cards again. "And you had a lousy hand."

"That, too," Davy said.

"So did I," Andrew said. "Toss your cards in, ladies and gentlemen. It's a new deal."

"That also is not fair," Tilda said, but she gave Andrew her cards.

"Of course not, honey," Davy said, rubbing her shoulder. "You're playing with me."

Andrew dealt again and Davy watched them all pick up their cards, more from force of habit than from any real interest. He was going to win anyway unless Nadine decided to take her vengeance with cards and even then—

Across from him, Louise tapped her finger on one of her cards three times and sighed.

Davy put his cards down and stared.

"What?" Eve said to him from behind Louise's contacts.

"I'm out," Davy said, standing up. "And so is Tilda."

"What?" Tilda said. "Hey I—"

"*Now*, Betty," Davy said. "Say good night to the family."

Tilda looked up at him. "Good night," she said to her staring family, and he led her through the door and up the four flights of stairs to her room.

"About Louise," he said when the door was closed behind them.

"Oh, for heaven's sake," Tilda said. "That's what this is about? Look, I know she's practically devouring Simon at the table, but she's perfectly sane, she won't jump him. There's no reason—"

"Louise is perfectly Eve," Davy said. " 'It's the same dame.' "

Tilda went still.

"That's a movie quote," Davy said.

"I know it's a—"

"From *The Lady Eve*," Davy said. "Louise's favorite movie. How dumb am I?"

Tilda's crazy blue eyes widened as she looked up at him, and he thought, *Here comes a lie*.

"I don't know what you're talking about," she said. "Eve's at a class. Meeting. Thing."

"When will you learn?" Davy said. "You do many things well, Matilda, but you cannot lie to me. Give it up."

"No, really," Tilda said.

"No, really," Davy said. "Face it, once somebody's on to it, she can't pull it off anymore. It's a miracle she's managed it this long."

Tilda sighed. "Well, she only had to fool you and Simon," she said, letting her eyes go back to normal. "She kept Louise away from you and Eve away from Simon and neither one of you was paying much attention."

"Simon is not going to be happy about this."

"You can't tell him," Tilda said, sounding shocked. "It's none of your business."

"Well, *somebody's* got to tell him," Davy said.

"Why?" Tilda said, and Davy didn't have an answer. "Look, once Simon finds out she's Eve, it's over for them. Eve is real, not Louise. They can't exist in the same world. Plus Simon has that stupid mother rule. How does he think women *become* mothers?"

Davy sat down on the bed. "Okay, I'm not used to being the voice of sanity in the room, so bear with me here, but has it occurred to you that Eve might need some therapy?"

"No," Tilda said. "Eve knows perfectly well who she is. She's a single mother who's helping to keep a roof over her family's head while dealing with the fact that the great love of her life is living with another guy. Eve can't do the things that Louise does because Eve has to be practical. But four nights a week, Louise does the Double Take and for those nights, Eve is free." She frowned. "Which means she should be gone because it's Sunday. It's driving us all crazy. She's breaking her own rules."

"It's not healthy," Davy said. "Maybe this should be group therapy. Family rates."

"You're overreacting." Tilda sat down beside him. "Look, did you ever go to Mardi Gras?"

"Yeah," Davy said cautiously.

"Well, Eve has her own Mardi Gras Thursday through Sunday. She just does a better mask than most."

"Doesn't she ever get confused?"

"No. People think that wearing masks makes them different, but what happens is they become the people they were meant to be. Without the mask, they're Eves, doing the right thing, sacrificing for others. With the masks they're Louises, completely themselves, without guilt. They can do anything. It's that transformation thing." She smiled slightly, her lips curving like a wistful secret, and Davy sucked in his breath and wanted her more than he thought possible.

"Tell me you have a Louise," he said, "because I would *really* like to buy her a drink."

"Very funny," Tilda said, looking away. "I don't do that."

"That's what I was afraid of," Davy said. "Does Nadine know?"

"Of course Nadine knows," Tilda said. "Everybody knows. Except you and Simon."

"And Nadine is all right with it?"

"Why not?" Tilda said. "Louise isn't a drug addict or

a drunk or a child abuser. She's just another set of clothes."

"That sleeps with Simon."

Tilda shrugged. "Well, as Gwennie always says, if you can't be a good example, you'll just have to be a horrible warning."

"Ah," Davy said. "The Michael Dempsey School of Parenting. I'm going to tell Simon."

"You think he's going to thank you?" Tilda said, sounding exasperated.

"I don't—"

"You think he's going to say, 'Thanks, buddy, for screwing me out of the best sex of my life?'"

"That's not—"

"Face it," Tilda said. "You want to tell him because it's the right thing for you to do, not the right thing for him to hear."

Davy frowned at her. "So I'm a selfish bastard for wanting to do the right thing?"

"Yes," Tilda said.

"I know that's wrong." Davy stood up. "Let me get back to you on why."

"Well, until then, keep your mouth shut," Tilda said. "You honest people can make life hell for everybody else."

ON MONDAY morning, having finally accepted that the gallery was going to be restored whether she helped or not, Gwen moved the stepladder to the side wall and climbed up, determined to hammer that damn piece of ceiling tin back into place once and for all. Of course the ceilings had to be a mile high. Tony had explained to her that it was because the artwork had to breathe. Well, the damn artwork should have put the ceiling back then. She climbed up as high as she could go, held the hammer by the very end, and took a whack at it, but she overbalanced and dropped the hammer, grabbing the ladder at the last minute and swinging her weight to the left to stop it from toppling. When she had her breath back, she realized she hadn't heard the hammer hit the floor and looked down.

Ford was standing there, holding it with one of those this-woman-is-a-moron looks on his face.

"I wanted to do it myself, okay?" Gwen said, not in the mood to be condescended to.

"Why?" Ford said.

"Because I've been staring at it for years, and it's been sneering back at me, and I wanted to put it in its place."

"So order me to do it," Ford said.

"Not the same thing," Gwen said.

"It's all you've got," Ford said. "Take it or leave it."

"I'm leaving it," Gwen said. "Give me that damn hammer."

"No."

"It's my hammer."

"Not anymore," Ford said.

"It's so unlike you to be playful," Gwen snarled. "Give me that hammer."

"I'm not playful," Ford said. "I'm preventing injury

and possible death. You almost killed me with this thing. Get your ass off the ladder."

"You weren't supposed to be standing there," Gwen said, and then she frowned at him. "Why were you standing there?"

"You're making a lot of noise," Ford said. "I thought you might need help."

"I need no help."

He sighed. "Get off the ladder, Gwen. Let me look at the ceiling and see what it needs."

"It needs to get whacked," Gwen said viciously, and then remembered what he did for a living.

"Get down," Ford said, and unable to think of any way to take back the "whacked," Gwen climbed down.

He climbed back up, tall enough that he could touch the ceiling. "It needs a nail," he said as he climbed back down. "The old one fell out. Whacking it will not help."

"Good to know," Gwen said brightly.

"Where are your nails?"

"Nails?" Gwen said.

"Where's Davy?"

"Out front."

"Good," he said. "Go do something that does not require tools."

"Hey," she said, but he was already heading out the door to Davy. "And what makes you think that Davy has nails?" she said to him through the plate glass, only to see Davy reach in his shirt pocket and hand over something that looked like nails.

Sometimes, she purely hated men.

Ford came back in, climbed the ladder, tacked the ceiling back up with two precision taps, climbed back down, folded the ladder and carried it to the back.

"For all you know, I still need that ladder," Gwen called after him.

"Not after your last performance," Ford said, coming back out of the office. "What else has to be done?"

"Nothing," Gwen said, moving in front of the cracked side window.

"Got a tape measure?" Ford said.

"Why?"

"So I can measure that window."

"We have somebody coming in to do that," Gwen lied.

"Give me the damn tape measure, Gwen," Ford said, and Gwen gave up and went in the office for the measure.

"I don't see why you're doing this," she said when she'd handed it to him.

"It's a nice building," Ford said, stringing out the measure. "I like seeing things put right."

"You do?" Gwen said, trying to square that with the hit man thing.

"That's my game. Write down twenty-seven and a half inches."

Gwen went for paper and wrote it down. When she went back to him she said, "Your game is remodeling old buildings?"

"By thirty-two and a quarter," Ford said, retracting

the tape. "No, my game is restoring justice to the world." He handed her the tape.

"Oh," Gwen said. "Justice."

"And order," Ford said. "Where's the nearest glass place?"

"Glass place?" Gwen said.

"Where's your telephone book?" Ford said, with infinite patience.

"I'm not an idiot, you know," Gwen said.

"I know."

"This isn't my idea, all of this."

"I know."

"I'm not even sure I want this," Gwen said.

Ford sat down on the edge of the table. "So why are you letting them do it?"

"We need the money," Gwen said, looking around. "And the place really is shabby. And Tilda wants it. Tilda's the one who gets things done around here."

"Why don't you leave?" Ford said, and Gwen jerked her head back to look at him.

"Leave?"

"Take a vacation," Ford said.

"A vacation." Gwen looked at him, stumped. "Where would I go?"

"The Caribbean," Ford said. "Aruba. Scuba diving."

"I don't know how to scuba dive."

"I'll teach you," he said, and Gwen lost her breath. "This is my last job," he went on. "I'm retiring and heading south for good. Taking the boat to Aruba. You could come along."

"Scuba diving," Gwen said, grabbing onto something concrete. "Isn't that dangerous? Don't people die?"

"People die in their beds, Gwen," Ford said. "Doesn't mean they don't hit the sheets." He stood up. "It's a big boat. Plenty of room. I'll get your window glass."

"Thank you," Gwen said, still a little breathless, and when he was out the door, she sat down at the counter, looked at the nine brightly colored umbrellas in her pencil cup, and thought, *I want to go.*

Well, that was ridiculous. She couldn't leave the family, and she'd never had the slightest desire to scuba dive, and the only thing she knew about Ford was that he was a hired killer who brought her piña coladas and fixed her ceiling. Of course, he was retiring, and she was all for forgiveness and forgetting the past, especially if it was her past, but if his last job was going to be killing Davy, that would pretty much be her sticking point.

Tilda came in carrying a can of blue paint, her hair standing up all over her head in little curls. "Are you okay?" she said. "You look sort of poleaxed."

"I'm fine," Gwen said. "Stop running your fingers through your hair. You look wild." Tilda patted her hair, which did nothing, and Gwen said, "Do you ever think about staying home and taking over the gallery?"

"No." Tilda squinted at her reflection in the office window and patted her hair again.

"Okay," Gwen said, feeling hugely disappointed even though she'd known that was what was coming.

"Because I've got at least another decade of murals to finish first. Do you want me to?"

"No," Gwen said. "But I didn't want to stand in your way."

"Nobody stands in my way," Tilda said and carried the paint can out through the office.

I should be like that, Gwen thought, and imagined announcing to Ford, "Nobody stands in my way." Although why it had to be Ford was a mystery. She should say it to Mason. "Mason, you're a nice person, but I don't want you to run the gallery." Although if he'd get them out of debt, the whole family would be free. He could have the gallery if he'd get them out of debt. At this point, he could have *her* if he'd get them out of debt.

Davy came in from the street, whistling, and went into the office.

Of course, that would mean she'd never scuba dive. But the family would be safe.

That was the problem. Once you'd given birth, you never really thought "I" or "me" again. It was always "we." What's best for "us." Even though what's best for "us" was often lousy for "me." She had two beautiful children and an equally beautiful grandchild, all of whom were fairly happy and healthy and who loved and supported each other. She didn't have to go to a horrible job every day, she could work Double-Crostics whenever she wanted, and nobody ever said, "Gwennie, don't do that." At least not for the past five years anyway. It was all good.

Well, mostly good. While it was true that Tony had been domineering, there'd also been some very nice things about him. Like sex, for example. That was a loss. She'd been okay with celibacy, but then it had started raining men at the Goodnights' and suddenly she was getting a lot of lunches. And piña coladas. Maybe she should think about it, make a plan. She was only fifty-three. Mason was clearly interested, a good steady man who understood finance and loved the gallery. Really, it was a no-brainer. She closed her eyes and tried to seriously imagine a life with Mason.

Scuba diving, she thought, and her mind washed through with blue-green water and bright-colored fish, like one of Homer's paintings, only real, with sun on her face, and the water flowing over her body, and Ford—

Oh, for heaven's sake, she thought and got up to move the chairs into the office. She could sweep the floor. That didn't involve tools. Or a great deal of thought.

Tilda came out of the office with a paintbrush. "You okay?"

"Fine," Gwen said. "Couldn't be better."

"Davy wants to paint the front today." Tilda nodded her head back at the office where Davy was now looking doubtfully into an open paint can, Nadine frowning over his shoulder. "We might have to block off the entrance."

"And that would be a problem because so many people come in?" Gwen said. "I don't—"

The street door to the gallery opened, and an older man with dark red hair and darker eyes came in, something about him very familiar. "Hello?" Gwen said, trying to place him.

"Hello, darling," the man said, and Gwen had one horrible moment when she thought he might have been somebody she'd slept with before Tony and had now completely forgotten. He was somewhere between fifty and eighty, so the age range was right.

"Do I know you?" Gwen said, fingers crossed that she didn't.

"Call me Michael, love," he said, so innocently her eyes narrowed. "I'm looking for Davy Dempsey. Tall boy, dark hair. Is he here?"

"Davy?" Tilda said, surprised. "He's back—" She stopped because the man smiled at her warmly and detoured around her to open the office door. "Uh, wait—"

Inside the office, Davy looked up and froze, and Gwen thought, *It can't be another hit man. How many people hate this guy?*

"I should have known," the man said to Davy, his voice light. "Me on the road, running for my life, and you here with a daisy hand."

"Daisy hand?" Gwen said.

"Three queens," Davy said grimly. "Hello, Dad."

CHAPTER · FIFTEEN

"*How* the hell did you find me?" Davy said, when he was staring at Michael across the table in Simon's room. It seemed odd that there was nothing on the table. He kept expecting Michael to pull out a deck and start dealing.

"That friend of yours, Simon," Michael said. "I called him in Miami a couple of weeks ago, looking for you."

"And he gave me up," Davy said, planning on having a talk with Simon later.

"It took some persuading," Michael said.

Davy sighed. It was Michael. Simon hadn't had a chance.

"And then it took me a while to get here," Michael went on. "I had commitments. And Greyhound is not the Concorde."

"You took the *bus*?" Davy said, dumbfounded. "That's not like you."

"I am temporarily embarrassed of funds," Michael said, with the ghost of a grin.

"I would gladly pay you Thursday for a hamburger today! My father, Wimpy."

"I have to keep a low profile," Michael said. "There appears to be a warrant out for me."

"That also is not like you." Davy sat back, unconcerned. "You usually don't get caught."

"There was a woman," Michael said darkly.

"There always is."

Michael grinned at him. "You should talk. I walk in and find you with three. You're me all over again, boy."

"I am *nothing* like you," Davy said.

Michael laughed. "You're right, you're nothing like me, you *are* me. Of all my children, Davy boy, you're my heir."

"Oh, good. I've always wanted to own two decks of marked cards and a pennywhistle."

"Now, Sophie," Michael went on as if he hadn't heard, "she had the skill, right from the beginning. She could look at you with those big brown eyes and take you for everything you had. But she didn't have the heart for it."

"She has morals," Davy said, thinking, *And because of that, she's a soft touch, which you know all too well.*

"And little Amy, she loved it, but she didn't have the skill. Too scatterbrained. But you, you were born for this. You have the skill and the heart, you have it all, you could be greater than I am—"

"Oh, spare me," Davy said, fed up. "Look at you, the Great One. On the lam at sixty, scamming for quarters, playing monte for motel money, that's your idea of greatness?"

"It's action, isn't it?" Michael said. "That's what Nick the Greek said."

"Yeah, that's what Nick the Greek said when he was washed up, playing two-bit poker instead of high-roller," Davy snapped. "That's what he said before he died broke. Is that how you want to live?"

"It's *living*." Michael leaned forward. "It's not sitting around wishing you were living and denying what you were born for. It's not shilling for the freaking FBI." He shook his head at Davy. "You miss it. Don't tell me you don't. What are you doing for the kick these days, Davy my lad? Picking daisies?"

"Okay," Davy said. "Back off on the Goodnights. And in Gwen's case that means literally. She's got a steady guy with money who's getting serious. Stay away."

"Ah, that's not for her," Michael said. "Women like Gwen Goodnight do not go for steady men."

"She deserves somebody she can count on," Davy said. "That is not you."

"She deserves a damn good time," Michael said. "That's most definitely me. Besides, she can't count on anybody. Nobody can. You're born alone and you die alone, Davy. So you better know yourself, because you're the only one who ever will."

"I know myself," Davy said grimly, "and I'm happy."

"After all I've taught you," Michael said sadly. "How many times did I tell you, the guy to beat at the table is the one who doesn't know what makes him weak and what makes him strong. And now look at you, pretending you're someone else, shirking your gift." He shook his head. "Good thing for you I showed up."

"Oh, yeah," Davy said. "We're all thrilled when you show up. I have news for you. I'm not playing the game anymore, and neither are Sophie and Amy."

"Then you're not living," Michael said. "I'd worry, but I know you too well. You'll be back. You need the edge."

"Did you come here for a specific reason?" Davy said. "Or just to piss me off?"

"I'm on my way to see my grandson," Michael said, settling back.

Davy thought of the hell Michael could make for Sophie, her peace shattered, her reputation ruined in a small town that never forgot anything, not to mention the monetary damage he could do when he sang his song to her. "No you are not."

"A man is entitled to see his grandson," Michael said, expanding a little. "Sophie would want me there. I hear she named him after me."

"She named him Dempsey, which is not specifically you. And you are staying out of her way, the same way I do. She has a good, law-abiding life and she doesn't need us screwing it up for her." He stood up. "The fun's over. You're leaving now."

"I thought we'd both go," Michael said, not getting up. "This weekend. Family reunion. You could keep me in line." He smiled at Davy cheerfully. Too cheerfully.

"You don't know where she is," Davy said, relaxing.

"Of course I do," Michael said. "She's here in Ohio."

"It's a big state," Davy said. "You wouldn't think so, but it is. Have a nice time searching it."

"I'll find out," Michael said. "Good God, boy, it's not like I mean her harm. I love her. She's her mother all over again. And she has my first grandchild. I want to see the boy, see the men my girls married."

He said it with such sincerity that Davy was impressed. "You lie through your teeth and you make it sound like 'Danny Boy.' I'm amazed they ever got enough on you to arrest you."

"Technically they didn't," Michael said. "It was a bum rap. And I'm telling the truth. I want to see this boy."

"This boy was born a year ago." Davy folded his arms and stared down at his father grimly. "Your girls were married three years ago. You're looking for cold cash, a warm bed, and a hot meal in a place the law won't find you, and once you get there you'll scam somebody, and it's a little town and everybody will know, and Sophie will be humiliated. And here's some news that may not have trickled down: Amy married a cop. I know this guy. He is not sentimental. He will not think you're a colorful old grandpa. If there's a warrant out for you, he will can your ass without blinking."

"You have such a cynical view of human nature," Michael said thoughtfully.

"Gee, wonder why," Davy said, feeling like a thirteen-year-old even as he said it.

"It was that woman," Michael said. "I warned you about her."

"What woman?" Davy said, legitimately confused.

"That Cleopatra blonde," Michael said. "That one you had in L.A. She had you so roped you couldn't have scammed a Sunday school. She was the worst thing for you. She made you bitter."

"Oh, I don't know," Davy said, surveying him. "There've been darker influences."

"Where is she now?" Michael said. "Still married to that anchor guy she dumped you for?"

"No," Davy said. "She killed him. Then she married somebody else and killed him, too."

"I'm not surprised," Michael said. "So where is she now?"

"Here," Davy said. "Stalking her third."

"I knew it." Michael sat back. "You're still chasing her."

"No," Davy said. "I'm chasing my money. She has it."

"That was careless of you," Michael said. "Leave her alone. Make some more."

"I'd rather get my old stake back, thanks," Davy said. "It's—"

"You know, this place is not bad." Michael looked around the room. "That gallery, it's a sweet setup. You could do some damage here."

"No," Davy said, trying to forget that he'd thought the same thing. "This is legit. And the Goodnights are another family you will not be ruining."

"So what are you doing here?" Michael said.

"They're my way to Clea," Davy said. "She needs them, and I can use them to get to her."

"That's my boy," Michael said. "So which one are you spending nights with? The kid's too young, and Gwennie's keeping company with a steady guy. That leaves the brunette with the glasses." He nodded. "Not bad. My guess is, she's not stupid and she won't fold in a pinch. Nice ass, too."

"I've never liked you," Davy said.

Michael's shoulders shook, which for him was roaring laughter. "I missed you, boy."

"I didn't miss you." Davy walked over to the door and opened it. "And now you're leaving."

"I don't think so," Michael said, looking around. "This is a nice room."

"It's Simon's," Davy said. "And he makes full use of it."

"So where are you sleeping?" Michael got up, and then nodded. "Right. With the glasses. And Gwennie has a stable guy."

"Which means there's no room in the inn." Davy pointed to the hall. "Out."

Michael ambled toward the door. "I think we should go next weekend," he said as he passed Davy. "I think—"

Across the hall, Dorcas opened her door. "I'm *painting* over here," she said, fixing Davy with her glare.

"An artist," Michael said, shaking his head at her in admiration. "And we broke your concentration. A thousand apologies."

"One's enough," Dorcas said. "That and shutting up."

"The artistic temperament," Michael said. "Fascinating. Could I see your work?"

Dorcas blinked at him.

"Dorcas, this is my father," Davy said. "He's a liar, a cheat, and a seducer of women, and he's looking for a place to stay. Avoid him at all costs."

"Michael Dempsey," Michael said, taking her hand. "Dorcas. Lovely name. It means 'lily' in Gaelic."

"It means "gazelle" in Greek," Dorcas said, but she didn't take her hand back, and Davy thought there might actually be color in her cheeks. She nodded toward Davy. "Is he telling the truth about you?"

"Sadly, yes," Michael said, smiling at her. "I am completely without redeeming value."

Dorcas smiled back at him.

"But I really would like to see your work," Michael went on. "I rarely meet artists and never artists at work. May I?"

And while Davy watched with a sinking heart, Dorcas said, "Yes."

"Don't do it, Dorcas," he said.

"Oh, please," Dorcas said. "Like you're a prize." Then she stepped back and let Michael in.

"Jesus," Davy said and went downstairs to warn the Goodnights about his father.

DAVY SPENT the rest of the week painting and hauling furniture and watching Michael with an eagle eye while Nadine and Ethan followed his every order. Gwen planned the details of the opening with skill if not pleasure, and made sure that the advertising was in place and that there would be a reporter to cover the preview. Simon worked on the security, still missing Louise, and on Tuesday, part of his wardrobe. "Your dad borrowed a shirt from me," he said. "Evidently neither one of you knows how to pack."

And Tilda came in after work on her mural and painted with Davy, saying, "You know, I never get enough of painting walls."

"You don't have to do this," Davy said. "You worked all day."

"It's the least I can do for you," Tilda said. "You're working your butt off for us."

"Actually, the least you could do for me," Davy began and then stopped when Tilda looked at him over her glasses. He did not want to hear about her damn vibrator again. "Never mind."

Tilda nodded and went back to painting. "I can't believe your dad moved in with Dorcas an hour after he got here."

"Yes. I know. He is without morals."

"But he's efficient," Tilda said. "It took you a good twenty-four hours to get into my bed."

"Hey," Davy said. "If I'd wanted in earlier—"

Tilda looked at him over the tops of her glasses again.

"Right," he said and kept painting.

Eve and Jeff and Andrew ran errands and did odd jobs and generally oiled the wheels, while Ford pitched in whenever they needed a repair that required actual skill, especially if it meant sharing space with Gwen. Even Mason showed up to monitor the action, so happy about the opening that he cheered everybody else up, with the possible exception of Ford. They were a team, albeit a strange one.

Michael was another matter. When Davy caught him playing monte outside a local high school, he dragged him off, threatened him with death, and gave him a job of his own to do.

"Where's Michael?" Tilda said when she got home from mural painting on Wednesday.

"Don't go looking for trouble," Davy said.

"I like him," Tilda said. "I wouldn't give him money, but I like him. What did you do with him?"

"Two birds with one stone," Davy said. "I told him about Colby."

"And?"

"And he took him for a quick five thousand this morning," Davy said. "He's dropping off half of it at Mrs. Brenner's as we speak."

"Five thousand *dollars*?" Tilda said.

"The old man is good," Davy said, trying not to feel proud.

"What is it he does again?" Tilda said.

"Sales," Davy said.

"Right. You really think he's going to give the money to Mrs. Brenner?"

"Half of it," Davy said. "He'll do it. He has a strong sense of justice. Just no morals."

"How you managed to turn out so honest . . ." Tilda's voice trailed off as she shook her head.

"It's a miracle," Davy said and went to work on the outside of the gallery before God struck him dead.

After that, since he had a stake, Michael stayed home with Dorcas and kept finding his way down to the gallery, and Davy kept an exasperated eye on him, as did Ford, every time Michael went near Gwen.

"That Ford is no fool," Davy told Gwen on the day of the preview showing. "I like him, even if he is going to kill me."

"Don't joke," Gwen said. "It's too upsetting."

"I was kidding. He's not going to kill me," Davy said, patting her shoulder.

"You don't know that," Gwen said.

"Sure I do," Davy said. "If he was going to do it, he'd have done it by now."

"Then why is he still here?" Gwen said, and Davy grinned at her. "Me? But he's a hit man."

"I've heard they're a hot date," Davy said. "You know, guys who are bent go the extra mile."

"Speaking of which," Gwen said, "your father borrowed a twenty from me."

"Oh, hell," Davy said, and reached for his wallet.

"And then he brought me back fifty," Gwen said. "He said he'd been playing pool and it was my cut."

"Oh," Davy said. "He didn't stick it in your T-shirt, did he?"

"Of course not," Gwen said. "He's a gentleman."

"Right," Davy said, and went back to the office to plan the next night's heist.

Later that day, when Gwen had gone out to lunch with Mason, Davy saw Nadine out at the gallery counter, with three cards spread in front of her, laughing at Ethan.

"What the hell?" he said and went out. "What are you doing, young lady?"

"Your dad taught me this cool game," Nadine said, flipping three cards down in front of him on the counter. "Here's the queen—"

"Nadine," Davy said, "I told you to stay away from my father. The only way to win at three-card monte is to cheat. That's bad."

"I wouldn't play for money," Nadine said, trying to sound shocked and half-succeeding.

No wonder Dad taught her to play, Davy thought. *She's a natural.* "Forget it."

"I love it," Nadine said. "It's a sure thing."

"There are no sure things."

"Oh, yeah?" Nadine said. "You can't beat me."

Davy took a five out of his pocket and slapped it on the table. "Where's yours?"

Nadine held out her hand to Ethan, and he sighed and dug a five out of his pocket and handed it to her. "You'll get it back, Ethan," she said.

"No you won't, Ethan," Davy said. "Deal 'em." He watched her shuffle the cards, show him the queen, and then palm it while she moved the rest around. For only having practiced a couple of hours, she was damn good.

"Okay," Nadine said, still moving cards. "Now, where's the queen?"

"Right here," Davy said, putting his finger on the middle card.

"Well, let's look and see," Nadine said, smug with her queen up her sleeve.

"Let's," Davy said, keeping his finger on the middle card. He turned over the eight of clubs to the right and the four of spades to the left. "Will you look at that? Neither one is the queen, so it must be the middle one." He took the two fives on the table.

"That's not fair," Nadine said, looking outraged.

Davy took his hand off the card and grabbed her wrist. "Neither is this," he said, sliding the queen out of her sleeve and flipping it at her. "Don't let me catch you pulling this on anybody ever again."

"Can I practice it on Ethan?" Nadine said.

"You're screwing Ethan over enough," Davy said. "You don't need to take him at cards, too. Put the last coat of paint on the door instead."

"I'm really tired of painting," Nadine said dangerously.

" 'We keep you alive to serve this ship,' " Davy said to her. " 'Row well and live.' "

Ben Hur," Ethan said, evidently not too perturbed about being screwed over.

"Honestly," Nadine said, and stuffed the cards in her pocket.

Davy went back into the office and found Tilda watching through the door. "Your niece has a real knack for crime."

"And yet I feel certain that you also can play that game," Tilda said.

"Can," Davy said. "I don't."

"So law-abiding," Tilda said. "Such an example to us all."

"Now about this burglary tomorrow night," Davy said. "Definitely wear that Chinese thing. I like it."

Michael was nowhere to be found that evening, but the next night, on his way to meet Tilda for one last theft, Davy knocked on Dorcas's door. When Michael answered, Davy said, "Do not teach Nadine con games."

"You've got to teach them when they're young," Michael said. "That's another reason I have to go see Sophie. Dempsey's a little underage yet, but doesn't Sophie have a stepdaughter?"

"Dillie," Davy said. "You will not be teaching her to con."

"Why not?"

"Because . . ." Davy stopped, remembering Dillie's practice swing. "You just won't."

"Already taught her, huh?" Michael clapped him on the shoulder. "That's my boy."

"I really wish you weren't here," Davy said. "I'm going straight, damn it."

"Nice black shirt," Michael said. "Robbing somebody?"

Davy closed his eyes and went down the stairs.

*

THE GALLERY looked beautiful and Gwen hated it.

She looked at her watch to check the time. Ten minutes to the preview. Maybe if she threw up on the cash register, they'd let her go upstairs and do a Double-Crostic.

Then she kicked herself. The entire family had worked their fingers to the bone for this place and it gleamed now, filled with the color and fun in Tilda's furniture and a beautiful buffet that Thomas the Caterer had laid out, and they were going to make money, and she was whining because she wanted to be scuba diving. No, that wasn't right. She wanted to go upstairs and pull the covers over her head.

"Mrs. Goodnight?" Thomas said, and Gwen looked up startled.

"Oh, Thomas, I'm sorry," she said, trying not to stare at the two yellowing bruises on his forehead. "The buffet looks wonderful. You—"

"Could I talk to you for a moment?" he said, putting his hand on her arm, and Gwen was so startled, she let him draw her into the office. He took out a leather case and showed her a badge. "Thomas Lewis, FBI."

Gwen squinted at it. "You're FBI?"

"Shhh." Thomas looked around. "I'm here undercover, Mrs. Goodnight, *no one* can know. Can you keep a secret?"

Oh, honey, Gwen thought.

"I'm investigating Clea Lewis," he told her, keeping one eye on the door. "We think she murdered her husband."

"Oh." That actually sounded plausible.

"And stole his art collection," Thomas went on. "Cyril Lewis was a very wealthy man, but when he died, the estate was bankrupt."

"Well, Clea's not cheap," Gwen said. "Maybe they just spent it."

"They did," Thomas said. "On paintings. Cyril Lewis bought over two million dollars' worth of paintings in the last year of his life."

"Wow," Gwen said, calculating the commissions.

"They were stored in a warehouse," Thomas said. "But it burned to the ground the day before Cyril Lewis died."

He was beginning to sound like a bad radio play. "And you think Clea killed him?"

"He wouldn't be the first husband she killed," Thomas said. "We could never get any evidence on her, but her first husband died under very suspicious circumstances. She's a vicious woman. We have every reason to believe she's put a contract killer in this very building."

"Really," Gwen said, trying to sound surprised.

"We think she's trying to kill an ex-lover," Thomas said.

"*Really,*" Gwen said, not faking anymore. "Huh." She wondered if Tilda knew. Probably. Tilda didn't miss much.

"The reason I'm talking to you," Thomas said, "is that she's showing a lot of interest in your gallery."

"Not really," Gwen said. "She's—"

"If she tries to sell you the paintings," Thomas said, "we'd like to know about it."

"I don't buy paintings," Gwen said. "Galleries take artwork on commission. We don't buy anything."

"If she talks to you about paintings at all," Thomas said, "we want to know."

"We."

"The Bureau."

"Right." The Bureau. "Well, I'll certainly keep you informed," Gwen said, thinking, *If you're FBI and Ford's the bad guy, this country is in trouble.* Hell, if he was the law and *Clea* was the bad guy, they were in trouble. "Have you been working for the Bureau long?"

"No," Thomas said, straightening. "But I'm fully qualified."

"Good," Gwen said, getting to her real concern. "Can you cater, too?"

"I buy the food from restaurants," Thomas said, a little shamefaced. "It gives me time to investigate the case."

"Oh, excellent," Gwen said, brightening. "Restaurants."

"Don't tell anyone."

"Not a soul," Gwen said.

"And keep your eyes open for those paintings," Thomas said as he opened the door to the gallery.

"Story of my life," Gwen said, and went back to the gallery as the first customer opened the door.

*

HALF AN hour later, Tilda watched the gallery from the office, feeling odd, as if she were watching an old movie. She'd stared at a hundred previews like this, some so long ago she'd had to stand on a footstool to see through the window in the door. There was something wrong this time, and it took her a minute to realize that there was nobody out there being a ringleader, nobody standing in the middle of the room laughing and directing the show.

Then Mason made his entrance wearing a brocade vest, Clea on his arm looking magnificent in a black halter dress cut to her waist and huge gold hoop earrings. Mason moved to the center of the room, laughing and gesturing like a parody of Tilda's father, and she thought, *Poor guy. He just doesn't get it.*

Davy came in from the hall. "And Vilma's wearing her Chinese jacket. Must be time to steal something and neck in a closet."

"Mason and Clea are here," she told him.

"Then we're gone." Davy picked up Jeff's keys, glanced through the office door, and said, "Whoa."

"What?" Tilda followed his eyes back into the gallery.

Clea had turned around. Her dress had no back. As they watched, she turned to smile up at Mason, her perfect profile overshadowed only by her equally perfect bustline.

"Oh," Tilda said, trying to keep the snarl out of her voice.

"Back off, Veronica." Davy grinned down at her.

"I'm just enjoying the scenery. I know she's a hag from hell."

"Yes, but she was good in bed, wasn't she?" Tilda said, watching Clea walk across the floor, every movement liquid with grace. *I don't like you.* "Better than me."

"Yes," Davy said. "Can we go?"

"*Lots* better than me?" Tilda said.

Davy closed his eyes. "Why do you ask this stuff? You know it's going to be bad."

"Tell me," Tilda said.

Davy sighed and looked out at the gallery. "You see the stuff you painted? How every move you made painting it was just right because you worked really hard at it and because you have a genius for it?"

"Thank you," Tilda said, touched in spite of herself.

"Clea fucks like you paint."

"Oh," Tilda said.

"If it's any consolation, she probably paints like you—"

"You're never touching me again," Tilda said.

"Oh, and there was a chance I was going to *before* I said that?" Davy said. "Can we go now?"

"Absolutely," Tilda said, trying to remember what was important. She was getting the painting back. Davy would get his money back. Then the show would be over and he'd go to Australia and she'd go back to her nice, calm mural-painting life.

"Now what's wrong?" Davy said.

"You know, I was *happy* before you came here," Tilda said and headed for the door.

"No you weren't," Davy said, following her. "You—"

Ethan came in carrying Steve, who was wearing a brocade vest and a black bowtie and looking a little perturbed about the whole thing. "Nadine made the vest," he said. "She said it was a gallery-opening tradition."

"That should perk Mason right up," Tilda said. "Don't bite anybody, Steve."

"You leaving now?" Ethan said.

"Yes," Davy said. "We're—"

"Well, 'have fun stormin' da castle,' " Ethan said and carried Steve out into the gallery.

Davy looked at Tilda. "Does everyone know we're committing a crime tonight?"

"Jeff doesn't," Tilda said. "We try to keep him pure for the defense."

"Good to know," Davy said and went out to the parking lot. "You should have lights out here," he told her when they were in the car.

"We should have the money to put in lights out here," Tilda said. "Let me get Simon paid off for the gallery paint first. And, oh yeah, the mortgage."

"Right," Davy said. "This is the perfect life I screwed up?"

"I know." Tilda let her head fall back on the seat. "Not your fault. Except it is."

"I did not—"

"Before you came, I didn't know I was unhappy,"

Tilda said. "I just put my head down and kept moving. And then you grab me in a closet and, all of a sudden, I notice that I'm miserable painting murals and lousy in bed."

" 'Lousy' was your word, not mine," Davy said. "And I'm willing to coach you on that."

She rolled her head to look at him. "I was not happy about you fixing up the gallery."

"I know," Davy said.

"I am now. It's beautiful, it's actually more beautiful than I remember it. And seeing all that stuff I painted in there makes me want to paint again, for real. It makes me *happy*. And when you're gone, that'll be gone, too, because we can't keep it going, we don't have the time and we don't have the . . ." She waved her hand. "The razzle-dazzle. That was my dad. And Gwennie'll go back to the Double-Crostics, and Nadine'll go back to dating careers, and I'll go back to painting murals. So thank you for giving me back the gallery, but you're ruining my life."

"I know," Davy said.

She frowned at him. "You do not know."

"Yeah, I do," Davy said. "I know you're a great painter, I know you hate painting the murals, I know you love your family, I know you're really mad at your dad for something, and I know that the gallery is where you belong. I know you."

Tilda lost her breath. "Not as much as you think," she said, looking out the window. "Shouldn't we be moving or something?"

"Yes." Davy started the car. "There will be closets, Vilma. Control yourself."

"There is one thing," Tilda said.

"What now?" Davy said, sounding wary.

"If something goes wrong tonight," Tilda said, "I'm staying. No more me leaving you to carry the can, no more you shoving me out the door. Tonight, we're in this together."

Davy was quiet for a minute. "Okay."

"I don't want to do this," Tilda said. "But I don't want you doing it, either."

"I know," Davy said. "But tonight is the last time. It's all over tonight."

"I know." Tilda looked out the window again. "Let's go."

BACK AT the gallery, Gwen was watching Mason and thinking, *He's such a sweet man. Maybe I can have Ford kill him.* No, that wasn't funny, but it would have been nice if somebody knocked him cold because he was single-handedly screwing up her gallery preview. And as much as she hadn't wanted it, if she had to have it, she wanted it to be a success.

She watched him now, telling some bewildered woman that buying a chest of drawers painted with tangerine-colored zebras was a good investment. "Art appreciates," he said, and Gwen went around the counter and took his arm.

"Mason, honey," she said.

"I think I'll wait on that," the woman said, backing away. "Can I pet the dog?"

"Of course!" Gwen said cheerfully.

Mason shook his head. "That dog is going to ruin the whole thing," he whispered to Gwen. "Can't we get it out of here? Nobody will take us seriously with it around."

We're selling furniture with orange zebras on it, Gwen thought. "The thing is," she told him, "this furniture is not an investment. You buy this kind of art because you love it, not because it appreciates."

He looked at her fondly and patted her arm. "You leave this to me, Gwennie. I know what I'm doing."

No you don't, Gwen thought, but he wasn't harassing that poor woman about the zebras anymore, so she went back to the counter.

At the back of the gallery, Michael was laughing with a woman who was holding a Finster but looking at Michael. Miraculously, the man had sold three Finsters since the doors had opened. *Maybe we should keep him around to run the place,* Gwen thought, and then thought, *No.* Michael would sell everything they had including Steve and then leave with the money. Sweet man, but completely immoral.

Across the room, Nadine was smiling and laughing, too, and selling furniture, and for a moment, Gwen could see Tony in her, or at least his charm. Then the woman Nadine was laughing with came over and paid a hundred dollars for a footstool painted with dancing cats and Gwen thought, *She got his gift for selling damn near anything, too.*

She smiled at the woman and took her money and looked around for Mason. He was talking to a graying man in a suit about a table covered in red beagles. Gwen could have sworn she heard him say "investment" clear across the room.

It was going to be a long night. *My gallery for a piña colada*, she thought, and went to rescue another customer.

THE BASEMENT window was still broken so Tilda and Davy got in without a problem, and it was like old times, climbing the stair to Clea's closet in the dark.

"Very nostalgic," Davy said, echoing Tilda's thoughts. "Go on upstairs to the room with the paintings and find your Scarlet. I'll hit Clea's bedroom for the laptop."

"Okay." Tilda looked up the next dark staircase with no enthusiasm whatsoever.

"Unless you want to search the closet with me," Davy said. "That's always interesting for us."

"Upstairs it is," Tilda said, and spent the next hour on the next floor with a penlight, flipping through dozens of wrapped paintings looking for eighteen-inch-square paintings or something that might be an eighteen-inch square framed. Some of the paintings had been clumsily unwrapped, and she gave in to curiosity and looked. There were some nice pieces, but nothing startling. As a collector, Mason didn't have much flair, which was pretty much in line with the rest of Mason, poor man. Maybe Gwennie could liven him up some.

She found the last square painting, carefully unwrapped a corner of it, and saw a checkered night sky, but not one of hers. *What the hell?* she thought and unwrapped it completely. It was eighteen inches square with a blue checked sky, but it was a forest scene, and she'd never painted a forest. She moved the penlight to the corner to make out the name, printed in block letters in the lower right corner: Hodge.

Huh, she thought. *Homer. I never saw this one.* She'd forgotten that she'd copied the checkerboard skies from Homer, maybe because she'd liked doing them. Well, that made sense. She was a forger. She moved the penlight over the painting to see what else she might have copied. The trees certainly weren't anything she'd have done, but in between the trunks were little animals, and she'd always liked painting animals, although not like these, they were too small and they had . . .

Tiny sharp white teeth.

CHAPTER · SIXTEEN

"OH, GOD," TILDA SAID, AND SAT DOWN ON THE FLOOR. It couldn't be. It was a coincidence. Maybe Gwennie had gotten the idea for the teeth from Homer. Except that Gwennie had been embroidering teeth long before Homer showed up. Now we're going to have to steal back all the Homers, she thought and then realized the impossibility of it. Homer had painted dozens and dozens of paintings. No, Gwennie had painted dozens and dozens. Some were in museums. There was no way she could get them all back.

Gwennie was Homer. That was enough of a mind-bender right there, even without the museums. Tilda shoved herself up off the floor and rewrapped the painting to take it with her. One floor down, she found Davy waiting for her. "I couldn't find—" she began and then she saw what he was holding, a package about twenty inches square.

"This it?" he whispered, handing it to her. "Believe it or not it was actually in her closet this time."

She pulled the painting out of the frame-store package by its cheap new frame and saw the Goodnight building. "This is it," she said, sadness seeping into her bones. The first Scarlet, the start of the whole mess. Except not, because there was Gwennie.

"Are you okay?" Davy whispered.

She stuffed the painting back into the box before Davy noticed that Scarlet had painted the gallery building. "Boy, what a relief," she whispered, trying to fake happiness. "I can't thank you enough. And now you've got your money and you can go." When he didn't say anything, she said, "You did get your money, didn't you?"

He looked down at her, his face hard to read in the dark hall. "No. I'll have to think of something else."

"I'm sorry," she said, meaning it. "I'll help you. Whatever it takes."

"Good," Davy said. "What's in the other package?"

"A souvenir for Gwennie," Tilda said. "Let's go home."

WHEN THEY got back to the gallery, Davy carried the wrapped Scarlet into the office behind Tilda. He wasn't sure what was wrong with her, but something had happened, and it wasn't good. It had to be the painting she was carrying, another wrapped square, so maybe she'd found a seventh Scarlet, maybe there were more to steal. Maybe it wasn't time for him to go yet.

That was not as annoying as it should have been.

Tilda went out to Gwennie, and across the room, Nadine saw Davy and waved. He motioned her over.

"Did you get the painting?" she said when she came in. "Is that it?"

"Yes," Davy said, watching Tilda. "I need your laptop."

"Okay." Nadine ran upstairs and came back with her computer.

"Get me on-line," Davy said.

Nadine plugged in the phone line and tapped a few keys. "Anything else?"

"Nope," Davy said, sitting down. "How's it going out there?"

"Your dad is amazing," Nadine said. "Mason is a horse's ass."

"I'll help tomorrow night," Davy said. "I lied, there is one more thing. Where does Gwennie keep the bankbooks?"

"What are you doing?"

"Embezzling your college fund."

"Right," Nadine said. "Like I have one. They're in the top left-hand drawer."

"Thank you. Go play." When the door closed behind her, Davy logged on to his account and looked at the balance. Two point five million, a nice round number. There had been a little more in Clea's account but he liked round numbers.

For some reason, this one wasn't much fun. Not as much fun as being without had been. *Some people aren't meant to be rich,* he thought. *Some people need the edge.*

And some people need college funds.

He grinned to himself and began to move money.

"HOW'S IT going?" Tilda said to Gwen when she'd finished selling a chair covered in ducks to a woman who seemed thrilled with it.

"Except for Mason, pretty well," Gwen said. "We're not mobbed but . . ." Her voice trailed off as she saw the painting Tilda held up. "Where'd you get that?"

"Mason's storeroom," Tilda said. "Look familiar?"

"Of course," Gwen said. "It's a Homer Hodge."

"No, it's a Gwen Goodnight," Tilda said.

"No," Gwen said. "I painted the kits. Homer painted those."

"Gwennie, I know . . ." Tilda said and then stopped as light dawned. "Oh, hell, Homer was your Louise."

"Not really, dear," Gwen said. "Homer never had sex."

"Davy was right," Tilda said. "Group therapy. Now."

"He was like the Double-Crostics," Gwen said. "A different place to go, away from reality. And then I got tired of him, and I quit."

"Dad must have been upset."

"Yes," Gwen said, smiling.

"You didn't tell me," Tilda said. "You let me move out thinking Homer was real."

"I wasn't too proud of him," Gwen said. "It was those damn paint-by-numbers. Once I started to mess with them, Tony decided I was a great primitive painter, but that wasn't enough, he had to be Brigido Lara and create his own art dynasty. He kept saying it would be Grandpa Moses and he'd have exclusive rights." She sighed. "He wouldn't even let Homer be female, damn him."

"What happened?" Tilda said. "He told me that he and Homer had a fight."

"They did," Gwen said. "He came up with the child-of-Homer idea, and I could see him roping you into the fraud, too, and he was already making your life miserable with that damn Goodnight legacy. I kept saying, 'Why can't we just tell people the truth?' and he'd say, 'Because the truth won't make us rich, Gwennie.' He was getting damn good money for those Homers, but it wasn't enough. He had to have Scarlets, too."

"So you stopped and I started," Tilda said. "That's why he told me not to tell you."

"I didn't know until you left," Gwen said. "I didn't know until I went downstairs and saw that last smeared painting. He signed that one for you, you know. He sold it anyway."

"I can't believe you never told me you were Homer. You sent me money so I didn't have to come back home, but you never told me you were Homer."

"I wasn't," Gwen said. "He was just a mask. Bad drag, as Andrew would say. He didn't fit very well. I'm just not male."

"Yeah, but that's not why you didn't tell me. You knew I'd stay if I knew. I'd have gone on painting the Scarlets if I'd known you'd painted the Homers."

"Don't give me more credit than I deserve," Gwen said. "I didn't protect you. You painted those beautiful paintings and he made you put somebody else's name on them and I didn't see it, I didn't stop him. Just another part of the Goodnight nightmare."

"It's not all a nightmare," Tilda said.

Gwen lifted her chin. "Are you going to teach your children to paint?"

"Yes," Tilda said. "But I'm not going to teach them to forge. That's done. That ended with me."

"So you're leaving again," Gwen said.

"No," Tilda said. "I'm staying. That's one of the many things Davy has done for me. He gave me back the gallery. We can do some good things here. And I want to start painting again, my paintings. I'm going to try to get more mural commissions close to home. I want to stay home."

"I don't," Gwen said. "I want to leave."

"Oh," Tilda said. "Okay."

"I've been here for thirty-five years," Gwen said.

"Definitely time to leave."

"I'll come back."

"It's okay, Mama," Tilda said. "It really is."

"I don't know where I'm going, of course," Gwen said.

"I think it's someplace with a boat."

"The boat's like Homer," Gwen said, turning away. "Not real. This is real." She smiled at a woman who was approaching with a painting, and Tilda widened her eyes, when she saw what it was.

"We're selling *Finsters*?" she said to Gwen.

"Michael's selling Finsters," Gwen said. "I'm just taking the money. Those Dempseys can sell anything."

"Right," Tilda said. Davy had her Scarlet somewhere. "We'll talk about this tomorrow."

"Oh, let's not," Gwen said, and rang up the Finster.

DAVY CROSSED the wide, white echoing space of the half empty storeroom, feeling pretty damn good about the world in general. He flipped back the quilt on the Temptation Bed. Five paintings, the sixth one in his hand, finally together again. He took the one he had out of the box and leaned it against the wall, and propped the other five up beside it, one long row of Scarlet Hodges. Then he stepped back.

Cows, flowers, butterflies, mermaids, dancers, and the new one, the apartment building in the city. He looked again and realized that the paintings fit together in sequence, the cows flowing into the flowers that blew into the butterflies. The only one out of place was the city, that belonged at the beginning, and when he picked it up to move it, he looked at it closer.

It was the Goodnight building. All the furniture that he'd been hauling for the past week came back to him, and all the joy and light in them now before him in the Scarlet paintings.

"You are *kidding* me," he said and put it down at the beginning of the sequence, watching the progression from city to country to sea to night sky, and wondering how in hell he had missed it before that Tilda had painted them.

He sat down on the bed and thought, *She's a crook and a liar and she's played me for two solid weeks. Jesus.*

He'd never wanted her more.

He heard her step on the stair and sat back on the bed waiting for her, and when she came through the doorway, wearing that beat-up Chinese jacket, her eyes pale behind her bug glasses, her curls standing up like little horns, she took his breath away.

Then she caught sight of the paintings, all lined up in a row.

"Hello, Scarlet," he said.

UPSTAIRS, CLEA was having a miserable time.

First, Mason was not paying any attention to her. He was wearing that ridiculous blue brocade vest that she'd hunted all over Columbus to find for him, and he was acting like a circus ringmaster. He'd even bought her an ugly chair painted with sunflowers and birds, and what the hell was she supposed to do with *that*? She was ready to put up with a lot from the men who married her, but she did expect some dignity. Cyril had had dignity, she thought now with regret. If only he'd had money, too, he would have been the perfect husband.

Plus Thomas the Caterer was acting strangely. He kept glaring at her across the canapés. He'd never been friendly, but that was okay, he was the help. Maybe he had indigestion; the buffet was a little greasy. Maybe he had a headache; those bruises didn't look good. Maybe she didn't care, she just really wished he'd stop giving her the evil eye. It was distracting.

And then Ronald had shown up and tried to take her arm. Honest to God, men. She'd whispered, "Not here," to him and shot a glance at Mason, but fortunately he'd been all caught up in his own circus and wasn't paying any attention to her.

"I found out something about the gallery," Ronald whispered to her, and she let him steer her toward the canapés.

"There's something funny about the Scarlet Hodge paintings," Ronald told her when he had a plate full of finger food. "It isn't just that somebody's buying them, it's that there's no information on them at all. One newspaper article and then nothing. Tony Goodnight sold them off and never mentioned her again."

"She died," Clea said, exasperated with him.

"No death certificate," Ronald said, and bit into a shrimp.

"So?" Clea caught Thomas glaring at her again and said, *"Stop that,"* to him. When he'd smoothed his face out again, she turned back to Ronald. "That's it?"

"If there's no death certificate," Ronald said, "she didn't die."

"Maybe she died someplace else," Clea said. "Maybe—"

"I don't think she exists," Ronald said. "These shrimp things are really—"

"What do you mean," Clea said, "she doesn't exist?"

"No birth certificate, either. Not for Homer or Scarlet."

"Who's Homer?" Clea said, losing patience.

"Scarlet's father," Ronald said. "The Goodnight Gallery made a killing with Homer, but then they stopped and switched to Scarlet and then they stopped that. And the gallery pretty much went downhill from there. You were right, there's something going on here."

"There is?" Clea looked at him with complete approval for the first time since he'd stolen her money back. "Ronald, you are wonderful." Ronald flushed and forgot the shrimp. "Clea, I—"

She pressed his arm. "Find out what you can and come see me tomorrow morning at ten." She looked up at him under her lashes. "In my bedroom."

"Right," Ronald said, almost dropping his plate. "I'll get right on it. I—"

He kept talking but Clea looked past him and saw Mason with Gwen again.

"I have to go talk to people, Ronald," she said, patting him on the arm. "I'll see you tomorrow."

"*Clea,*" he said, sounding angry, but that was his problem. She drifted toward Mason, a smile plastered on her face. He was going to propose by the weekend, or she was going to take steps. And if this damn gallery got in her way, well, she'd take it down with whatever Ronald was digging up.

And she'd take Gwen Goodnight down with it.

DAVY WATCHED as Tilda stayed frozen in the doorway, staring at him.

"Figured it out, did you?" she said finally, sounding grim.

"I can't believe I didn't see it earlier," Davy said, hoping to make her smile. "I was really thick. It was obvious."

"It is now," Tilda said. "It's like Louise. Once you know the truth, it's always obvious." She sounded miserable, which was a lousy aphrodisiac.

He patted the bed beside him. "Stop looking like death and come here."

Tilda sighed and crossed the room to sit beside him. She held up her wrists. "Okay. Put me in jail."

Davy stared at her wrists, distracted. "If that's for handcuffs, thank you, I'll run right out and get some, but jail is not where I'll be taking you."

Tilda shook her head. "I know you have some. Your cover's blown, too. Simon told Louise you work for the FBI."

Davy closed his eyes and thought about strangling Simon.

She let her hands drop. "And I brought you here. That's how good I am. I brought the Feds to my own crime scene."

Davy took a deep breath. "Could that *possibly* have been the reason you've been saying no to me for the past two weeks?"

"Well, it didn't help," Tilda said. "I kept thinking I'd say something and you'd—"

"Do what? Arrest you on the spot? Coitus apprehendus? I'm going to *kill* Simon."

"You don't know how long I've been carrying this secret," Tilda said, looking at the Scarlets.

"Sure I do. Seventeen years." Davy shook his head. "Look, you can relax. Louise got it wrong. We are not Feds. They wouldn't have us as a gift. Every now and then they call and ask for some input, but we are not agents. We don't arrest people. Your secret is safe."

She swallowed. "Oh. So, to review here, just to make this perfectly clear, you're not going to bust me."

"First of all, I couldn't," Davy said. "I told you, I'm not an agent. Second, nobody's filed a complaint, so you're not wanted for anything." He looked at her jacket. "Well, you're not wanted by the law. Third, I'm not even sure you broke the law because I'm not sure that painting the Scarlets was a scam. Unless you know something I don't."

Tilda sighed.

"And even if you do," he added hastily, "I don't care. Fourth, I want you naked. And I figure I've got a fighting chance if you're relieved and grateful, and your vibrator is five flights up."

"You want me?" Tilda said.

"Hell, yes," Davy said. "I crave your crooked mouth."

She looked at him, dumbfounded. "I thought you'd never *speak* to me again."

Davy snorted. "Not a possibility. Take off your clothes, and I'll recite limericks if you want."

She put her hand on his arm and looked at him, immorality flickering in her weird blue eyes, and then she smiled that bent smile at him, the one that made him dizzy, and he lost his breath.

"You don't care that I'm a forger," she said, looking like crime made flesh.

"Honey, for the first thirty years of my life, I scammed everything that moved. Where do you think the FBI found me? Church?"

"You're twisted, too."

"Like a pretzel."

"So I can confess to anything and you won't—"

"Matilda," Davy said as her nefarious little art-forging hand warmed his shirtsleeve and his blood. "Tell me you have the Hope diamond stashed behind the jukebox, and I will fuck your brains out."

"Oh," Tilda said. "The Hope diamond is not behind the jukebox."

"That's what I figured." Davy sighed and took her hand, separating her slender cool fingers with his. "I can't believe you thought I'd bust you, Scarlet."

"It would have been fair," Tilda said. "I lied to you."

"No," Davy said. "It wouldn't have been. That's not us." She was quiet after that for so long that he ducked his head to look into her eyes. "What's wrong?"

"Us," she said, sounding a little breathless. "Oh. Well, there is one other thing."

Davy closed his eyes and laughed. "Of course there is. Let me have it, Scarlet. Then we'll go fix it."

"The Hope diamond."

Davy turned and saw her smile widen.

"It's behind the vodka."

He blinked at her, not sure he'd heard her right.

"It's hard to see because it's the same color as the vodka, and of course it's dark in the cupboard, but—" Her smile quirked a little. "It's there. Kiss me."

Davy's brain shorted out, and he lunged for her mouth, shuddering when her tongue touched his. She wrapped her arms around him and fell back on the bed, taking him with her, laughing against his mouth.

"*I can't believe this!*" She stretched her arms over her head. "You *know*. I'm *free!*"

"Oh, good." He slid a shaking hand under her jacket. "Anything I can do to help? Please?"

She wrapped her arms around him again, smiling at him. "You already did, Ralph, you hero, you. God, I feel *wonderful*. No more secrets." She looked around the half empty white basement. "At least no more secrets from you." She kissed him hard, her body sliding against his, and he held on as she began to unbutton his shirt. "I can tell you anything. *Anything.*"

"God, yes," he said, trying not to lose his mind as her fingers moved against his chest. Every cell in his body screamed, *Take her*, but he held back, wanting to make sure, wanting this time to be the time he got it right.

"I forged my first painting at twelve," she said, still trying to unbutton his shirt. "What is wrong with this shirt?"

He pulled it over his head and then sucked in his breath as she licked his chest. "Keep talking," he said as he started on the slippery knots of her jacket. This time they'd both get it right.

"My dad sold a Monet I faked when I was fifteen." She yanked her jacket over her head before he could start the next knot. "Your turn."

"I played three-card monte in Bible School." He stripped her T-shirt off, leaving her in her black bra, looking rounder than he'd remembered and hotter than he could believe.

"More," she said.

"When the teacher caught me, I told her I was doing it for the Lord and she gave me a gold star." He stared at her as she rose up to meet him, all black lace and round flesh, but she caught his hand as he reached for her.

"Con me," she said.

"I'll respect you in the morning."

She laughed, and he leaned in, but she pulled back. "*Con me.*"

Right. The con. First the smile, then the "yes."

He kissed her on the neck and then bit her softly where he'd kissed her, and she caught her breath. "More?" he whispered, and she said, "*Yes.*"

He bit harder, and she trembled under him, digging her fingers into his shoulders. *I want you now*, he thought, but she wanted conned. What was next? *Think*. Right, make her feel superior. He looked down at her beautiful crooked face and thought, *God knows, you are*. "I can't believe the way you played me," he said. "You're incredible."

She melted against him, breathing deeper, and he curved his hand around the firm heat of her breast and felt her tighten as she gasped. "Asthma?" he said, not sure, and she said, "*You*," and stretched against him. Lust rolled over him and blanked out everything but her.

"That's it?" Tilda said, her voice soft in his ear as he pulled her close. "That's the con?"

He smelled the cinnamon in her hair as he kissed her shoulder. Her fingers trailed down his chest, and he shook his head to clear it. *Come on*, he told himself. Smile, yes, superior . . . "I can't remember the rest," he told her. "You're ruining me, Scarlet."

She glowed with heat under him. "Ask me for what you want, but make me think you're doing me a favor."

"Right," Davy said. "Thank God you listen at doors."

She ran her hand down his stomach, and he lost his place in the conversation again.

"So what are you going to do for me, Ralph?" she whispered.

"Celeste," he said, searching desperately for something good, *anything* good.

"Yes, Ralph?" She kissed him, and he was lost in her heat again, and then she slid her hand lower and inspiration hit Davy everywhere.

He pulled back a little and looked down at her sternly. "Celeste, for your own good . . ."

She smiled that crooked grin at him, and the room grew hazy.

"Out of the kindness of my heart—"

She pressed closer, that lush mouth just millimeters from his.

"—I'm going to cure you of your vibrator addiction."

"*Save me*," Tilda said, and Davy moved to take her mouth and everything else she had.

UPSTAIRS, GWEN watched Clea try to collect Mason. The preview still had some time to run, but things were winding down. Nadine looked tired but happy, which wasn't surprising since she'd worked nonstop all night. Even Steve looked fairly content, stretched out on the snake armchair, waiting for another stranger to come by and pet him. Louise was safely back at the club, singing with Andrew. Tilda had her last Scarlet back.

Everybody's safe, she thought. *It's a good night.*

So why did she feel like smacking somebody with a blue armadillo footstool?

"This was so cool," Nadine said, coming up to her, Steve now in her arms. "I'd be bummed it's over, but we get to do it again tomorrow night."

"Yeah, lucky us," Gwen said. "How's Steve?"

"He *loved* it," Nadine said. "People kept coming up and petting him and calling him 'Steve Goodnight' and telling him he was a good dog and the *Dispatch* took his picture. He was born to be a gallery dog, weren't you, puppy?"

Steve looked up at her, patient as ever.

"And he didn't bite anybody," Nadine said. "He didn't even try to hump Ariadne when Dorcas brought her down. They sat in that armchair together and looked so cute. Except when Ariadne would swat him. And even then he just sat there."

"Good boy, Steve," Gwen said, and Steve sighed.

"I'm going to take him out before I put him upstairs. Do you know where Aunt Tilda is?"

"She's back," Gwen said. "She must be in bed by now."

The gallery door opened and Mason came back in, looking a little flustered. "Could I talk to you, Gwennie?"

"Of course," Gwen said, and thought, *Please let me get out of here soon.*

Nadine rolled her eyes behind Mason's back and took Steve out through the office.

Mason nodded at her. "She's a good girl. She was a little pushy tonight, I thought."

She made tonight, Gwen thought, and said, "She's a Goodnight. They don't hold back."

"I had a wonderful time," Mason said.

"Good," Gwen said, trying to be nice. Mason was sweet.

"I'd like to have a lot more wonderful times," Mason said, clumsily taking Gwen's hand across the counter.

"Oh," Gwen said.

"I love this place," Mason said. "And tonight I knew this is where I belong. Let me take Tony's place and take care of you."

"Oh," Gwen said again. "Well, I'm all right. I have family."

"That's not the same." Mason leaned closer. "Let me into your life, Gwennie. You'll never have to worry about money again, I swear."

"Uh," Gwen said, looking around. "Where's Clea?"

"In the car," Mason said. "That's over, there really wasn't ever much there. After her husband died, I took her out a couple of times just to be kind. I didn't mean for it to—"

"Mason," Gwen said, taking a step back. "You don't have to tell me this."

"Yes I do," Mason said. "I want you to understand, it was just that somehow we ended up together."

"Look, Mason," Gwen said.

"But she's not you," Mason said. "In fact, I'm beginning to think she's not even what I thought she was. I think she may have killed Cyril."

"Really," Gwen said, thinking Clea needed to do some PR fast.

"Look, I know Clea doesn't make me look good," Mason said. "I know I'm not Tony."

Gwen sighed. "Actually, that's not a drawback."

He leaned closer and kissed her.

It was a perfectly good kiss, and she was so surprised, she kissed him back because she hadn't done it in a while. It was nice, and she thought, *It's been too long since I did this.*

He leaned back and smiled at her, sweet as ever, and said, "I've been wanting to do that for weeks," and she thought, *He's not Tony*, but Tony had been a doughnut and look where that had gotten her, and Ford was a hit man—no more doughnuts, no more doughnuts—and she said, "Well, do it again," and kissed him back.

Muffins, she thought. *Better than passion. Really.*

When he left reluctantly, promising to see her tomorrow, Nadine came back in. "That man *kissed* you," she said.

"Yes, he did," Gwen said. "He wants to help us run the gallery." *And some other things, too.*

"No," Nadine said, with great conviction, as Ethan came to stand in the office doorway.

"What?" Gwen said.

"No. We run the gallery. No outsiders. This is family."

Gwen blinked at her, amazed by her fierceness. "You let Ethan help."

"Ethan is family," Nadine said, and Ethan looked as though he wasn't quite sure what to do with that. "He's like Davy."

"Davy?" Gwen shook her head. "Honey, Davy's leaving any day now."

"Nope," Nadine said. "He's going to stay and marry Aunt Tilda, and they're going to run the gallery until I get out of college. Then they're going to retire and I'm going to run it. I've decided that's my career."

Gwen sat down on the edge of the desk. "Nadine, honey, sweetie, your aunt hates the gallery. And she loves her murals, which means she has to travel. And Davy is a doughnut. I don't think they're even, uh, dating anymore."

"Adults can be so blind," Nadine said.

"Adults can be?" Gwen said, looking at Ethan. "You're a little nearsighted yourself."

Ethan wheeled around and went back into the gallery.

"I see everything," Nadine said.

"Ethan's crazy about you," Gwen said.

"I know," Nadine said.

"Not in the brotherly, best-friend way," Gwen said.

"I know," Nadine said.

"*Well?*" Gwen said.

"I don't know." Nadine frowned. "It's not like my heart goes *kathump* whenever he's around. You know?"

Gwen thought of Mason. "I know."

"And if I make the move to find out, and it turns out it isn't there, then what am I going to do? He's my best friend. I can't lose him. And if I lie to him and try to fake it, he'll know because he knows me better than anybody. We've been best friends for ten years."

"Oh," Gwen said. "Actually, that makes sense."

"And you're wrong about Tilda. Davy makes her laugh. I hadn't heard her laugh for a long time, but he does it."

"You're right," Gwen said. "But Nadine, a long-term relationship is not about laughing."

"I bet it's a good start," Nadine said. "They don't pretend with each other. They know each other."

"They don't have a clue about each other," Gwen said. "Your aunt Tilda has a lot to hide, and Davy's no choirboy."

"I know what I know," Nadine said. "And I don't think you should kiss Mr. Phipps again."

"Hey, even grandmothers get to date." Gwen went back into the office, annoyed.

Nadine followed her. "It's such a shame Mr. Ford turned out to be a hit man."

"Nadine, you do not know that Mr. Ford is a hit man." Gwen felt exhausted, her headache back in full force. "I'm going to bed," she said, heading for the hall door.

"Maybe he only killed people who had it coming," Nadine said, from behind her. "Like John Cusack in *Grosse Pointe Blank*. Maybe if he showed up at their doors, they deserved it."

"Good night, Nadine," Gwen said, and opened the door and sucked in her breath.

Ford was standing there, broad as the doorway. "Sorry. How'd the preview go?"

"Oops." Nadine faded back into the gallery.

"Pretty good," Gwen said, working on keeping her breathing even.

"It looked good from the street," he said. "When I left. Through the window."

"Oh." Gwen nodded. "Thank you."

"The whole place looks good," Ford said.

"Thank you," Gwen said again, still nodding like an idiot.

"Good night," Ford said.

"Good night," Gwen said. He went up the stairs, and Gwen thought, *I'm going to pass out. Breathe, for heaven's sake.* She was such a fool. Mason kissed her and nothing happened, and Ford turned up behind a door and she hyperventilated.

"Do you think he heard me?" Nadine said, coming back in a little breathless herself.

"I think he hears everything," Gwen said. "I'm going to bed now. If you change your mind about Ethan, don't have sex on the office couch."

"Yeah, and I won't put beans up my nose, either," Nadine said, annoyed now, too.

Gwen waved her away and went upstairs to bed to not think for a while.

DOWNSTAIRS, TILDA kicked off her jeans and rolled naked against Davy, who'd lost his, too. "There's more," she said, feeling his heat as he touched her. She wanted to crawl into him, he felt so good.

"God, yes," Davy said, pulling her tighter against him.

"I mean about me." She closed her eyes, feeling her body slide on his, the bite of his hands on her hips, wanting all of him, hot inside her, as soon as possible. "More things to tell."

"Keep talking." Davy bent his head.

"My grandfather sold a Pissaro to the Metropolitan." She gasped as he reached her breast and sucked hard, and she felt the pull everywhere. "It's a contemporary." She laced her fingers through his hair and arched against him to ease the prickle in her veins. "Oh, God. My great-grandfather painted it. It's really good."

Davy moved up to her neck, kissing her there. "My grandpa sold the Brooklyn Bridge for scrap iron," he said in her ear. "Three times." He bit her earlobe and she moaned. "To the same guy."

Tilda ran her tongue along the beautiful line of his collarbone. "My great-grandpa scammed the Louvre," she said, letting her hand stray south as he shivered. "We have a Goodnight in there." She found him, hard against her, and stroked him until he caught her hand.

"Stop that," he said, breathless, "or this'll be over before the end of my rap sheet."

"Your rap sheet's that long?" She kissed him, stealing his mouth, scamming his tongue.

"No. Your hand's that hot." He slid his hand between her thighs. "I remember this. I've been here before."

"Not like this." Tilda shuddered as he touched her. "Don't wait. Don't—"

He slipped his finger inside her and she cried out.

"My great-grandpa conned a Vanderbilt out of a railroad," he said in her ear. "*Christ*, Tilda."

"I know. I know." She closed her eyes and bit her lip and lost herself in the heat he was stroking into her. "Listen to me." She drew her breath in rhythm with his hand, rocking against him. "Listen to me. Listen to me.

My family . . . have been forgers . . . for—Oh, God, *fuck me*."

He rolled between her legs, and she arched up to meet him, and he slid inside her solidly, making her cry out and clench around him, biting his shoulder while he held her down and rocked into her. The heat rolled over her and she shuddered with it, frantically catching his rhythm as he moved inside her. "Oh, *God*, that's good. Don't stop. *Don't stop*."

She moved with him, feeling the pressure build, rolling in his heat. "I'm a forger," she whispered in his ear, and he held her tighter and pulsed deeper. "My family . . . has been bent . . . for four centuries." He bit her neck and she shuddered under him. "We've been wrong . . . forever."

He raised himself up over her, pressing harder and making her gasp, and then he smiled down at her, his eyes hot and his face flushed. "Matilda," he said, moving against her. "My grandmother was a Gypsy. We stole nails at the Crucifixion. *Beat that*."

She rolled her hips to bring him closer, putting him on his back, rising up to straddle him, feeling him deep inside her as his fingers bit into her again.

"I painted the Scarlets," she said, rocking them both toward mindlessness, feeling him everywhere as her body flushed and swelled. "My mother painted Homers. My grandmother painted Cassatts. My great-grandmother—"

"Thank *God* there were a lot of you," Davy said, gripping her tighter.

"My *great-grandmother*," Tilda said again as her muscles tightened inside. She stopped, savoring the tension, knowing the screaming would start soon. *Oh, this is going to be good*, she thought, and looked down at Davy, strong and hot and holding on to her as if he was never going to let go.

"Don't tell me Great-grandma was straight," Davy said, his breath coming hard. "I was hoping for centuries here."

She leaned down slowly, feeling her blood thicken in her veins, and she kissed him, long and deep. "My great-grandmother Matilda," she whispered against his mouth as she began to move against him again, "sold a fake van Gogh . . . to Mussolini."

"Good for her," he whispered, watching her.

"It was a *bad* fake," she said, the edge sharpening inside her.

He arched against her, and she choked as she felt him deep inside.

"It was a *terrible* fake." She breathed in again, her skin damp with anticipation, her eyes on his. "*Anybody* could have told it was fake." *There*, she thought as he moved, *there*. "He must have been *insane*."

He moved against her, intent on her mouth. "Did she look like you?" he whispered.

"Yes," she said, her eyes half-closed. *Almost, almost. There. There.*

He curled up against her, making her cry out as he wrapped his arms around her. "Was she naked when she sold it to him?"

"Yes," Tilda said, choking on the heat. *"Yes."*

"I'd have bought it, too." He rolled to trap her underneath, and she felt herself against him, digging her nails into him and biting his shoulder as the spasm started, clutching at him as he held her down, trying to consume him, devour him, possess him, taking him for everything he had while he took her and she lost it all, over and over and over again.

When she could think again, she felt him shaking on top of her and realized he'd come, too, that part of the shaking was her, that he was holding on to her like death, and that she didn't care about anything except having him again.

"Christ," Davy said finally, still trying to breathe.

"I want to do that again," Tilda said, around her own gasps.

"Yeah," Davy said, gasping into her neck. "Me, too. Maybe next week."

"That was *so good*," Tilda said, stretching under him. "Oh, God, that was *really* good."

"Have I mentioned," Davy said, still trying to breathe, "how pleased I am . . . to meet your family? God, I hope there are thousands of them." He kissed her hard. "You're good at this, Scarlet."

"Not lousy," Tilda said.

"World class." He dropped his head back into the hollow of her neck. "I think you left marks."

Tilda held him tighter as her breathing slowed. "I think you did, too."

"That's so I can find the way back. Damn, you're good."

"Oh, stop." Tilda tilted her hips so he rolled off her, and then followed him to keep his heat. "You'd think you'd never had sex before." She licked into his ear, so besotted with his body that she wanted to start at the top and keep going.

"Not like this," he said, and she lifted her head to look at him. "There was a real quality of insanity there, Scarlet." He took a deep breath. "I usually don't fear for my life during sex but . . ."

"Oh." Tilda grinned at him, exhausted and exhilarated. "Thank you. That's so sweet."

He laughed and pulled her back to him, holding her close. "Maybe we could pace ourselves. There were so many things we could have done that we didn't get to."

"Really?" Tilda said, brightening at the thought. For the first time the unknown seemed interesting and inviting instead of dangerous. "Give me some examples. I'm suddenly feeling very open-minded." When he didn't say anything, she propped herself up on one arm and saw him frown. "What?"

"That was it, wasn't it?" he said, and she tensed again. "That's what's been wrong all along. You've been scared this whole time, haven't you? Of me finding out." He waved his hand to take in the basement. "About this."

"Yes," Tilda said. "God, this is such a relief. But you can't tell anybody. Not even Simon. Promise."

"I promise," he said. "Why?"

She thought of the Scarlets and the shame and the disaster of being found out, and the glow slipped away.

Davy held her tighter. *"Never mind, forget I asked, don't look like that, Jesus."*

He pulled her back down and kissed her hard, and she said, *"Just don't tell,"* and he said, "Never," and kissed her again and again until she relaxed beside him.

"It's okay." She pushed herself up again. "I'm okay."

"You're better than okay," he said, following her up, not letting go. "You're . . ."

"What?" she said, and realized he was looking past her, at the Scarlets lined up along the wall. *"What?"*

"They're you," he told her, still holding on to her as he stared at them. "All that color and light and anger and sex. They're all you."

She looked at the paintings, trying to see them the way he did, without guilt and pain, and they were beautiful, full of laughter and passion and joy.

"God, you're beautiful," he said, still looking at the paintings.

"Oh," Tilda said and felt something give way inside.

He turned back to her and smiled into her eyes. "Scarlet," he said, savoring her name as if he were tasting it. He bent close to her. "Matilda Scarlet Goodnight. Her work." He kissed her gently.

I love you, she thought and kissed him back, naked and unashamed.

CHAPTER · SEVENTEEN

THE NEXT MORNING, TILDA MET EVE OVER MUFFINS IN the office.

"My God," Eve said when Tilda smiled at her, practically bouncing on her heels. "What happened to you?"

"Me?" Tilda tried to tone down her beam. "Davy got the last Scarlet back. I'm free."

"And what did he do after that?" Eve said.

Tilda got the juice out and poured. "Oh, we talked some. He figured out I'm Scarlet."

"Really." Eve's smile faded. "Was he upset?"

"Not so's you'd notice," Tilda said. "It turned him on."

"Everything about you turns Davy on," Eve said. "This is not news."

Tilda choked on her juice, surprised. "Davy? No."

"Yes," Eve said. "He's blind with it, and he doesn't know what to do about it."

"Well, last night he figured it out," Tilda said, grinning again in spite of herself.

"Really," Eve said. "That good?"

"Really that good," Tilda said, looking out the door to the gallery. It was still full of her furniture, but it was also bright and clean and full of light, and she thought, *I love this place. Thank you, Davy.*

"He wasn't mad," Eve said.

Tilda put her glass down. "Tell Simon you're Louise."

"No." Eve got up and put her own glass in the sink so Tilda couldn't see her face.

"It was a real turn-on for me, too, Eve," Tilda said. "I didn't have to be afraid anymore once he knew it all."

"That's when I'd start to be afraid," Eve said.

"No," Tilda said, leaning closer. "That's when you're free. When there's one person you can tell anything to, and it won't matter because he understands you."

Eve took a step back and shook her head. "I think you may be overreacting here."

"I don't think so," Tilda said. "I think—"

"That this is it?" Eve rolled her eyes. "You've known this guy two weeks and this is it? The real thing?"

"I don't know about that," Tilda said, a little taken aback by how cold Eve was. "I don't know if it's true love forever. He's definitely not a fairy-tale prince. But I trust him. I know him."

"No you don't." Eve turned away from her again. "You never know anybody. You just guess."

"All right," Tilda said, more worried than insulted. "Are you coming to the opening tonight?"

"I think Simon is expecting Louise," Eve said, sounding a little tired. "She told him she was getting off early because she wanted to catch the last of the opening."

"That doesn't sound like Louise."

"I want to catch the last of the opening," Eve said.

"Well, give Louise the night off, then," Tilda said. "Come as you are."

Eve shook her head. "She's got a really nice dress." She straightened a little. "You know, she's got a dress that would be good for you, too."

"Like I could get into Louise's stuff," Tilda said. "The only reason I can wear yours is that you buy everything two sizes too big."

"This one's loose," Eve said. "Sort of drapey."

"Drapey?"

"Well, it doesn't have a back."

Tilda thought of Clea Lewis. "What color?"

"Blue," Eve said. "Midnight-blue like the Scarlet skies."

"I'm in," Tilda said and started to follow her out the door, only to stop when they met Gwennie, very pale, carrying the bank bag.

"What's wrong?" Tilda said.

"The mortgage." Gwen dropped the bank bag on the desk and sat down on the couch. "I tried to put the money from last night on the principal, and they wouldn't let me."

"Why not?" Tilda said. "Nobody could buy that mortgage, we've been making the payments."

"It's been paid off," Gwen said, looking like death.

"Paid off?" Tilda said.

"Really?" Eve said, cautiously delighted. "Really, it's gone?"

Gwen looked at her and shook her head.

"Who?" Tilda said.

"Mason," Gwen said. "It has to be Mason. He's the only person we know with six hundred thousand dollars and a yen to run an art gallery. It has to be him. And I think he wants to marry me."

"Oh," Eve said, sitting down beside her. "Well, we'll just give the money back. Unless you like him."

"He's nice," Gwen said.

"Nice." Tilda sat on her other side. "Gwennie, you cannot marry for nice. Or for six hundred thousand dollars. Tell me you're not thinking about doing this in some insane bid to save the plantation. Because it's not necessary. We can give the money back. We'll be out of debt in—"

"About forty years," Gwen said. "But no, that's not why I'm thinking about doing it. Mason is sweet."

"Sweet is good," Tilda said doubtfully. "I mean, definitely when I decide to settle down, I'm doing the muffin thing." She thought about Davy. If she stretched the definition of "muffin" . . .

"That's Mason," Gwen said. "All muffin."

"I'm just saying, maybe not *this* muffin." Tilda took her hand. "He's just a little . . . bland for you. He's bran, you're orange-pineapple."

"Muffins are bland," Gwen said. "If they're not bland, they're just doughnuts without holes."

"Well, take him for a trial run first," Eve said. "Even

for six hundred thousand dollars, you shouldn't have to be bored in bed."

"Right," Tilda said, looking at her sister in disbelief. "Good advice, Louise."

"We'll be just fine," Gwen said, standing up. "Uh, how exactly do I ask him if he paid the mortgage?"

"He'll tell you," Eve said, still channeling Louise. "Guys love to tell you stuff like that."

UPSTAIRS IN Simon's apartment, Davy said, "What would you think if I paid off the mortgage on this place? Don't tell Tilda."

"I'd think you were insane," Simon said. "Why would I tell Tilda?"

"You told Louise we worked for the Feds," Davy said.

"It seemed like a good idea," Simon said. "You're not serious about that mortgage?"

"Pretty much. I gather you told Louise you were a Fed, but you didn't tell her you were a thief?"

"Good God, no." Simon sat on the edge of the table. "About that mortgage. I think we've been here long enough. What do you say we go back to Miami?"

Davy felt like punching him. "You know, the thief thing would have turned Louise on a lot more than the FBI."

"She'd have told Eve," Simon said. "It's been two weeks. Time to go home."

"She did tell Eve about the FBI," Davy said. "Who told Tilda. Who told me last night, which is when I realized why she's been avoiding me. She thought I was an agent. You screwed up my sex life."

Simon got up and pulled his suitcase out from under the bed. "I don't see how."

"I feel strongly," Davy said, "that if somebody is going to lie to my girl, it should be me. That way none of us gets confused."

"Your girl." Simon shook his head. "We are definitely going back to Miami."

"And leave Louise?" Davy turned to go.

"I'm ready to go," Simon said. "You got your money back—"

Davy turned back. "Do *not* mention that to *anyone*."

"Interesting," Simon said. "I would think that would turn Tilda on even more than the FBI."

"You don't know Tilda," Davy said. "I mean it. *Nobody* finds out."

"You're a lot easier to live with in Miami," Simon said. "Ohio makes you tense."

"Not really," Davy said, thinking about Tilda upstairs. "Have you ever met a woman you wanted to give everything to? Just turn over everything you had?"

"No," Simon said. "Being of sound mind, of course not."

"Me, either," Davy said. "I'd have told you that Clea was the great love of my life, but I never felt the slightest urge to buy her a diamond."

"Smart boy," Simon said.

Davy sat down on the edge of the bed. "I looked at

that money in my account last night and suddenly felt this overwhelming need to pay off Tilda's mortgage."

"So we should be leaving now," Simon said, opening his suitcase. "A good time was had by all. Cheerio."

"It was only six hundred thousand." He shook his head. "And then later . . ." He looked at Simon. "Did you ever watch a woman in glasses strip to 'I Can't Stay Mad at You'? Dumb song, but Tilda can sing the hell out of it."

"I'll make the reservations." Simon picked up the phone. "Would you like me to hold on to your checkbook for you?"

"No," Davy said. "Look, I can afford it. It would be a generous thing to do. I still haven't paid for the bed."

"Do not give money to women," Simon said as he dialed. "They either take it badly, or they take it and want more. You can't win."

"I could tell her it was an investment."

"In a broken-down art gallery that is rapidly going to the dogs that even she doesn't want anything to do with? No." Simon spoke into the phone. "Hello, love, it's me, your favorite client. How fast can you get Davy and me on a flight to Miami? Out of Columbus."

"I have to go see my sister on Sunday," Davy said.

"Out of Columbus on Sunday night," Simon said into the phone.

"You know, a smart guy could make this place work," Davy said. "Put in a little capital, start the old razzle-dazzle—"

"Absolutely not," Simon said to him, and then spoke

into the phone again. "No, not you, darling, that sounds brilliant. Two tickets, one-way."

"Simon, I already did it," Davy said and Simon hung up.

"Sandy's got us on the ten o'clock direct flight on Sunday," he said briskly. "That'll give you time to see Sophie, and me time to say good-bye to Louise. In fact, why don't you go see Sophie now? Spend the weekend?"

"Because the opening is tonight," Davy said. "Did you hear me? I transferred the money to the Goodnights' loan last night. It's done."

Simon crossed his arms. "You did. And what did Tilda say?"

"I didn't tell her," Davy said. "It's going to be hard to explain."

Simon nodded. "Because many women, when given large sums of money, expect that the giver will stay around for a while."

"Well, yeah." Davy stood up. "Actually, I'm thinking about staying."

"No you're not," Simon said with heavy patience. "You're thinking about sex."

"Go away," Davy said, wanting to punch him because he was probably right. "It's Friday. I have to call my sister."

"Much better to go see her," Simon said, *"now,"* but he left as Davy punched the numbers into his cell phone.

"Tucker residence," Phin said, and Davy thought, *Oh, hell, not you.*

"Harvard, old buddy," he said. "It's me. Sophie around?"

"Nope," Phin said. "Council meeting. She's going to come home bitchy, though, so I'd try again tomorrow."

"Okay," Davy said. "Don't tell her I called in case I can't get back right away."

"You in trouble?"

"Dempseys are never in trouble," Davy said loftily. "We just have stretches of life that are more interesting than others."

"How interesting is your life right now?"

Davy thought of Tilda, singing "You've got me where you want me" a cappella as she shimmied her bra off. "Very."

"How bad is it?" Phin sounded as calm as ever. "You just in trouble with the law or is somebody trying to kill you?"

"That's not the problem," Davy said. "For once, I'm innocent and everybody loves me." Clea's face rose before him, not to mention Ford's. "Well, almost everybody." And then there was Michael. "Did Sophie ever tell you about our dad?"

"Yes," Phin said and then a beat later said, "Oh, no."

"Yeah," Davy said. "I can handle it, he doesn't know where you are, but it's Dad, so he'll find out eventually. And then he'll boost the kids' college funds and sell the town council land in Florida and take Sophie for every dime she has."

"The kids don't have college funds. The rest would be bad."

"I'm hoping he'll get tired and wander off, but if he heads your way, lock the door. And don't tell Sophie or she'll feel like she has to invite him in."

"Right," Phin said.

"Oh, and in case you find out anyway," Davy said, "the kids now have college funds." He hung up and gave one last thought to Temptation. It didn't matter how safe it was there, if he had to go back, he'd con somebody just from the boredom. The thought of what his father could do there was worse.

Plus, Scarlet wasn't there.

"Worthless place," he said and went to see what Tilda was doing.

WHEN TILDA came downstairs that night, she found Davy in the middle of the gallery, surveying the place with a frown. "What now?" she said from the office doorway.

"I can't tell if it's too crowded or not," he said. "You want it to look like there's a lot here without it looking like we'll never unload all of it, and I don't know enough about galleries to . . ." His voice trailed off as he looked at her. "Whoa."

Tilda smoothed her skirt down and fought back a smile. "Exactly the right word, thank you." She turned around so he could get the full effect of the dress's backlessness. "Do you like it?" When he didn't say anything, she turned back. "Hello?"

He nodded.

"Is it too much?"

He shook his head.

"Speak."

"Could I see you upstairs?" he said finally.

She smiled and crossed the room to him, and he reached for her before she was close. She slid into his arms and felt the world settle around them.

"You're beautiful, Scarlet," he whispered in her ear, and she knew she should say, "Me?" and be modest, but she just nestled closer and said, "Yes, I am." He laughed and kissed the top of her head, and then Gwen came in and he let go.

She could still feel his arms around her while Gwen marveled at the dress. Louise stopped in on her way to the Double Take and took her glasses off—"*Not* with that dress, Tilda,"—and Ethan said, " 'That's not a dress, that's an Audrey Hepburn movie,' " and Nadine smacked him on the back of the head before he could tell her it was a movie quote. Even Steve seemed respectful, although that may just have been because he was wearing his brocade vest again. "He was in the *Dispatch*," Nadine said, showing Tilda the picture of Steve on the back of the Accent section, looking weirdly intellectual in his bow tie, like a furry Woody Allen. "What do you think?"

And Tilda looked across the top of the paper at Davy and said, "I think he's amazing."

Davy was even more amazing when people began to come in. He smiled, and laughed and made them say yes, steering them to different pieces, watching their faces to see which things they responded to and then moving in for the sale. "What a wheeler-dealer," Jeff had said halfway through the evening when he'd brought out the last of Thomas's potstickers. "The guy's an ace."

"You have no idea," Tilda said, keeping an eye on Davy in case he needed her. She thought her face was going to crack from smiling, but Davy was still relaxed and easy.

"It's not just him," Jeff said. "His dad sold three more Finsters."

"You're kidding," Tilda said, looking around to see.

"Back there." Jeff jerked his head toward the left. "He must be drugging the customers."

"He's conning them," Tilda said, squinting to see. "I don't have my glasses on. He doesn't have them backed into a corner, does he?"

"No," Jeff said, grinning. "And they're all women. Do you think that's significant?"

Tilda looked back at Davy, very tasty in Simon's dress shirt and tie. "No, I'm sure that has no relevance at all."

She threaded her way through the crowd to stand beside him and then waited until he'd made his sale and turned to her. "You're my hero," she said.

"Why?" he said, suddenly cautious.

She slipped her arm through his. "You got back all my Scarlets and now you're getting rid of all this furniture."

"Oh." He looked relieved. "Listen, this stuff sells

itself. There's almost nothing left downstairs. Ethan and I even loaded the bed into the back of your van. You're sure you don't mind me taking it to Temptation on Sunday?"

"As long as you come back," she said, trying not to tighten her grip on him.

"Yeah, that's all my rap sheet needs," Davy said, looking over her head. "Grand theft auto. I have to go. There's a woman over there who is trying to buy that chair with the purple bats."

Tilda turned to follow his eyes. "Then why isn't she? I can't see details without my glasses."

"Because Mason is helping her," Davy said grimly. "He is undoubtedly telling her it will appreciate and add to her retirement income. Look at him, he's standing there with his arms folded smiling because he thinks he's sold her."

"He does that when he plays poker, too." Tilda squinted in his general direction. "When he thinks he has something. Which he never does. Bats are going to add to her retirement income?"

"Yeah, I'm not seeing the logic, either." He pulled his arm away, kissed her cheek, and started across the floor.

"Hey," Tilda said.

He stopped and came back.

"You're not getting tired of me, are you, Ralph?" she said, trying to keep her voice light. "Leaving me for purple bats and Temptation. We're in a rut already?"

"We don't do ruts, Celeste," he said. "We're inventive. If we start to pall on each other, we'll improvise."

Tilda moved closer, wanting his warmth. "Like how?"

He bent to her ear. "Like sometime before I go, you're going to be Grandma, and I'm going to be Mussolini." Then he straightened and she realized he was looking over her shoulder at Mason. "Oh, hell," he said, and took off without looking back.

"Before you go?" Tilda said to his back. Did that mean before he went to Temptation or before he went forever? "Australia," she said with loathing and turned her back on him to help a man who had a question about a lavender frog bookcase.

DAVY'S EVENING went beautifully, even with his dad coming by every half hour or so to say, "Damn, what a setup."

"I'm impressed with the Dempseys," Louise said to him before she left for work. She was dressed in tight, stretchy black, and even though he knew she was Eve in a black wig and dark contacts, he couldn't help thinking of her as Louise because Eve would never wear that dress. "Your dad is selling Finsters almost as fast as you're selling Matilda Veronicas."

"Don't say it," Davy said, knowing what was coming.

"Two of a kind," Louise said and drifted away.

A few minutes later, Michael came up to Davy. "Why is Eve dressed up like Elvira Queen of the Night?"

"What?" Davy said.

"And calling herself Louise. It's a con, right?"

"Oh, hell," Davy said. "It took me two weeks to get that."

"You were distracted," Michael said sympathetically. "Sex will do that to you."

"You're not sleeping with Dorcas?" Davy said, surprised.

"A gentleman never tells," Michael said.

"You're sleeping with Dorcas," Davy said. "And selling her paintings, I understand."

"They're works of art," Michael said seriously, and anybody but Davy would have believed him.

"Well, I hope she appreciates the work you're doing. Nobody else but you could move those things."

Michael put his hand over his heart. "Why, thank you, my boy, I'm touched."

Davy shrugged. "Have to give the devil his due. You're good."

"Yes," Michael said, smiling back at Dorcas, who was looking pale but lovely in gray crepe. "I am." Then he went back to selling Finsters.

Davy watched for a moment to see Michael's newest mark turn to him and expand under the light in his smile and the glint in his eye. *That's wrong*, he thought, but she looked so happy as she bought a Finster that it was hard to explain why it was wrong.

Maybe when she woke up the next morning and

realized she'd bought a watercolor of sadistic fishermen drowning fish, maybe that was when it was wrong. Assuming she did. Maybe she'd look at it and remember how she felt when she bought it. Maybe it would make her happy.

Maybe he was rationalizing. He went to sell a woman a sideboard with green and blue elephants.

Ten minutes later, the sideboard sold, and feeling something was missing in his life, Davy went looking for Tilda and her blue dress and saw her over by the counter, talking with a tall, good-looking guy in an expensive suit. She looked happy.

I'm not jealous, Davy thought, and then grabbed Andrew as he went by. "Hey."

"I'm late for the Double Take," Andrew said. "Make it fast."

Davy nodded toward the counter. "Who's the suit with Tilda?"

Andrew looked over. "Scott. Old boyfriend."

"Oh." Davy watched Tilda laugh up at the guy and felt his jaw grow tight.

"He's a lawyer," Andrew said helpfully. "Very successful. Treated her like a goddess. They were great together."

"No they weren't," Davy said, watching Tilda put her hand on the suit's arm. "He's all wrong for her."

"Uh-huh," Andrew said, and turned away, almost running into Michael.

"Andrew," Michael said, "who's that idiot with

Gwennie? He was here last night, too. Worst salesman I've ever seen in my life."

Andrew looked over. "Mason Phipps. He treats her like a goddess. They're great together."

"No they're not," Michael said. "He's all wrong for her."

"Are you leaving soon?" Davy said to him. "Because if not, I'm going to get drunk."

"With Tilda in that blue dress? That's no way to treat a woman, son," Michael said. "No wonder she's flirting with somebody else." He went over to dazzle Gwennie and annoy Mason.

"I don't want to hear any 'two of a kind' crap," Davy said to Andrew, his eyes back on Tilda.

"He has a lot of good points," Andrew said mildly.

"He has a lot of bad ones, too," Davy said grimly.

"He is all wrong for her," Andrew said.

"Dad for Gwennie? Jesus, yes. So is Mason. She's doodling teeth on the sales slips. That's not a good sign."

"No," Andrew said. "I meant that Scott's all wrong for Tilda. You staying around?"

Davy opened his mouth to say something and then couldn't think of anything.

"That's what I thought," Andrew said, sounding disgusted. "Two of a kind."

"Hey," Davy began but Andrew walked off. "Okay, how did I get to be the bad guy again?"

Across the room, Tilda turned away from Scott, and Davy caught her eye. He folded his arms and raised his eyebrows, and Tilda looked confused for a moment and then pointed at Scott. Davy nodded. Tilda stuck her chin in the air, but she grinned, and when he crooked his finger at her, she crossed the room to him and made his pulse pick up.

"Stop flirting with strange men, Vilma," he told her, pulling her close.

"I wasn't flirting and he's not strange," she said as she snuggled under his arm. "In fact, he's very sweet. He's not even mad that I turned him down."

"For *what*?"

"Marriage," Tilda said, laughing. "What is with you?"

"He *proposed*?"

"Six months ago. I told you this."

"Oh," Davy said, feeling foolish. "Right. Sorry."

"Are you kidding?" Tilda said. "I *love* it that you're jealous."

"I'm not jealous," Davy said. "But if he comes near you again, I'm breaking his fingers."

"You have nothing to worry about, Ralph." She stretched up and kissed his cheek. "He doesn't have the fine understanding of living on the edge that you do. So few men do." She smiled past him and turned to see Michael handing over another Finster. "Of course, you had a great teacher." Before he could deny it, she slid out of his arms. "Furniture to sell," she told him. "Move that armadillo footstool and wonderful things will happen to you later."

Wonderful things are going to happen anyway, he

thought as she walked away from him. He looked back at Michael. Okay, maybe part of him was Michael. The charming part. He'd take that legacy. Across the room, a woman picked up the armadillo footstool, and Davy went to help her.

Three footstools, an armoire, and a garden bench later, Nadine came back into the gallery from the street, looking enraged.

"Your *father*," she said.

"Now what?"

"Kyle came by to see me," Nadine said, "and your dad scared him away. I didn't want to see him but *I* wanted to tell him that." She glared at Davy. "What is *wrong* with you people?"

"We're very protective of our womenfolk," Davy said, giving up.

Nadine's frown eased a little. "I thought you were on your way to Australia."

"I am."

"Then I am *not* your womanfolk," Nadine said, her scowl back in place. "If you're not staying with Aunt Tilda, *back off*."

"Right," Davy said. "I'm backing. Off. Go throw yourself away on a worthless male."

"Yeah. Goodnight women do that a lot," she said, and went to rescue Steve, who was being baby-talked to by a woman holding a giraffe side chair.

"I am not worthless," he called after her, and did not look over at his father, who was undoubtedly leaving Dorcas shortly.

Clearly Fate had brought him to the Goodnights to make him see that he really was Michael and, in so doing, ruin his life. And he'd fallen for it. He should have walked away when Tilda said, "Steal it for me," in the closet; he'd known that when she'd asked him. He should not have rented the apartment; he'd known that when he'd seen the sign in the window. He should—

"What's wrong with you?" Michael said from behind him. "You look like the last grave over by the willow."

Davy shook his head. "I should have listened when you said, if it's too good to be true, get out."

"Sometimes," Michael said, "it's better to stay and get taken."

He nodded across the room, and Davy followed his gaze to Tilda, laughing with the customer over Steve, showing Nadine and everybody else in the room how to charm anybody.

"She's something," Michael told Davy. "She really is."

Tilda turned to see them, her curls rumpled and her smile crooked and her eyes . . .

"Yes," Davy said to her.

"Are you sure she's not bent?" Michael said. "Because if she was, she really would be too good—"

"Forget it, Dad," Davy said, and crossed the room to buy whatever she was selling.

GWEN'S EVENING was a little rockier. It was clear to her that the show was a success; people weren't exactly clawing their way through the door, but there was a nice crowd, thanks in no small part to the article in the *Dispatch*. People dropped by to meet Steve and stayed to have a good time, buying at a fast enough clip that Simon and Ethan spent the evening bringing up pieces to replace the things they'd sold. At ten, Ford came in and helped, and shortly after that, he brought her a dog-covered end table and said, "That's it. You'll have to start on the furniture in my room next," and she'd said, "We'll wait until you leave for Aruba for that." He nodded, and she felt disappointed, and then some woman bought the end table—it had paws and a face that looked just like her Pete, she said, and Gwen had wondered if Pete was a dog or a husband—and she'd gone back to smiling until her face ached.

Shortly after that, Thomas came up to her and put his hand on her arm again. "Mrs. Goodnight?"

Oh, hell, Gwen thought, *it's the FBI.* "Yes?"

"I was cleaning up the office," he said, a fake smile pasted on his face, "and I found an interesting painting. A forest."

"A forest," Gwen said and thought, *Damn it, Homer, why weren't you in the basement with Scarlet?*

"It's a painting by an artist named Homer Hodge," Thomas said. "And it was part of Cyril Lewis's collection that burned in the warehouse fire."

"Oh." Gwen sat down on her counter stool. That explained why Mason had it even though he'd given his Homer collection away. So how had he gotten it?

"Did you get that from Clea Lewis?" Thomas said, sounding stern in his white jacket.

"I don't know what painting you're talking about," Gwen said. "It's in the office? We don't store paintings in the office."

"It was stuck behind the desk," Thomas said.

"What were you doing behind the desk?" Gwen said.

"What are you doing with this painting?" Thomas said.

"Is there a problem?" Mason said, and they both jerked their heads around to see him standing on the other side of the counter. "Thomas," he said severely, "you shouldn't be annoying Mrs. Goodnight with catering details. Just handle whatever it is."

Clea drifted up, her face grim, as she linked her arm through Mason's. "You know, every time I go looking for you," she told him, smiling tightly, "I find you over here."

Mason disentangled his arm from hers, and Thomas, his face pale under his bruises, said to Gwen, "I'll talk to you later."

"*I* need to talk to you later," Mason said to Gwen as Thomas turned away. "In the office. Privately."

Clea's face went stormy, and Gwen said brightly, "Oh, good. I'll look forward to that. Now if you could move, there's a lady with an armadillo footstool behind you."

By the end of the evening, Gwen had a raging headache, due in equal parts to Mason revolving by every fifteen minutes to pat her arm, Clea sending her death looks every five, Michael selling Finsters with outrageous promises ("Is she really going to be the next Wyeth?" one woman whispered to Gwen, and Gwen thought, *Oh, hell, Michael,* and smiled), and Ford looking bored and temporary as he hauled furniture out to waiting cars. *Always on your way out the door,* she thought as she watched him carry a ferret chair. *Which is good because you're a doughnut. Not to mention the hit man thing.* Across the room, Louise, back early from the Double Take, looked at Simon as though he was the answer to her prayers which was very Eve-like of her, and over by the butterfly chairs with the big SOLD tag, Davy kissed Tilda's cheek and made her blush. *No good,* Gwen thought, *neither one of these guys is going to stay. Why can't my daughters see that? Doughnuts. They're all doughnuts.* By the time Thomas went AWOL around ten-thirty, she really didn't care.

"Do you know where Thomas is?" Jeff said. "We're out of potstickers. I asked Mason, and he said the last he saw of him, he was talking to Clea Lewis, and now she's gone, too."

"Maybe they're having sex in the basement," Gwen said, watching Tilda lean into Davy. "That's popular lately." Then she shook her head. Enough whining and negativity. Her family had been amazing all night, especially Nadine, back in full form from the night before, and Tilda, wonderfully gracious and efficient, the center that held things together.

Davy, though, was the real revelation.

"That Davy," Andrew said to her at the end of the show. "The last person I knew who could con people into buying like that was—"

"Tony," Gwen said.

Davy smiled and people nodded. He leaned forward and spoke, and they considered the furniture. He leaned back and spread his hands and they bought, clearly delighted with their purchases, themselves, and him.

But there was no tension in Davy when he approached people. And when Tilda talked to someone, calm and knowledgeable, he stepped back and smiled at her, listening to every word. Tony would have shouldered her aside, but Davy brought people to her. "You have to talk to Matilda," she heard him say to one buyer. "She knows everything." He revolved around the room all night, selling everything in his path, but Tilda was his sun, the one he kept turning to.

He's not Tony, Gwen thought, and felt relieved and wistful at the same time. Thinking about the past could do that to a woman. She turned the cash register over to Nadine and said, "I think we're almost done. Check with Tilda, and if she says yes, we'll start closing up."

"Cool," Nadine said, surveying the money.

"Was that Kyle I saw earlier?"

"Michael scared him off," Nadine said. "Those Dempseys."

"Good for Michael," Gwen said. "Don't let him near the cash drawer."

Back inside the office, she was pouring vodka into her pineapple-orange, when Mason came in.

"This was great," he said, rubbing his hands together nervously. "Gwen, honey, this was really *good*."

"I know," she said, toasting him with her glass. Mason had spent the evening reinforcing her suspicions that he was the most abysmal salesman she'd ever met in her life. On the other hand, the last thing she wanted was another salesman, and he'd paid off her mortgage, and he was a muffin. And he'd gotten "peccable" right. Clearly that was a sign.

"The only thing is," Mason said now, darting a glance over his shoulder, "we're going to have to watch that Davy."

"Davy?" Gwen said, her glass at her lips.

"He doesn't understand gallery etiquette," Mason said. "He kept laughing and talking like he was just anybody. He doesn't realize how *serious* a gallery is. He has to go, Gwen."

He's jealous, Gwen thought.

"I mean it," Mason said, trying to sound stronger and only sounding weaker. "He has to go."

"That's pretty much up to him and Tilda," Gwen said. "So where's Clea?"

"She went home a while ago," Mason said. "I saw her talking to Thomas, and then she said she was going home and that's the last I saw of either of them." Mason took a deep breath. "I didn't want to tell you this, I was hoping Davy would just move on."

I'm going to hate this.

"He's a con man, Gwen," Mason said, and he said it gently enough that she knew he wasn't lying, wasn't trying to sabotage Davy, not that Mason would. He wasn't that kind of man. "Clea knew him in L.A. He scammed everybody out there with these bogus land deals and movie deals. She said the last she saw of him, he was working for a porn producer, kind of his right-hand man. He's not the right guy for Tilda."

Oh, hell, Gwen thought. *And he was so good tonight.* Of course, if he was a con man, he would be good. And poor Tilda, so happy. "Maybe he'll leave on his own," Gwen said. "Don't tell Tilda."

"Of course not," Mason said. "I wouldn't have mentioned it to you except . . ." He trailed off, clearly upset, and she moved over to him, putting her hand on his sleeve.

"I appreciate it that you told me," she said. "It's right that I know that."

"Thank you," he said, moving closer. "I really didn't want to be the one to tell you."

"You're very sweet," she said, and he bent and kissed her again, and it was nice. He was such a nice guy, not a con man or a hit man or anything but a good man, and it was time she stopped falling for the flashy cowboy doughnuts and grew up.

Then he said, "I was going to wait for this, but . . ." and pulled out a ring box.

"Oh," Gwen said, and she said it again when he opened it and showed her a rock that lit the room, at least ten carats.

"We can run the gallery together, Gwennie. It'll still be the Goodnight Gallery. Everything will be the same as it always was. It'll just be with me instead of Tony. Marry me, Gwennie."

Mason's voice shook a little when he said it, and Gwen said, "Did you pay off the gallery?"

"What?"

"I know it's rude to ask, but somebody paid off the mortgage," Gwen said, "and I know it must be you."

"Oh," Mason said, looking taken aback. "Uh, well, yes."

That's it then, Gwen thought. It was a good offer. It wasn't as if she was ever getting out of here anyway. Mason was very sweet, he wasn't bragging about the mortgage at all. Tilda would be free. Nadine could go to college. She leaned forward and kissed him again, grateful but depressed.

"Is that a yes?" he said, and she nodded, and he slid the ring on her finger, and put his arms around her. "We're going to be so happy," he told her as he held her, and she crooked her finger to keep the ring on because it was too large.

"Yes," Gwen said into his shoulder. "Can we go scuba diving for our honeymoon?"

"Of course," Mason said. "Anything you want."

"Just not to Aruba," Gwen said.

Nadine opened the door and said, "Uh, Aunt Tilda says it's time to close," and Gwen pulled back. "Also, we can't find Thomas the Caterer. Did he leave? Because all his stuff is here."

"I'll be right there," Gwen said, and straightened

her dress, which didn't need straightening. "I have to go—"

"I understand," Mason said.

"So, tomorrow," Gwen said, smiling at him as brightly as she could.

"Oh," he said, and looked up at the ceiling, toward her apartment.

"Because we have to . . . you know . . . shut down the gallery," Gwen said, trying to think of a reason not to invite her fiancé upstairs. "For the night. Clean up. You know."

"Of course," Mason said, looking confused. "I'll see you tomorrow." He kissed her again, and over his shoulder, Gwen could see Nadine scowling.

Yeah, I kind of feel that way, too, she thought.

OUT IN the gallery, Davy had come up behind Tilda, put his arms around her, and whispered in her ear, "I have plans for you, Vilma."

Oh, good, Tilda thought. "There's one last woman over there thinking about buying that awful wombat chest." She snuggled in closer. "Don't you think you should go sell it to her?"

"No," Davy said. "I'm tired, the show's over, and I want to clean this place up and then see how easy this dress is to get off."

"Extremely easy." Tilda shoved her shoulder strap up again. "The trick all evening has been to keep it on. I don't know how Louise manages this stuff."

Back in the office, Nadine started the jukebox, and some woman began to sing about saving the last dance.

Davy frowned. "What is this song? And why do I have good feelings about it?"

Tilda laughed. "You were winning a bet the last time you heard it." Her shoulder strap fell down again.

"We can clean tomorrow." Davy took her hand and pulled her toward the office door.

"You were great tonight," Tilda said, following him.

"You haven't seen anything yet, Celeste."

Tilda stopped at the door for one last look around the gallery. About half of the furniture was gone, and the rest would go in the next couple of weeks as word spread. She wasn't going to set the art world on fire, or even the furniture world, but people had liked the things they bought, the Finsters notwithstanding. And they'd bought them because of Davy. The basement was empty because of Davy.

No, she thought. *Only half-empty.*

"Okay, long silences make me nervous," Davy said from the office doorway. "Also, you have that look on your face again."

She turned back to him. "You're solving all my problems."

"I can do it all," he said, not really listening as he tugged at her hand. "Come upstairs and I'll show you."

"Come downstairs first," she said.

Davy shook his head. "The bed's packed in the van. And that concrete floor is cold."

"I have something to show you." She pulled her hand out of his and headed for the basement.

"Can't you show it to me in the attic?" he said, but he followed her down the stairs and stopped behind her as she punched in the code for the studio.

"Til, you don't have to," he said, his voice serious.

"Yeah," she said. "I do. Here's the last of my secrets, Dempsey. Let's see how good you are with a big problem."

And then she opened the door.

CHAPTER · EIGHTEEN

UPSTAIRS, THE LAST CUSTOMER LEFT WITH HER WOM-
bats, and Nadine and Ethan walked around picking up
cups. "We'll clean up the office and then head
upstairs," Nadine told Gwen. "We have things to talk
about."

"You didn't bug anybody else, did you?" Gwen said,
alarmed.

"No," Ethan said. "But the investigation is ongoing."

"What things, then?" Gwen said, looking at Nadine
with narrowed eyes.

"We're going to discuss the future of Matilda
Veronica furniture," Nadine said. "We're going to run
out pretty soon, and we were thinking that if we went
around to dumps and collected stuff on trash day, that
Tilda could draw the lines and we could paint them."

"I don't know if Tilda wants to." Gwen looked
around the depleted gallery. Mason wouldn't be happy
about more furniture. He'd want to sell paintings. Her
head throbbed harder. "I don't even know when Tilda is
leaving again on her next mural."

"That's why we need to talk about this first," Nadine

said. "It's still fuzzy, but once Ethan and I work out the details, I don't think she'll say no. After all, we'll be doing most of the work. Right?" She nudged Ethan and grinned up at him affectionately. "It's not like Ethan has anything else to do."

"And how do you feel about that, Ethan?" Gwen said, exasperated with them both.

Ethan shrugged. "It's summer."

No, it isn't, Gwen thought, *it's Nadine.*

"You look tired, Grandma," Nadine said. "Go to bed. Ethan and I will take care of everything down here."

"Maybe you're right," Gwen said and then someone banged on the street door to the gallery. "Who could that be? It's after midnight."

"Want me to get it?" Ethan said.

"No." Gwen went toward the door. "You stay here and clean."

When she lifted the shade on the street door, Mason was standing there. "Hey, we're closed," she said, opening the door for him.

"Thought you might be able to spare another drink," Mason said, a little sheepishly, as he came in.

"Hello, Mr. Phipps," Nadine said politely, when they came into the office. "Come on, Ethan, let's do the gallery." She picked up the sweeper and went into the gallery, Ethan following her with a trash bag and a pained expression.

"Cute kids," Mason said, while Gwen got out the orange juice and vodka.

"Good kids," Gwen said, failing to see how anybody

could call either Nadine or Ethan cute. She glanced through the glass into the gallery. Nadine was attacking the floors with the sweeper while Ethan gathered up miscellaneous cups and plates, keeping one eye on Nadine's rear end. Maybe it was time to send Ethan home.

"I thought maybe," Mason began and hesitated. "I don't want to go home to Clea tonight, Gwen," he blurted finally. "Let me stay with you."

"Oh," Gwen said.

"I don't want to rush you." Mason said, moving closer. "I know you're tired."

Oh, good, I look tired. Gwen stood up. "You're a very generous man, Mason."

"I'm not generous," Mason said. "I get a lot, too. It's lonely back at the house."

Gwen thought, *I know. It's lonely where I am, too. And sooner or later . . .* "Would you like to see my apartment?" she said.

"Yes," he said solemnly. "I would like to very much."

"Great," she said and stood up. "It's this way."

THE BASEMENT room was big when Tilda turned on the light. Davy saw three walls lined with expensive-looking metal cabinets and the fourth with shelves full of tools and equipment, some of it standard artist's supplies but a lot of it unfamiliar. The whole place was white, just like everything else in the basement.

Tilda pulled out a bentwood side chair that had seen better days and said, "Sit," and Davy sat, facing the longest wall of cabinets. She opened the first cabinet and pulled out a painting, cornfields under a heavily painted, swirling blue sky.

"Do you know what this is?" she said.

"A van Gogh?" Davy said, not caring. "You have great legs."

"A Goodnight," Tilda said. "My great-grandpa painted it. Of course, he signed it van Gogh."

Davy squinted at it. "Why didn't Great-grandpa sell it?"

"Because it was lousy," Tilda said and began to open more cabinets, her body moving under the slippery fabric of her dress. Davy watched as she pulled out painting after painting, her body tensing with each canvas until she had dozens of them propped against the walls and lying at her feet, and he wanted her so much he was dizzy with it.

"All Goodnights," she said, looking at them. "They've been down here for decades, in the family for centuries. Our great secret. We should burn them, but we can't. They're history. They're part of us."

"Burn them?" Davy said, not caring. "Why didn't you sell them?"

Tilda put her hands on her hips and looked at him sternly, which made him stop thinking about the paintings entirely. "They're forgeries. That's illegal."

"Really, Scarlet?" Davy said. "Come here and tell me about it."

"Okay, because most of them are really bad," Tilda said, dropping her hands. "And because some of them were intended for future generations. We pass them down."

"Why?" Davy said, trying to gauge how much longer he had to talk to her before he could get that dress off.

"I told you," Tilda said, "the hardest forgeries to break are the contemporaries, the ones painted during the time the real artist worked. Science can't touch them. So every generation of Goodnights paints for the next generation."

"Because once the artist is dead, nobody can tell," Davy said, gaining new respect for the Goodnights. "How many of these do you have?" A small part of him was interested from a purely financial point, but most of him was praying she wasn't going to make him look at all of them. It would take hours and there was very little blood left in his brain.

"Over two hundred if you include the drawings and prints," Tilda said. "We have some that go all the way back to Antonio Giordano, who is supposed to be the first of us. We switched to Goodnight when we came to America."

"To fit in?"

"To cover up the fact that we were related to my great-uncle Paolo Giordano," Tilda said. "He sold a Leonardo off the wall and got caught."

"Off the wall," Davy said, interested in spite of his lack of blood. "He just pointed to it and said—"

"No," Tilda said. "He lined up a client and said, 'I'll

• 411 •

steal the Leonardo for you.' And he did. And he told the client he was painting a copy for the police to find so that they'd stop looking for it and they'd all be safe."

"Who got the copy?" Davy said.

"The client," Tilda said. "Well, clients. He told the same story to four different collectors. My great-uncle would never keep a national treasure. Borrow, yes, steal, no. And the clients deserved it because they were stealing a national treasure. Greed."

"Classic con," Davy said. "As long as the mark is crooked, he can't go to the cops. Come over here and discuss this with me."

"And if he's crooked, he deserves to be taken," Tilda said. "I know this part. My dad used to drill it into me." She went over to the last of the cabinets and pulled out another painting.

"What if they buy it because they like it?" Davy said, wishing she'd come back to him.

"Then they're getting what they paid for, aren't they?" Tilda said, turning the painting so he could see it. It was of a woman with protruding eyes hovering over a well-fed mother and her disturbing-looking baby. "This is our prize, a Durer Saint Anne," she said. "A Goodnight Durer, of course, but still."

"Okay," Davy said.

"Antonio painted it in 1553," Tilda said. "But it wasn't his usual good work, so the family kept it. For four hundred years. If it was good and we sold this as a Durer, analysis of the paint and canvas would show that it was real. It would go for millions at auction, and nobody would ever catch on."

"But it's bad?" Davy said, tilting his head to look at it. "It looks okay to me. Old."

"It's not bad," Tilda said, "but it's not good enough. There are half a dozen paintings down here, any one of which would solve all our problems if we could sell it. But we can't."

"Your morals do you justice," Davy said. "Give them a vacation and come upstairs with me."

"It's not my morals," Tilda said. "We can't afford to get caught. Nobody has ever tied the Goodnights to fraud, if you don't count Great-uncle Paolo. If a fake turns up, everybody starts looking at everything they've ever bought from us. And we can't afford to give decades of dissatisfied customers their money back." She put the Durer back. "And I'm not good enough to stonewall them on it. I'm just not the wheeler-dealer my dad was. The guilt . . ." She shook her head. "I get upset. So this stuff stays down here, and it drives me crazy. I'd burn it all if I could, I really would, but I can't. My family made these." She picked up another canvas to put it back. "And a lot of them are good. They're not good forgeries, but they're good paintings. They should be on people's walls."

"Sell them as fakes."

"Right," Tilda said. "Nobody will notice that." She bent over to slide another painting away.

"You have a great butt," Davy said.

She straightened, and he waited for her to snap at him.

"Thank you," she said, and picked up another painting. "But I also have this problem here."

"Sell them," Davy said again, waiting for her to bend over again. "Publicize the sale as all the paintings that Goodnights bought thinking they were real and then couldn't sell when they found out they were fakes. That's why there are so many of them, because the Goodnights are such honest dealers." He looked around at the riot of color.

"Yeah," Tilda said. "I could bring that off. Because honesty is so easy to fake."

She looked down at the forgeries, so much pain on her face that Davy forgot he wanted her. "Okay, there's something else going on here. This is the thing that got you last night, isn't it? I'm not getting why this is so awful, or how the Scarlets fit into it."

"What?" Tilda looked up from the Durer. "Oh. They don't. I wasn't trained to paint the Scarlets, I was trained for this."

Davy shook his head. "I don't get it."

"My dad trained me as a classical painter," Tilda said. "The same way his dad trained him and his dad before that. But then one day Dad showed up with a Homer Hodge and said, 'Paint like this,' and they were so simple that—" She broke off. "I painted six of them and left." She shrugged. "No big deal."

"Why did you leave?" Davy said.

Tilda bit her lip. "It was a bad time," she said

offhand, but her voice shook a little. "I was a kid. It doesn't matter. Long time ago, all over now." She started to put the paintings away.

"How old a kid?"

"Seventeen."

Davy straightened. "What the hell happened?"

"You know, it really isn't—"

"Tilda, stop lying and tell me."

Tilda pressed her lips together in a caricature of a smile. "I wasn't lying. It doesn't matter. Eve and Andrew found out they were pregnant, that's all. He was my best friend, we were the way Nadine and Ethan are now, but he was Eve's friend, too, and she was so beautiful, and he took her to the prom, and . . ." She waved her hand. "No big deal."

"That's why you left?" Davy said back. "No. It's something else. What happened with your dad?"

Tilda turned her back on him and put another painting in the cabinet.

"We're not going upstairs until you tell me," Davy said. "Spill it."

"It wasn't anything," Tilda said. "We found out Nadine was on the way, and I came down here to work on the last Scarlet." She forged a smile for him. "The one you scammed from Colby. The dancers."

"The lovers," Davy said.

Her smile disappeared and she nodded. "I was working on it, down here, crying, and Dad came in and said . . ." She swallowed. "He said, 'When will you learn you were born to paint and not to love?' "

"I hate your father," Davy said, rage slicing through him.

"No," Tilda said. "He was trying to . . . make me see my destiny. And, really, he was pretty much right. I mean, I've been loved. Scott loved me."

Davy felt that spurt of jealousy again.

"But Dad was right," Tilda went on, trying to smile. "I was happier painting than I was with people. I loved painting the furniture and the Scarlets, even the forgeries I was doing were more interesting than people. I just . . ." She sighed. "I just really loved Andrew. And I loved Eve. There weren't any bad guys. It just didn't work out for me, I'm just not . . . But I didn't want to hear it then." She gave Davy a wobbly smile. "My dad had really bad timing."

"He was an exploitive son of a bitch," Davy said.

Tilda took a deep breath. "So I scrubbed the paintbrush through the faces in the painting and threw it at him and walked out. I took the bus to Cincinnati, and found a job waitressing there and let Eve know, and she told Gwennie, and Gwennie sent money, every week, and never told Dad where I was, and it turned out okay. I'd graduated from high school the year before because he'd had me test out of a bunch of stuff so I could paint, and that meant I could work if I lied about my age. Eventually he found out and called and yelled and disowned me, but by then, the scary part of being on my own was over." Tilda's face eased a little. "And one day, the guy who owned the restaurant was talking about fixing up the place, and I said, 'I can paint a mural for you,' and I did, and one of the people who came into the restaurant saw it and wanted one, and the mural business just sort of evolved. And there I was, painting forgeries for a living just like all the other Goodnights." She looked down at the paintings at her feet. "Just like my dad said I would. He was right."

"He was wrong," Davy said grimly.

"The bad thing," Tilda swallowed. "The bad thing was that the Scarlets . . . were . . . the way . . ." She swallowed again. "The way I really paint. So when he sold them, I couldn't paint that way anymore unless I was Scarlet for him, so I couldn't paint."

"How could he *do that*?" Davy said. "He was an artist. He knew what that meant. How could he do that to *his own kid*?"

Tilda took a deep breath. "He wasn't an artist."

"What?"

"He was a terrible painter." She leaned against the cabinets and slid down until she was sitting on the carpet, collapsing there like a rag doll in her pretty, silky dress, looking so tired Davy ached for her. "You can learn all the craft you want," she said. "But if you're not born with a sense of light and color and line and mass, you cannot paint. And he couldn't paint. He was a great teacher, but he couldn't . . . It was like being born tone-deaf in a family of musicians." Her face crumpled. "Eve couldn't paint, either, he tried to teach her but she couldn't. But I could."

I can't stand this, Davy thought and went over to sit beside her.

"I could paint before I could write my name," Tilda said as he put his arm around her. "I loved everything he taught me." She sniffed, trying to hold back tears, and he tightened his hold on her. "I think he resented me for it. He loved Eve so much, but he couldn't . . . I couldn't . . . I didn't get it. I thought if I just painted better, he'd love me more. I didn't get it that he . . . So I tried harder and harder and got better and better and he—"

"Oh, God, Tilda." Davy held her close. "I'm so sorry. And I really hate your father."

"No," Tilda said into his shirt. "He did his best. And I got out. I walked away. I just didn't get to take Scarlet with me." She lifted her head. "Do you know that he wanted me to sign them as James? James Hodge, Homer's boy. I was the one who named me Scarlet. I signed them Scarlet."

"Good for you," Davy said, holding her tighter.

"No," Tilda said, her pale eyes swimming as she looked at him. "Good for you. He sold them, but you got every damn one of them back for me. Every damn one."

"Oh, honey," he said and kissed her, feeling her tears on his face, and then he held her tight as she wiped her face on his shirt.

"I'm sorry," she said. "I know I look like hell when I'm soggy."

"Yeah, that's an issue now," Davy said, still holding her. "Christ, Tilda." He looked around at the Goodnight forgeries and suddenly they looked like bodies to him. "We have to get rid of this stuff."

"I can't," she said tiredly. "I want to, so much, but I can't even talk to you about them without sobbing all over you. Imagine me trying to—"

"I can," Davy said grimly. "And you're getting out of this damn basement, too."

"It's a good studio," Tilda said.

"It's the pit of hell," Davy said. "I don't care how white you paint this place, there's blood on the walls. We're moving your stuff up to the attic. Tonight. There's plenty of room up there. You can paint in the sunlight tomorrow."

"He wasn't a bad man," Tilda said. "He—"

"Right. He just couldn't paint. Fuck him." Davy let go of her and pushed himself off the floor. Then he held out his hand to her and hauled her to her feet. "What stuff do you need from down here?"

"Davy, I don't—"

"Upstairs, Matilda," he said. "All of it. I can't beat up your father because the son of a bitch died on me, but I can get you out of this basement. Pack."

He started shoving Goodnight forgeries back into their crypts, and Tilda said, "Did you mean it?"

"Mean what?" he said, giving a van Gogh a shove.

"That you could sell them."

"I can sell anything," he said. "But I don't want to touch this stuff. I'm thinking we consign it to an auction house."

"I had thought of that," Tilda said. "People collect forgeries. We could do it anonymously. But somebody will find out and ask about them. Somebody always finds out, and then I'd—"

"I'll take care of it." Davy slammed another painting into a cupboard. "Pack." When he didn't hear her move, he turned around.

"I'm sorry," she said, standing there in misery. "I didn't mean to unload all of this angst on you. I didn't mean to be so..." She waved her hand. "*Melodramatic. Drama queen.*" She tried to laugh. "You must hate weepy women."

"Yeah, I do." Davy walked over to her and put his arms around her and held her tight. "But not you, Scarlet." He kissed the top of her head. "You can do anything you want, and I'll still love you." She went still in his arms, and he said, "I know. I can't believe I said it, either."

"You can take it back," she said into his shirt. "It's just because I cried all over you, and you're feeling sorry for me."

"No," he said. "It's because you kissed me in a closet and adopted Steve and support your family and painted armadillo footstools and really hot mermaids. It's because you're Matilda Scarlet, and I was born to love you as sure as I was born to con people, damn it." She lifted her head to look at him and he added, "And I love you with everything I've got, which means your rat bastard father was wrong."

She came up on her toes to meet him, slippery in his arms as her dress slid between them, and when she kissed him, her lips were soft and open on his, no more secrets, and if Davy hadn't already been in love, that would have done it. "Pack your stuff," he whispered against her mouth, holding her as close as he could. "We're getting out of here."

Tilda looked around. "You're right." She sighed and relaxed against him, pliant in his arms. "It's a shame, though. It's a good space."

"I know," Davy said. "I'm thinking we paint a mermaid mural in here and put in a pool table. And a jukebox with music from this century." He felt Tilda laugh into his shirt. "I love you, Matilda," he said into her curls, breathing in cinnamon.

"I love you, too," she said, and he felt his own tension go because she'd finally said it. "But I don't play pool."

"You will," he said. "It's your kind of game. Now pack."

HALF AN hour later, upstairs, Gwen was trying to figure out what to do with Mason. He was a nice man and a competent lover and she wanted him out of her apartment, out of her building, and possibly out of her life, although that was probably an overreaction. Why couldn't he be like other men and leap out of bed, citing morning meetings or something?

"That was wonderful, Gwennie," he said, kissing her again.

Get off my leg. "It was," she said, "but I think you should go. Nadine is downstairs, and I don't want her to think—"

"Of course," Mason said, pulling her close. "You're absolutely right." He kissed her again, and then got out of bed, which gave her a chance to grab her robe, wondering why she was so cranky. Mason had been very sweet, and first times were always a problem, or at least they had been in her teens which was the last time she'd had a first time—

"You don't need to see me out," Mason said when he'd dressed, coming around the bed to kiss her again. "I'll see you tomorrow." He looked at the clock that said twelve-thirty, and added, "Or I guess I'll see you today." He smiled at her, almost shy. "It's a brand-new day, Gwennie."

"Yep," she said, smiling back and thinking, *Leave.*

She walked him to the door, and patted his arm, and he had started down the hall, when Ford came up the stairs, passing him on the way. He stopped when he saw her.

What? Gwen thought, sticking out her chin. *You're a hit man. Cut me a break.*

He shook his head at her and went inside his apartment, slamming the door behind him, and she felt like hell, which was ridiculous.

She went back into her apartment and into the bedroom and looked at the rumpled bed, all white in the lamplight, like the site of a virgin sacrifice. Which was damn funny when you considered how long it had been since she'd been a virgin and the kind of track record she'd had before she'd married Tony.

Maybe another vodka was in order. She was turning

into a real lush, but at least she had good reason. She had *problems*. She tied her robe tighter, and went back into the hall, and Ford opened his door.

"Listen," she said, before he could say anything. "Don't give me any crap. I'm having a hard life."

"You're an idiot."

"Hey, I get to make my own choices."

"Not when they're that bad," Ford said. "You couldn't wait another week, could you?"

"Why another week?" she said, and thought, *Davy*. "Listen, you have to stop killing people."

"Killing people?"

"Someone overheard a phone call," Gwen said, looking at the ceiling.

She heard him move, and when she brought her eyes down he was there, and then he kissed her, his body blocking out all light and his mouth blotting out all thought, and she should have slapped him silly.

Instead she almost crawled inside his shirt in her enthusiasm for his mouth, and when he finally broke the kiss, he had to push her away to look her straight in the eye. "Okay, it's only a mistake if you do it again," he said.

"Hey," she said, holding up her left hand. "I'm *engaged*."

He took the ring off her finger as she pulled her hand away. "And now you're not," he said, pocketing it.

"Who the hell do you think you are?" she said, trying not to be the kind of woman who was turned on by domineering men, which was a laugh, considering

Tony. "I'll kiss anybody I want. I'll get engaged to any-body I want. I'll *sleep* with anybody I want. Give me back that ring."

"No," he said.

"I'm still engaged," she said and went back into her apartment, slamming the door in his face, suddenly feeling pretty damned good. The world had swung around and two men had jumped her in one night, not bad for a middle-aged former singer and grandmother of one. It was almost like the old days, guys lining up, and all she had to do was choose. And it was happening because she wanted it to, because she needed the change, because she was done sleeping through life.

And Tilda was fine with her leaving. She could go.

For the first time in years, Gwen felt no interest in a Double-Crostic.

But just because she wanted it to happen, that didn't mean she was with the right guys. *Okay, definitely not Mason*, she thought. *What was I thinking?* Well, she'd been thinking about the mortgage, but maybe they could work something out. And definitely not the hit man across the hall, either. She'd done the charming-crook thing with Tony. Forget it.

But definitely somebody. There will definitely be somebody. Definitely, I am back in the game.

She went to change the sheets, and found herself humming one of those obnoxious songs with forget-table lyrics and an unforgettable tune, chachaing around the mattress with a spring in her step as she reclaimed her bed. When the bed was smooth and new again, she picked up the phone and called down to the office. "Ethan?" she said, when he answered. "What is this?"

She hummed a few bars and Ethan said, "Wait. Let me get Nadine."

"What?" Nadine said when she picked up the phone and Gwen hummed again. "It's that Beach Boys thing," she said. "Something, Jamaica, oooh, I'm gonna take ya."

"Aruba, Jamaica," Gwen said, the song dying on her lips.

"Where is Aruba anyway?" Nadine said.

"The Caribbean," Gwen said. "Bring me up the vodka, would you, honey?"

"ABOUT MUSSOLINI and Grandma," Tilda said, later that night in bed, as Davy was dozing off, his arms around her.

"You have to ask before we do it," he said sleepily into her neck.

"Right," Tilda said, trying to free her arm from under him. "When do you think we'll be playing that one?"

"Whenever you want," he mumbled.

"No," Tilda said, "I meant *when* . . ." Her voice trailed off as he began to snore.

Steve took that for a signal and jumped up on the bed.

"What I want to know," Tilda said to Davy's unconscious body, "is *when* are you leaving me, you bastard, and are you coming back?" She swallowed. "Because

I'm believing in you and that can't be good." He snored again and she had a moment's suspicion that he was faking it. Then she remembered that he hadn't had any sleep the night before, that he'd sold furniture for hours straight, that he'd moved the entire contents of her studio up five flights of stairs, and that he'd just made athletically passionate love to her. "He's really out, Steve," she said to the dog. "But tomorrow we ask him. We are not going to be those people who dillydally and then regret it. He said he loves me. He said he's going to get rid of the forgeries. He's staying. Right?"

Steve sighed and stuck his nose under the quilt. Tilda lifted the edge for him and he tunneled under.

"You'll never leave me, will you, Steve?" she said to him. Then she looked over at Davy and said, "You never will, either."

She looked around the attic, now stacked full of easels and foam core board and paint and canvas, even her drawing board in one corner, and she thought, *This is so much better. This is so right.*

She looked at Davy again, asleep beside her, and leaned over to kiss him on the cheek. Then she slid down under the covers between the two men in her life and fell asleep.

THE NEXT morning when Tilda went down for muffins, Eve was sitting in the office, looking like death.

"What?" Tilda said, still on a high from the night before. "What happened?"

"Can we go someplace else?" Eve said. "I want to get out of here."

"Sure," Tilda said. "What's wrong?"

"I told Simon I was me," Eve said.

"Oh, boy," Tilda said. "Let's go."

CHAPTER · NINETEEN

"WHAT HAPPENED?" TILDA SAID WHEN THEY WERE sitting in a booth at the diner and had ordered omelets.

"He's leaving," Eve said, her voice husky.

"Oh." Tilda took her hand. "Is that good?" She ducked her head to see Eve's face. "No?"

"He didn't believe me," Eve said. "Not at first. I had to get the wig and show him."

"And then?"

"And then he was mad as hell," Eve said. "So I told him if he'd been paying attention that he'd have noticed, the way Davy knew you. I told him he was getting two for one. I told him he probably had secrets from me, too, but that I'd understand."

"And he didn't buy it," Tilda said, scrambling to think of a solution. "Maybe if you give him time—"

"He's a thief," Eve said flatly.

"Oh." Tilda regrouped.

"He told me all about it when I said that thing about his having secrets I'd understand. He said he didn't think I would, that he'd been a thief for years before the

FBI asked him to consult. Since he was a teenager. He stole from everybody."

Tilda swallowed. "Everybody makes mistakes."

"He *stole*, Tilda," Eve said, taking her hand back. "He went into people's houses and he took their things. He just *took* them. He still doesn't think it was wrong. He says he only took from people who could spare it." Eve shook her head. "That's like Ford only killing people who deserve it. It's what he did that counts, not who the victims were."

"Well, he's reformed," Tilda said. "Maybe—"

"People don't reform," Eve said. "Not like that. There's a piece of him missing that let him do that. And he's not even sorry. He's just mad about Louise. He says I lied to him, which I didn't. I never said I wasn't Louise."

"I don't think that's the point," Tilda said. "I think—"

"We just stood there and looked at each other," Eve said. "Like we were looking at each other for the first time."

"Well, you were."

Eve shook her head. "All I could think of was, I slept with him and he was a thief. And he kept saying that he couldn't believe he'd slept with Nadine's mother. Except he didn't say 'slept with.' I didn't even tell him that it wasn't me, it was Louise. He wouldn't get it. And I didn't care."

Tilda sighed. "Look, you hit the sheets about fifteen minutes after you met, and then you lied to each other for almost three weeks so you could keep on doing it. It's not a huge surprise that it didn't work out. Can't you just chalk it up to experience and great sex?"

"Is that what you're going to do with Davy?" Eve said, her mouth set in hard lines.

"No," Tilda said. "Davy is forever. But that's because we know the truth about each other."

"Davy's a con man," Eve said. "Did you know that?"

"Yes," Tilda said. "He told me."

Eve looked at her in outrage. "And it doesn't bother you?"

"He is what he is," Tilda said. "He's not breaking the law anymore, and neither am I, and we can make our peace with that."

Eve shook her head. "I don't see how you can stay with him knowing the truth."

"I think it's like a litmus test," Tilda said. "If you're going to make it, you can tell each other anything, and it may not be what you want to hear, but it doesn't matter. Even if you cry all over him and end up a soggy, pathetic mess."

"So it's love," Eve said, clearly not buying it. "Well, that's very optimistic of you, but you're still trusting a con man."

"And he's trusting an art forger," Tilda said, exasperated. "Nobody's perfect. Everybody who's ever loved anybody has had some stuff to get past. So you get past it because you really don't have any other choice. You can't leave."

Eve shook her head. "I just can't be that way." She

sounded almost smug, and Tilda lost what little sympathy she had left.

"You love Andrew," she said.

"Well, of course, I—"

"And sixteen years ago he used you to convince himself he wasn't gay," Tilda said. "He knew he was gay, he's always known, but he didn't want it to be true, and he knew you loved him and would do anything he asked, and he slept with you to lie to himself."

Eve's face was like stone.

"And he's felt like hell about it ever since," Tilda said. "As much as we all adore Nadine, she stopped your life in its tracks at eighteen."

"Andrew stopped, too," Eve said.

"No," Tilda said. "He went on and found the love of his life and the career he always wanted. Andrew doesn't stop for anybody. And good for him, too, he's doing it right, but he still screwed up in the past, and you've forgiven him."

"I screwed up, too," Eve said miserably. "I knew he was gay and I thought I could change him, if I just loved him enough." She stopped and swallowed. "I lied to him. I told him I was on the pill. I should have let him be him. I used him, too."

"So neither one of you should love each other," Tilda said, completely exasperated. "You did lousy things to each other, just like you and Simon, so—"

"It's not the same," Eve said.

"I know it's not the same," Tilda said. "You don't

love Simon. *Which is my point.* Let it go. Kiss him good-bye, wish him luck, move on."

The waitress brought their omelets and Tilda busied herself with salt and pepper, waiting for Eve to say something. When her omelet was half gone and Eve's was still untouched, Eve finally spoke.

"I thought you'd be there for me," she said. "I thought you'd be on my side."

"I am on your side, always," Tilda said. "But you don't love him. That means it's good that it's over. That means that it worked out right."

"Then why do I feel like hell?" Eve snapped.

"Because you wanted it to be right," Tilda said, feeling sorry for her again. "You wanted Simon to be a law-abiding FBI stepfather to Nadine and the perfect husband for you, and it wasn't ever going to happen. It was Andrew all over again."

Eve sat silent for a moment, staring at her congealing breakfast, and then she pushed her plate away. "It still hurts."

"Oh, baby." Tilda went around the table and slid into the booth beside her. "I know it does," she said as she put her arms around her sister. Eve put her head down on Tilda's shoulder. "Poor baby. I'm sorry, I *really* am."

"I can't believe how dumb I am," Eve said, her voice muffled.

"You're not dumb," Tilda said, tightening her arms. "Poor baby. Poor, poor baby."

"Am I ever going to get this right?" Eve said, holding

on to Tilda. "I'm *thirty-five*, for God's sake, and I'm still screwing up."

"Gwennie's fifty-three and getting ready to shoot herself in the foot," Tilda said. "I don't think there's an age limit. Let's just hope Nadine has not inherited our lousy track record with men."

"I thought you and Davy—"

"I have great hope," Tilda said, "that he will break the Goodnight curse. But if he doesn't, I'll survive. And he'll be leaving me in a *much* better place. Maybe Simon's leaving you in a better place, too."

Eve was silent for so long that Tilda leaned over to look in her eyes.

"Do you ever wonder if you're Tilda pretending to be Scarlet or Scarlet pretending to be Tilda?" Eve said.

"No," Tilda said. "But it's a damn good question."

"Because I think I'm Louise."

"Oh, boy," Tilda said.

"Eve doesn't love him. Louise might."

Tilda leaned over her to call to the waitress. "Is it too early to get a drink here? Can we . . . No?" She opened her purse and put bills on the table for the omelets. "Come on, cookie," she said, pulling her sister out of the booth. "We're going home for some pineapple-orange."

THREE BLOCKS away, Clea sat across the breakfast table from Mason, mad as hell. First Thomas didn't show up to make breakfast, then Ronald stood her up, and now

Mason was sitting there drinking coffee, just as if he hadn't come home late and then turned her down when she offered to help him relax.

He'd slept with Gwen Goodnight.

He looked up at her now and she smiled and thought, *You fucking bastard.* "More coffee?" she asked him.

"Clea, it's over," he said, not unkindly.

"What's over?" she said brightly, as her entire body went cold.

"Us," he said. "It was fun, I had a good time, you had a good time—"

Want to bet?

"—but it's over. I'm in love with somebody else."

"Gwen Goodnight," Clea said.

"I'm sorry, Clea," he said, and he sounded as though he meant it. "I just fell in love."

"With her gallery," Clea said before she could stop herself.

His face darkened. "I knew you wouldn't understand. Gwen's the real thing."

"And what am I?" Clea said. "I'm real, damn it. I'm a human being, I'm somebody you've talked to, made love to, made plans with, and now I'm just supposed to be *understanding*?"

"We didn't make plans," Mason said firmly. "We never—"

"We were going to build an art collection together," Clea said, her throat closing at the unfairness of it all. "We talked about it, we went to museums, we bought paintings—"

"I did all of that," Mason said. "You were just along for the ride."

Clea put her napkin on the table. "Funny you didn't mention that in the beginning."

"I thought you knew," Mason said, looking surprised.

"Knew what? That you were just using me?" Clea felt the tears start. "This is so unfair of you."

"Clea," Mason said, sounding stricken, and Clea let the tears flow. They were real ones. He deserved them.

"I love you," she said on a sob and ran for the stairs. Crying was hell on a woman's complexion, and she needed a tissue.

A ball bat to smack Mason with would be good, too.

AT ABOUT the same time Clea was thinking of bashing Mason, Davy came downstairs to find Tilda and found Nadine instead.

"Hey, Lucy," he said to her. "Nice job last night."

"I know," Nadine said. "I think it's going to be my career."

"Good choice," Davy said. "So where's your aunt? I've misplaced her."

"I think she went somewhere with Mom," Nadine said.

"Okay," Davy said, and then remembered he hadn't seen Michael since the night before, either. "Have you seen my dad?"

"Yeah," Nadine said. "He and Dorcas went to visit your sister."

Davy went still. "He doesn't know where she is."

"He got Ethan to look her up on the computer. You can find anybody on the Net. She's in some little town with a weird name."

"Temptation," Davy said.

"That was it," Nadine said. "They took off in Dorcas's car about half an hour ago."

"Oh, hell," Davy said, exasperated, and grabbed the phone.

Dillie picked it up on the first ring.

"Get me your dad," Davy said.

"I was sort of hoping you'd be Jordan," she said. "Listen, the stuff you told me—"

"Your dad," Davy said. *"Now."*

He heard Dillie drop the phone, and a minute later, Phin picked up.

"What's wrong?" he said. "Dillie says it's an emergency."

"It is," Davy said. "Dad figured out where you are. He's heading your way. Hold the fort until I can get there and remove him. Do not let him alone with Sophie and do not give him money."

"I'm not stupid," Phin said.

"Neither is he," Davy said. "I like to think of him as washed up, but the man can talk anybody into anything."

"You know, he's starting to sound interesting," Phin said.

"Famous last words," Davy said. "Head for high ground."

★

UP IN her bedroom, Clea dabbed the last of her tears away and faced the unavoidable truth: Mason was leaving her for a fifty-three-year-old woman who didn't moisturize. It was a slap in the face of her entire worldview. She'd spent forty-five years taking excellent care of herself, only to lose to a nobody who was going to have jowls at any minute. God knew how long it had been since Gwen had done a sit-up. One hundred. That was how many Clea did every morning and every night, one hundred damn sit-ups, and what had it gotten her? Dumped for a grandmother, for God's sake. The woman had given birth, she had stretch marks, she had a stomach—Clea put her hand on her own supernaturally flat abdomen—and still she was winning. That was so wrong.

Well, Gwen had messed with the wrong woman this time. "This is not over," she said out loud. "This is *not* over."

She dumped her purse out on the bed until she found Ford Brown's number. When he answered, she said, "We had a deal."

"What?" he said.

"You were to keep Gwen away from Mason."

"Look, you brought him to the gallery," Ford said. "She hasn't come to the house, has she?"

"No," Clea said. "And I did not bring him. He went on his own."

"I can't stop him," Ford said. "That's up to you."

"And Davy's still there," Clea said.

"Is he bothering you?" Ford said.

"Yes," Clea said. "His *existence* bothers me."

"I can take care of that if you want," Ford said. "Just say the word."

Clea swallowed. "Gwen is the bigger problem." She looked around to make sure no one was listening.

"Gwen?" He sounded taken aback. "You want me to hit a woman?"

"No, I don't want you to hit her," Clea said, exasperated. "I want you to—" Her eye fell on the open closet door, the place where she'd hidden the painting. She stretched the phone cord over and looked inside.

The Scarlet was gone.

"What?" Ford said.

"Wait a minute," Clea said, her heart in her throat. She put down the phone and went to the closet and then over to her laptop. Three minutes later, she picked up the phone, her heart hammering, and said, "Do *not* do anything to Davy Dempsey. I need him alive."

Oh, God, Davy had her money. She sat down on the bed, trying not to shake. He'd taken it all. Mason was slipping away and she had no money and she was forty-five.

"Are you okay?" Ford said.

"No," Clea said, her voice shaking. "I'm not okay. And you did not keep Davy Dempsey out of this house. He stole a painting from me and he took my money. And if you kill him, I'll never get it back. Just *watch* him." She bent and put her head between her knees, trying to keep from fainting. She had no money. And you couldn't find men with money unless you had money. Or youth. Oh, *God*.

"For how long?" Ford said.

"What?" Clea said, trying to keep the tears out of her voice.

"For how long do I watch him?"

"Until I get the money back," Clea said, swallowing. No need to panic. She still had time. She could still bring this off. She deserved to bring this off, damn it. Zane had left her with nothing, Cyril had left her with nothing, it was *her turn*. "Watch him until I get the money back and then you can finish the job." She straightened and caught sight of her reflection in the mirror and tried to smooth out her face. Terror made her look old. She couldn't be old. Oh, *God*—

"All right," Ford said. "Exactly what does 'finish the job' mean?"

"What?" Clea said, still trying to cope with the mirror. "I have to go. Just *watch* him, damn it, and do a better job than you did last night. I can't believe—"

"He never left the gallery last night," Ford said. "I watched him the entire time. When the gallery closed, he went downstairs with Tilda."

"Maybe it wasn't last night then," Clea said. "But it was him." She thought about Davy, impossibly young with her all those years ago, just impossible with Tilda now, and she wished she'd never met him, in spite of all the good times and good sex. It hadn't been that good, not good enough for the price she was paying now. "I wish he was dead."

"Is that an order?" Ford said.

"*No*," Clea said. "For Christ's sake, pay attention. He's got my *money*. He has to stay alive until I get it back. If you kill him, his sisters will inherit everything, and I'll never get it back." She thought about Sophie, implacably efficient and not a little obsessive about her baby brother. "Do *not* kill him."

"Just checking," Ford said and hung up.

Clea hung up the phone and sat, thinking fast. She didn't have the know-how to embezzle the money out of Davy's accounts, Ronald had done that, so maybe—

She straightened. How had *Davy* had the know-how? How had Davy gotten the numbers, the password? How—

She picked up the phone and dialed again, and when the phone clicked, she said, "Ronald, we had an appointment. Get your ass over here. You have some explaining to do."

WHEN TILDA and Eve got back to the gallery, Nadine was bagging trash in the gallery.

"Have you seen Davy?" Tilda asked.

"He left," Nadine said. "He went to Temptation to see his sister."

Tilda took a deep breath. "Did he say anything? About me?"

Nadine shook her head. "Michael and Dorcas left, and Davy took off after them."

"Did he leave a note?" Tilda said.

"No," Nadine said. "He was in a hurry. What time are we opening the gallery?"

"I don't know," Tilda said and turned to see Eve, standing behind her, radiating sympathy and suppressing "I told you so." "He's coming back," she told Eve.

"Of course he is," Eve said.

"I have to go work," Tilda said and headed for the attic.

He was coming back. She was not going to be an idiot and panic because he went to see his sister and didn't leave a note, for heaven's sake. He'd come back to sell the fakes. They still hadn't played Grandma and Mussolini. He'd promised her that. He always kept his promises.

He was a con man.

He's coming back, you dummy, Tilda told herself.

He had to. He had her van.

RONALD DID not look guilty when he showed up, and that made Clea even madder. She dragged him into the bedroom and shut the door, even though it was pointless since Mason wanted Gwen Goodnight, the bastard.

"You gave Davy Dempsey my account numbers," she said, practically spitting her rage. "You *betrayed* me."

"He beat me up," Ronald said, looking untouched. "And who are you to talk about betrayal? You're living with another man. You—"

"Davy took my money, Ronald," Clea said, stepping closer. "He took *all of it*. Every man I've ever trusted has left me penniless and now I'm penniless again, and you helped the man who did it."

"You're not penniless," Ronald said. "You can sell your art collection."

"He took that, too," Clea said, remembering the Scarlet with increased rage. "He wiped me out."

"Well, there's that," Ronald said, pointing to the starry-night chair Mason had insisted on lugging home from the gallery for her.

"Ronald, pay attention, that's *junk*," Clea said. "I lost a fortune here, and you want me to be a *junk dealer*?"

"That's not junk," Ronald said. "That's a Scarlet Hodge."

"No it isn't," Clea said. "That's . . ." She looked at the chair again. It did look a little like the Scarlet. "It's not the same artist," she finished, not snapping anymore.

"Yes it is," Ronald said. "It was obvious when I looked at the show at the gallery last night after you ditched me by the catering table." He sounded put out. "But I couldn't tell you because you had to talk to the important people. Like *Mason*."

Clea tuned him out to look at the chair again. It could be a Scarlet.

"Look at the motifs," Ronald was saying. "The color choices. Look at the brushwork. It's the same painter. Now about Mason."

Clea waved him off and sat down, thinking fast. Maybe Ronald was right. Suppose Tilda Goodnight was Scarlet Hodge. Was that illegal?

"Clea, you're not listening to me."

"Ronald, if somebody painted under somebody else's name, would that be illegal?"

"Yes," Ronald said. "It's forgery. And I don't care. Clea, Mason isn't what you think he is. He's—"

"Going after Gwen Goodnight, I know," Clea said. "Give me a minute here."

Why would Matilda Goodnight forge Scarlet Hodges? There had to be money in it somewhere, but for right now, the important thing was that she had something on Tilda Goodnight, and Davy was sleeping with Tilda Goodnight. And nobody knew better than Clea how Davy was about the women he slept with.

"Clea—"

"Quiet. I'm thinking."

So all she had to do was threaten to expose Tilda, and Davy would have to give the money back. Clea frowned. No he wouldn't, not if she couldn't prove it, and she couldn't prove it without the painting. So first she had to get the painting back.

And Davy would have given Tilda Goodnight the painting, she was sure of it.

"How do you prove something's a forgery?" she asked Ronald.

He frowned at her. "Lots of ways. Clea, we have to talk about us."

"Give me one of the ways," Clea said.

"Show it to the artist who is supposed to have painted it," Ronald said, exasperated. "I've been very patient, Clea, but it's time—"

"What else?" Clea said.

"Show it to somebody who worked with her, who saw her paint it," Ronald said. "Now, about *us* . . ."

Homer Hodge, Clea thought. Mason hadn't found Homer yet, but that didn't mean she couldn't. She was excellent at finding men. And if she couldn't find him, well, Tilda wouldn't know that, would she?

"Clea, are you listening to me?" Ronald said.

Clea focused on him. "Ronald, you betrayed me."

Ronald flushed. "He forced me."

"But I will forgive you," Clea said, "if you can keep Davy Dempsey away from me for the next couple of days."

"He's gone," Ronald said. "I called him this morning and he was gone."

Got my money and took off, Clea thought. *Poor Tilda Goodnight.* "All right, then," she said. "Ronald, I have to get my money back."

"I don't know what his account numbers are," Ronald said, backing up. "He changed them all. He doesn't trust me anymore."

"*I* will get it back," Clea said. "But I need time to work. So go away."

"Clea, you can't keep shoving me away like this," Ronald said, taking a stand. "I know things you need to know."

"Ronald, because of you I just lost three million

dollars," Clea said. "Be grateful I'm not having Ford drop you off a building."

Ronald swallowed.

"Now be a good boy and go away," Clea said. "I have to think."

He tried to protest and she ignored him. First, she'd get the painting back, as many paintings as Tilda had. There'd been six, Mason said. If Davy was on the job, Tilda would have all six. So she'd get six Scarlet Hodges to give Mason; let Gwen Goodnight try to top that.

Then she'd call Davy and tell him Tilda was going to jail unless he gave her the money back. Even if he'd left Tilda, he wouldn't let her go to jail. Not Davy. Davy took care of his women. The thought gave her a pang, a brief moment when she wondered if maybe she'd made a mistake cutting him loose all those years ago, and then she remembered that he'd been broke and that Zane had had money, that the only reason Davy had money later was that he'd stolen hers, and that the only person she could really count on to take care of her was herself.

So first she'd get the paintings from Tilda.

Then she'd get the money from Davy.

Then she'd take the paintings to Mason and seduce him until he forgot about Gwen entirely.

And if he didn't, she had Ford to take care of Gwen.

"All right," she said out loud and looked around.

Ronald was gone.

"All right," she said again, and dressed to go see Tilda.

*

"HE'S INSIDE," Phin said when Davy met him on the front porch of the farmhouse. "He likes Temptation. He's thinking of retiring here. And he brought this albino woman with him."

"She's not albino," Davy said. "She just doesn't get much sun. Has he asked for money?"

"Not unless he's doing it now," Phin said. "I've been there the whole time. God, he's exhausting. I'd be willing to pay him off just to make him go away."

Davy stopped with his hand on the door. "You know, that might be his plan."

"It's reasonable," Phin said. "It's working."

"No it's not," Davy said, opening the screen door. "Hey, Dad," he called as he walked in. "Funny meeting you here."

"Davy," Sophie said, springing up from the couch where Michael was dandling a rosy baby on his knee. She threw her arms around Davy and hugged him hard, and then slapped him on the shoulder. "Where have you been?"

Davy kissed her on the cheek. "Great to see you. Your anniversary present's in the van. Take your husband and go look at it."

"Our anniversary isn't until September," Sophie said, as he pushed past her.

"Well, let's go look anyway," Phin said, taking her hand.

"But—" Sophie said, and then she was gone, towed out the door by her husband.

"We need to talk," Davy said to Michael. He picked Dempsey up and transferred him to a startled Dorcas who'd been sitting bemused through the whole process.

"I'm going home," Dorcas said, looking at Dempsey as if he was an alien.

"His mother will be back in a minute," Davy said and took Michael's arm and pulled him to his feet. "You'll like the back porch here," he said to him. "It's private. *Move*."

CHAPTER TWENTY

"Now, LISTEN," MICHAEL SAID, BUT DAVY FROG-marched him out through the kitchen.

"Hi, Uncle Davy," Dillie said when they went past her at the refrigerator. "Want a DoveBar?"

"Hi, sweetie," Davy said. "No." He opened the back screen door and shoved Michael out on the porch.

"Now, look," Michael said, straightening. "I—"

"Have you looked around here?" Davy said.

Michael looked taken aback. "I don't—"

"This place is every little town you ever dragged us to," Davy said. "It's every place you ever screwed up for us. Only this time, Sophie belongs. She's got a husband and two kids and a great reputation, she's *mayor*, for Christ's sake, but you can screw that up in a minute, just like you always did."

"I would never hurt my daughter," Michael said, and there was no con in his voice.

"You never mean to," Davy said. "But you always do. You can't help it. You mean to go straight, but it's in your blood."

"I never mean to go straight," Michael said, confused.

"Well, I did," Davy said. "The point is, it doesn't work. You'd have to take somebody just to keep your blood moving. You'll ruin Sophie. With the best intentions in the world, you'll ruin her."

"You're overreacting," Michael said. "Now I'm going back in there—"

"How much are you going to hit her up for?" Davy said.

And for the first time in his life, Davy saw his father flush.

"Just a small loan, right?" Davy said.

"Seed money," Michael said. "A stake. Not much."

Davy took an envelope out of his back pocket and held it up. "There's a hundred thousand in here," he said, and Michael grew very still. "I was going to give it to you today to bribe you to leave. Now it's yours if you promise to never come back here without me."

"My family's here," Michael said, outraged. "That's my grandchild in there."

"Listen to me," Davy said. "I've learned a lot in the last couple of days, among other things, that everything you said to me last week was right. If I don't accept who I really am, I'm the mark. And what I am is your son."

"You say it like it's a bad thing," Michael said. "I gave you an education no one else on earth could give you."

"I know," Davy said. "I'm grateful. But Sophie comes first. She saved us after Mom died, she saved *me*, and I will do anything to keep her safe, even if it means dropkicking you into the river with a brick around your neck." He held up the envelope again. "This is for you if you go away and leave her in peace. You can count it if you want."

"No," Michael said. "I trust you."

"There's irony for you," Davy said.

"Honor among thieves," Michael said.

"Take the money," Davy said. "But from now on, when you come to Ohio, you come directly to me. You do not try to come down here without me."

"You're going to be *here*?" Michael said, his appalled expression saying everything anybody needed to know about Temptation.

"I will be in Columbus." Davy held the envelope toward Michael. "Take it. Maybe you can make a killing with it. If nothing else, it'll give you a couple of good months."

Michael took the envelope. "I wasn't going to stay," he said, sounding tired. "I just wanted to see Sophie and Amy. And the kid. Dempsey." He grinned ruefully at Davy. "I didn't want to see the name die out."

"It's not going to," Davy said. "I've got that covered for you."

"Tilda." Michael nodded. "Good for you." He cocked his head at Davy. "Maybe I can come back for Christmas. Just to see how things turn out."

"Call first," Davy said. "We may be busy."

"You're a ruthless son of a bitch." Michael put the envelope in his jacket pocket. "You get that from your mother's side of the family. Ministers. They'll save you even if it kills you."

"You and Dorcas can go back tonight," Davy said.

"Dorcas is heading back now," Michael said. "She says it's been fun but she wants to paint. She should be missing me again by about Christmas. But I have to stay here tonight." He held up his hand as Davy leaned down on him. "No, I do. Amy's having us to dinner tomorrow, she's all excited about it. Dillie has a softball game tomorrow afternoon I promised I'd go to. I won't do anything, Davy." He patted his breast pocket. "I don't have to now. Give me today and tomorrow."

"If you so much as play Crazy Eights with Dillie," Davy began.

"You have my word," Michael said, and Davy stopped, surprised.

"Okay, then," he said, just as Sophie came out on the back porch.

"That bed is *wonderful*," she said, and then she caught sight of Michael's face. "What's going on?"

"Nothing," Davy said, turning to smile at her. "I hear we're going to a softball game tomorrow and then getting ptomaine at Amy's." Over her head, he saw Phin standing inside the screen door. "And then on Sunday, we've got to go," he said, a little louder.

"That's not long enough," Sophie said. But she was looking at him, not Michael. "So how's your landlady?"

"Her name's Matilda," Davy said. "Let me tell you all about her."

*

UP IN the attic, Tilda looked at her six Scarlet paintings, all lined up in a row. They were a motley lot. The first one had a horrible cheap frame on it, and while the second and third ones were in good shape, the other three needed to be cleaned.

And the sixth one needed to be finished.

She sat down on the floor in front of it and touched the smeared heads of the dancers. She remembered the hurt, but she didn't feel the pain anymore. Andrew was a good man. She loved him. But he wasn't Davy.

You may be overreacting, she tried to tell herself. It wasn't hard to convince yourself that you were in love with a guy who stole paintings for you, who resurrected your art gallery, who made you feel like a partner, who told you that you were magnificent and beautiful, who made love to you until you passed out, who told you he loved you with everything he had . . .

No, she really was in love with him.

She touched the painting again. Maybe it was time to do it right. Maybe it was time to be Scarlet again, only this time—

"Here you are," somebody said from behind her, and she jerked around to see Clea Lewis, looking impossibly lovely in the middle of the attic.

"What are you doing here?" Tilda said, so shocked she forgot to be polite.

"And there they are," Clea said, looking past her to the Scarlets. "Davy got all six of them for you, didn't he?"

"Uh," Tilda said, not sure how she was going to lie her way out of this one.

"I knew he would," Clea said, coming closer. "He always gets what he wants." She smiled down at Tilda, not unfriendly. "He's gone, isn't he?"

"Just for a day or so," Tilda said, lifting her chin.

"No," Clea said. "When he goes, he's gone. But he left you the paintings, that's like him. He's a very generous man." She looked regretful for a moment. "It's such a shame he's not rich."

"He's coming back," Tilda said firmly. "Now what are you doing in my bedroom?"

"I've come for the paintings, of course," Clea said.

"And I would give them to you because . . . ?" Tilda said, amazed by her gall.

"Because if you give them to me, I won't tell the world you're Scarlet," Clea said. "And those people you conned out of the paintings, they won't find out who you are. And you won't go to jail. And since you're pretty much supporting your entire family, they won't starve. I think it's a good trade."

She sounded perfectly friendly but there was ice in her eyes, and Tilda thought, *She knows about Gwennie and Mason.*

"You think these paintings are going to get Mason back?" she said, and Clea's face twisted.

"I think it's none of your damn business," she snapped.

Tilda nodded, trying to buy time to think it through. "They need to be cleaned. And I have to get the cheap frame off the first one. Mason would spit on that frame. And . . ." She turned back to the last painting, the dancers she'd smeared with her brush and thrown at her father when he'd told her she was born to paint not to love. "I have to finish this one. I'll bring them to you tomorrow."

"Tomorrow," Clea said, clearly suspicious.

"The paint will be dry by tomorrow," Tilda said. "I'll bring them to the house." She looked up at Clea. "You can trust me."

"I can't trust anybody," Clea said. "But I guess I have to here. Tomorrow morning then."

"Yes," Tilda said, looking at the last Scarlet. "Tomorrow you can have them."

DOWNSTAIRS, THE afternoon passed with a respectable number of customers, and when the last one left the gallery at five, and Gwen had sent Mason home, she locked the front door and turned to Nadine. "Do we have a number for Thomas the Caterer? His stuff is still here. Oh, and can you take the garbage out?"

"Sure," Nadine said, patting her on the back. "I don't know about Thomas, but we have to take Steve out anyway so we can do the garbage then. Wasn't he a good gallery dog today?"

Gwen looked down at Steve, who lay down on the floor and sighed. "I know," she told the dog. "Hell of a life."

"He loves it," Nadine insisted and held the office door open. "Come on, puppy, let's go take the trash out and pee on the Dumpster. You like that."

Steve trotted out after her and so did Ethan, and Gwen shook her head at her granddaughter's mastery of her life. Nothing bothered Nadine.

Except a minute later, Nadine was back, shaking. "Call 911," she said, and Gwen froze. "There's a dead body behind the Dumpster."

"*Davy*," Gwen said, her heart clutching.

"No," Nadine said. "Thomas the Caterer."

AN HOUR earlier, upstairs in her new studio, Tilda had finished cleaning the paintings and taking the frame off the first one. Now she set the last unfinished one up on her drawing table, tilted the light to see it better, and studied it. She was going to have to match her style to her old way of painting. No careful sketches or under-painting, just free strokes. It was the worst kind of painting to forge because any hesitation would be caught in the paint, scream out "I'm a fake," and ruin the painting.

She didn't want to ruin the painting.

Practice, she thought, *I need to practice who I used to be.* She tried a few sample strokes on newsprint, but it wasn't the same, they looked stupid, clumsy. She wasn't Scarlet anymore. She wasn't sure who she was.

Davy knows who I am, she thought. But he was in Temptation. She was on her own, faking again, out in the cold.

I can do this, she thought and looked around the all-white room. *I just need to remember.* She picked up her largest chunk of charcoal and drew the outlines of leaves in big slashes on her walls, channeling Scarlet, keeping her arm free and fluid. When she had walls full of outlines, she started to paint in the colors, making them round and full and warm, leaves you wanted to touch. That was what Scarlet had done, she'd made paintings you wanted to move into. She'd been young and happy and in love and she'd painted it all into . . .

That was the key to the last painting, Tilda realized, in the middle of a leaf stroke. Scarlet had stopped because Andrew loved Eve and she couldn't paint joy anymore. She'd stopped because she couldn't love Andrew; maybe it was time to start because she loved Davy. Maybe it was time because she believed in the future again. Because Davy was coming back.

She looked at the jungle drawn on her walls.

And because she'd been born to paint like this.

She brought the last Scarlet into the light, and this time she saw exactly how to finish it, two dark-haired lovers with the moon behind them, reaching for each other, forever.

It was going to be the story of her life.

GWEN HAD dialed 911 and then run out to the parking lot. It really was Thomas the Caterer, stretched out behind the Dumpster, looking pale as death with blood on his head.

"Are you sure he's dead?" Gwen said to Nadine. "Never mind. We'll wait and we won't touch the body and . . ." She stopped. "I have to go upstairs. Turn your back on him or something and don't touch anything."

"We're not idiots," Nadine said, still shaking.

"Just don't look at him," Gwen said and ran back inside and up to the second floor.

"Funniest thing," she said, her voice trembling, when Ford answered his door. "Nadine just went to take out the trash and there was a body behind the Dumpster."

"Anybody we know?" Ford said.

"That's it?" Gwen said, her heart sinking. "You don't sound surprised."

"I'm surprised," Ford said. "Anybody we know?"

"Thomas the Caterer," Gwen said. "Except he wasn't a caterer. He was with the FBI."

That got him, she saw with satisfaction. It was only for a minute, a flicker in his eyes, but it was there.

"He catered for the FBI?" Ford said, deadpan.

"Oh, funny," Gwen said. "The police are on their way. You might want to do better than that."

"You're a little hostile today," Ford said.

"Yeah. Finding a dead caterer behind my Dumpster will pretty much do that for me." She folded her arms across her chest, took a deep breath, and said, "You don't, by any chance, know how he got there, do you?"

"Haven't a clue," Ford said. "How'd he die?"

"There was a dent in his head," Gwen said. "I'm guessing that was it."

"Pretty much rules out natural causes and suicide, then."

Gwen set her jaw. "Did you kill him?"

Ford looked at her, disappointment plain on his face. "You think that little of me?"

Gwen was taken aback. "Well—"

"Hell, Gwen, if I'd killed him, he wouldn't be behind your Dumpster," Ford said. "I'm not *stupid*."

"Oh," Gwen said, appalled and relieved at the same time. "No, you're not."

"You could give me a *little* credit," Ford said.

"Right." Gwen took a step back. "I'm sorry."

"Anyway, the only guy I want to kill is Mason," Ford said. "He still walking around?"

"I think so," Gwen said, not sure what to do with that.

"Too bad," Ford said, stepping back. "Send up the cops when they get here."

He closed the door before she could say anything. "You know," she yelled through the door, "I'm not feeling better about this."

After a moment, when he hadn't answered, she drew a deep breath and went downstairs to meet the police.

TILDA FOUND out about Thomas when the police found her in the attic. She went downstairs to Gwennie and said, "What the hell?"

"It's not as bad as we thought," Gwen said brightly over her vodka and pineapple-orange. "He's not actually dead."

"You thought he was *dead* and you didn't come get

me?" Tilda poured herself a drink and tried to be upset. Poor Thomas. The man was practically a piñata.

I want to paint, she thought.

"He looked so awful," Gwen said. "Of course, he'd been lying behind the Dumpster for twenty-four hours. The police think he was talking to somebody out there and the other person just bashed him with a rock. Unpremeditated."

"Oh." Tilda nodded. "So how's Ford?"

"He says he wouldn't have left a body behind my Dumpster," Gwen said. "And I really think if he tried to kill somebody, they'd die. I mean, he's efficient."

"Right," Tilda said. "So who do they think did it?"

"Well, there's us," Gwen said. "And everybody at the gallery. They'd like to talk to Davy and Michael since they took off like that."

"Davy," Tilda said.

"I think they called the police in Temptation," Gwen said.

"Oh," Tilda said. "Maybe that'll bring Davy back."

"That's good," Gwen said. "Concentrate on the *important* stuff."

"I have to go paint," Tilda said, and went back upstairs to the jungle in her studio.

TILDA FINISHED the last Scarlet as the moon rose overhead in her skylights. When it was done, she looked at it, feeling tired and peaceful and finished, the end of one chapter and the start of a new one. Then she looked around at the charcoal lines on her walls, while Steve lay in the middle of her bed, exhausted from watching her. "We should keep painting, Steve," she said to him. "We're on a roll."

She turned the stereo on and painted to Dusty Springfield singing "I'd Rather Leave While I'm in Love" and Brenda Holloway doing "Every Little Bit Hurts." She remembered Davy saying she needed music from this century and switched to the Dixie Chicks, mattress-dancing while she applied gold leaf to her headboard, and ended up at four in the morning painting huge, happy, non-insane sunflowers over her bed as Pippy Shannon sang, "I Pretend." "Our song," Tilda told Steve, tired enough to be able to laugh, until Pippy sang, "Who am I foolin'? I'm foolin' myself." "Really my song," she told him. "I should pay more attention to what these women are saying."

She stepped back to look at the sunflowers, and they made her think of Clarissa, waving her Sharpie, saying, "Sign it bigger."

"Steve," she said, and Steve picked up his head from the bed and looked at her blearily. "It's very important to sign your work."

She put down the broad brush she'd used to lay in the leaves and picked up a number 1 paintbrush instead. She hunted out a tube of cadmium red from her paint box, squirted out a dime-sized drop, dipped the brush into the paint, and took a deep breath. Then, with a trembling hand, she signed the first painting again, writing "Matilda" above the "Scarlet" and "Goodnight" under it.

"Matilda Scarlet Goodnight," she read out loud. "Her work."

She dipped the brush into the paint again and moved to the cows. Her hand was steadier this time, her strokes surer. "Matilda Scarlet Goodnight," she read, conviction in her voice this time. "*Her* work." She kept on until she signed the lovers, and then she sat back and looked at what she'd done.

She felt wonderful.

"These are *my paintings*," she said to Steve. "Nobody's ever going to take that away from me again."

Except for Clea, she remembered bleakly. Well, she'd think about that tomorrow.

Then she put her brushes in water and climbed into bed with Steve and fell into a dreamless sleep.

WHEN TILDA woke up at nine the next morning, she packed up the paintings, put Andrew's "Bitch" cap on for good luck, and dropped Steve off with Eve and Gwennie, telling them where she was going.

"You shouldn't do this," Eve said. "This is wrong."

"Maybe not," Tilda said. "Maybe this is right. Maybe I was just supposed to get them back so I could sign them."

"No," Eve said, but Tilda hugged her good-bye, drove to Clea's in Jeff's car, and parked outside.

I don't want to give these up, she thought as she looked at the case she'd packed the paintings in. *I don't want to stop painting like that.*

And I don't want to do any more murals.

She sat there for a moment, and then dug in her purse for her cell phone and her day planner and turned to her work list: six more murals scheduled with the contact numbers written beside them.

She dialed the first one and said, "Mrs. Magnusson? This is Matilda Veronica. I'm going to have to cancel your mural. Something has come up and . . ." She went on, soothing her wounded clients, offering them paintings or furniture, feeling the tightness between her shoulder blades ease. It took her over an hour, and when she was done, she looked at the case and thought, *If I have to give these up, I should get more for them.*

And even though she was late, she shifted deeper in her seat and began to plan.

"WHERE'S TILDA?" Davy said, when he came through the office door.

"Where have you been?" Gwen said, annoyed with him. "All hell's been breaking loose here and—"

"The police," Davy said. "They're still talking to Dad. Where's Tilda?"

"At Clea's," Gwen said miserably. "She's taking her the Scarlets."

"*Why?*" Davy said, exasperated.

"Somebody told Clea she was Scarlet," Gwen said. "It's blackmail, but there's not much—"

"Fuck," Davy said. "I leave for one day and you

people fall apart." He went out again before Gwen could think of something cutting to say.

"Well, *the hell with you*," she finally said to the empty doorway and went upstairs to get her puzzle book.

Ford met her in the hall. "What now? I heard you yelling."

"Davy," she said.

"He's back?" Ford said. "Good, I need him. Where is he?"

"He left again," Gwen said. "He's going to Clea's to save Tilda." She felt waspish about that.

"Clea's." Ford went back inside his apartment and Gwen followed him.

"What are you doing?" she said, and saw him pick up a shoulder holster. "No, I can't let you do this." She stepped in front of the door.

"Do what?" Ford said. "I'm running late here—"

"Look, I know that the people you've . . . well, I know if you showed up at their door, they were probably asking for it—"

"*Grosse Pointe Blank*," Ford said.

Gwen deflated.

"All hit men know that movie," Ford said. "It's our *Casablanca*."

"It's not funny," Gwen said. "That's what Tony always used to say, 'If they're going to buy art they don't like just to show off, they're asking for it.' But it's wrong, and I . . ." She shook her head at him. "Can't you just move to Aruba and open an orphanage?"

"Why the hell would I want to open an orphanage?" Ford said, clearly mystified.

"To atone," Gwen said. "If you stop now, maybe—"

"Gwen."

"Because Tilda really loves Davy and we don't want him . . ." Gwen stumbled over the word again. "Like Thomas."

"Catering is no life for a man," Ford agreed.

"Damn it, Ford." She slammed the door behind her. "I have had enough of you goddamn men not taking me seriously. First Tony patted me on the head for thirty years, and then Mason wants to marry me for my gallery, and now you're making jokes before you kill my future son-in-law, and I'm sick of it. I am somebody to pay attention to, damn it, and I am not putting up with any more goddamn patronizing and mediocre sex and . . ." She stopped as she saw his face change. "If you make fun of me," she warned him, "you're a dead man."

He walked toward her until he had her trapped against the door.

"Mediocre sex, huh?"

Gwen sighed. "I'm not going to marry him."

"That I already knew," Ford said. "And I am not patronizing you. But you have to get out of my way so I can finish this one last job."

"No," Gwen said, sticking her chin out. "You'll have to go through me to get to him. He's my daughter's future and nobody messes with my daughters' happiness."

He stared down at her, his face inscrutable. "Gwen,

how much do you want to save Davy Dempsey's worthless life?"

Gwen swallowed. "Quite a bit."

He bent his head until his lips almost touched hers. "How much of a sacrifice are you willing to make?"

Gwen bit her lip to keep from kissing him. "Damn near anything," she said nobly.

He moved around to her ear, and she closed her eyes. "What if you didn't have to sacrifice anything?" he whispered.

Gwen took a deep breath. "I'd insist," she said.

"Davy Dempsey owes you," Ford said, and dropped his holster.

DOWNSTAIRS, SIMON caught Davy on his way out. "You're back. Good. We can leave."

"I'm staying," Davy said. "Gotta go. Talk to you later."

"I'm not staying," Simon said. "I had a chat with Eve yesterday."

Davy stopped. "Right. Meant to tell you, Louise is Eve."

"I know," Simon said, looking grim. "Do you have any idea of the things I did to Nadine's mother?"

"Roughly, yes," Davy said.

"I'll never be able to face that child again," Simon said.

"Get over it," Davy said. "I have to go. Come back for the wedding."

"Wait a minute," Simon said, but Davy was already heading for the van.

CLEA WAS sitting at her dressing table, waiting for Tilda and making plans to give Mason six paintings and the best sex of his life, when Ronald walked into her bedroom and closed the door behind him. "I have to see you," he said, looking as firm as somebody like Ronald could.

"Not now, Ronald," Clea said. "I have an appointment."

"It's time for you to choose, Clea," Ronald said, sticking what little chin he had out. "It's him or me."

Clea closed her eyes. Jesus, the men in her life. Maybe it wasn't too late to become a lesbian. There must be rich older women somewhere. "Ronald, I told you, this is not a good time—"

"It's the only time, Clea," Ronald said, making another stab at firmness.

"*Look*, Ronald," she began and then the doorknob rattled. "That could be Mason," she told him, standing up. "You are screwing up my life, Ronald."

Ronald looked around. "I can't—"

Clea took his arm and dragged him to the closet again. "Stay far back," she whispered as she shoved him in. "Get behind the clothes, and be *quiet*." She shut him in and then opened the door again and whispered, "Stay to the *right*." Then she went to deal with Mason, running her fingers through her hair to give it a little volume first.

But when she opened the door, she saw Davy Dempsey.

"*Jesus*," she said and yanked him in. "What are *you* doing here?"

"Lotta good memories in this room," he said, recovering his balance.

"We never had sex here," Clea said.

"I wasn't talking about you," Davy said. "I have a proposition for you."

He looked pretty good in the soft bedroom light, tall and broad and sure, but Clea had had enough propositions to last a lifetime. And besides, very shortly, she was going to have a proposition for him. "No. Get out—"

He took her chin in his hand and yanked it up, and Clea felt a thrill she hadn't felt in a long time. Mason was a real gentleman in bed, and Lord knew Ronald was no firecracker. But Davy had been worth sleeping with even when he didn't have money.

"I will give you one million dollars—" Davy said.

"Okay," Clea whispered, glancing toward the closet. "But we have to be quiet."

"—if you let Tilda keep her paintings and never go near the Goodnights or their gallery again," Davy finished.

"Oh." Clea pushed his hand away. "I need the paintings. I'm giving them to Mason. He's been—"

"Proposing to other women," Davy said. "Gwennie

Goodnight to be specific. He asked her to marry him. I don't see why you're so fixated on him. Rabbit wants you."

"Shhhh," Clea said. "Who the hell is Rabbit?"

"Ronald Abbott, your partner in crime," Davy said. "He wants you. God knows why." He looked down the neck of her robe and said, "Okay, God and I know why."

"Ronald is broke," Clea whispered. "And—"

"Rabbit has money," Davy said. "And even better, he knows how to make money."

"Keep your voice down." Clea tried not to look at the closet. "And don't try to con me. He told me. He said he wasn't rich but he loved me. He said we could live on love." Even the memory of it made her indignant. "Look at me. Do I look like somebody who could live on love?"

"No," Davy said. "But you have to learn to speak Rabbit's language. He thinks ten million is rich and anything under that is just wanna-be."

"He's right," Clea said. "Look, I'll talk to you later, but right now—"

"Pay attention. Rabbit has enough to buy you dinner several times," Davy said. "More than that, he *wants* to buy you dinner, which Mason doesn't seem to. Even more than that"—he leaned closer, those crazy brown eyes on hers, and she thought, *Maybe I should have held on to him*—"he can take the million I'll give you and make it ten. He knows the market, Clea. He's your best bet."

Clea considered it. It would be nice not to have to work so hard to keep a guy. Maybe—

"There you go," Davy said. "Now all you have to do is promise me two things."

"Two?" Clea said, regrouping.

"One is you let Tilda keep her paintings and leave her and everyone she loves alone," Davy said. "You never darken her doorway again."

"I do *not* see what you see in that woman," Clea said. "She has no muscle tone."

"You have no idea," Davy said. "And the second thing is you have to stop killing people, Clea."

Clea glared at him. "I do not kill people."

"I watched you let Zane die," Davy said grimly. "He was a son of a bitch—"

"I thought he was drunk," Clea said. "And then when I realized he wasn't, I needed to get that bankbook. But I didn't kill him. Not calling 911 is not murder."

"Then there was your last husband," Davy said.

"I didn't kill Cyril, either," Clea said, exasperated. "The only person I ever slept with that I wanted to kill was you."

"And now there's Thomas," Davy said.

"Thomas?"

"I know he was blackmailing you," Davy said. "But I can't prove it, and I don't want to prove it. I want you gone from here. Just swear you'll let Rabbit live or I'll come after you for all of them."

"*Listen to me,*" Clea began, and then the doorknob

turned and rattled. "That's Mason," she said to Davy, looking around for a way to get rid of him. Tilda was on her way over with the paintings, and with the paintings she still had a chance with Mason, and she definitely could get more than a million out of Davy—"The closet," she said, shoving him toward it. "It's deep."

"Really?" Davy said, as she opened the door. "Who knew?"

"And stay to the *left*," she hissed as she closed the door on him. "I have stuff stored on the right."

Clea straightened her robe and answered the door, her best I-forgive-you-Mason smile plastered on her face, but it faded when she saw Tilda standing there, her dark hair standing up on end as usual, this time around a black ball cap that said "Bitch," her face half-hidden behind those ridiculous glasses, holding up a large package that looked to be about six paintings thick.

"You're late." Clea drew her into the room, locking the door behind her again. "You were supposed—"

"Did you know your front door was open?"

"The paintings," Clea said, reaching for them.

Tilda held the package away from her. "There's a condition."

Clea frowned at her in disbelief. "You're in no position to make conditions."

"Yes I am." Tilda walked past her and sat on the bed. "You can't turn me in because if you do these paintings are worthless and you lose Mason. Oh, and you might want to make sure he doesn't get a good look at the signatures until after the wedding."

Clea clenched her jaw. "Did Mason propose to your mother?"

"Yes," Tilda said. "But it's not going to happen. She was momentarily confused. You're still in the game. *If* you have the paintings and *if* nobody knows they're fakes. It's in both of our interests that these stay out of sight."

"Okay." Clea realized she was frowning and smoothed out her forehead. Honest to God, these people and their conditions, it was enough to make a woman turn to Ronald. She held out her hand. "So I'll take the paintings and never see you again."

"I like that," Tilda said, not handing over the paintings. "But there's one more thing."

Clea sighed. "What?"

"You have to give Davy his money back."

"What?"

"The money you had Rabbit embezzle from him," Tilda said patiently.

"Who?"

"Clea, don't play dumb. If you want these paintings, you have to give Davy his money back."

"He has it," Clea said. "He took it Thursday night, the night of the gallery preview." Tilda's mouth dropped open, which was satisfying. "So there you go," Clea said. "Give me the paintings."

"I don't believe you," Tilda said. "He stayed so he could get the money. If he had the money, why did he stay?"

"You're sleeping with him, right?"

"Uh," Tilda said. "Yes."

Clea nodded. "He puts up with a lot for sex. Give me the paintings."

"Wait a minute," Tilda said, but the door rattled again, and this time, Mason called out, "Clea?"

"Under the bed," Clea said to Tilda, trying to get the paintings away from her.

"What?" Tilda said, holding on. "Why?"

"Because I don't want him to know I got the paintings from you." Clea yanked the case out of her hands. "I don't want him to know there's any connection to you and that damn gallery at all."

"Hey," Tilda said, but Mason called out *"Clea?"* again. "Okay, but I'm not going under your bed. I'll go in the closet."

"No," Clea said, but Tilda had already opened the door and Mason was calling to her, so she gave up and went to let him in.

CHAPTER · TWENTY-ONE

THE CAB HONKED OUT FRONT, AND SIMON HEADED FOR the gallery door, grateful to be leaving a madhouse, but just as he reached the door and freedom, he heard Louise say, "Wait a minute, damn it."

Only when he turned around, she was Eve.

"I have nothing to say to you," he said.

"Well, I have something to say to you," she said, and hearing Louise's sharp, red-lipsticked voice coming from Eve's soft pink lips was so disconcerting he stopped. "Listen, bucko," she said as she came toward him, a spun-sugar angel channeling a dominatrix, "You *owe me.*"

"I'll send you a check." He pushed on the door, but she slid between him and the glass, and she was too short to be Louise, and too fresh-faced to be Louise, and too blonde to be anybody he'd spend carnal time with, but she definitely felt like Louise against him.

"My sister is giving away her paintings to your best friend's ex-lover so she can get his money back for him," she said, fixing him with pale blue eyes that made him dizzy. "And you are a thief."

"I'm not seeing the connection," Simon said, beginning to reconsider his position on mothers.

She leaned toward him, lovely as Eve, hot as Louise, lethal in combination, and fixed him with those weird eyes. "Steal them for us," she whispered, and for a moment, Simon felt light-headed. *Get on that plane, you fool,* he told himself.

"Certainly," he said to Eve, and pushed the door open for her.

TILDA PUSHED her way to the back of the closet, still coping with the realization that Davy had stayed when he hadn't had to. Maybe—

A hand pressed over her mouth and made her jerk. "I need you to be very quiet," Davy said in her ear, and her body melted into relief as she turned to face him.

"I thought you'd left," she whispered back, trying to keep her voice steady. "I thought you were on your way to Australia."

"We have to work on your concept of me." Davy bent and kissed her, all that heat on her mouth, in her mouth, everything she was afraid she'd never have again, and she grabbed onto his shirt and said, *"Don't leave me."*

"I'm not going to." He bent to kiss her again, and she gripped his shirt tighter.

"I mean *ever*, don't *ever* leave me." She tried to swallow some of her desperation. "I'm sorry, I know this is a huge turnoff—"

"Yeah," Davy said, close to her mouth. "I hate it when women want me."

"—but I really need you forever, the whole thing, for always—"

"You got me," Davy said and kissed her again, and she breathed him in and felt lust and relief and gratitude, all at once, and wrapped herself around him.

"Maybe I'll just take short trips," Davy whispered, coming up for air, "so we can do this again."

"We can do it without the trips." Tilda went up on her toes to reach his face. "Anytime."

"How about half an hour from now, your place." Davy slid his hand down her back.

"How about now?" Tilda shuddered because he felt so good. "How about here? Oh, God, I can't believe you're here, I want you now."

"Right, you and closets," Davy whispered.

"We should build a closet in the attic," Tilda said and bit his ear.

"Ouch," Davy said, and tightened his arms around her.

"You are moving in, right?" Tilda whispered, pulling away a little. "We are living in the attic? You're okay staying with my family?"

"Yes," Davy said, but he seemed distracted. "I'm okay with the attic, the family, and you. Can you hear what they're talking about out there?"

Tilda moved back to him. "The hell with them. Take me now."

He leaned toward the closet door. "Believe me, I want

to, but I think that's Mason out there with Clea, so if you could—"

"Do we *care*?" Tilda whispered, pressing closer.

"I don't, but there may be some stuff going on out there I'm not getting."

"I'll give you some stuff." She kissed his neck.

"Yes, you will. But—"

"Do me now, against this wall," Tilda whispered, only half-kidding.

"Do you *mind*?" somebody whispered, and Tilda jerked in surprise just as Davy tightened his grip on her.

"Rabbit?" Davy said, turning around in the dark.

"Your financial manager's in this closet?" Tilda whispered.

"It's bad enough I have to listen to what's going on out there," Rabbit said, his voice bleak with betrayal. "I don't need to listen to people talking dirty in here."

"You think that was dirty?" Davy said. "Rabbit, you have no idea—"

"I heard everything you said to her," Rabbit said.

"I didn't say anything dir—"

"That woman is a gold digger," Rabbit said.

"Considering where her hand is, I don't think my money is what she's after."

"He's talking about Clea," Tilda said to Davy.

"That's all she ever wanted was the money," Rabbit went on, pain in his voice.

"Oh, Clea," Davy said. "Hell, yes, she's a gold digger. You're just noticing that now?"

"I loved her," Rabbit said.

"Well, then it doesn't matter," Davy said. "Now could you leave? Because—"

"She just wanted the money," Rabbit said sadly.

"Rabbit, you only want sex," Davy said. "And God knows, Clea can deliver."

"Hey," Tilda said, "I can deliver."

"Yes, you can, but not to Rabbit," Davy said, and the door opened.

"What the *hell* is this?" Mason said.

"Hi, Mason," Davy said. "I've been meaning to tell you, you have good closets."

BY THE time they were all out of the closet, Mason was speechless, and Davy felt for him. It must have been like watching a clown car at the circus.

"What the *hell* is going on here?" Mason said.

"I think you had to be here," Davy said.

"I can explain," Clea said, and then looked at the three of them standing in front of her closet. "No, I can't. I have no idea what's going on."

"Tilda," Mason said. "Honey, what are you doing here?"

"Delivering paintings," Tilda said. "Clea bought paintings for you, and she wanted it to be a surprise so . . . I hid." She pointed to the case of paintings leaning against the bed. "See?"

"Paintings?" Mason said, cheering up.

Clea slipped her arm through his. "All six Scarlets, darling. They're my wedding present to you."

"That's very generous of you, Clea," Mason said, patting her hand but still looking at the paintings. "I know Gwennie will appreciate it, too."

"Not your wedding to *her*," Clea snarled. "Your wedding to *me*."

"I'm not marrying you," Mason said. "What's Davy Dempsey doing in your closet?"

"He came with me," Tilda said. "He's very protective."

"What are you doing?" Davy said to Tilda. "Stop trying to save her. Let her rot."

"And who is he?" Mason said, pointing to Ronald.

"I'm Clea's lover," Ronald said, looking betrayed. "But that's all over. She's only interested in money."

"You have a lover?" Mason said to Clea.

"Not exactly," Clea said, but then somebody banged on the door, and she brightened. "I'll just get that."

When she opened the door, Gwen was there, looking mad as hell. "Did you know your front door is standing open?" she said to Clea. "That's dangerous. Anybody could get in here. *Like a hit man*." Clea stepped back, and Gwen caught sight of Davy and pushed past her.

"Thank God, you're alive," she said to him.

"Gwennie!" Mason said, but she ignored him to concentrate on Davy.

"Listen, you have to get out of here," she told him. "Clea sent Ford to kill you."

"No I didn't," Clea said.

"He's on his way," Gwen said. "I delayed him for a

little while, but then I fell asleep. He's probably here already. You have to get out."

"Thank you," Davy said, disentangling her fingers from his shirt. "But that won't be necessary."

"You fell asleep?" Tilda said to Gwen. "Ford was coming to kill him and you *fell asleep*? What are you, narcoleptic?"

"It was probably the sex," Davy said.

"Sex?" Mason said.

"He's just being funny," Tilda said to Mason.

"Ford's going to *kill* you," Gwen said to Davy, ignoring them both. "He has a gun. Clea has paid him to kill you and he's not going to retire until he's finished."

"I did *not* pay him," Clea said.

"Usually she just kills her husbands," Davy said, "so I don't—"

Clea stood up, incandescent with rage. "For the *last time*, I did not kill my husband. *Either one of them.* They both died of *heart attacks.*"

"Not according to the FBI, they didn't," Mason said. "At least Cyril didn't. He was poisoned."

Clea blinked at him. "Somebody poisoned Cyril?"

"That would be you," Davy said to her and looked at Mason. "When did you talk to the FBI?"

"They exhumed the body a couple of weeks ago, according to Thomas." Mason shook his head. "He told me at the gallery opening Friday night. He said the FBI had evidence that Clea had killed Cyril and had stolen his collection. He seemed serious, but I just can't stop thinking of him as the caterer."

"Why would anybody poison Cyril?" Clea said, outraged past the point of caring. "He was eighty-nine, for Christ's sake."

"Well, there was all the money you inherited," Davy said, watching her. "Patience has never been your strong suit."

"I *did not kill*—"

"I believe you," Tilda said to her. "Just ignore him."

"Hey," Davy said.

"Well, pay attention," Tilda said. "Why would she kill him if he was eighty-nine and rich?"

"*He wasn't rich,*" Clea said, evidently goaded beyond endurance. "*He died broke, okay?*"

"Really?" Davy said. "What a disappointment for you. You suppose the warehouse fire you set had anything to do with that?"

Clea glared at him. "Do I *look* like somebody who would set a warehouse fire?"

"No," Tilda said. "You don't look like somebody who could light her own cigarette."

"It was just my lousy luck," Clea said miserably. "He was supposed to have all this money and then it turned out he'd spent it on his art collection and then most of that burned—"

Davy turned back to Mason with renewed interest. "So you talked to Thomas Friday."

Mason nodded. "He came to warn me about Clea."

"About me?" Clea sat down, almost in tears. "What did *I* do?"

"You know, the list is so long," Davy said to her.

"He told me you kill your husbands," Mason said to Clea. "And that the Homer Hodge you gave me was from the warehouse fire. How did that end up at the gallery? Did you take it there?"

"What Homer Hodge?" Clea said. "I don't kill people!"

"Look," Mason said. "I have no interest in seeing you in jail, Clea. I'm about to marry the woman I love, and I don't want to make anybody suffer. If you leave now, I won't turn you in. The police don't know what Thomas knew."

"Clea, when did he get home on Friday night?" Davy said.

"After midnight," Clea said, glaring viciously at Gwen. "Because of *her*."

"She doesn't know," Mason said to Davy, dismissing her. "She wasn't here. She's just trying to use me as an alibi for Thomas."

"What?" Tilda said. "How did you know—" And then Davy stepped on her foot. "Ouch?"

Mason stayed focused on Gwen. "Look, I can understand why this is confusing, honey, but it's okay. I'll take care of everything, even the gallery. We'll run it together. I'll be just like Tony."

"I don't want the gallery," Gwen said. "I hate the damn gallery. I want to get *away* from the gallery, not be buried there for rest of my life. I'm sorry, Mason, I'm grateful you paid off the mortgage, but—"

"What?" Davy said.

"Mason paid off the mortgage," Tilda told him. "Don't interrupt, she's dumping him."

"He didn't pay off the mortgage," Davy said. "I did."

"You didn't pay off the mortgage?" Gwen said to Mason.

"I can explain that," Mason said to Gwen.

"You paid off my mortgage?" Tilda said to Davy.

"No," Davy said. "That would be presumptuous of me. I paid for the bed and applied the payment to the mortgage."

"This should be good," Gwen said to Mason, crossing her arms. "Explain."

"You paid six hundred thousand for a bed?" Tilda said to Davy.

"Considering what happened on that bed, it was a bargain," Davy said.

"I thought it was a mistake at the bank," Mason said to Gwen. "I was going to go over there and pay it off. I thought—"

"With what?" Ronald said bitterly. "You're broke."

"*What?*" Clea said, going beyond outrage now.

"I was trying to tell you," Ronald said, looking at her with distaste. "I investigated him when I investigated the Goodnights."

"*Hello?*" Tilda said.

"I don't know who you are," Mason said to Ronald, "but you have no idea of my resources."

"Actually," Davy said to Mason, "he probably has a better idea of your resources than you do. It's pretty much his thing."

"Gwennie." Mason reached for her hand. "Let's get out of here, go someplace where we can talk."

"No," Gwen said. "I wasn't faking about the other guy. I slept with him. I loved it. I plan on doing it again. In Aruba. And I'm going to learn to scuba dive."

"Go, Gwennie," Davy said. "So, Mason—"

"All right," Mason said, scowling at them all, clearly going for the Stern Patriarch look. "You people don't realize the position you're in, but that's all right, I do. You could all go to jail for perpetrating a fraud. Gwennie might be willing to go, but she'll never let Tilda be arrested. And Tilda might go, but she won't let Gwennie be hurt." Mason smiled at Gwennie. "And neither will I. We're getting married, Gwennie, and I'm running the gallery, just like old times."

"She *cheated* on you," Clea said to him, virtue making her voice shrill. "With a *hired killer*. Mason, darling—"

"Prewedding jitters," Mason said, and turned to Tilda. "It'll be all right, Tilda. I'll protect you like a father."

"The hell you will," Tilda said to Mason. "I've had enough of that."

"Of course, Davy's a different story," Mason went on. "With his record, they'll throw away the key and board up his cell."

"I don't know why everybody assumes I have a record," Davy said to Tilda. "I was actually pretty careful about that."

"I think he's completely out of touch with reality in general," Tilda said to Davy.

"I'm *serious*," Mason said.

"Chasing money'll do that to you," Davy told Tilda. "Did somebody say he was Cyril's money manager? Because you can't trust those guys."

"There were extenuating circumstances in my case," Ronald said.

"Getting your brains fucked out by a greedy blonde is not an extenuating circumstance," Davy said to him.

"*Enough*," Mason said. "I've made plans and we're going to follow them." He nodded at Tilda. "You're a very good painter, Scarlet. I caught on to that at the gallery opening. You're going to do a lot more paintings for the gallery." He turned to Gwen. "It'll be like old times, Gwennie. You had Tony, and now you have me."

"Mason," Gwen said. "It's not happening."

"Yes it is," Mason said, leaning back and folding his arms.

"Oh, look, he thinks he has something," Davy said to Tilda. "He never does, but he's always optimistic. Terrible poker player."

"I have something," Mason said. "I've found Homer Hodge."

"*Who?*" Tilda said.

"And he's not happy about your daughter pretending to be Scarlet," Mason went on to Gwen.

"*What?*" Gwen said.

"So I've talked him out of having you arrested—"

"You miserable little *rat*," Gwen said, glaring at him. "You did not talk to Homer. The only one who talks to Homer is me. And he thinks you're a jerk. And a liar. And *boring in bed*."

Mason took a step back.

"And a murderer, I bet," Tilda said. "Although if you hit Thomas, you're not a very good one."

"You're all bluffing," Mason said. "Well, I'm calling. You have nothing. Game's over."

"I don't think they're bluffing," Davy said. "And even if they are, we have an ace in the hole. Or in the hall."

"Damn, boy, you're usually a better poker player than this," Ford said from the doorway.

"Nope," Davy said without turning around. "I'm just putting my cards on the table. Arrest him. Or if I've got it wrong and Clea really did hire you to kill me, shoot him."

"I *did not* hire him to kill you," Clea said.

"She pretty much left that part up in the air," Ford said. "I tried my damnedest, but she never would come right out and say it. It was Rabbit who hired me. Through his Bureau connections." He shook his head at Rabbit. "What were you thinking?"

Davy turned to Ronald. "You put out a hit on me?"

"Not exactly," Ronald said, shifting away from him.

Davy looked at Clea. "You know that second condition, about not killing him? Forget it. Have at him."

"I don't know who you are," Mason said to Ford, "but get out of my house." He nodded at Clea. "And take her with you."

"No, thanks," Ford said. "The Columbus police are on the way to arrest you. Thomas finally came to, and you're the last thing he remembers."

"Whoops," Tilda said to Mason.

"So I'm just watching things until the cops get here," Ford said. "I was kind of hoping you'd all keep talking so I wouldn't have to mention that." He looked at Gwen. "Especially you. Aruba?"

"The Columbus police?" Gwen said to Ford. "*You* called the police? Who *are* you?"

"I think he's the FBI," Davy said to Gwen. "The only real one in the bunch. You finally picked a winner."

"Mason killed Cyril?" Clea said, more perplexed than upset. Then she perked up. "To get me?"

"Pay attention," Davy said to Clea. "Mason burned an empty warehouse so he could steal Cyril's art collection and sell it. I'm guessing Thomas figured it out and confronted him, and Mason bashed him."

"That's ridiculous," Mason said, but he sounded too confused to be convincing.

"I told you he was broke," Ronald muttered to Clea. "People don't realize how hard it is to sell art."

"The hell we don't," Tilda said with feeling.

"You're *FBI*?" Gwen said to Ford, focusing on the essentials.

"Well, there's Thomas the Caterer, too," Tilda said to Gwen.

"Thomas the Caterer is not FBI," Ford said to Tilda. "We have some pride. He's Cyril Lewis's grandson."

"Cyril had a grandson?" Clea said to Ford.

"I slept *with the FBI*?" Gwen said to the room in general.

"Not all of it," Davy said to Gwen. "Just him."

"Mason killed Cyril, Thomas was stalking me because he thought I did it, and Ford's the FBI?" Clea said to Davy.

"That's about it," Davy said.

"Oh, well, that's just *fine*." Clea looked around the room, so mad she was spitting. "All of you people are just—" Her voice broke off as she searched for the word.

"Liars and cheats?" Tilda said.

"*Yes*," Clea said, and turned to Ronald, putting her hand on his arm. "Ronald, darling, these people are *horrible*."

"Just what you deserve," Ronald said.

"*Ronald*," Clea said, her beautiful eyes filling with beautiful tears as she moved closer. "*How could you!*"

Ronald cleared his throat. "Well . . ."

"After all we've been to each other," she said, pressing against him. "After all our plans for the future."

Ronald whimpered.

"Go for it, Rabbit," Davy said. "Only the good die young. You're covered."

Clea smiled up at Ronald, and Ronald sighed.

"I just want to make it clear," Tilda said, casting a cautious look Ford's way, "that if we get out of this unjailed, we're all going straight." She smiled at Ford as honestly as she could fake. "Really."

"Don't worry about me," Ford said as official

sounding feet started up the stairs. "I'm taking your mother to Aruba."

"WELL, THAT was interesting," Davy said, following Tilda up the stairs to the attic an hour later.

Tilda nodded. "The only thing I regret is that I lost the Scarlets. I went back for them after the police left, but they were gone. Do you think they took them for evidence?"

"No," Davy said, looking past her to the case of paintings balanced on the top stair of the last flight.

Tilda turned. "What?" She ran up the last flight and opened the case.

"They're all here," she said, delighted. "And there's a note from Simon."

Davy took it from her to read it.

"Here's your wedding present, Dempsey. I'd stay to explain but those Goodnight women are too damn dangerous. Best wishes, Simon."

Tilda picked the case up and hugged it to her. "Davy, he stole my paintings back for me."

"Believe me," Davy said. "The pleasure was all his. Open the door."

"About that." Tilda widened her eyes.

Betty, he thought, and moved closer, only one step below her now.

"I want you to know . . ." She pushed her glasses up the bridge of her nose. "That I understand that you're on your way to Australia . . ."

Davy grinned at her. "Frankly, Scarlet, I—"

"Oh, don't," Tilda said, frowning. "You're a better person than that."

"You're right, that one's too easy." Davy put his arms around her and the Scarlets. "Vilma, I am no longer on my way to Australia. Open the door."

She put her head down, and he held her closer, and she bit his shoulder softly, and he lost his breath.

"Could we just go in there?" he said. "Because I'm willing to do this on the steps, but it's harder that—"

"Tell me you're on your way to Australia," she said in his ear.

"Fine," he said. "I'm on my way to Australia." He reached around her and opened the door, pushing her and her paintings through as he spoke. "Now can we—"

He stopped in the doorway.

The walls weren't white anymore.

Huge green leaves grew around the bed, wild lush leaves, tapering off into charcoal sketches as they rounded the corners of the room, clearly a jungle-in-progress. Outlines of sly little animals peeped out of the bushes, laughing snakes and seductive flamingos and Steve, looking fairly calm, drawn near the floor in front of a large banana leaf. On the wall behind the bed, van Gogh–like sunflowers grew up in wild bursts of color like mutant suns, looming over Tilda's headboard that was now covered in more green leaves that wreathed one word in the center, written in huge Gothic letters, burnished in gold leaf:

Australia.

"So, sunflowers," Davy said, looking down into the crazy blue eyes of his one true love.

Tilda stepped into the room and put the paintings down. He followed her, kicking the door closed behind him, and she slid her hand up his chest. "Zey are by Van Gogh," she said in a terrible Italian accent. "Would you like to buy zem, Il Duce?" She went up on her toes to kiss him, her hot little mouth just millimeters away from his, the scent of cinnamon making his head light.

"I can't," Davy said sternly, pushing her away. "Really sorry. Out of the question."

"Oh." Tilda rocked back on her heels. "Hey, I spent *hours* on those things so you could play this dumb game—"

He bent and scooped her up in his arms, and she flailed for balance, smacking him in the nose and knocking him back a step. He bounced her once to center her, and she shrieked and hung on to his neck.

"I can't buy it because I'm leaving," Davy said. "I'm taking my wife, Matilda Scarlet Celeste Veronica Betty Vilma Goodnight to Australia. It's a touching story. We met in a closet—"

Tilda stopped struggling. "Are you proposing?"

"Yes," Davy said. "I love you. Marry me, Matilda, and make me the most confused man on earth."

She blinked at him, her lips parted, and for one horrible moment, he thought she was going to say no.

Then she smiled that crooked smile, and he breathed again.

"Ravish me, Ralph," Tilda said.

"I'll take that as a yes," Davy said, and did.

BET ME

*He may be the king of hearts . . . but she's got
an ace up her sleeve*

From *New York Times* bestselling author Jennifer Crusie
comes an addictive tale of long shots, risk management, true
love, and great shoes

Minerva Dobbs knows that happily-ever-after is a fairy
tale – especially with a man who asked her out to dinner to
win a bet . . .

Cal Morrisey knows commitment is impossible – especially with a woman as cranky as Min Dobbs . . .

When they say good-bye at the end of their evening,
they cut their losses and agree never to see each other again.
But Fate has other plans – and it's not long before Min and
Cal are dealing with a jealous ex-boyfriend, Krispy Kreme
donuts, a determined psychologist, chaos theory, a freak-
ishly intelligent cat, Chicken Marsala, and more risky
propositions than either of them ever dreamed of . . .
including the biggest gamble of all: true love.

**Here is the mouth-watering first chapter of *Bet Me*
to whet your appetite . . .**

Chapter One

Once upon a time, Minerva Dobbs thought as she stood in the middle of a loud yuppie bar, *the world was full of good men*. She looked into the handsome face of the man she'd planned on taking to her sister's wedding and thought, *Those days are gone.*

"This relationship is not working for me," David said.

I could shove this swizzle stick through his heart, Min thought. She wouldn't do it, of course. The stick was plastic and not nearly pointed enough on the end. Also, people didn't do things like that in southern Ohio. A sawed-off shotgun, that was the ticket.

"And we both know why," David went on.

He probably didn't even know he was mad; he probably thought he was being calm and adult. *At least I know I'm furious*, Min thought. She let her anger settle around her, and it made her warm all over, which was more than David had ever done.

Across the room, somebody at the big roulette wheel–shaped bar rang a bell. Another point against David: He was dumping her in a theme bar. The Long Shot. The name alone should have tipped her off.

"I'm sorry, Min," David said, clearly not.

Min crossed her arms over her gray-checked suit jacket so she couldn't smack him. "This is because I won't go home with you tonight? It's Wednesday. I have to work tomorrow. You have to work tomorrow. I paid for my own drink."

"It's not that." David looked noble and wounded as only the tall, dark, and self-righteous could. "You're not making any effort to make our relationship work, which means . . ."

Which means we've been dating for two months and I still won't sleep with you. Min tuned him out and looked around the babbling crowd. *If I had an untraceable poison, I could drop it in his drink now and not one of these suits would notice.*

". . . and I do think, if we have any future, that you should con-tribute, too," David said.

Oh, I don't, Min thought, which meant that David had a point. Still, lack of sex was no excuse for dumping her three weeks before she had to wear a maid of honor dress that made her look like a fat, demented shepherdess. "Of course we have a future, David," she said, trying to put her anger on ice. "We have *plans.* Diana is getting married in three weeks. You're invited to the wedding. To the rehearsal dinner. To the *bachelor party.* You're going to miss the *stripper,* David."

"Is that all you think of me?" David's voice went up. "I'm just a date to your sister's wedding?"

"Of course not," Min said. "Just as I'm sure I'm more to you than somebody to sleep with."

David opened his mouth and closed it again. "Well, of course. I don't want you to think this is a reflection on you. You're intelligent, you're successful, you're mature. . . ."

Min listened, knowing that *You're beautiful, you're thin* were not com-ing. If only he'd have a heart attack. Only four percent of heart attacks in men happened before forty, but it could happen. And if he died, not even her mother could expect her to bring him to the wedding.

". . . and you'd make a wonderful mother," David finished up.

"Thank you," Min said. "That's so not romantic."

"I thought we were going places, Min," David said.

"Yeah," Min said, looking around the gaudy bar. "Like here."

David sighed and took her hand. "I wish you the best, Min. Let's keep in touch."

Min took her hand back. "You're not feeling any pain in your left arm, are you?"

"No," David said, frowning at her.

"Pity," Min said, and went back to her friends, who were watching them from the far end of the room.

"He was looking even more uptight than usual," Liza said, looking even taller and hotter than usual as she leaned on the jukebox, her hair flaming under the lights.

David wouldn't have treated Liza so callously. He'd have been afraid to; she'd have dismembered him. *Gotta be more like Liza*, Min thought and started to flip through the song cards on the box.

"Are you upset with him?" Bonnie said from Min's other side, her blond head tilted up in concern. David wouldn't have left Bonnie, either. Nobody was mean to sweet, little Bonnie.

"Yes. He dumped me." Min stopped flipping. Wonder of wonders, the box had Elvis. Immediately, the bar seemed a better place. She fed in coins and then punched the keys for "Hound Dog." Too bad Elvis had never recorded one called "Dickhead."

"I knew I didn't like him," Bonnie said.

Min went over to the roulette bar and smiled tightly at the slender bartender dressed like a croupier. She had beautiful long, soft, kinky brown hair, and Min thought, *That's another reason I couldn't have slept with David*. Her hair always frizzed when she let it down, and he was the type who would have noticed.

"Rum and Coke, please," she told the bartender.

Maybe that was why Liza and Bonnie never had man trouble: great hair. She looked at Liza, racehorse-thin in purple zippered leather, shaking her head at David with naked contempt. Okay, it wasn't just the hair. If she jammed herself into Liza's dress, she'd look like Barney's slut cousin. "*Diet* Coke," she told the bartender.

"He wasn't the one," Bonnie said from below Min's shoulder, her hands on her tiny hips.

"Diet rum, too," Min told the bartender, who smiled at her and went to get her drink.

Liza frowned. "Why were you dating him anyway?"

"Because I thought he might be the one," Min said, exasperated. "He was intelligent and successful and very nice at first. He seemed like a sensible choice. And then all of sudden he went snotty on me."

Bonnie patted Min's arm. "It's a good thing he broke up with you because now you're free for when the right man finds you. Your prince is on his way."

"Right," Min said. "I'm sure he was on his way but a truck hit him."

"That's not how it works." Bonnie leaned on the bar, looking like an R-rated pixie. "If it's meant to be, he'll make it. No matter how many things go wrong, he'll come to you and you'll be together forever."

"What is this?" Liza said, looking at her in disbelief. "Barbie's Field of Dreams?"

"That's sweet, Bonnie," Min said. "But as far as I'm concerned, the last good man died when Elvis went."

"Maybe we should rethink keeping Bon as our broker," Liza said to Min. "We could be major stockholders in the Magic Kingdom by now."

Min tapped her fingers on the bar, trying to vent some tension. "I should have known David was a mistake when I couldn't bring myself to sleep with him. We were on our third date, and the waiter brought the dessert menu, and David said, 'No, thank you, we're on a diet,' and of course, he isn't because there's not an ounce of fat on him, and I thought, 'I'm not taking off my clothes with you' and I paid my half of the check and went home early. And after that, whenever he made his move, I thought of the waiter and crossed my legs."

"He wasn't the one," Bonnie said with conviction.

"You *think?*" Min said, and Bonnie looked wounded. Min closed her eyes. "Sorry. Sorry. *Really* sorry. It's just not a good time for that stuff, Bon. I'm mad. I want to savage somebody, not look to the horizon for the next jerk who's coming my way."

"Sure," Bonnie said. "I understand."

Liza shook her head at Min. "Look, you didn't care about David, so you haven't lost anything except a date to Di's wedding. And I vote we skip the wedding. It has 'disaster' written all over it, even without the fact that she's marrying her best friend's boyfriend."

"Her best friend's *ex*-boyfriend. And I *can't* skip it. I'm the maid of honor." Min gritted her teeth. "It's going to be hell. It's not just that I'm dateless, which fulfills every prophecy my mother has ever made, it's that she's crazy about David."

"We *know*," Bonnie said.

"She tells everybody about David," Min said, thinking of her mother's avid little face. "Dating David is the only thing I've done that she's liked about me since I got the flu freshman year and lost ten pounds. And now I have no David." She took her diet rum from the bartender, said, "Thank you," and tipped her lavishly. There wasn't enough gratitude in the world for a server who kept the drinks coming at a time like this. "Most of the time it doesn't matter what my mother thinks of me because I can avoid her, but for the wedding? No."

"So you'll find another date," Bonnie said.

"No, she won't," Liza said.

"Oh, *thank you*," Min said, turning away from the over-designed bar. The roulette pattern was making her dizzy. Or maybe that was the rage.

"Well, it's your own fault," Liza said. "If you'd quit assigning statistical probability to the fate of a union with every guy you meet and just go out with somebody who turns you on, you might have a good time now and then."

"I'd be a puddle of damaged ego," Min said. "There's nothing wrong with dating sensibly. That's how I found David." Too late, she realized that wasn't evidence in her favor and knocked back some of her drink to ward off comments.

Liza wasn't listening. "We'll have to find a guy for you." She began to scan the bar, which was only fair since most of the bar had been scanning her. "Not him. Not him. Not him. Nope. Nope. Nope. All these guys would try to sell you mutual funds." Then she straightened. "Hello. We have a winner."

Bonnie followed her eyes. "Who? Where?"

"The dark-haired guy in the navy blue suit. In the middle on the landing up by the door."

"Middle?" Min squinted at the raised landing at the entry to the bar. It was wide enough for a row of faux poker tables, and four men were at one talking to a brunette in red. One of the four was David, now surveying his domain over the dice-studded wrought-iron rail. The landing was only about five feet higher than the rest of the room, but David contrived to make it look like a balcony. It was probably requiring all his self-control to keep from doing the Queen Elizabeth Wave. "That's David," Min said, turning away. "And some brunette. Good Lord, he's dating somebody else already." *Get out now*, she told the brunette silently.

"Forget the brunette," Liza said. "Look at the guy in the middle. Wait a minute, he'll turn back this way again. He doesn't seem to be finding David that interesting."

Min squinted back at the entry again. The navy suit was taller than David, and his hair was darker and thicker, but otherwise, from behind, he was pretty much David II. "I did that movie," Min said, and then he turned.

Dark eyes, strong cheekbones, classic chin, broad shoulders, chiseled everything, and all of it at ease as he stared out over the bar, ignoring David, who suddenly looked a little inbred.

Min sucked in her breath as every cell she had came alive and whispered, *This one.*

Then she turned away before anybody caught her slack-jawed with admiration. He was not the one, that was her DNA talking, looking for a high-class sperm donor. Every woman in the room with a working ovary probably looked at him and thought, *This one.* Well, biology was not destiny. The amount of damage somebody that beautiful could do to a woman like her was too much to contemplate. She took another drink to cushion the thought, and said, "He's pretty."

"No," Liza said. "That's the point. He's *not* pretty. David is pretty. That guy looks like an adult."

"Okay, he's full of testosterone," Min said.

"No, that's the guy on his right," Liza said. "The one with the head like a bullet. I bet that one talks sports and slaps people on the back. The navy suit looks civilized with edge. Tell her, Bonnie."

"I don't think so," Bonnie said, her pixie face looking grim. "I know him."

"In the biblical sense?" Liza said.

"No. He dated my cousin Wendy. But—"

"Then he's fair game," Liza said.

"—he's a hit and run player," Bonnie finished. "From what Wendy said, he dazzles whoever he's with for a couple of months and then drops her and moves on. And she never sees it coming."

"The beast," Liza said without heat. "You know, men are allowed to leave women they're dating."

"Well, he makes them love him and then he leaves them," Bonnie said. "That is beastly."

"Like David," Min said, her instinctive distrust of the navy suit confirmed.

Liza snorted. "Oh, like you ever loved David."

"*I was trying to,*" Min snapped.

Liza shook her head. "Okay, none of this matters. All you want is a date to the wedding. If it takes the beast a couple of months to dump you, you're covered. So just go over there—"

"No." Min turned her back on everybody to concentrate on the black and white posters over the bar: Paul Newman shooting pool in *The Hustler*, Marlon Brando throwing dice in *Guys and Dolls*, W. C. Fields scowling over his cards in *My Little Chickadee*. Where were all the women gamblers? It wasn't as if being a woman wasn't a huge risk all by itself. Twenty-eight percent of female homicide victims were killed by husbands or lovers.

Which, come to think of it, was probably why there weren't any women gamblers. Living with men was enough of a gamble. She fought the urge to turn around and look at the beast on the landing again. Really, the smart thing to do was stop dating and get a cat.

"You know she won't go talk to him," Bonnie was saying to Liza. "Statistically speaking, the probable outcome is not favorable."

"Screw that." Liza nudged Min and sloshed the Coke in her glass. "Imagine your mother if you brought that to the wedding. She might even let you eat carbs." She looked at Bonnie. "What's his name?"

"Calvin Morrisey," Bonnie said. "Wendy was buying wedding magazines when he left her. She was writing 'Wendy Sue Morrisey' on scrap paper."

Liza looked appalled. "That's probably why he left."

"Calvin Morrisey." Against her better judgment, Min turned back to watch him again.

"Go over there," Liza said, prodding her with one long fingernail, "and tell David you hope his rash clears up soon. Then introduce yourself to the beast, smile, and don't talk statistics."

"That would be shallow," Min said. "I'm thirty-three. I'm mature. I don't care if I have a date to my sister's wedding. I'm a better person than that." She thought about her mother's face when she got the news that David was history. *No, I'm not.*

"No, you're not," Liza said. "You're just too chicken to cross the room."

"I suppose it might work." Bonnie frowned across the room. "And you can dump him after the wedding and give him a taste of his own medicine."

"Yeah, that's the ticket." Liza rolled her eyes. "Do it for Wendy and the rest of the girls."

He was in profile now, talking to David. *The man should be on coins,* Min thought. Of course, looking that beautiful, he probably never dated the terminally chubby. At least, not without sneering. And she'd been sneered at enough for one night.

"No," Min said and turned back to the bar. Really, a cat was a good idea.

"Look, Stats," Liza said, exasperated, "I know you're conservative, but you're damn near solidifying lately. Dating David must have been like dating concrete. And then there's your apartment. Even your furniture is stagnant."

"My furniture is my grandmother's," Min said stiffly.

"Exactly. Your butt's been on it since you were born. You need a change. And if you don't make that change on your own, *I will have to help you.*"

Min's blood ran cold. *"No."*

"Don't threaten her," Bonnie said to Liza. "She'll change, she'll grow. Won't you, Min?"

Min looked back at the landing, and suddenly going over there seemed like a good idea. She could stand under that ugly wrought-iron railing and eavesdrop, and then if Calvin Morrisey sounded even remotely nice—ha, what were the chances?—she could go up and say something sweet to David and get an intro, and Liza would not have movers come in while she was at work and throw out her furniture.

"Don't make me do this for you," Liza said.

Standing at a roulette wheel bar sulking wasn't doing anything for her. And with all she knew ahead of time, it wasn't likely that he could inflict much damage. Min squared her shoulders and took a deep breath. "I'm going in, coach."

"Do not say 'percent' at any time for the rest of the night," Liza said, and Min straightened her gray-checked jacket and said a short prayer that she'd think of a great pick-up line before she got to the landing and made a fool of herself. In which case, she'd just spit on the beast, push David over the railing, and go get that cat.

"Just so there's a plan," she said to herself and started across the floor.

Up on the landing, Cal Morrisey was thinking seriously about pushing David Fisk over the railing. *I should have moved faster when I saw them coming*, he thought. It was Tony's fault.

"You know, that redhead has great legs," Tony had said. "See her? At the bar, in the purple with the zippers? You suppose she likes football players?"

"You haven't played football in fifteen years." Cal had sipped his drink, easing into an alcohol-tinged peace that was broken only slightly when somebody with no taste in music played "Hound Dog." As far as he was concerned the only two drawbacks to the place were the stupid décor and the fact that Elvis Presley was on the jukebox.

"All right, it's been a while since I played, but she doesn't know that." Tony looked back at the redhead. "I got ten bucks says she'll leave with me. I'll use my chaos theory line."

"No bet," Cal said. "Although that is a terrible line, so that would shorten the odds." He squinted across the room to the roulette wheel bar. The redhead was flashy, which meant she was Tony's type. There was a little blonde there, too, the perky kind, their friend Roger's dream date. Behind the bar, Shanna saw him watching and waved, but she didn't smile, and Cal wondered what was up as he nodded to her.

Tony put his arm around Cal. "Help me out here, she's in a group. You go over and pick up her chubby friend in the gray-checked suit, and Roger can hit on the short blonde. I'd give you the short blonde, but you know Roger and midget women."

Roger jerked to attention at Cal's elbow. "What? What short blonde?" He peered across the room at the bar. "Oh. *Oh.*"

"Suit?" Cal looked back at the bar.

"The one in gray." Tony nodded toward the bar. "Between the redhead and the mini-blonde. She's hard to see because the redhead sort of dazzles you. I bet you—"

"Oh." Cal squinted to see the medium-height woman between the redhead and the blonde. She was dressed in a dull, boxy, gray-checked suit, and her round face scowled under brown hair yanked back into a knot on the top of her head. "Nope," he said and took another drink.

Tony smacked him on the back and made him choke. "Come on, live a little. Don't tell me you're still pining for Cynthie."

"I never pined for Cynthie." Cal glanced around the crowd. "Keep an eye out for her, will you? She's in that red thing she wears when she's trying to get something."

"She can get it from me," Tony said.

"Great." Cal's voice was fervent. "I'll even go pick up that suit if you'll marry Cyn."

Tony choked on his drink. "Marry?"

"Yes," Cal said. "She wants to get married. Surprised the hell out of me." He thought for a moment of Cynthie, a sweetheart with a spine of steel. "I don't know where she got the idea we were that close."

"There she is." Roger was looking over Cal's shoulder. "She's coming up the stairs now."

Cal got up and tried to move past Tony to the door. "Out of my way."

Tony stayed in his chair. "You can't leave, I want the redhead."

"So go get her," Cal said, trying to get around him.

"Cynthie's got David with her," Roger said, and there was great sympathy in his voice.

"Cal!" David's voice grated over Cal's shoulder. "Just who we were looking for." He sounded mad as hell, but when Cal turned, David was smiling.

Trouble, Cal thought and smiled back with equal insincerity. "David. Cynthie. Great to see you."

"Hello, Cal." Cynthie smiled up at him, her heart-shaped face lethally lovely. "How've you been?"

"Great. Couldn't be better. You, too, looking great." Cal looked past her to David, and thought, *Take her, please*. "You're a lucky man, David."

"I am?"

"Dating Cynthie," Cal said, putting all the encouragement he could into his voice.

Cynthie took David's arm. "We just ran into each other." She turned her shoulder to Cal and glowed up at David. "But it is nice seeing him again." Her eyes slid back to Cal's face, and he smiled past her ear again, radiating no jealousy at all as hard as he could.

David looked down into her beautiful face and blinked, and Cal felt a stab of sympathy for him. Cynthie was enchanting up close. And from far away. From everywhere, really, which was how he'd ended up saying yes to her all the time. Cal glanced at her impeccably tight little body in her impeccably tight little red dress and then took a step back as he jerked his eyes away, reminding himself of how peaceful life was without her. Distance, that was the key. Maybe a cross and some garlic, too.

"Of course," David was saying. "Maybe we can do dinner later." He glanced at Cal, looking triumphant.

"Well, don't let us keep you." Cal took another step back and bumped into the railing.

Cynthie let go of David's arm, her glow diminished. "I'll just freshen up before we go." Tony and David watched as her perfect rear end swung away from them, while Roger ignored her to peer across the room at the pixie blonde, and Cal took another healthy swallow of his drink and wished he were somewhere else. Anywhere else. Dinner, for example. Maybe he'd stop by Emilio's and eat in the kitchen. There were no women in Emilio's kitchen.

"So David," Tony was saying. "How'd our seminar work out for you?"

"It was terrific," David said. "I didn't think anybody could teach some of those morons that new program, but everybody at the firm is now up to speed. We've even . . ."

He went on and Cal nodded, thinking that one of the many reasons he didn't like David was his tendency to refer to his employees as morons. Still, David paid his bills on time and gave credit where it was due; there were much worse clients. And if he took over Cynthie, Cal was prepared to feel downright warm toward him.

David wound down on whatever it was he'd been saying and looking toward the stairs. "About Cynthie. I thought that you and she—"

"No." Cal shook his head with enthusiasm. "She left me a couple of months ago."

"Isn't it usually the other way around?"

David arched an eyebrow and looked ridiculous. And still women went out with him. Life was a mystery. So were women.

"Aren't you supposed to be the guy who never strikes out?" David said.

"No," Cal said.

"He's losing his edge," Tony said. "I found an easy pickup for him, and he said no."

"Which one?" David said.

"The gray-checked suit at the bar." Tony motioned with his glass, and David looked at the bar and then turned back to Cal, smooth as ever.

"Maybe you *are* losing it." David smiled at him. "She shouldn't be that hard to get. It's not like she's a Cynthie."

"She's all right," Cal said, cautiously.

David leaned in. "After all, nobody says no to you, right?"

"What?" Cal said.

"I'm willing to bet you that you can't get her," David said. "A hundred bucks says you can't nail her."

Cal pulled back. *"What?"*

David laughed, but there was an edge to his voice when he spoke. "It's just a bet, Cal. You guys love risk, I've seen you bet on damn near everything. This isn't even that big a bet. We should make it two hundred."

That was when Cal had contemplated giving David a healthy push. Tony turned his back to David and mouthed, *Humor him*, and Cal sighed. There must be something he could ask for that would make David back down. "That baseball in your office," he said. "The one in the case."

"My Pete Rose baseball?" David's voice went up an octave.

"Yeah, that one. That's my price." Cal slugged back the rest of his scotch and looked around for a waitress.

David shook his head. "Not a chance. My dad caught that pop-up for me in seventy-five. But I like your style, upping the stakes like that." He leaned in closer. "Tell you what. The last refresher seminar you ran for us set me back ten grand. I'll bet you ten thousand in cash against a free seminar—"

Cal forced a smile. "David, I was kidding—"

"But for ten thou, you have to get her into bed. I'll play fair. I'll give you a month to get her out of that gray-checked suit."

"Piece of cake," Tony said.

Cal glared at Tony. "David, this isn't my kind of bet."

"It's *my* kind," David said, drawing his brows together, and Cal thought, *Hell, he's going to push this, and we need his business.*

Okay, clearly booze had shut down David's brain. But once it was back up and working again, David would back down on the ten thousand, that was insane, and David was never insane about money. So all he had to do was stall until David sobered up and then pretend the whole thing never happened. He stole a glance across the room to the bar and was delighted to see that the gray suit had disappeared some time during their conversation.

Cal turned back to David and said, "Well, I would, David, but she's gone." *And God bless you, gray suit, for leaving*, he thought and picked up his drink again.

Things were finally going his way.

Min had walked across the room, telling herself that it was a real toss-up as to which would be worse, trying to talk to this guy or enduring

Di's wedding unescorted. When she neared the landing, she edged her way under the rail, catching faint snatches of conversations as she went, not stopping until she heard David's voice faintly above her, saying, "But for ten, though, you have to get her into bed."

What? Min thought. It was noisy up there by the door, maybe she hadn't heard him—

"I'll play fair," David went on. "I'll give you a month to get her out of that gray-checked suit."

Min looked down at her gray-checked suit.

"Piece of cake," somebody said to David, and Min thought, *Son of a* bitch, *the world is full of sex-crazed bastards,* and forced herself to move on before she climbed the railing and killed them both.

She headed back to Liza and Bonnie, fuming. She knew exactly what David was up to. He assumed she wouldn't sleep with anybody because she'd turned him down. She'd warned him about that, about the rash assumptions he made, but instead of taking her advice, he'd kept asking her out.

Because he thought I was a sure thing, she realized. Because he'd looked at her and thought, *Overweight smart woman who'll never cheat on me and will be grateful I sleep with her.* "Bastard," she said out loud. She should have sex with Calvin Morrisey just to pay David back. But then she'd have no way of getting even with Calvin Morrisey. God, she was dumb. Fat and dumb, there was a winning combo.

"What's wrong?" Liza said when she was back at the bar. "Did you ask him?"

"No. As soon as you finish your drinks, I'm ready to go." Min turned back to the balcony and caught sight of them, just as they caught sight of her.

David's face was smug, but Calvin Morrisey clutched his drink and looked like he'd just seen Death.

"There she is," David crowed. "I told you she'd be back. Go get her, champ."

"Uh, David," Cal began, consigning the gray-checked suit to the lowest circle of hell.

"A bet's a bet."

Cal put his empty glass down on the rail and thought fast. The suit did not look happy, so the odds weren't impossible that she'd go for a chance to get out of the bar if he offered dinner. "Look, David, sex is not in the cards. I'm cheap, but I'm not slimy. You want to bet ten bucks on a pickup, fine, but that's it. Nothing with a future."

David shook his head. "Oh, no, I'll bet on the pickup, too, ten bucks if you leave with her. But the ten thousand is still on. If you *lose* . . ." He smiled at Cal, drawing out the 'lose,' "you do a seminar for me for free."

"David, I can't make that bet," Cal said, trying another tack. "I have two partners who—"

"I'm good for it," Tony said. "Cal never misses."

Cal glared at him. "Well, *Roger* isn't good for it."

"Hey, Roger, you in?" Tony said, and Roger said, "Sure," without looking away from the blonde at the bar.

"Roger," Cal said.

"She's the prettiest little thing I've ever seen," Roger said.

"Roger, you just bet that I could get a woman into bed," Cal said with great patience. "Now tell David you don't want to bet a ten-thousand-dollar refresher seminar on sex."

"What?" Roger said, finally looking away from the blonde.

"I said—" Cal began.

"Why would you bet on something like that?" Roger said.

"That's not the question," Tony said. "The question is, can he do it?"

"Sure," Roger said. "But—"

"Then we have a bet," David said.

"No, we do not," Cal said.

"You don't think you can do it," David said. "You're losing it."

"This is not about me," Cal said, and then Cynthie slid back into the group and put her hand on his arm. She leaned into him, and he felt his blood heat right on cue.

"She's over there waiting for you," David said, an edge in his voice.

"She?" Cynthie's glow dimmed. "Are you seeing somebody?"

Oh, hell, Cal thought.

"Cal?" David said.

"Cal?" Cynthie said.

"I *love* this," Tony said.

"What?" Roger said.

Cal sighed. It was the suit or Cynthie, the rock or the soft place who wanted to get married. He detached her hand from his arm. "Yes, I'm seeing somebody. Excuse me."

He pushed past Cynthie and David and headed for the bar, wishing them both the worst fate he could think of, that they'd end up together.

Min watched Calvin Morrisey move toward the stairs. The beast. He thought that he could get her in a month, that she was so pathetic she'd just—

Her brain caught up with her train of thought, and she straightened.

"Will you tell us what's wrong?" Liza said.

"A month," Min said.

He walked down the steps and made his way through the crowd, ignoring the come-hither looks of the women he passed.

He was coming to pick her up.

Suppose she let him.

Suppose for the next three weeks she made him pay by stringing him along and then took him to Di's wedding. He wouldn't leave her; he had to stick for a month to win his damn bet. All she had to do was say no to sex for three weeks, drag him to her sister's wedding, and then leave his ass cold.

Min settled back against the bar and examined the idea from all sides. He more than deserved to be tortured for three weeks. And in that three weeks she could figure out a way to make David suffer, too. And her mother would have somebody beautiful to point out to people at the wedding as her date. It was a plan, and as far as she could see, it was all good.

The bartender came back and Min said, "Rum and Diet Coke, please. A double."

"That's your third," Liza said. "And fourth. The aspartame alone will make you insane. What are you doing?"

"Was he mean to you?" Bonnie said. "What happened?"

"I didn't talk to him." Min waved them away. "Move down the bar a couple of feet will you. I'm about to get hit on and you're cramping my style."

"We missed something," Liza said to Bonnie.

"Move," Bonnie said, and pushed Liza down the bar.

Min turned away when the bartender brought her drink, so when The Beast spoke from beside her, she jerked her head up and caught the full force of him unprepared: hot dark eyes, perfect cheekbones, and a mouth a woman would betray her moral fiber to bite into. Her heart kicked up into her throat, and she swallowed hard to get it back where it belonged.

"I have a problem," he said, and his voice was low and smooth, warm enough to be charming, rich enough to clog arteries.

Dark chocolate, Min thought and looked at him blankly, keeping her breathing slow. "Problem?"

"Well, usually my line is 'Can I buy you a drink?' but you have one." He smiled at her, radiating testosterone through his expensive suit.

"Well, that is a problem." She started to turn away.

"So what I thought," he said, his voice dropping even lower as he leaned closer to her and made her heart pound, "was that we could go somewhere else, and I could buy you dinner."

The closer he got, the better he looked. He was the used car salesman of seducers, Min decided, trying to get her distance back. You could never get a good deal from a used car salesman; they sold cars all the time and you only bought a couple in a lifetime so they always won. Statistically speaking, you were toast before you walked on the lot. She could only imagine how many women this guy had mutilated in his lifetime. The mind boggled.

His smile had disappeared while he waited for her answer, and he looked vulnerable now, taking a chance on asking her out. He faked vulnerable very well. *Remember*, she told herself. *The son of a bitch is doing this for ten bucks*. Actually, he was trying to do *her* for ten bucks.

Cheapskate. Suddenly, breathing normally was not a problem.

"Dinner?" she said.

"Yes." He bent still closer. "Somewhere quiet where we can talk. You look like someone with interesting things to say. And I'm somebody who'd like to hear them."

Min smiled at him. "That's a terrible line. Does it usually work for you?"

He froze for a second, and then he segued from sincere to boyish again. "Well, it has up till now."

"It must be your voice," Min said. "You deliver it beautifully."

"Thank you." He straightened. "Let's try this again." He held out his hand. "I'm Calvin Morrisey, but my friends call me Cal."

"Min Dobbs." She shook his hand and dropped it before it could feel warm in her grasp. "And my friends would call me foolhardy if I left this bar with a stranger."

"Wait." He got out his wallet and pulled out a twenty. "This is cab fare. If I get fresh, you get a cab."

Liza would take the twenty and then dump him. There was a plan, but Liza didn't need a wedding date. What else would Liza do? Min plucked the twenty from his fingers. "If you get fresh, I'll break your nose." She folded the twenty, unbuttoned her top two blouse buttons, and tucked the bill into the V of her sensible cotton bra so that only a thin green edge showed. That was one good thing about packing extra pounds, you got cleavage to burn.

She looked up and caught his eyes looking down, and she waited for him to make some comment, but he smiled again. "Fair enough," he said, "let's go eat," and she reminded herself to ignore what a beautiful mouth he had since it was full of forked tongue.

"First, promise me no more lame lines," she said, and watched his jaw clench.

"Anything you want," he said.

Min shook her head. "Another line. I suppose you can't help it. And free food is always good." She picked up her purse from the bar. "Let's go."

She walked away before he could say anything else, and he followed her, past a dumbfounded Liza and a delighted Bonnie, across the floor and up onto the landing by the door, and the last thing she saw as they left was David looking outraged.

The evening was turning out *much* better than she'd expected.

JENNY CRUSIE

Fast Women

PAN BOOKS

Love, marriage, friendship – only one of these is a sure thing

Nell Dysart is living a too small life in a too small apartment. Her marriage is finished, her career is in limbo and she feels she has the sex appeal of a skeletal giraffe. But things might be about to change, because Nell has landed a job at a down-and-out detective agency with huge potential for redecoration and a boss who looks easy to manage.

A quick spot of dachshund-napping, blackmail and embezzlement later and Nell can scarcely believe her life was ever dull. But when somebody starts killing people and unprofessional sex becomes a sticky situation, she starts to wonder just how many thrills one woman's life can withstand.

JENNY CRUSIE

Welcome to Temptation

PAN BOOKS

She's the talk of the town – for all the wrong reasons

Sophie came to Temptation, Ohio, to help her sister make a movie. Now she's making trouble for the town council, making love with the mayor and making lemonade for a murderer . . .

WELCOME TO TEMPTATION:
Population 2,158 and falling.

JENNY CRUSIE

Tell Me Lies

PAN BOOKS

Sometimes the truth can be scandalous . . .

Your husband is an adulterer and a crook.
Your best friend has a devastating secret.
The love of your life just showed up, twenty years too late.
Your worst day is the best time to start a new life . . .

Maddie Faraday knows she's having a bad day when she finds a
pair of black lace knickers under the front seat of her husband's car.
To make matters worse, her first true love has just reappeared, and
in a small town where little happens it's prime-time news. When her
husband mysteriously disappears, Maddie becomes the most talked
about person in town. She is on a quest for answers, but will she survive long enough to discover the truth?

OTHER PAN BOOKS

AVAILABLE FROM PAN MACMILLAN

JENNY CRUSIE

TELL ME LIES	0 330 42648 6	£6.99
CRAZY FOR YOU	0 330 42647 8	£6.99
WELCOME TO TEMPTATION	0 330 42649 4	£6.99
FAST WOMEN	0 330 42650 8	£6.99

SUE GRAFTON

Q IS FOR QUARRY	0 330 48833 3	£6.99

All Pan Macmillan titles can be ordered from our website,
www.panmacmillan.com, or from your local bookshop
and are also available by post from:

Bookpost, PO Box 29, Douglas, Isle of Man IM99 1BQ
Credit cards accepted. For details:
Telephone: 01624 677237
Fax: 01624 670923
E-mail: bookshop@enterprise.net
www.bookpost.co.uk

Free postage and packing in the United Kingdom

Prices shown above were correct at the time of going to press.
Pan Macmillan reserve the right to show new retail prices on covers
which may differ from those previously advertised in the text
or elsewhere.